CHANGELING

THE TERRA MIRUM CHRONICLES

KIRI CALLAGHAN

Genre Punk Publishing

Published by
Genre Punk Publishing, an imprint of Doce Blant
Publishing, Bradenton, Florida 34208
www.doceblantpublishing.com

Cover by Fiona Jayde Media
Interior Design by The Deliberate Page

ISBN Paperback: 978-1-955413-02-2
ISBN Hardbound: 978-1-955413-03-9
ISBN ePUB: ISBN: 978-1-955413-04-6

Library of Congress Control Number: 2021940746

Printed in the United States of America
www.doceblant.com

To Sandy and Brent, my loving parents, who raised a strange child and loved her all the more for it. I owe every ounce of independence, cleverness and creativity to the both of you.

A deep thank you to my wife, Angelique, whose support extended to everything short of literally chaining me to my desk. Without her, this book would not exist.

Thank you to Alan, Ana, Bethany, Clare, Dez, E, James, Jo, Kristian, Kristi, Nat, Melissa, Melanie, Ren, Vivka, Zoe, and so many others that I will feel guilty later for not naming, who helped me create this story. Your insight, your knowledge, and your friendship are invaluable.

You make me a better person, and a better writer.

PROLOGUE

Alys had lost the time.

She'd been perched on the brocade settee for what felt like ages; her stomach churning so strongly she'd been forced to hunch over herself, resting her elbows on her knees.

Twice, she'd risen and attempted to retreat through the mirror she came through. Her reflection always stopped her. A visual manifestation of her conscience, it guarded the way home until she had done what she'd come to do.

The amber of her eyes stared back at her, and the longer she looked, the less she recognized them. Self-consciously, she smoothed her shirt down over her stomach, but it did nothing to alleviate the heavy weight dragging her sternum down toward the floor. Her fingers played with the pocket watch dangling from a chain around her neck, and she moved back to sit on the settee once more.

How much longer? Was he even in the palace?

She released the watch and let the weight of it pull on her neck as she hunched over again. She clasped and unclasped her hands. They were cold. Her right thumb traced the lines of her left palm, then pressed in a little deeper: back and forth, anxiously following the life-line crease as if she could create a rut.

Home-grown worry stone.

The door opened.

She froze.

It closed hurriedly behind him.

"Alys?"

There had always been something different about how he spoke her name. It did not demand attention, it courted it. His voice made it seem so much more intimate; like a secret between them. It was a quality that always made him hard to ignore.

So Alys found herself grinding her teeth when, instead of looking to him, her focus sharpened on the settee opposite her. She wasn't ready.

This was a terrible idea.

"Is everything alright?"

It was a question of courtesy, and so she did not feel the need to answer it.

His footsteps were so deliberate that the sound of each as he drew closer tightened the knot in her chest. "Alys…" His voice was too kind, too gentle, too concerned…

She wasn't ready.

He gingerly stepped into her line of sight, easing down to sit on the low table between the two pieces of furniture.

She was looking past him—through him.

"What's wrong?"

Alys bit her lower lip.

Oswin took a moment to examine her posture, the hunch of her shoulders and the indescribably blank expression. Disconnected. He clasped his own hands in front of him and tried again. "Did something happen?"

Alys' eyes moved sharply to his, like a camera aperture shifting to focus on the foreground. "No."

"You're upset," Oswin said, unclasping his hands to offer them to her, palms up, his fingers lightly beckoning hers. "Tell me why."

Alys stood. The proximity to him which had once been comforting felt suffocating under these circumstances. She played with the chain around her neck, taking calculated, slow breaths. She shifted slightly so that she could see the light reflect off the mirror in the alcove almost like a glowing exit sign. She swallowed. Her voice could not shake. She could not waver. Her resolve needed to be firm and unbreakable. "I think this needs to be my last visit to Terra Mirum."

Silence. She wasn't looking at him, but she'd imagined the expression on his face enough times to know she wouldn't be able to bear it.

"…I'm sorry?"

Another deep breath. Alys reluctantly turned her body back around toward him, her gaze dropping to the floor. A measured inhale and her eyes rose to meet his. "We have to end this."

Oswin's mind was racing, she could see him trying to make sense of this moment by the way his brow knit closer together and how his eyes took her in. In their short time together, he had always been a logical man. He approached his problems with a studious mind. He was clever, brilliant even… but no matter how much he attempted to study this scenario, she knew he would not find the satisfying resolution he was looking for. At last he spoke, his voice hoarser than she'd ever heard it, barely above a whisper. "You're not serious."

Alys could feel her throat tightening, her eyes stinging, and she forced a pained smile. "I'm sorry."

Oswin chuffed in disbelief and walked a few paces away from her. He raked his fingers through his hair, pausing as his palms rested on his temples. He stared forward, scanning the objects of his room as if they would provide clues to how he found himself in this moment. Finding none, his hands dropped in frustration as he whirled around to face her once more. "*Why?*"

Alys' fingers interlocked, and her thumb found the opposite palm again, rubbing along the same crease in her palm. She met his gaze easier this time. If this was going to work, she had to be believable. "We have to be practical."

A beat.

"*Practical?*" The word didn't seem to have a place between them—so much, he felt suspicious of it.

Alys made a point to maintain eye contact. "Did we really think we could keep this up forever?"

He had. At least, he'd *hoped*. Oswin's eyes averted to the side, but he could feel her gaze never leave him. He pursed his lips, sucking them in slightly in thought. He could see the mirror from here. He exhaled and rubbed the back of his neck before looking back to her. He took her in. She was fidgeting. She was also uncomfortable. His gaze softened and his hand dropped to his side again. "I know all this secrecy hasn't been fair to you... I do."

Alys sighed and she looked down at her own hands. "It's not... We're not kids anymore."

Oswin moved to her, closing the distance between them. "Just give me time. Just a *little* more time. I'll figure something out, I promise." He was pleading with her. It made her heart ache.

"Oswin..." She looked to him. He was close again. Deliriously close. She could smell the familiar scent of sandalwood and petrichor. "You're a king." She swallowed, hard. Lying felt impossible this close to him. It was easier to look someone in the eyes when you couldn't catalogue every shade of blue intermixed in the iris. So, she didn't lie. She relied on her truths. "I can't keep being selfish. I can't keep taking you away from that."

The relief on Oswin's face was almost more painful than his desperation. "Is that what this is about?" He almost laughed as he reached out to take her face in his hands. "Alys, you're not taking me away from *anything*." He kissed her forehead and she felt tears fall down her cheeks. "If it weren't for you, I wouldn't be the man I am today. You make me a better King for them. You challenge me, you give me different perspectives, you…" His brow furrowed. "You're crying."

"I've forced you to lie to everyone for the past two years."

"Then we'll stop lying to them," he said simply as he leaned in to kiss her cheek.

"Oswin…"

"It's not like you're a danger to Terra Mirum anymore," his head tilted to kiss the other cheek.

"Aren't I?"

Oswin paused. He shifted back to look her in the eyes, his brow furrowing once more. "Something's happened."

Alys broke from him to raise a hand to wipe at the tear streaks on her face. "Nothing happened."

Oswin persisted. He'd found the puzzle piece he'd been looking for, now he simply had to identify it. "Someone said something to you—"

"No—"

"Did they find out? Was it Basir?"

Alys put a few paces between them again. "No one said anything to me. *Nothing* happened."

"Why are you lying to me?"

Alys whirled around to face him, her heart pounding as their eyes met once more. "I'm not *lying* to you."

"Then *why* are you doing this?"

"*Look* at us, Oswin," Alys seethed, gesturing to the room around them. "Is *this* a way to live our life? We have no hope for a future together. You have your responsibilities to your kingdom, and I…" She caught sight of herself in the mirror again and self-consciously smoothed down her shirt. "I have to wake up."

"Do you still love me?"

Alys' gaze fell from her reflection to the floor. Her throat felt tight again. "It's not about that."

"Alys," he said her name so gently she couldn't help but meet his gaze. Oswin searched her expression, the way the light shined off her eyes. He took a breath and asked again, afraid of what the answer might be, but deliberate in his questioning. "Do you still love me?"

She pursed her lips, quirking them to the side. There were many lies she would tell to keep this secret. But this could never be one of them. "…of course, I do, idiot."

"Then don't go."

She breathed something between a laugh and a sob. "This is bigger than us, Oswin. Sometimes love just isn't enough."

"Bullshit," he dismissed. "If I have you with me, I'm invincible. I've beaten back armies of Nightmares, I've stared the end of the world in the face… Alys, if you *love* me, there isn't anything I can't do."

Her throat was tightening again, and she felt the tears rising. "God, I wish it were that simple."

Oswin stepped toward her, taking her hands in his own. "It is," he insisted. "It *can* be, I promise. Let me show you. Please."

She looked down at their joined hands, struggling to find her resolve again. "You… have to marry and provide your kingdom with an heir."

"Alright," Oswin agreed, dropping to his knee. "Marry me."

"Oswin," Alys breathed.

"We've overcome so much more than this before. We can do this. We'll figure it out." He kissed her knuckles repeatedly, murmuring reassurances into her skin. "We could be open about this, come out of the shadows."

Alys' hands turned to gently run her fingers along the side of his face.

He looked up at her, hopeful. "You could come and live with me, and I could find and appoint an heir outside of my bloodline."

Reality came crashing back to Alys' senses and her hands froze their motion. An heir. His bloodline. *Their* bloodline.

"You could stay *here*, with me."

She broke away from him, moving closer to the mirror. She couldn't afford to let herself get swept away in such daydreams. They might have been an option. Possibly. Once. No more. "And I would wither and die in a breath of the time it took you to," she dismissed the idea.

Oswin remained on one knee and spoke simply. "I'd rather have a moment with you than nothing at all."

"Then let it be *this* moment!"

"Please. Don't go."

"We have to live our lives. You have to find a Queen; you have to have children—" Her breath caught in her throat, and she forced it out with a frustrated exhale as her hands came up to rub her face. Her heart was pounding in her ears. "I could never give you that, as both of your advisors so pointedly made clear years ago. A Changeling between Dream and Dreamer would have... unthinkable consequences. And it would always be a risk."

Oswin slowly rose to his feet again. "You're not a Dreamer anymore."

Alys visibly flinched.

"We don't know what sort of child it would be if... Maybe we *could*..."

"Maybe we could what?" Alys snapped incredulously. "Raise someone in a world that would fear them simply for who they were? Possibly give god-like power to a baby. If you thought *my* moods were mercurial when we first met—"

"Why are you *fixating* on this?"

"Because they aren't things we can afford to ignore anymore, Oswin!"

Silence fell between them.

Oswin was the first to relax his posture, and following his lead, so did Alys. Their eyes never left each other's, and they merely took in the way the other let their guard down. It was in those small details that both understood these were truly their final moments together, and they were to be savored, not squandered in a fight neither was really going to win.

"…I'm not going to be able to convince you to stay, am I?" he asked, his voice back to nearly a whisper again.

Alys shook her head ever so slightly and shrugged a little helplessly. "…I have to live my life." She looked back to the mirror at the reflection of the woman she didn't recognize now, though she spoke when she did and mimicked her movements. "I need to make a plan for how I'm going to survive in *my* world. Set a foundation, start working on something…" Her heart wrenched and she looked back to him. "Real."

Oswin breathed in sharply.

Alys took a deep breath and removed the Coleridge clock from around her neck, letting the watch face rest in her palm before she held it out to him as an offering. "I have to stop dreaming."

Oswin thought a moment before he approached her, his eyes focused on the Coleridge clock before closing his hand around her own, tightening her hold on the watch in her palm. Only then did he dare meet her eyes again. "Perhaps I cannot change your mind, but one day, though it will be nothing short of a miracle, *you* might change yours."

Alys looked down at their hands.

"If that day ever comes, I want it to be a door you can open." He paused a long moment, and finally shrugged his shoulders with a wry sort of smile. "Besides, I don't think I could trust myself to stay away."

She laughed. A bittersweet sort of sound.

He took a breath and his hand moved from hers to gently tip up her chin. "You really won't visit? Not even infrequently?"

"Every time I did; it would get that much harder to leave."

A sad smile. "I was hoping you'd fall into that trap anyway."

She chuckled despite herself. "I will miss you."

Oswin's smile slowly faded as he searched her face, the lingering sadness in her eyes, the sense that she was guarding something. "...you'd tell me, wouldn't you? If there was something else? If it... you'd *tell* me?"

Alys swallowed, knowing that if she looked away now she'd never convince him. "There's nothing else."

His brow furrowed. Frustration. He didn't understand. None of this made sense to him. "I will always love you; you know. Time cannot wither that; death cannot extinguish that—"

"Oswin—"

"Let me say it." His volume did not rise, but the intensity in his voice was so heartbreakingly full of desperation. "If I am never truly going to ever get a chance again, please, just let me say it. I *need* you to know."

Alys' free hand rose to the hand beneath her chin, carefully guiding his to cup her cheek, her palm layering over it. "I *do* know." She bit her lower lip, and the hand over his gave it a gentle squeeze. "It will be better this way..."

Tears fell from Oswin's eyes. "I can't fathom how."

She kissed his palm. "You're just going to have to trust me. One last time. That's all I ask." She released him and took a step back, then another, and another until she could see all of him clearly.

Oswin swallowed, but this did little to alleviate the lump in his throat. "At least tell me this will all make sense someday. That at some point in the future I'm going to understand."

Alys bit her lower lip again.

He chuffed and hung his head. "You can't even do that, can you?"

Her grip on the Coleridge clock tightened, then released the latch. She turned toward the mirror, turning the clock so that the golden hand hit the 6, and the large mirror rippled outward, opening the door back to Earth.

He was losing her. In a moment she'd be gone. "Don't make me say goodbye," he asked. "It's too final."

Alys frowned. "I'm not coming back, Oswin."

"Let me at least have my hope."

Her breath trembled. "…I'll see you in your dreams."

1

CHARLOTTE / "CHARLIE"

There was a crack in the sky. A thick black line that splintered upward from the horizon with limbs and long gnarled fingers grasping at the thundering clouds overhead. Emptiness seemed to spill from the void, as if the very concept of being hollow had suddenly found a way to take physical form and spiderweb outward.

Lightning mimicked the void's jagged shape and forced illumination through the spaces between the cracks. It brightened the ground, scattering branches of shadows, the darkest formed by the break in the atmosphere itself. It was a shadow not cast from an object obstructing the light, but rather a space where light had never been. Could never be. A space born of and from the darkness. Another flash of lighting and her attention drew to the surrounding trees, and a single brass orb in the near center of the dark vacuum.

She moved toward it, drawn by the curiosity that tempts us all into the unknown and potentially dangerous. It beckoned her across the barren ground, and as she approached, the wind began to stir. Cold, bitter, and whispering words she couldn't quite make out.

Then came the snow. It was soft, floating down delicately in a manner that seemed completely inappropriate for her surroundings. Serene and peaceful. Grace juxtaposed with chaos. Unlike the air, it was surprisingly warm—some flakes were even hot to the touch, and she had to shake them from her hand, worried they'd burn if left to linger.

Thunder rumbled once more and the lightning flashed behind her, casting her shadow long across the ground before her. Once more, light danced across the orb, and now at a closer distance, she could identify it. A doorknob. A simple, unassuming brass doorknob, seemingly hanging onto nothing.

She took another step forward, and another blaze of lightning gave her just enough clarity to give context to a haunting creaking sound as the floating brass doorknob swayed to the side.

The air shifted from within the void, creating a vortex of swirling wind that inhaled the world around her. It pulled at her, snatched at her hair, skin, and clothing, and began to drag her forward by the force. She reached out, arms flailing to grasp something, finally catching hold of a tree branch. Her feet kicked the air, as if she could shake the wind's hold on her. Giving up on this she held tighter to the tree, trying to hug her body closer to it.

The wind howled around her, and her eyes shut tightly. It was starting to sound like screams. And it was getting louder.

A wail streamed by like a passing siren, sounding more human, and it was joined by more. Her eyes slowly opened, and to her horror, discovered the sound she'd been hearing was not the wind at all.

It was people.

Dozens of people being dragged screaming through the trees around her. Whatever power pulled at her from the void seemed to have a grip on them through a silvery-white cord that extended from each of their backs. It raked them over the forest floor, on their stomachs, their fingers digging into the ground, grasping at roots, or clawing at the bark of the trees. They kicked and flailed, twisting desperately as if trying to separate themselves from the cord, but it was a fruitless effort.

She watched as each one was pulled through the door, but even as each vanished from sight, their voices lingered in the air.

A hand snatched around her leg, and she looked down into the wide eyes of a young blonde woman. The woman's fingers bit into her with desperation.

Her breath caught, suspended in the moment, and as the two stared at each other, her grip on the tree tightened.

"Don't let go," the woman begged.

"I won't," she promised. She wanted to mean it. She carefully tried to bend the leg the woman held onto, hoping to bring her closer so they could both grip the tree—*both* take hold of the more solid anchor.

The force from the void seemed to tighten its grip around the young woman, and she could swear she saw the vague ghostly outline of a clawed hand wrapping its forearm around the blonde woman's silver cord before gripping tightly and yanking her towards the void.

She felt the branch snap under the pressure of her arms, and her own back hit the forest floor. Her brow furrowed and she coughed, barely aware as she felt herself being dragged by virtue of the young woman's grip still on her leg. She flailed her limbs outward, and something—no, *someone*, caught her forearm and held it tightly.

The grip on her leg faltered, slipping to catch around the ankle. "No. Please!" And then hand was gone.

Her senses were groggy as she tried to find her bearings. Her head was pounding. She arched her neck upward to blink at the figure above her in silhouette. Her eyes couldn't focus, only make out a dark grey shadow.

"What's going on?" she cried out to it, her voice barely reaching out over the wailing sounds around them.

Her answer came in one statement—one truth that she could not place if it were spoken by the man in silhouette, or merely a sensation of knowledge that passed between them through other means in that moment. "The door to the Nothing has *opened*."

"Charlotte!" A voice barked, and one last flash of light-ning flooded her vision, melting into a harsh white, fluorescent hue.

She squinted, her eyes peering through the abrupt change of scenery, and raised a hand to block out the intruding beams of government-funded light bulbs. She could hear a chorus of giggling hyenas around her as she blinked her way back into reality. Her mouth felt dry. Her heart was still pounding.

The nightmare and terror that had surrounded her moments before had been replaced by the dull hum of poorly wired electricity, and a mix of mildly amused faces, relieved for a break in the overwhelming monot-ony that normally occupied first period.

At last, her eyes rested on the one not-amused face. "Mr. Keats?" She responded with the nonchalance of someone politely nodding to an acquaintance in the hallway.

Darrel Keats was a man who had dedicated his life to a career in education and little else. This was a decision he clearly regretted, and this fact was obvious to no one more than to his students. It's possible he'd assumed there would be time later for things beyond his work, or perhaps he thought he'd find a more pros-perous position than teaching sophomore English in a high school that would always prefer athletics over academics. Whatever the case, he had decided it was too late to change reality, and so reality had painted him as a short, unhappy bald man, bitter with his life decisions.

"Did we have a nice nap?" Keats asked, his voice taking on the rising inflection of someone barely clinging to polite behavior.

"Not particularly," Charlotte admitted, hoping he was done attempting to shame her and would move on.

Keats exhaled through his nose sharply and adjusted his stance, his head slightly cocking to the side before leveling once more as he clasped his hands behind his back. "Are we *boring* you?"

"Yes." It was an honest answer, albeit an unwelcome one.

Keats gave an incredulous and strained laugh. "Perhaps you require something more challenging than one of the most celebrated writers in American history, young lady?"

Charlotte's heartbeat had not calmed, and so she took a deep breath.

Keats leaned over ever so slightly, his voice affecting a false saccharine quality as if addressing a very stupid young child. "Is Faulkner just too simple for you? Hmm?"

Charlotte ran the tip of her tongue along the sharp edge of her upper teeth behind her lips before giving an even, clarifying answer. "Our discussion of Faulkner is too simple for me, Mr. Keats." She exhaled through pursed lips, keeping the flow even and slow.

Keats' entire head reddened. It started somewhere in his cheeks, flushing outward all over his face and up through his bare scalp. "Well, then, Miss Carroll, perhaps you can assist us poor, unfortunate simpletons. We've been discussing why Faulkner chose the title for his story."

Charlotte blinked at him. "A Rose for Emily?"

"Yes." His gaze leveled with hers in a challenge, his jaw visibly tightening. "Why. That. Title?"

Charlotte could feel the eyes of the class on her, daring her to fail. It was a familiar scene, played out much the same way in multiple classes throughout the years. Sadly, familiarity had not increased her comfort with those moments. She laced her fingers on the desk in front of her. It was here that she focused her gaze, and here she settled the butterflies in her stomach. She took another deep and measured breath. "Well, in an interview he was quoted to have said the title was allegorical—claiming that Emily's story was a tragedy, and to show condolence to a woman in tragedy, you would hand her a rose…" She pursed her lips as the man's condescending tone replayed over in her mind, anxiety melting into anger as her fingernails dug into the backs of her hands. "But I don't think that's the reason at all."

Keats chuckled disdainfully. "Don't you?" He folded his arms. "Please, Miss Carroll, by all means, grace us with your wisdom."

This man had every intention of humiliating her, making her look like an absolute idiot, and Charlotte was going to be damned before she let him. "I think it refers to the practice of hanging flowers upside down to dry them—killing them prematurely to preserve them rather than putting them in water to prolong their life but ultimately allowing the bloom to run its course and drop its petals. Emily murdered Homer rather than letting him live his life—'dried him out,' so to speak. In doing this, she 'preserved him,' giving him no option to leave her like everyone else, and she could keep him with her always. This is why they find one of Emily's hairs on his corpse. It suggests that, at the very least, she had slept in the same bed with his dead body. If not more."

There was discomfort among her classmates, and she could feel them recoil from her, coupled with a chorus of hushed murmurs of "gross," "freak," and "ew."

Keats, on the other hand, merely blinked, puffed out his cheeks as he looked from her to the board, and sighed, visibly deflating as he made his way back to the front of the room. "Tomorrow we'll be continuing our study of American authors through famous short stories."

Charlotte felt the knot in her sternum release, and she relaxed her hands.

"Wait, Mr. Keats—she's *right*?" Shelby Ferris, or Shelby "Fairest" as she was often nicknamed by her admirers for her jet-black hair, alabaster skin, and unparalleled winning streak when it came to running for any kind of school dance royalty, indignantly raised her hand, despite having spoken before waiting to be called upon.

Keats sighed once more. "It is a popular theory among academics." It wasn't clear if his palpable remorse was regarding the twisted nature of Faulkner's chosen title or that he wouldn't be failing the girl who managed to breeze through his class without ever seeming to be awake during it. "As I was saying, we'll be continuing our short story segment, so I want all of you to have read and be familiar with Glaspell's 'A Jury of Her Peers' by tomorrow. We will be starting the class with a quiz, so come prepared."

He wrote the assignment on the board along with the page numbers, and as he placed the last punctuation, as if on cue, the bell rang.

First period ended and began the dreary slog characteristic of a Seattle Monday in winter, complete with a new rumor that Charlotte Carroll slept with dead people.

It was raining that day. It never rained in Seattle as much as the rest of the world seemed convinced it did. It was overcast more than anything—and moist; a constant mist in the air that made your skin slick and damp if you stood in it for too long. But today it was raining.

Charlotte liked the rain. It was soothing; a steady patter on the windows and roof that had a vaguely lullaby-like quality. It was enough to put you to sleep. It *had* put her to sleep.

She sat up in her seat, angling forward to prevent any comfortable slump that might draw her back to… to… whatever that had been. She looked down to her notebook and realized she'd been absently doodling the crack and the door in the margin of her notes. She blinked and tilted her head, realizing that from this perspective, it rather looked like a tree. She pursed her lips.

"Door to the Nothing…" she repeated quietly to herself. What did it even mean?

The thoughts were abandoned almost immediately as Mrs. Robertson swirled into the room. She had that sort of quality, entering a place like a force of nature. Her voice had a pleasant and dramatic booming quality. Unlike Keats, Robertson attacked every class with an elaborate lesson plan, usually complete with costume or prop. It was a theatrical performance, and even if you knew her script by heart, you'd find it impossible to look away. She wrapped an embroidered robe around her regular clothing and enthusiastically continued her lecture on the fall of Tsarist Russia. Her nimble hands miming the many assassination attempts on Rasputin, occasionally reaching over to strike a key on her laptop, changing through the many visual aids, photographs, and paintings being projected on the screen. It created a staccato rhythm of sharp taps accompanying her impassioned tale of the assassination of Nicholas II by the Bolsheviks.

Tap.

Tap.

Ta-

Then the phone on her desk rang.

A few kids startled, a few glared at it as if it were the lone person in a movie theater who forgot to silence their cell phone, and Mrs. Robertson herself stared blankly as if she wasn't entirely sure what to do with it. She was suspended in motion, her finger still hovering over the key as if she didn't dare move.

The phone rang again, and Robertson sighed in frustration, an actor forced to break character as she huffily picked up the receiver. "Laura Robertson," she spoke with a brisk tone. She was ordinarily an impossibly energetic and cheerful woman, but needless interruption of any performance was never tolerated. "I am in the middle of an important lecture." Her eyes raised to meet Charlotte's, and they shared an understanding of exasperation. "Can't it wait?"

Charlotte slid to the edge of her seat; certain she knew how this conversation would end.

"Yes. I understand." The phone was placed back on its cradle with a twinge of indignation and a disregard for pleasantries or phone etiquette. "Charlie, you're to go directly to Mr. Blake's office."

Charlotte stood and slipped her bag onto her shoulder in one fluid motion. She could feel an unkindness of looks upon her as a congregation of whispers broke out among her classmates.

Unlike everyone else in the counseling office, Mr. Blake was not a counselor. He was the school *psychologist*. He didn't help you sign up for classes, he didn't advise you about colleges or scholarships. He had one purpose and one purpose only: to *fix* you. So, when you were called in to see him, everyone knew exactly why.

"*Class,* quiet…" Robertson rubbed her temples with a slow exhalation. "You can find my lecture and study questions on my website." It was a frustrated, out-of-habit statement that she had repeated to Charlotte far too many times than either of them liked.

Charlotte was sent to see Mr. Blake a lot—almost always after first period.

Were it any other day, Charlotte would have retreated to a corner of the quad near the outdoor basketball hoops. It was secluded enough that she wouldn't get caught out of class and quiet enough that she could peacefully stream the lecture online that she'd been pulled out of in the first place. But it was pouring by now.

Instead, she lingered outside Mrs. Robertson's door and leaned against the lockers. There was the library, but that meant walking past the Counseling Office, not to mention the unfortunately large windows that left little to be desired in terms of privacy and made any bookworm feel something akin to a zoo animal.

Left with few other options, Charlotte walked down the abandoned halls and out the back doors that lead to the annex used for auto shop. She positioned herself under the small awning over the door, leaning artfully against the small portion of dry brick.

She'd barely situated when the door opened, nearly knocking her from her perch. Charlotte flailed and caught the railing to prevent herself from falling down the three concrete steps.

"Charlotte?"

Charlotte froze. She knew that voice too well. She slowly looked up and smiled sheepishly. "Vice Principal Raphus."

"Are you alright?" the sensibly dressed woman asked, her brow furrowing.

Charlotte righted herself slowly, no longer concerned with the rain pelting down on her. "Yeah, totally fine."

"I'm so sorry, I didn't see you."

That had, regrettably, been the point. "No worries."

"What are you doing out here in the rain?"

"I was…" *Lie.* "On my way to the counseling office."

"Oh." Ms. Raphus took a step to the side to allow her to pass.

Reluctantly, Charlotte took a deep breath and walked inside, giving a polite, albeit tight-lipped smile as she did. "Thanks." She dipped down slightly, giving a small awkward sort of curtsey before turning to walk down the hall.

"I didn't realize you took auto shop," Ms. Raphus called after her knowingly.

Charlotte hesitated and looked over her shoulder at the older woman. She pursed her lips together and forced another anxious smile. "Yep."

She let the lie hang between them, a small yelp of deceit unsuccessfully drowned out by the rapid tap dance of the raindrops outside the door the vice principal still held open.

Ms. Raphus straightened to her full height and tugged down the hem of her blazer. "Give Mr. Blake my regards," she said pointedly.

"Sure."

So, Charlotte went to the counseling office.

It had the false aspartame-like sweetness found in centers like it: motivational posters right and left, encouraging the depressed masses of teenagers as they were pushed from the thralls of childhood to deciding on the foundation that would support their adult existence.

There were three counselors for three different sections of the alphabet, except for Mr. Merida, who also handled the foreign exchange students, regardless of their last names. Well-lit rooms, brightly colored, and full of phrases you'd imagine plastered on a cat poster. Hang in there. You can do it. Life is a journey.

Mr. Blake's office, on the other hand, was a different kind of motivation. It was filled with brochures about abstinence, teen pregnancy, eating disorders, drugs, and alcohol. He also had framed posters on his walls, but while their goal was essentially the same of those that belonged to his colleagues, they seemed to take more of a scare tactic: what could happen if you didn't stay in line.

There was a psychology thesis somewhere in this office; she was certain of it.

The dark-haired man at the desk was somewhere in his mid-forties, but his hair had acquired a salt-and-pepper quality around the temple early. This gave him a somewhat distinguished appearance and a false sense of wisdom. The sleeves of his collared shirts were undone and rolled up to the elbow, and a pair of thick, black-rimmed glasses perpetually sat on the bridge of his strong nose in a way that made Charlotte suspect they were purely for aesthetic.

Charlotte had inherited her mother's short stature, eyes, and nose, but seemingly her father's everything else. Copper skin drew out the warmer tones in her honey-colored eyes, camouflaged a smattering of freckles across her cheeks, and made the impossibly white hair on top of her head stand out even more. It was long and layered in a way that gave the impression a lot of care went into its maintenance. Her ears were accented with silver from three ringed piercings that trailed up each lobe. Her jeans were simple but ripped at the knee from age, and the hoodie that covered her Ramones T-shirt had been decorated around the pockets with a variety of silver safety pins. It was comfortable attire, but given her current situation, she felt a tad cliché. She hovered in Mr. Blake's doorway, like a vampire unable to cross the threshold. Her face felt hot, and she cleared her throat.

Mr. Blake startled at the sound and looked up, but Charlotte noticed his uneasiness did not dissipate even after his surprise wore off. It was the same discomfort she'd noticed in countless others through the years—a discomfort no one had ever been able to explain beyond that something felt "off" about her. Something they couldn't put their finger on that kept them on their guard. The two stared at each other a moment before finally, Blake spoke up. "Do you need something?"

Charlotte raised an unimpressed eyebrow. "You called me in."

His blank stare did not falter.

"Charlie Carroll?" she offered unenthusiastically.

He blinked. Realized. Straightened in his seat. "Oh! *Charlotte.* Yes." He moved to adjust the files on his desk. "You'll have to forgive me; I wasn't expecting you to actually…"

"Show up?" Charlotte filled in the blank for him.

"…Yes," the man admitted, and she couldn't quite tell if he was uncomfortable about this admission, or that she had in fact shown up after all.

"Me either," Charlotte answered honestly. She was equally uncomfortable.

"This is a first for you."

Charlotte could see he was examining her, trying to size her up for who she was, finding what box he could put her in. "Let's make it the last, too."

"Sit," Blake gestured as if he was commanding a dog rather than inviting her to take one of the chairs in front of his desk.

Charlotte didn't move.

"Please."

Reluctantly, she pushed off from the door frame and removed the shoulder bag to set it beside her as she sunk down into a chair.

Blake smiled at her. "So."

She didn't like that smile. She didn't trust that smile; it made her nervous.

His head tilted ever so slightly to the side, trying to seem more genial. More familiar. "What's going on, kiddo?"

It was the 'kiddo' that made her bristle. The sort of language one heard from a distant parent, or someone attempting to fill some sort of familial role of authority. Simultaneously belittling and endearing. A key tool in any manipulator's belt. "*You* called *me*," she reminded him humorously.

He folded his hands on his desk and spoke in an irritatingly soft, tender sort of voice. "Mr. Keats informed me that you disrupted his class again."

"Mr. Keats disrupted his own class," Charlotte scoffed.

"He also said you've…" Blake paused to check his notes, "a pattern of falling asleep in his class—"

"Okay," Charlotte raised a hand in protest. "Today was the first time I've actually fallen asleep—"

"And when confronted, became hostile."

"Hostile is a gross exaggeration—as an English teacher, I'd expect him to be more careful with his word choice," Charlotte argued quietly, folding her arms. "Irritatingly precocious? Fine. Too candid? Definitely, but *hostile* implies *I* was antagonizing *him*."

Blake adjusted the glasses, which at this proximity, were most assuredly for purely aesthetic use only. "And you weren't?"

"He asked me questions, I gave honest answers. He didn't *like* them, but I was perfectly polite, whereas *he* was rather condescending. I'm a little offended *he's* not in here, actually."

"You weren't paying attention to his lesson."

"It didn't *deserve* my attention."

Blake blinked, stunned by this assertion. "I… beg your pardon?"

"It was a *bad* lesson," Charlotte explained candidly. "He was just droning right out of the textbook. I'd already read everything he was going over—*more* even."

The man's jaw tightened.

Charlotte dug her thumbnail into the palm of her opposite hand.

He turned back to his notes, and she could see a vein in his neck that was now far more prominent than it had been five minutes ago. "He's not the only one of your instructors who have reported that you seem extremely distracted in class. Reports that follow you all the way back to elementary school. Yet your grades… are in the top percentile… Do you feel you're being challenged in your schoolwork?"

Charlotte laughed. "No."

Calmer, with what he assumed was his solution, she watched him exhale and the vein seem to relax as he folded his hands languidly on the desk. "Perhaps you'd be happier and more engaged in our more advanced classes."

"I *am* in your more advanced classes."

He blinked.

Charlotte gave him a pursed-lip smile and a shrug.

He glanced back down at his notes to confirm this was indeed correct. "What about…" he carefully skimmed quickly over the file as best he could. "Skipping ahead? Looking into some college courses. We have the Running Start program… You're more than qualified."

"Would it mean never having to talk to you again?" Charlotte asked a little too hopefully.

Mr. Blake sighed heavily and looked up from his notes, using a tone far too gentle to be genuine. "I really don't know where this hostility comes from, Charlotte, do *you*?"

Charlotte's back stiffened. It was a tone far too often employed by adults who weren't her parent when they were attempting to parent her. Like she was a puppy.

His brow furrowed in what she assumed was his attempt at genuine concern—he was a poor actor at that. She could see the way his eyes glazed over, focusing on something in the distance, probably on whatever he'd rather be doing than speaking to her in that moment. "Are you having trouble adjusting to the environment, perhaps?"

Charlotte blinked and glanced slightly to either side of herself. "Adjusting to the environment?" she repeated, unsure.

"It's not easy when you're in a new place, is it?"

"New pl... I'm not sure what you're talking about," Charlotte confessed, feeling a little off base. Was she going mad?

"As I'm sure Mr. Merida has counseled you before, America works a little differently than possibly how you did things back home. It can be a hard adjustment, make you feel lost, even angry at those around you."

Charlotte squinted slightly, her head tilting to the side as she examined this person across the desk from her. Her lips parted slightly, and she exhaled a laugh, anxiety abating. "Where do you think I'm from exactly?"

Mr. Blake seemed to freeze in that moment, knowing he'd made an error but not entirely sure where. "Well, you're... I mean you have... Your features are reminiscent of..." He was floundering.

And she let him flounder. It was not an unheard-of mistake, even in Seattle, but it would be the first time she'd encountered this sort of behavior from someone who had literally been handed a file of her personal information, a file that no doubt stated quite plainly that she was an American citizen. It was that ridiculous oversight that prompted her to let him drown in a few moments of silence before she spoke up. "Mr. Merida is my assigned counselor because my last name starts with the letter C, Mr. Blake. I've literally lived in Washington State my entire life."

"Ah, well…" He floundered, shifting in his seat. "Even when your home environment is a little different, it can cause a cultural disconnect." He was grasping to excuse his behavior.

Charlotte wasn't about to let him. "My mother was *also* born in Washington." She felt her upper lip curl in amusement. "She's also probably even whiter than you are."

"And your father?"

"Who fucking cares?"

"You're upset, so I'll let that language slide this once."

"I'm not upset," Charlotte spat.

Blake paused, and as he leaned forward, adopted that far-too-soft voice once more. "…aren't you?"

Charlotte shrugged. "No."

"Why not?"

"He's not a part of my life, he's *never* been a part of my life."

"And that's hard," he concluded in synthetic empathy.

Charlotte exhaled loudly. "He's *never* been here, he's irrelevant."

"An absent father in a child's life—"

"*Look*," Charlotte interjected sharply as she leaned forward in her seat. "I *get* it. You want this to be some sort of touching, 'I'm like this because I never had a dad' kind of thing." Her brow furrowed as she focused hard on the man across from her who still seemed to be looking through her rather than at her. He didn't care. He was looking for a box to put her in so he could go about the rest of his day. "But. It's. *Not*." She articulated firmly. "I've *never* known him, I've never even seen a *picture* of him, and his absence is *only* noticeable when people like you try to make me feel bad about it. You're asking me to be upset about something I've no concept of. Do you get that? I can't miss a thing that's *never* been there."

For a moment, she wondered if she might have hit her point home…

But then, "You never thought life might be different?"

Charlotte huffed and slumped back into her chair. "Not really," she dismissed, fingers massaging her temple. "I mean… *maybe* my mother wouldn't have had to work her ass off as—"

"Miss Carroll, I will not ask you to keep a civil tongue in my office again. This is the exact hostility I'm sure Mr. Keats is at his wit's end with."

Charlotte flexed her fingers. She could feel a burning sensation on the skin of her right thumb. "I'm sorry. My point is, I've never felt like I've been lacking anything."

"No?" He was skeptical. And smug. It made his face seem infinitely more akin to something meant to be punched. "Did your mother never even attempt to provide you with a strong father figure?"

"Stop." Charlotte rasped, her eyes focusing on the far wall. Her hand slowly moved down her face as she tried to inhale a second wind for her patience again. "*Don't* make this about my mother." It was a warning, not a request. She slowly turned her attention back to the sham psychologist in front of her. "For whatever reason, she decided to raise me completely on her own. I would ask you respect that, because I believe she made the best choice for both her and me. I have never regretted only having one parent. She's done an amazing job—far better than most people in her situation—far better than most nuclear families ever manage, frankly. I was always the top priority, and not having a father figure in my life has had no impact on my mental development. I didn't sleep well last night, okay? The lesson was boring, and then he decided to talk down to me about it. I've never done great with condescending tones, *that* is why I was irritable and falling asleep. So please, stop trying to blame either of my parents for why you don't like my poor behavior."

Another beat of silence that gave Charlotte some hope that she might have gotten through to him.

"...Why didn't you sleep well?"

Charlotte groaned and leaned forward, letting her head fall into her hands. Her heart was racing again, and it was starting to create a headache. "I don't know, I just didn't."

"Is this a common occurrence for you?"

"I don't know," Charlotte murmured, impatient. "Maybe. Sometimes."

He leaned farther over his desk toward her. "Have you talked to your mother about perhaps participating in a sleep study?"

Charlotte blinked. Talked to her mother. She raised her head from her hands, focusing bleary eyes on him. "Have *you* talked to my mother about pulling me out of class and inhibiting my education? Don't you need her permission for this sort of intervention?"

"You are not obligated to stay in my office, Charlotte. No one is holding you here. I was merely following up on concerns vocalized by your teachers."

Charlotte's eyes narrowed. "So, you haven't talked to her."

Mr. Blake skirted around her direct assertion and adopted his counterfeit concern once more. "I don't think you *want* to be like this, Charlotte. I don't think you're mean. I think, deep down, you're a sweet young girl, and you just don't know how to process all of these things going on inside you right now."

"What *things*, exactly?"

He smiled. "Well, I was hoping you would tell me."

His mannerisms made Charlotte wonder if he might not be the unwilling stepfather to some unfortunate child on whom he used these same tactics. This disingenuous buddy-buddy sort of attitude that was just one cliché shy of calling her 'sport' or 'pal.' "…Mr. Blake," she began evenly. "The way I see it, you're going to do one of two things. A, you are going to call my mother and *she* will give you an earful on the legal boundaries you currently seem to be skirting around right now, or B, you're going to let me go back to class without further interrogation or interruption."

Mr. Blake's mouth pursed slightly, and she could see the irritation in his eyes that the mask of 'parental-like compassion' had poorly attempted to conceal. "Thank you for speaking with me, Charlotte."

"You're very welcome, Mr. Blake." Charlotte stood, slinging her bag over her shoulder once more. She paused on her way to the door. "By the way, this? *This* was me being antagonistic. You might want to explain the difference to Mr. Keats."

The day might have finished without further incident had the rain ceased by lunch. Rain is a glorious spot of weather, but if one were to trace the domino effect that is action, circumstance, and consequence, it would have been the undeniable instigator of the whole business. Had it not been raining that Monday, had it been what locals insisted was 'nicer weather,' or if by perhaps a less radical stretch the school had amended its rule that only seniors were permitted to leave the campus during the lunch hour to retrieve meals, the entire incident could have been avoided entirely. But the truth of the matter is it was raining, and like most bureaucracies, the school was mired in the idea of rules that had always been and thus had no discernable inclination of ever changing. Therefore, conflict was inevitable.

Charlotte sat on the floor in the great room that served as a cafeteria because no other space would do. The open room was a testament to the recent "modern" reconstruction the school had undergone that seemed to be trying just a bit too hard to relate to student life rather than providing practical needs such as tables and chairs. There were some, of course, but they only covered half of the room, so most of the student body sat on the floor like Charlotte. A select few, those who were out of class quick enough but didn't possess the social standing to risk claiming a table, sat on the steps of a carpeted circular six-tiered mini-amphitheater-shaped hole in the ground affectionately referred to as "the pit." The purpose behind its design had never been entirely clear, but students had decided it did decently as a substitute table by sitting on a lower step and using the next tier up as their flat surface to eat on.

The entire space, while created with the best of intentions (as such things often are), created a hierarchy, where those of sufficient status took over the tables, leaving the "lower class" to find seating on the floor. A floor which was often still slightly damp from the excessive cleaning it had to go through for the staff to justify allowing the students to eat their lunch on it.

Charlotte, being one of those many groundlings, leaned her back against the great square pillar behind her, her lunch untouched and abandoned in favor of her phone. She didn't often use it for its designed purpose. She made occasional calls to her mother and godmother, and she occasionally surfed the internet for research, but she never touched any brand of social media. She hadn't downloaded any games. More often than anything, Charlotte used it for one single application: Geocaching. It was, like most of her activities, one that could be done in solitude but didn't leave her lonely.

When searching for a cache, Charlotte felt part of something bigger. She felt adventurous, exciting—like she was more than just a high school sophomore with high test scores and too much anxiety to make friends her own age. She scrawled through the app, searching for anything new in the area, anything she could seek out on her way home if she opted to not take the bus.

"Hey Charlotte."

She'd found all these caches. And looking at their last updates, on quite a few of them, she'd been the *last* person to find them.

"Hey." A beat. "Hey Charlotte!" More insistent this time.

Her eyes flickered to a nearby table.

Leaning back in his chair was a boy looking like a pleased chimpanzee about to throw his own feces.

His football jersey placed him among those Charlotte had come to know as the faceless gold-and-blue-clad army that they held nearly weekly assemblies to celebrate. She didn't know his name, which made it more surprising that he seemed to know hers. "Shelby tells us you got a thing for dead guys."

The table laughed, and Shelby popped her gum.

Charlotte blinked slowly at him, expressionless, before slowly looking back down at her phone and continuing to scroll through the listings, broadening her search radius.

"Hey," he started again between stifled hyena giggles.

There was nothing new. She needed to find a new area. Maybe this weekend she'd take the bus out to Ballard. Search for caches and celebrate her victory at Hotcakes with her mother or Diana.

"How do girls bang a corpse, anyway?" Another burst of laughing and elbow nudging.

Charlotte clicked her phone off and placed it back into her book bag before then gathering her lunch. Her movements were slow, calm, and deliberate, as if the cackling hyenas at the table to her would pounce if she made any sudden movements. *Ignore them. Ignore them, and eventually they'll get bored and leave you be.* She stood, slinging her bag onto her shoulder.

"Hey Charlotte, why won't you answer us, huh?" Another boy—Danny, she thought his name was— with his arm around Shelby's shoulders taunted.

"She likes to be called *Charlie*," Shelby purred smugly as if revealing some great secret.

"Maybe that explains how she gets it on with dead bodies. Wednesday Adams' got a dick!" Another one of them crowed.

"That one doesn't even make sense," Charlotte muttered to herself, bending down to pick up the lunch bag as well.

Danny removed his arm from around Shelby so he could lean forward. "Explains the tranny that picks her up from school."

Charlotte stopped cold.

He continued, "Who is that? Her dad? Have you seen that freak? Does he really think he's pa—?"

Charlotte's ten-pound book bag swung violently into his face, knocking him out of his chair. She was on him only an instant after, balling her fists to wail on the offender.

"Holy shit!" Danny choked, a crimson geyser exploding from his nose. Noses were always dramatic when it came to blood, but never so dramatic as Shelby.

"Oh my god!" Shelby's scream was the last girl standing in a horror film.

"APOLOGIZE!" The red liquid was gushing. She could feel it on her hands as they fought around his flailing limbs to land another hit, and then another.

"Fight, fight, fight!" A chorus of voices ecstatically chanted.

Then they swarmed on her like angry bees. Exceptionally large, uncoordinated, and objectively stupid, angry bees. Two grabbed her by the elbows and lifted her off with some difficulty due to her flailing limbs. Her elbow jabbed back into something, and she heard a string of curses from one of the boys. Then someone grabbed her by the hair at the root, nails scraping against her scalp as they pulled back roughly.

"APOLOGIZE!" Charlotte growled against her restraints, trying to yank her head and arms free to attack again.

Danny scrambled to his feet, blood gushing down from his nose. He stared at her, wide-eyed, as if he were looking upon some feral creature, realizing their initial assessment of her had been wrong. This was not prey. This was something else entirely. And it unnerved the hell out of him. He reached up, wiping at the blood, then, upon seeing the amount of it on his hands, felt shaky and pale. "The hell did you do to me, you crazy b—"

"Break it up!" a voice barked, and Charlie felt everything release her at once. The hand grasping at her hair released, then pushed her head forward, causing her to stumble forward and grasp the pillar for balance.

The vice principal glowered at the lot of them. "My office. *Now*."

2

ALYS

Charlotte felt like she was awaiting execution sitting outside the vice principal's office. She slowly kicked her feet back and forth, wondering if parents had been called yet. Would this be proof to Mr. Blake that she was indeed in heavy need of therapy? Would this be reason enough to force her to take it?

She felt like she'd swallowed a cannonball the size of her fist. It sat heavily and uncomfortably in her stomach, and she idly wondered if it were possible to vomit psychosomatic projectiles—or if they could also somehow be responsible for iron-poisoning. Imaginary cannonballs causing iron poisoning. A kind of irony poisoning.

She chuckled at the stupid thought and the stretch of her lips caused her to wince ever so slightly. Her tongue cautiously ran along her bottom lip. It was swollen, but not quite split. She poked at her right knee. It was bruised. So were her arms where they tried to wrench her away from Danny.

Still, all in all, she was rather impressed with herself for being nearly unscathed. At least, until the door opened, and she remembered why she was sitting there.

Right.

Look penitent.

She watched the last of her blue-and-gold tormentors file out—Shelby fairest of them all. Raphus had kept everyone separate in some attempt to get a straight story without collaboration: a noble effort, but Charlotte had seen the hive mind work before. It undoubtedly had again.

The Queen Bee herself leveled her gaze at Charlotte, her eyes narrowing ever so slightly as a smile tugged at the corner of her lips. Then with a regretful gaze she turned back to the office, and with a hand poised over her heart to better sell her remorse, she said, "Again, I am so sorry for any part I had in this, Vice Principal Raphus."

It was a feigned innocence she'd seen every student before her perform, but Shelby was the real pro at it. It was impressive, albeit revolting.

Charlotte shook her head as she watched the smugness return while Shelby exited the office without another glance or word. She felt her temper simmer. She knew she wasn't blameless, but dammit, neither were they.

Vice Principal Raphus stepped into the threshold of her doorway and motioned with two fingers for Charlotte to follow her inside: "Charlotte."

The cannonball sunk further, and Charlotte felt herself shaking as she pushed herself into a stand, following the tall woman into her office. She set down her bag softly beside a chair opposite the vice principal before carefully taking a seat. She clasped her hands in her lap, then unclasped them, then once again. Nothing felt right or comfortable. Her heart was pounding.

Ms. Raphus' complexion was smooth and well cared for, save for the seemingly permanent wrinkle between her brows from a constant furrow either in bewilderment or disappointment. She fixated this mixture of deep thought and dismay on Charlotte for a long moment, seemingly trying to puzzle something out of the odd-looking girl before finally breaking the silence with a heavy sigh. She leaned back in her chair. "You should know, you have all fingers pointing to you saying you started the fight."

Charlotte exhaled sharply through her nose, her eyes averting indignantly. She'd expected it, and yet that did little to alleviate the frustration.

Ms. Raphus did not break her intense focus on Charlotte. "Is this true?"

"No."

"No, it's not true?"

Charlotte felt the cannonball start to simmer with a sort of righteous indignation. "I finished the fight."

There was a moment, ever so brief though it was, where the vice principal almost smiled. A smile that did not quite reach her mouth but glimmered in her eyes as she regarded the tiny girl before her. She held that look before glancing down at what Charlotte recognized was an awfully familiar file sitting on the desk.

The cannonball dropped further in her stomach.

"Mr. Blake thought it was important that I look at your file before speaking with you."

Charlotte gnawed on her lower lip.

"His notes detail you have a bit of a history with hostility." She looked up to Charlotte, the amusement gone from her eyes. She was expectant.

Charlotte's fingers twisted against each other in her lap. "With all due respect, I don't think being a smartass should really qualify as being hostile, ma'am."

The corner of the vice principal's lips twitched, and she closed the file, folding her hands on top of it as if she had no intention of opening it again during their meeting. "Why don't you tell me what happened?" she asked quietly.

The closed file folder admittedly eased the tension in her stomach, but Charlotte found herself hesitant to recount anything. It was their word against hers... and who the hell was she in all of this? Some fatherless weirdo with impressive test scores, a catalogued bad attitude, and an inexplicable knack for making quite a few people almost as uncomfortable as they made her. What was even the point in trying to defend herself?

Ms. Raphus tilted her head to the side slightly and gently added, "Understanding is a two-way street, Charlie."

Charlotte's eyes lifted, and now her own mouth involuntarily quirked toward a smile. "Eleanor Roosevelt."

Ms. Raphus smiled and nodded affirmatively. "That's right."

Charlotte evaluated the woman across the desk from her now, not as a figure of authority but as a human being. A human being that at one point might have also been a weirdo with impressive test scores. At the very least, a human being that understood what it was like to be bullied. You did not become a high school vice principal if you had never encountered firsthand the unkindness in a student body that often required the attention of a high school vice principal. She took a deep breath and leaned slightly forward in her chair. "Ms. Raphus, do you... remember high school? Like, *really* remember it?"

The woman nodded, uncertain.

"Were you..." Charlotte paused, debating how to pose this question politely, "...well-liked?"

Ms. Raphus' lips parted slightly as she realized where this particular line of questioning could be leading. "I... had a lot of friends," she offered evasively.

"I don't," Charlotte admitted bluntly. She could feel her hands trembling, so she tightened her grip on them in her lap. She could feel that cannonball, that fear, returning, cold and heavy. "So, the friends I do have are very precious to me. Family, even. People I would do anything to protect."

"Charlotte," Ms. Raphus began softly but firmly. "Did you start the fight?"

Charlotte clamped her mouth shut, squirming a little in her seat. "...I was provoked."

The vice principal sighed again.

"They accused me of necrophilia, they were being lewd and gross and making gestures, and *then* they started off on my godmother, and I couldn't let that stand, okay?"

Ms. Raphus used her thumb and forefinger to massage that deep and permanent wrinkle in her brow. "We cannot let the bullies of our lives get the better of us, Charlotte. That's how they win."

"Really? I'm fairly sure letting them get away with hate speech and bigotry is how they win."

There was a pause. "Hate speech and bigotry?"

"My godmother is a transwoman. Danny Stead called her a *slur*."

"I see. Well, I will investigate that, Charlotte. I promise you."

It was a tone that meant well, a tone meant to be diplomatic, but it was a tone she'd heard too often, always ending in nothing. It set the cannonball in her stomach on fire, no longer a remnant of ammunition against her but something she fully intended to fire back. "*No one*, especially the likes of that meathead, is going to talk about my family like that. They don't get to disrespect her; they don't get to use *that* word."

"Alright." Ms. Raphus raised her hands in a manner Charlotte thought was befitting of calming an animal. "I agree with you, but unfortunately, I don't have any proof of what was said to you. What I do have is several witnesses that saw you hit Daniel Stead in the face with your book bag."

Charlotte stared in disbelief. "So... what? They get to walk away with *nothing*?"

Ms. Raphus' eyebrows raised. "I wouldn't call a black eye and bloody nose *nothing*."

Charlotte grinned involuntarily, realized she was grinning, and dropped her gaze to her lap, pursing her lips together. She tried to remember what it looked like to feel remorseful.

The vice principal took a deep breath. "Charlie, I'm afraid we're going to have to administer a suspension from campus."

Charlotte's head shot up; eyes wide.

"Just three days," Ms. Raphus assured, "for violent behavior, on the recommendation of Mr. Blake."

Charlotte's mouth fell agape.

"Your return will also be dependent on some anger management counseling. I'll be speaking with your mother about possible options."

"You can't be serious."

Ms. Raphus glanced down at the closed folder in front of her. "Your file shows a record of being consistently antagonistic, even toward your teachers, and today we saw what that hostility could become if not properly dealt with."

Charlotte blinked, feeling betrayed to have her file used against her after all. She repeated the scenario to the woman, attempting to contain her frustration through a tight jaw. "He. Called. My godmother. A. *Slur*."

"It's just a word, Charlotte."

"Fuck you, it's just a word!" Charlotte rose to her feet, the fury within her rising.

"Charlotte!" Ms. Raphus leaned back in her chair, shocked.

"No," the young girl insisted. "I've been hearing this since I was in grade school, and I just *can't* anymore, okay? I just *can't!* Sticks and stones, and all that—it's such bullshit. It's not *just words*, it's abuse, and it takes its toll on kids like me *every day*. It's lies like that that make us statistics, Ms. Raphus. Junkies, anorexics, suicides... We all deal with it differently, but we all know the phrase 'words will never hurt me' is a mantra invented by people who don't know what words can really do."

They stared at each other a moment, both equally surprised by the outburst.

Finally, the vice principal cleared her throat. "Charlotte," she started gently. "I can appreciate your frustration, but try to understand my position. All I have is your word against a majority, and instead of coming to one of your teachers about being bullied, you took it into your own hands and attacked a fellow student. Despite what I'm sure you believe, I'm not an idiot."

"I don't—" Charlotte started apologetically.

"Let me finish," Ms. Raphus said firmly, and Charlotte sank back into her chair. "*Your* version of these events makes far more sense than theirs; don't think that the reason you're getting punished and they aren't is because I don't believe you. But when you act out like this, you hinder our ability to help you. You attacked a student. Regardless of how justified you may feel about your actions, you cannot work outside of the system. We would have helped you."

Charlotte scoffed and stared down at her feet.

"*Now*," Ms. Raphus began pointedly, trying to get Charlotte to look back at her. "All we can do is respond to the actions you took on your own." She let that sink in before looking down to the folder on her desk. "I've already called your mother."

Charlotte's back stiffened.

"She's on her way to discuss the next steps required to get you back to class and take you home. Until then, I suggest you wait in the nurse's office and let her patch you up."

The fire was extinguished, and the lead weight pulling her downward had returned. Her mouth felt dry and as she looked back to the vice principal. "... did she sound mad?"

"She didn't sound particularly happy."

Charlotte mouthed a curse to herself before reaching down to grab her bag and move to the door. Was she imagining the funeral march, or did some eavesdroppers have a sadistic sense of humor? She'd attacked a student, she'd cursed at her vice principal, she… was screwed. She placed her hand on the door handle and paused with a sigh. She looked back at Ms. Raphus and did feel remorseful—at least for the cursing. This woman was just trying to do her job. "I *know* I shouldn't have hit him," she admitted. "I do know that…" She bit her lower lip, before she continued, unable to leave it at that. "But the system doesn't work, ma'am. I'm sorry, but it *doesn't*. That group has been doing this kind of stuff to kids like me since second grade. I have *never* retaliated until now, yet ignoring them or turning the other cheek or whatever has never deterred them. *Never*."

The wrinkle in Ms. Raphus' brow returned.

"What you don't do can be a destructive force," Charlotte tried to reason. Not seeing a look of recognition in the vice principal's face, she clarified. "Also Eleanor Roosevelt."

The wrinkle relaxed as Ms. Raphus raised a critical eyebrow. "Do you think Eleanor Roosevelt would have wanted you to sucker punch a student in a school cafeteria?"

Charlotte quirked her mouth to one side, raising her own eyebrow to answer this challenge. "Eleanor Roosevelt was very dear friends with a Russian sniper famed for killing over 300 Nazis… So, yeah, I think she would at least have been *okay* with me smacking a bigot with my book bag."

Ms. Raphus simply looked dumbfounded, unsure what to say.

Charlotte sighed, knowing she had again said a thing she should not have said. "What I mean to say in all of this is… We need a better system, Ms. Raphus. Because right now? We're damned if we do, and we're damned if we don't."

Still, she received no answer.

"Anyway, thank you for your time." Charlotte shrugged a little awkwardly and exited through the door.

It was eerily quiet as the door clicked behind her. A ghost-town quality followed the bustle of students filing back into class, not a soul in sight save for the janitor carefully re-mopping the floor to remove any food particles that may have fallen during the lunch hour.

Charlotte sighed heavily, feeling that growing weight in her stomach as she scuffed her boots along the floor, shuffling across the hall reluctantly into the nurse's office. Mrs. Stevens was not within immediate sight, but Danny Stead, whose nose had finally stopped bleeding, was sitting on the cushioned examination table. His head was cocked back slightly, an icepack in one hand, held over a black-and-purple discoloration that had overtaken most of his nose.

Charlotte resisted smiling. Barely.

He caught sight of her, and she saw the smugness return to his eyes. "Heard you're getting suspended," he smirked, then winced, realizing this action aggravated his injury.

Charlotte nonchalantly moved to idly examine some of the nurses' pamphlets. Teen pregnancy, abstinence, STDs, depression, eating disorders… "Not sure why *you're* so happy. If I got my ass kicked publicly by someone half my size, I would have welcomed a chance to hide my face for a few days."

Danny moved his head back again, so he didn't have to look at her. "Shut up."

Charlotte shrugged. "I mean, it sucks—it's not like you can lie about it. At least half the student body must have seen that you needed three people to help you fend off a small girl." She "hmmed" at the pamphlets and stepped away. "Nothing on toxic masculinity. Pity."

Danny glared at her, scowling through the pain. "Bite me."

"You wouldn't survive it," Charlotte met the gaze with a deadpan stare.

It was an uncomfortable sort of eye contact. Danny couldn't help but feel something wasn't quite right the more he looked at her, like if he blinked, she might in fact not actually be there and vanish from sight. It made him even more on edge and frustrated. "What the hell is *wrong* with you?"

"I wish I knew," Charlotte answered, surprised by her own sincerity.

Mrs. Stevens, the school nurse, re-entered from her office. She was a much older woman, the sort you imagined at one point might have worn the white dress and hat in her prime when she worked at an actual hospital and had authority over more than a few cuts and bruises. Her wiry grey hair was curled and vaguely reminiscent of the Farrah Fawcett style it had likely been trained to do since she was first enamored with it in the 1970s. Despite choosing a profession that had her on her feet most of the day, by stubbornness alone, it had not seemed to wither her as expected—a woman well past retirement who persisted in her profession, where she was allowed simply because she could not stand the idea of no longer being useful. "Danny, I've called your mother. She's going to take you to the hospital to get your nose looked at. It should be fine—don't worry—but in the likely event that it's broken, you should have a doctor look at it. You can wait for her here if you like, or outside. Cool air might help." Her eyes shifted to the white-haired girl now standing in her office. Her brow furrowed. "How can I help you?"

Charlotte shifted uncomfortably. "Ms. Raphus sent me."

Mrs. Stevens blinked at her, unsure if her memory was indeed finally going. "You are…?"

"Charlie Carroll."

Another blink from the elderly woman. "You."

Charlotte nodded.

"You're Charlie."

"Yup."

"You're…" Mrs. Stevens took another moment, her face scrutinizing this small teen before her, then looking to Danny's stature and the deep bruise before looking back to Charlotte. "What? Ten pounds? If that?"

Charlotte snerked.

Danny grumbled and slid off the table. "I think I'll wait outside, Mrs. Stevens. Thanks for patching me up."

The two women on either side of him watched his exit before their attention refocused on each other once more.

Mrs. Stevens was still puzzled by Charlotte. "…are you even injured?" She asked flatly.

Charlotte shrugged. "My lip kind of hurts?"

Mrs. Stevens closed the distance between them to take Charlotte's hands. She ran her thumb over the knuckles and prodded the webbing between them. "This hurt?"

"Not really."

"Any of this blood yours?"

Charlotte had been given a wipe to clean the blood off her hands earlier, but she'd missed some of the crevices in her knuckles and between her fingers. Her nose scrunched. "Doubt it."

Mrs. Stevens' brow furrowed, and she glanced from Charlotte's hands to her face. "Hmm."

Now Charlotte was starting to feel a little uncomfortable. "What?"

"You can wash your hands up in the sink." Mrs. Stevens released Charlotte's hands and moved to the tiny little refrigerator beneath the table to retrieve another ice pack.

Charlotte squinted. "What's 'hmm'?"

"Bruised, but no broken skin. I can't remember the last time I saw that after a fight broke out." Stevens held out the ice pack.

Charlotte took it cautiously and tucked it under her arm as she walked to the sink. "What's your point?"

"Where'd you learn to punch?" It was more accusation than question.

Charlotte took a moment to fully lather her hands in liquid soap. "I was taught by a wise elderly Japanese man who works maintenance for my apartment building."

The two stared at each other a moment.

Mrs. Stevens' face didn't so much as twitch. "Cute." She moved back toward her personal office. "I can see why you have so many friends."

Charlotte rinsed her hands and hopped up to the examination table. She begrudgingly placed the icepack on her lip. Stevens had hit a nerve, but she was going to pretend to be far more interested in the murmuring TV mounted on the wall.

"Funny though," Mrs. Stevens continued, returning with a clipboard in hand to make some notes, "first time I think I've seen both a black eye and a broken nose delivered by someone with so few injuries themselves."

"Is this where you reveal to me that you were once a prized boxer and you've just been waiting for someone to come along to train to be the best around and thus give you a new lease on life and renewed hope about the world?" Charlotte didn't look away from the TV, and Mrs. Stevens didn't so much as look up from her clipboard

"I'm going to go out on a limb here and wager your mouth gets you into a lot of trouble."

Charlotte shifted uncomfortably and looked back at the nurse. "I just don't get where these questions are coming from."

Mrs. Stevens peered over her clipboard at her. "Did you start the fight on purpose?"

"What?!" Charlotte nearly dropped the icepack. "No! I was trying to walk away!"

Mrs. Stevens squinted at her. She carefully examined every aspect of her expression and blinked, half expecting this specter of a child to no longer be there. But still she sat. "So, I'm not going to see a lot more broken noses in here any time soon?"

Charlotte sighed. "In all honesty, I'm sure my bag is what broke his nose, and I think someone's eye hit my elbow when they were trying to pull me off him. It wasn't… super intentional."

Mrs. Stevens gave her a skeptical 'hmm' and retreated to her office.

Charlotte scooted back to lean on the wall and stared miserably at the ceiling. This was not how she wanted to spend her Monday.

The small television in the corner quietly murmured on and filled the quiet room.

"Is your family safe? For the first time in almost 100 years, we may be facing a curious spread of Encephalitis

lethargica, otherwise known as sleepy sickness," the news anchor on the tv said in that strange intonation anchors always seemed to use.

Charlotte lethargically adjusted her attention to the screen.

"*Not to be confused with the parasitic disease known as Sleeping Sickness, found often in Sub-Saharan Africa, this disease has a history of leaving people in a catatonic or even coma-like state, immobilizing both speech and motor functions. While doctors say there have been sporadic cases since the initial 1915 epidemic—*"

A knock on the door frame drew Charlotte's attention away from the TV.

Alys Carroll was not a particularly tall woman, and even at age 36, she looked like it hadn't been too long since she had been in high school herself. Her light blue hooded sweatshirt was spotted with raindrops, and the old black boots looked like they might have encountered one or two puddles in the dash from visitor parking to the main entrance. She waggled her fingers in a small wave. "Hey you."

Charlotte remembered to breathe. "…Hey."

The two Carroll women stared at each other, one waiting for the other to explain herself, the other terrified by what the other already knew.

"Have you…" Charlotte started warily, "…talked with Ms. Raphus yet?"

"No," Alys answered softly. "Was just about to head in. I wanted to see if there was anything you wanted to tell me first yourself, about what happened?" Her brow furrowed, and somehow the amber color of her eyes seemed to catch the light like a flicker of flame as they drew to a sharp focus. "Or why you have an icepack on your face?"

Charlotte became keenly aware of the dull pain in her lip as she cautiously lowered the icepack to give her mother a view of the swelling. "It's no big deal."

Alys folded her arms, and her gaze seemed to intensify.

It spilled out of her in that moment, rapidly, and with little breath or punctuation. "Some dumb jock called Diana a—well he called her a—*that word*, Mom. He called her that freaking word and I just—I lost it, and I hit him. A lot. He got in a few, sort of, or—well— *they* got in a few, but because *I* technically started the fist fight, they're going to suspend me for it." And with it completely out there, with the story spread out, she felt her jaw slam shut and her body press back against the wall as if she were scared what she would unleash with this feverish admission.

Alys' eyes averted as she processed this information. She was eerily still, save for the slight tightening of her jaw, and when she finally did speak, there was a soft protective growl. "Are you alright?"

Charlotte nodded wordlessly.

Alys took a deep breath, exhaled, and straightened her back. "Okay. Wait here. I'll be back."

With her mother's departure, Charlotte felt her anxiety increase. Her heart began to pound, and she leaned her head back and closed her eyes.

She could see flashes of The Nothing when she did. The crack in the sky, the lightning, and as she tried to breathe steadily to calm her heartbeat, she could swear she heard the distant wails of those being dragged to some unseen hell on the other side.

The feeling of burning snow on her skin.

The smell of smoke, and ash.

A world on fire, but still no illumination survived, as if that too had burned up.

"Just a dream," she muttered to herself. She couldn't get the terrified pale blue eyes of the blonde woman out of her mind. She flinched, and her breathing quickened. "Just a dream." She inhaled a five-count and exhaled on six, then repeated. Inhale one, two, three, four, five. Exhale one, two, three, four, five, six.

Repeat.

Repeat.

Re—

"Hey. Ready to go home?"

Charlotte opened her eyes, surprised to see Alys had returned. She blinked, hard. "I need the assignments for the days I'll be gone," she murmured.

Alys held up a red folder in answer that she hadn't had when she'd arrived. "Do you have all the books you'll need, or are they in your locker?"

Charlotte shakily slid from the table to pick up her hefty book bag. "I have all of them."

Alys gestured with her head for Charlotte to follow as she dug her keys out of her purse. "Okay, let's go."

The rain was pounding as they stepped outside. Alys put her hood up, but Charlotte, dragging her feet behind her, didn't bother. She was too depressed. There were a lot of things she could endure, but a rift between her and her mother was not one of them.

It wasn't too far from visitor parking, but it was enough to get substantially wet if you took your time getting to it. Charlotte still preferred the downpour to talking.

Alys had unlocked the doors to the Honda Civic and settled into the driver's seat by the time her daughter finally caught up and opened her own door.

Charlotte put her bag on the floor before sitting down and pulling the door closed quickly behind her. She shivered as she locked her seat belt into place. Seattle rain had a talent for chilling you down to the bone in a way that only a hot shower was likely to steam out.

The car was silent but for the rainfall on the roof.

Charlotte tentatively peeked toward her mother, who was staring out windshield, past the curtain of water, as if memorizing something far in the distance. Her expression was stoic and perhaps contemplative, but Charlotte couldn't pinpoint it to any one emotion.

"So," Alys at last began in a thoughtful tone. "Your school record is… impressive."

"I have a 4.0," Charlotte tried to evade.

"I'm not talking about your grades, Charlotte," Alys said heavily.

Charlotte gnawed her lower lip, looking down at her own knees. The weight in her stomach was unbearable. "Are you going to yell at me?" she asked quietly.

Alys paused before putting the keys in the ignition, pondering the reason the question was asked rather than what it was asking her. "No."

Charlotte blinked. "You're not angry?"

"Angry isn't really the word." She started the car.

Charlotte watched her mother's expression carefully, finally finding the word that described that look in her mother's eyes. Disappointment. Almost sadness. It made her stomach lurch. "*Please* yell at me?"

Alys sighed again, her brow knitting together. "You know better than to start fights, Charlie. Or to talk back to teachers."

"Mom, Mr. Keats is—"

"Oh, I've no doubt the man's a complete tool. But he's still one of your teachers." Alys carefully backed them out of the parking lot, and they were on the road back toward home.

"So that means I have to respect him no matter what?"

"No," Alys answered. "But it does mean you don't *disrespect* him, especially in front of the entire class. There is a difference. It's hard enough being a teacher, Charlotte, how do you think it looks when your top student can't even be bothered to pretend like she's paying attention?"

Charlotte leaned back in her seat, her throat tight and her eyes watering. This was worse than being yelled at. Being yelled at gave her the luxury of being angry in response. This... There was no defense for this other than not caring, and Charlotte wasn't particularly good at not caring when it came to her mother.

"As for the fight..." Alys shook her head a little, bewildered. This was out of her depth. It wasn't the sort of thing she'd seen coming, that was for sure. "As much as I hate to admit it, your vice principal is right. If you'd gone to a teacher with your concern, you wouldn't be in this situation."

"A teacher like Keats?" Charlotte asked resentfully, trying to find some high ground in the conversation.

Alys shot her daughter a skeptical look. "You're telling me there isn't a single teacher you trust in your entire school?"

Charlotte looked out her window guiltily. There was always Mrs. Robertson.

"That's what I thought."

Charlotte could feel the frustration increase the tightness in her throat, and she reached up to wipe at her eye surreptitiously. "You seriously think tattling on those assholes would have helped?"

Alys waffled over how to answer this question. "No. But I think it *would* have kept you from being suspended."

"What was I supposed to do after they spoke about Diana like that? Just ignore them?"

"Sometimes, yes, it's better to ignore people like that. Especially," Alys gave another pointed glance, "when you know they're saying it to specifically get a rise out of you."

"That's just—" Charlotte stopped herself, sighed, and folded her arms as she leaned back in her chair. "It seems cowardly," she said, deflated.

"Well, it's not exactly brave to beat someone up simply because they say something you believe is wrong."

Ah. Finally. Moral high ground. "It's not something I believe is wrong, mom. It IS wrong."

Alys exhaled slowly, patiently. "I'm sorry, I misspoke. You're right. It's very wrong to treat anyone like that, or to use that word. *However*, pummeling someone to the ground isn't exactly going to get them to see that is it?"

Charlotte grumbled in frustration, her arms falling to her sides.

"I'm not explaining this very well, am I?" Alys asked more to herself than her daughter. She took a moment, drumming her fingers on the steering wheel as they navigated the neighborhood just north of downtown Seattle proper. She reached her right hand out to gently place it over Charlotte's. "Charlie, I love Diana just as much as you do. She's my best friend. I've known her since I was your age. But even she wouldn't want you getting into fist fights with some dumbass boy at school for calling her names."

Charlotte looked at the hand that laced its fingers with her own and gave it a soft squeeze. She frowned and looked at Alys helplessly. "I don't understand what you expect me to do."

"I expect you to do the right thing," Alys answered, and she could practically feel her daughter's brow furrow in frustration at that, and so she elaborated. "I expect you to stand up for her, with *words*. You want to talk about what's brave? It takes a lot more bravery to tell someone *why* they're wrong than it does to punch them in the face for being it."

Charlotte took her hand back grumpily so she could fold her arms again. "Mom, people like Danny stead aren't going to listen to me. The moment I say anything, they have more ammunition to make fun of me."

"Then say your peace and walk away. He's not worth risking your education."

Charlotte gripped the air in frustration. "Ugh, that's so…"

"I know, I *know*." Alys agreed with emphasis. "The high road sucks. But if you don't take it, they're just going to use it as ammunition to ruin your life. You don't get to sink to their level. You have to be better than them for the rest of the world to even consider hearing you. It isn't right. And it isn't fair. It really, *really* sucks."

Charlotte's hands dropped to her lap, and she felt her fury deflate. "Yeah. It does."

"But it's how our broken world is right now. And unfortunately, you're going to continue to experience that on a level I can't even imagine. Definitely more than I ever do. Maybe even more than Diana. But I promise you, no matter what, we will have your back."

Charlotte smiled weakly. "Thanks mom."

"So," Alys concluded with authority. "No more fighting at school?"

"No more fighting at school," Charlotte agreed dejectedly.

Alys gave a firm nod. "Good." She exhaled in a way that made Charlotte think she might have found the whole discussion just as uncomfortable as she did. "Now we can get on to far more important things."

Charlotte blinked. "Like... what?"

"Like how we're going to spend your three days of vacation."

The younger Carroll choked on a laugh. "Mom, I'm *suspended.*"

"For vigilante justice!" Alys exclaimed. "You're practically Batman, and that doesn't deserve three days of *punishment.* You just need to learn a way to safely work *with* the authorities, not leave them out of the loop entirely. Figuratively speaking, of course—I do not expect you to start cleaning up the streets of Seattle in cahoots with the SPD—I don't care if you find your Jim Gordon or not. College first and all that." She pointed at Charlie with this last sentence, a growing grin on her face.

It was in that moment Charlotte realized the reason her mother had been so hard to read in the first place. There was a part of Alys, regardless of how inappropriate she knew it was... that was proud of her daughter.

"You learned your lesson, and you're not going to do it again, right?"

Charlotte smiled with uncertainty. "Right…"

Alys shrugged. "So, then why dwell on it? Then you feel bad all night and *I* feel bad all night, and then we both are in foul moods for nothing."

Charlotte shook her head. Despite that she knew most households didn't work this way, she couldn't quite find the words to explain why they should dwell on it, and she was hard-pressed to argue with her mother's logic. So instead, she laughed. "I don't… think you parent right."

Alys scoffed. "Nonsense! I parent excellently." She pulled into a parking spot on the street just a little off from "The Ave," the main street that ran through the University District. Alys had explained many times to Charlotte that even though the street was named University Way, and in fact a University Avenue *did* exist in downtown proper of Seattle, it was still called by all "The Ave." She'd agreed that it didn't make sense, but it was just one of those things you simply had to accept, or you would forever be getting them confused and going to the wrong addresses. "I think… Thai 65 and a marathon of something we can make fun of on Netflix…"

It was at this moment that Charlotte realized they hadn't been on their way home from the start. She looked at her mother incredulously. "Okay, now you're just *rewarding* bad behavior."

Alys pursed her lips at this accusation as she turned the car off. "What if… I only let you order *one* entree?"

"You. Monster."

3

HEAD CASE

Charlotte woke up on the couch. Her head was hanging off the edge toward the floor, and her torso twisted so that her knees pointed toward the back cushions. She shifted her head groggily, the duvet that had been draped over her tickling her nose. She fought to free her left arm from beneath the heavy comforter to push it away and rub her face. She took in the upside-down room blearily.

It was still dark, even with the blinds of the great living room window still partially open. She could hear the rain still dropping off the roof from the porch.

She kicked her legs to pull the duvet off her, but in her tangled state, this made the matter worse. She kicked again, and again, and the twist of the duvet around her legs rolled her upper half off the couch completely.

Her left hand cushioned her fall by placing down on the rug, while the right caught the coffee table in time before her face smacked against it. She blinked, and as her vision focused, she took in the glorious mess of empty takeaway containers of Thai food, the empty popcorn bowl, and just beyond the coffee table on the tv, Netflix suspended in an eternal question of "Are You Still Watching?"

Using the table and floor as leverage, she carefully wiggled her legs to untangle from the comforter before pushing herself into a more upright position. Alys was nowhere to be seen, and Charlotte imagined she had been the smarter of the two and gone to sleep in a bed, being spared the strange crick that now presented itself in Charlotte's neck.

She rubbed at her neck with her left hand and used her right to hover over the forest of take away boxes and find her phone among them.

6:05 a.m.

If she got up now, she could surprise Alys with coffee from down the street. True, they had made amends the night before, but a little extra effort would help ease the sting of why a woman who worked from home would be having an unexpected coworker during hours she normally had alone. She found the remote and turned off the TV. She took in the evidence of takeout and made note to get a trash bag to collect it after she was dressed. That way, she could just pop it into the large trash can outside on her way to the coffee shop. She crossed the hardwood floor and padded up the stairs to the upstairs bathroom. Habitually, she turned on the small MP3 music player sitting on the bathroom counter.

The shower took a few seconds to steam up, and she was inside. She sighed contently, allowing the weight of yesterday to wash off her. She closed her eyes, simply enjoying the moment. Her fingers ran through her hair as she leaned back into the water stream. She was warm, happy, and… She stopped as her fingers caught, finding what felt like the worst knot she had ever had at the base of her skull. She pinched at it, trying to decipher how she'd managed to create something so unmanageable.

The hair felt… matted and… sticky?

Charlotte stumbled out of the shower, to the mirror, as water dripped haphazardly on the tile floor and bathmat. She slid her hand across the fogged-up surface and turned her head, craning to see if she could get a look at the issue, to no avail.

She opened the cabinet below to retrieve the smaller standing mirror below, making sure the magnifier wasn't currently facing toward her so she could get a clear view. She twisted her hair up and turned her back toward the bathroom mirror, raising up the standing mirror to reflect the image of the back of her head to her.

Sure enough, right near the base of her skull, plunged deep into her roots, was a giant wad of dull pink goo.

She stared, numb and confused.

Then slowly, through the morning fog, she remembered the pop of Shelby's bubble gum the previous day, then the feeling of a hand with manicured nails grabbing the back of her head. "Oh no."

Charlotte hopped back into the shower, shaking, and poured a large dollop of shampoo on her hand before vigorously lathering her hair, desperately working at the gum, where it seemed to only pull more. "Oh no, oh no, oh no." Her heart started to pound.

She poured on the conditioner and carefully tried to dislodge the gum. A few small pieces seemed to come off, but it did little to the bulk of the thing. She turned off the shower and stepped out once more to move to the mirror and get a better look at it once more. "No…"

The pink mass of goo seemed to mock her.

Maybe it was the panic, maybe it was hormonal, maybe she wasn't fully awake. But the most logical action Charlotte could think of at the time was to snatch up the small manicure scissors from the drawer and try to cut the gob of chewing gum from her hair. She had already taken out a small chunk of hair about two inches from the root before she realized her mistake. She looked at the small fistful of long white hair in her hand before her eyes welled with tears. "Oh no…" She shook her head. "No, no, no, Charlie you idiot—what did you just do?"

There was a soft knock on the door. "Charlie?" Alys' voice was tired.

"Shit," Charlotte hissed under her breath, feeling her heartbeat quicken as she reached frantically for a towel and wrapped it around herself.

"Sweetheart, what's wrong?" Alys asked gently.

"Nothing!"

"Lie better," Alys advised, worry starting to creep into her voice.

Charlotte tried to stifle what sounded like something between a laugh and a sob.

"Charlotte Aislynn Carroll, open this door, please."

Charlotte hesitated a moment, then reluctantly did as she was told, her head low. "Mom… I did something stupid."

Alys looked at her daughter, then to the silvery white clump on the counter. "What happened?"

Charlotte's eyes welled with tears, and she started to shake.

Alys carefully reached forward and took the scissors out of her daughter's hand, placing them on the counter before gathering her in her arms. "Okay, hey… deep breaths."

"I'm getting water all over you," Charlotte half-heartedly protested.

"You used to get a lot worse all over me when you were a baby. I think I can handle water." Alys hugged her tighter. "Talk to me. What's going on?"

Charlotte took a deep breath and exhaled her reply without taking another breath. "Shelby Ferris put freaking gum in my hair, and I didn't notice it until this morning, and it wasn't coming out, so I thought maybe I could cut it out, but I think I cut more than I wanted to, and I ruined everything, and I can't do anything right, and I'm a complete idiot." Then she broke into a loud sob.

"Hey, hey…" Alys rested her head on the top of Charlotte's. "Take a breath. It's okay. I promise. It's okay. We can fix this, and it's going to be *okay*. You're not an idiot."

Charlotte sniffled into Alys' shoulder. "I ruined everything."

"Can I see it?"

"No."

"Charlie."

Charlotte slowly released her and turned around, lifting her wet hair to show her mother where the rest of the gum was stubbornly fixated.

"Okay…" Alys said to herself, thinking a moment. "Put on your robe, and I'll be back with some peanut butter."

"Peanut butter?"

"Mmhmm," Alys affirmed, pointing to the toilet. "Get cozy and sit down, we'll have this out in no time."

Charlotte watched Alys leave before closing the door enough to pull her bathrobe off the hook and put it on over the towel. She shut down the toilet seat cover and sat, fingers idly playing with the ends of her hair.

Alys returned with a jar of smooth peanut butter usually only employed when baking cookies. The Carroll household had decided on the superiority of chunky peanut butter when it came to sandwiches and the like and would fight you with a surprising level of vehemence on the subject if you attempted to argue otherwise. "I learned this trick when you were really little and liked to go to sleep with gum in your mouth. The Internet is a wonderful thing."

"This will get the gum out?"

"Well, *this*, patience, and a little elbow grease," Alys answered, clipping the unstuck hair out of the way.

Charlotte sighed and shook her head. "Stupid."

"Hey, stop. You panicked, and you didn't know. Besides, it's just hair, it'll grow back."

"Yeah, but in the meantime—"

"In the *meantime*, I'm going to give Diana a call and see if she has time to sneak you in today. Let's let the expert assess the damage, okay?" Alys took a gob of peanut butter and applied it to the gummy area, carefully working it in with her fingers. "Now… Who's Shelby?"

"Stupid cheerleader who told people I have sex with corpses."

Alys choked on a startled laugh. "What?"

"It's what started the whole thing in the first place, and I tried to ignore them, mom, I *really* did, and then Danny said that thing about Diana, and I just lost it. Then the rest of them, including Shelby, were on me until Ms. Raphus broke it up."

"Okay…" Alys paused, trying to figure out just how she should approach the question she knew she needed to ask but was admittedly a little afraid of the answer.

"Is there any specific reason how that *particular* rumor got around?"

"A Rose for Emily."

Alys felt her muscles relax in surprise. "Your assignment?"

"Shelby is in my AP English class. Apparently doing my homework by applying critical thinking on a short story where a woman kills her lover so she can sleep with his corpse is damning evidence about my own personal life?"

Despite that she had been certain she knew her daughter, and that such rumors were never based on any fact, Alys couldn't deny the relief that the origin of the rumor had nothing to do with sex with *anyone*, or dead things in any capacity. She paused. "Are you... with... *anyone*?"

"What? Mom!"

"It's alright if you are. I just want to make sure you're being safe—"

"No! I... No! I'm not even dating, and even if I... No."

"You know you could tell me if you were."

"Yes, I *know*."

"I promise I'd be... cool or whatever."

"Like you were cool about Kimiko?"

Alys laughed. "Oh, that was just teasing. It was cute."

"What if she heard you?"

Alys huffed through her nose. "From outside the coffee shop? In our car?"

Charlotte flustered slightly. "I... maybe?"

Alys nodded, deciding it was best to simply accept that it was possible a barista had superhuman hearing rather than try to reason with a sixteen-year-old girl about her first crush. "So, this... Shelby person. Why is she so threatened by you?"

"...what?"

Alys shrugged. "In my experience, when someone goes out of their way to make someone else feel smaller or lesser, it's because they feel insecure, or threatened. *Especially* kids your age."

Charlotte took a moment to think this over. "...I don't know. Maybe she's jealous because I'm acing a class I don't even have to pay attention to?"

Alys nodded slowly to herself, sucking in her cheeks thoughtfully. "Yeah, about that... You want to tell me what's going on?"

Charlotte growled in frustration and rolled her eyes. "Mr. Keats clearly doesn't enjoy teaching and uses boring, predictable, and formulaic lesson plans pulled directly from the textbook instead of trying to engage his students. Frankly, I don't understand how they get by calling that Advanced Placement ANYTHING. The entire class should be able to breeze through it."

"I meant with you."

Charlotte blinked. "...what about me?"

Alys let the peanut butter sit and turned to rinse her hands in the sink before she leaned back against the bathroom counter. "Ms. Raphus let me read your *file*."

Charlotte looked down. "I *don't* have an anger problem."

Alys began carefully. "I'm not saying you have an anger problem, honey, but clearly *something* is going on with you. Something changed. You used to love school. You were practically the teacher's pet all through elementary."

"I have the highest grade average in my class."

"I'm not talking about grades. I'm talking about the attitude that has apparently riled enough teachers that they told me you needed to agree to see a counselor before going back to school."

Charlotte flinched.

Alys folded her arms, her head tilting to the side to try to catch Charlotte's gaze. "You've always been able to talk to me. And if that's changed for some reason, I will try to understand... But I want to help."

"No, it's not that," Charlotte assured.

"So, what's going on then?"

Charlotte averted her eyes and looked down at her fingers in her lap. It wasn't that she didn't *want* to tell her mother or feel like she couldn't tell her... she just simply wasn't sure how. "I don't know... I just... feel weird lately."

"Depressed?" Alys suggested quietly.

"No... not exactly. More anxious than anything, but..." Charlotte tilted her head from one side to another, choosing her words carefully. "Do you ever feel... *stuck*?"

"Stuck like a jealous cheerleader put gum in my hair?"

Charlotte laughed and shook her head. "No... Like... You're still half-asleep."

Alys' smile faded.

"I feel like more and more I'm not really here. Disconnected..."

Alys rubbed her arms subconsciously as if a chill had set into the room. "That kind of sounds like depression, honey."

"But I'm not upset about it. I don't feel emotionally disconnected; I feel..." Charlotte sighed. "I know it sounds stupid, but I literally feel like part of me isn't here. Like when you stand between an open door and part of you can feel the breeze from outside and the other part can feel the heat of your house. I don't feel sad or lost, I just feel... split? And sometimes I get this feeling like... I'm not in the right place. Like I'm supposed to be somewhere else." She looked up at Alys. "Do you ever feel like that?"

Alys seemed to be looking more through her daughter than at her. Her gaze seemed distant and her eyes glossy as her fingers absently toyed with the golden pocket watch that hung on a long sturdy chain around her neck. "Yes," she answered softly. "I know exactly what you mean..."

"I keep thinking..." Charlotte laughed half-heartedly as she found the words, "the *mothership* has got to come back for me at some point, or something, like there's no possible way this is where I'm meant to be."

She drew her knees up to her chest, wrapping her arms around them. "I don't fit in here, Mom. I've tried, I really have. I've tried for years, and I just... I just *don't*. I feel like I don't really fit in *anywhere*."

Alys took a moment to listen, letting the silence fall between them for a moment. Her brow furrowed and her lips pursed in that telltale manner that said she was deciding something. She inhaled slowly and shrugged on the exhale. "Okay, so maybe you don't."

Charlotte blinked. "Huh?"

"Maybe... you *are* different from all the other kids at school. Maybe you'll never be able to blend in like the others and be truly one of them. Maybe you were never meant to belong here."

Charlotte was taken aback.

"But," Alys intoned pointedly, her voice softening, "...is that so terrible?"

Charlotte let that question sink in. She bit her lower lip and let her gaze drop to the tile just in front of her. Was this feeling of not belonging really that bad? It certainly felt that way. Sometimes, she would dare say it seemed nearly unbearable.

Alys moved to kneel in front of her. "You know... everything and everyone in the world is really nothing more than millions of atoms, vibrating at different frequencies?"

Charlotte stared at her.

"Really," Alys assured with a sad, almost nostalgic smile. "That's *all*."

"…so?"

"So, *maybe* you just vibrate at a different frequency than most people. And that's okay. It's just what makes you *you*."

Charlotte's gaze averted.

"And maybe it sucks now. Maybe it sucks *a lot* right now and you feel really lost and out of place in this world… but I promise you, it's temporary. Kids like Shelly Whatsherface? They usually peak in high school because they never had to really try at anything until they were out in the real world. And that's a harsh wake-up call not a lot of them get through on their own merit. But you?" Alys shook her head almost in wonder. "It's hard *now* because you were meant for so much more than high school popularity. And I can't *wait* to see what great things you'll accomplish."

It was a long sullen silence that warmed so gradually it was almost imperceptive. Then finally, with a reluctant return of eye-contact, "Yeah?"

"Yeah." Alys smiled reassuringly, but Charlotte noted there was something melancholic in her eyes. "And until then, you and I can wait for the mothership together. Conquer this world in the meantime. Okay?"

Charlotte smiled and nodded, wiping at her eyes with the back of her hand. "Okay."

Alys exhaled heavily and gently patted Charlotte's knee before using it to stand again. "Let's see how we're doing back here." She moved around her to check the status of the chewing gum, her fingers carefully beginning to pull the rest of the gum from Charlotte's hair piece by piece with relative ease. "Uh-huh. There we go…"

Charlotte could feel her heart quicken. "Really?"

"Really." Alys dropped the big pieces into the bathroom trash can and carefully removed any lingering bits of gum. "Now, I'll fix up some breakfast and give Diana a call to see if she can squeeze you in at the salon today. Okay?"

Charlotte stood and hugged her mother tightly. "You're the best."

"I bet you say that to all your mothers."

Like most things just off Broadway on Capitol Hill, Head Case Salon had no parking lot of its own. Thankfully, being a Tuesday morning, street parking was decently abundant, so the trek through the morning mist was a short one.

Alys knocked on the locked door as she and Charlotte huddled beneath the awning, waiting to be let in. It was 9 a.m. and still an hour before the salon was due to open.

The woman who opened the door for them could only be described as Amazonian in stature. Daintily resting on her strong nose was a pair of black-rimmed cat-eye glasses, accentuating her high cheekbones.

Her makeup was a flawless nod to pin-up style and nearly covered the faint smattering of freckles that naturally spread across her cheeks. "I hope you appreciate the pure amount of love it took to get me here this early."

"We love you, too," Alys answered, offering up a large latte they'd picked up on their way up the hill.

"Bless you." Diana took the cup and stood to the side to allow them both to pass inside. "How are you?" She asked a rather miserable looking Charlotte, slinging her free arm around her. Between her natural height and the four-inch heels, Diana was nearly an entire two feet taller than the teenager.

"Not great," Charlotte answered.

"Yeah... Mama told me what happened." Diana led her to one of the salon chairs. "Have a seat, kitten. We'll assess the damage."

Alys slipped into the chair in the station next to them. "It's not that bad, to be honest."

"Excuse me, Miss I-have-worn-my-hair-in-a-pony-tail-since-junior-high, you do not get to comment on anyone's hair." Diana carefully examined Charlie's hair by parting through it layer by layer with the tail of her comb, using a duck clip to secure it out of the way once she had inspected it. "Okay..."

"Okay?" Charlotte asked.

"Well, love, I can give you two options." Diana met Charlotte's eyes through their reflection in the mirror. "I can leave it be and it will grow back, and as long as you don't put your hair up, it will be unnoticeable… or we can cut it. But that will be a pretty drastic change."

Charlotte chewed her lower lip. "Can't you just work it into the layers?"

"It's too close to the center of your head and not close enough to the bottom of your hairline for that."

Charlotte sighed. "What would you do?"

Diana released the hair from the clip and let it fall around Charlotte's face and shoulders. "Y'know me. I love the dramatic. Give a chance to make a grand entrance and I take it in a heartbeat." She ran her fingers up through the girl's hair, scrunching it up near the root. "I'd cut it. Something high-end and edgy. Walk back into school with your head held high and renewed confidence. And if you don't completely love it, it'll grow back…"

Charlotte didn't look convinced. "Yeah, but won't that take forever?"

"It would take quite some time, yes, but there's also ways to supplement the length if you find you miss it too terribly much. How about I show you a few pictures of options we could do?"

Charlotte bit her lower lip as she considered this. She'd never done much of anything with her hair since she was a child… save for trim it. "Okay…"

Diana smiled and patted her shoulders before grabbing a book from the coffee table in the waiting room. "People are gonna try to tell you that cutting long hair means losing your femininity, and those people are full of patriarchal bullshit, okay?" She placed it on the counter in front of Charlotte and flipped through a few pages. "Some of the fiercest women I have ever met rock something above the shoulders, and I think with your hair we could do a very stylish updated inverted bob."

"A *bob*?" Charlotte's nose scrunched.

"Not those boring football helmet-shaped things you see on suburban soccer moms—I mean something like this." Diana pointed to a picture in the book. "This is an inverted bob with layers. It's asymmetrical, longer in the front, but the back is shorter and off your neck. We can flip it up. Give it a good punky flair. Like something out of those sci-fi movies you love."

"I don't know…"

"You're not going to look dated; I promise." Diana watched Charlotte's face. "But if you hate it, we aren't going near the cutting shears. I'm not going to try to talk you into something you don't want to do."

"I don't know… It's not that I don't want to… I've just… had this forever." Charlotte ran her fingers through her hair critically. "I don't know…" she repeated. "Maybe it's time for a change? I don't know."

"That's a lot of 'I don't knows,'" Diana pointed out skeptically.

"Probably be pretty cathartic to cut off all that weight," Alys offered. "You haven't had a real cut since what? Fourth grade?"

"Yeah…" Charlotte paused, weighing her options. On one hand, if she cut it, then Shelby Ferris would know she'd won. On the other hand, if it looked better than now, it would be an extremely hollow triumph. "You really think it'll look okay?"

"Kitten, you know I would never make you anything less than gorgeous. You'd look taller, it's going to make those amazing cheekbones of yours pop, and you'll probably actually get to see your ear piercings every once in a while, rather than them hiding under this unicorn mane."

Charlotte appraised her appearance in the mirror in front of her as Diana slowly took her hair in her hands and raised it to best give the illusion of the shorter length. She bit her lower lip. Cutting off all the weight... She took a deep breath. "Okay," she exhaled with as much confidence as she could muster. "Let's do it. *Whatever* you think is best."

"You're *sure*?" Diana asked firmly.

"Yes."

By the time Diana and Charlotte had returned from the shampoo room, Alys had turned on the TV. "Have you seen this?" She asked, pointing toward the screen, remote in hand. "First outbreak of this disease since 1926."

Diana nodded. "Made me afraid to go to sleep last night. They said it'd put 45 people in a coma so far."

"Closer to 150 now, by this report, all over the country."

"Jesus."

"What's weird..." Alys continued. "Is the only relative similarity in cases is that it's mostly women—and everyone affected is under 40."

"Keep your head still, sweetie," Diana reminded Charlotte as she pulled out her comb and scissors. "Things like that are enough to make you scared to eat anything, go anywhere, or talk to anybody." She carefully pulled Charlotte's hair back into a ponytail at the base of her neck and paused one last time. "Okay, no backing out after this. You're sure you're ready?"

"Do it." Charlotte closed her eyes tightly. She heard the snip of the scissors unnervingly close to her ears before she felt hair fall forward over her shoulders. Her eyes opened slowly, tentatively, and she moved her head from side to side, surprised by how light her head felt now. "Holy crap…"

"Bet you didn't realize how much weight you were carrying, did you?" Diana laughed, setting a long pony-tail of bright white hair on the counter off to the side. "In case you want to donate it, or mourn the loss later," she joked.

"Holy crap, there's so much of it."

"You know… I don't think this disease is infectious…" Alys, having completely missed the first cut, was fiddling with the watch around her neck again. She always did it when nervous or anxious. Charlotte could see her through the reflection in the mirror, and there was something about the inflection of her voice, or the look in her eyes, that just seemed… haunted.

"Can you tilt your head down for me?" Diana asked Charlotte, and in obeying, Charlotte lost sight of her mother again, staring down toward the floor. "Are you feeling particularly morbid today, or is there really nothing else on TV?"

"Sorry," Alys said, changing the channel reflexively. "Something about it seems so…" She shook her head. "It's just strange." She started flipping through the channels, more out of something to do than anything else, as she didn't pause long enough to observe what was playing to be truly searching for programming.

Charlotte listened intently, watching strands of white hair float down to the floor as they were severed from her. As more of it gathered on the floor, she began to think it rather did look like someone had sheared a unicorn.

Diana turned the chair away from the mirror. "Head up, try not to peek. You know how I love a big reveal."

"Who am I kidding, if working from home for ten years has taught me anything, it's that there's nothing good on regular TV before 6 p.m.," Alys turned the TV off and wandered back over to the chair by Charlotte.

"Then why are you almost always missing deadlines?" Diana arched a perfect eyebrow at her.

"I have Netflix," Alys answered obviously, picking up a magazine and flipping through it. "Oh, trashy magazine, what deliciously pointless information can you bestow on me today?"

"There's a pretty terrifying botched plastic surgery spread in there."

Alys' face scrunched, and she tossed the magazine back on the counter. "No thanks. If I want to see the face of terror, I'll just visit my mother."

"Good lord, that woman…" Diana paused. "Have you ever met your grandmother, Charlie?"

"No," Charlotte answered. She could feel her hair being pulled upward and snipped. "But Mom has told me a lot."

"Charlotte's never been to Appleweed… and I think that's probably for the best," Alys explained.

"The last time I saw your mother… around Christmas two years ago? Popped into Suzy's for pie and coffee with my mom and she was there with some guy I didn't recognize."

"Shocked face," Alys commented dryly, pointing to her own very obviously not-shocked expression.

"I don't know if she even still lives in Appleweed," Diana continued. "It was, however, pretty funny, because obviously she and my mom don't socialize? So, she had no idea about me, but you could tell she made the connection a few seconds after we waved by the way her entire jaw started to sag like the rest of her."

Alys cackled at the image.

"Doesn't that bother you?" Charlotte asked quietly.

"Chin up," Diana requested. "Doesn't what bother me?"

"When people act like that around you."

"When people act like rude assholes with no sense of compassion or manners? Of course, it bothers me. I wish we could just live and let live in this godforsaken world." Diana had moved on to defining the layers with her texturizing scissors. "But it's their problem, sunshine, not mine. I'm gonna do me and be happy. If they want to be miserable little close-minded shits, let them. They're a dying breed."

"You think so?" Charlotte asked.

"Baby, I know so. Hell, my health insurance covered my hormones, and I was able to get assistance for my surgery. You think that would have been the case a decade ago?" She shook her head. "Change is slow, but it's happening." Diana paused a moment, locking eyes with her goddaughter in the mirror. "So, don't you even think about letting them get to you again, okay?"

Charlotte smiled a little. "Okay."

"You're going to graduate, you're going to go to a top college, and then you're going to rule the world, am I right?" Diana glanced back at Alys.

"That is our official ten-year plan, yes," Alys answered.

"And I'm here to make sure that you're going to look amazing doing it." Diana turned on the hairdryer. "So, what else is up for you today?" She asked Alys. Charlotte could barely hear her over the hot air blasting her hair every which way.

"I have to get some last few pieces to my editor today, so I need to knuckle down in my studio for a few hours," Alys answered.

"Pushing the deadlines again, I see."

"I don't have that much to do. I would have been done last night but..." She pointedly looked toward Charlotte. "Someone seemed to need some emergency mom time."

Diana nodded slowly. "What's this one?"

"*Bottomed Out*. It's about William Shakespeare trying to cure his writer's block and encountering a very mischievous group of faeries. Supposed to be the story of how he got the idea for *A Midsummer Night's Dream*." Alys grinned suddenly and fiddled with the chain of her necklace again. "So basically, Donkey-Shakespeare wearing an Elizabethan ruff is my new favorite thing ever. He's adorable. I'm probably not going to paint anything else. My editor better love Donkey-Shakespeare because he's probably getting his own series."

"Close your eyes." Diana cackled and spun Charlotte back toward the mirror as she finished blow-drying her hair. "Well, here's hoping that's not career suicide."

"I'm fairly certain children will also see the genius of tiny Donkey-Shakespeare. I will likely be rich and heralded as this generation's Dr. Seuss."

"I can't tell if you're joking," Diana commented, heating up a flat iron.

"No," Alys mused. "Neither can I."

"How long do I have to do this?" Charlotte asked.

"You can see the finished product when I'm done styling it, love. I want you to have the full effect," Diana insisted. "No peeking."

"Does it look how you pictured it?" Charlotte asked.

"Looks better than how I pictured it," Diana answered. "We should have stuck gum in your hair years ago," she joked.

Charlotte smiled and sat up a little straighter.

"How late are you working tonight?" Alys asked.

"My last client is around 6:30, but it's just a quick razor cut. Why?"

"I figure I could prepare my best takeout for dinner and you could join us, since you went out of your way to help us." Alys shrugged. "Thank you again for coming in early and saving poor Charlotte from her own hormonal teenage whims."

"*Mom*," Charlotte shot Alys a look, causing Diana to jerk the chair in the other direction.

"I'm sorry, did you want to credit the Edward Scissorhands moment to rational thinking?" Alys raised a critical eyebrow at her daughter.

Charlotte's cheeks puffed out as if preparing a retort and then slowly deflated as she realized she didn't really have one.

"What did I say about peeking?" Diana sighed in exasperation.

"Sorry," both Carroll women apologized, and Charlotte closed her eyes again.

The flat iron passed through Charlotte's now much shorter hair multiple times, turning up at the ends to encourage the strands to do the same. "In regard to the dinner invitation, I will take any thanks and offering of free food, especially sushi, as soon as Charlie confirms that there is thanks to be had."

"Can I look?" Charlotte asked eagerly.

"Give me a moment," Diana laughed, and Charlotte heard aerosol hairspray as Diana's other hand lifted some of the top layers of hair by scrunching her fingers. "Okay, just a little longer..." She slowly turned Charlotte's chair back toward the mirror. "...Now."

Charlotte opened her eyes and blinked. The air was disturbingly silent as she leaned forward. She almost didn't recognize herself. Normally her face felt partially hidden beneath a heavy curtain of white, and now she felt she had a much clearer view of herself. No longer hiding her face, it framed it, highlighting her features. And while it was certainly much shorter, it was long enough that it left her with a lot of options. Diana had used the flat iron to flip out the strands in the back, giving it a kind of wild look. She smiled slowly and shook her head, watching the strands move. "It's so much lighter." And oddly, just as Alys had said, Charlotte felt lighter, too. Not physically, but emotionally. Her smile broadened and she looked back at Diana. "I love it."

"Yeah?" Diana breathed in relief.

"It's so cool."

"Good." Diana relaxed and reached back to the table to once again brandish the large can of aerosol hairspray. "Now hold still so I can make sure it doesn't move for the next ten hours."

4

NO MORE YIELDING,
BUT A DREAM

She was back in the woods again. It was dark, cold, and silent. The feeling of dread was becoming eerily familiar. There were no screams, no burning snow, and the crack in the sky was nowhere to be seen.

The most noticeably different aspect, however, was that she was standing on a staircase. She looked up ahead of her, and the stairs seemed to stretch to an impossibly long distance to some unseen second floor. Behind her it did much the same, going deep into the ground and winding downward along a worn brick tunnel that plunged deep beneath the ground's surface.

Charlotte's head snapped to look down at the sight of a glint of silver out of the corner of her eye, and she gazed out over the railing and down to the forest floor.

There it was again. Someone's cord. But this one was different.

It was a very dimly glowing silver cord, flowing behind a figure as if they were wading through water.

This one, however, looked thin and frayed, almost as if someone—or *something* had deliberately attempted to sever it.

She strained her eyes in the darkness, trying to focus on the figure, whose back was to her, below. They were wearing a familiar sweatshirt, and it almost seemed… "Mom?"

From the palpable darkness she saw the same clawed hand reached out toward the cord.

Charlotte's breath caught. She looked straight down in desperation. Too far to jump. And yet, maybe—

The hand perceptively curled its fingers just above the cord and plucked it like a harp string.

The figure turned around abruptly—too fast for Charlotte to see their face—and then it instantly vanished from sight as if they had never been there in the first place.

Charlotte blinked rapidly, trying to see if the darkness had perhaps merely increased like a fog, but no. She could see glimpses of the forest floor, but the figure who had walked along it below her was gone. She exhaled in frustration and looked back toward the tunnel, thinking if she could find a way down, she might find some sort of clue—

She froze.

The brick of the tunnel… appeared to be *growing*. It twisted, adding to its architecture, the brick formation climbing and curling up around the staircase and expanding toward her.

Charlotte quickly stumbled backward, her hand gripping the railing of the stairs to keep from falling.

"Don't be scared."

Charlotte's heart stopped and her gaze tore upward to the endless ascent ahead of her, but she saw no one. "Scared? Of *what*?" She looked back to the tunnel.

The bricks built themselves outward in winding-like motions, weaving together like vines to continue creating the tunnel so that the enclosed space was moving closer and closer. And now that she noticed it, it was hard to deny that it was increasing in speed.

Her heart pounding, she turned fully up toward the stairs to full on run.

"If you're scared, it will know you're coming."

"Shut up!"

"If you're scared, it will hear your heartbeat."

"*What* will?" Charlotte yelled in exasperation as she tripped forward, her knee slamming against the hard ironwork staircase. She gritted her teeth and planted her hands on the stair in front of her to launch back into a mad dash, but as her head turned upward, she found herself face to face with a pair of polished men's dress shoes.

They were a stormy grey that faded to a black at the toes, with a monk strap across the top that buckled in two places on the side. Perfectly tailored to fall right over these shoes were grey pants. She pushed herself back enough to crane her neck to look at the rest of him, but the dim light that had once been on top of the stairs now backlit his figure and obscured the face she was trying to focus on. It was a grey, misty morning sort of light.

"It's time to stop running, Charlie."

Charlotte was reminded of the growing tunnel behind them, and as she looked back down, the brick enveloped them. The wind from the rapidly moving tunnel blew her hair back, the light extinguishing all around them, becoming a distant glow in a shrinking circle up the stairs ahead of them.

"It's time to be brave."

"I don't understand…"

"The Dreamers need us now more than ever…" Perhaps it was another breeze that gave her the impression of his departure, but as Charlotte carefully and blindly pushed herself into a standing position, she knew she was alone again.

"Find her…" A chorus of quiet voices pleaded— or was it one voice simply echoing on top of itself? The sounds beckoned her to make her descent down the stairs.

"I can't see," Charlotte protested, feeling her throat tightening. She reached her hand out tentatively to touch the brick wall. It felt solid enough. Perhaps it could guide her. Her fingertips carefully fumbled along the lines of the grout, as her feet tentatively slid across the stair to gauge the distance between each and find a rhythm in stepping down them.

"Save her…" The voices beckoned again.

"Who?" Charlotte breathed in frustration, none of her questions answered. Was it getting colder as she descended, or was this a result of the brick tunnel sealing her in?

It seemed an endless pursuit. The more she walked, the more stairs that seemed to stretch below her.

Brave. What did she have to be brave about? While descending into pitch-black darkness was certainly unnerving, she hadn't been afraid of the dark for quite some time.

Something tickled across her palm. Her heart jumped, and she jerked her hand from the wall instantly. "Omigod, what the hell was that?!" She paused to calm her breathing and took a tentative step forward, hesitantly reaching a shaking hand out to touch the wall again. It was smooth… and springy, and… a little sharp like paper on one edge… "Ivy," Charlotte breathed in relief. "It's just ivy."

An indescribable screech echoed up the tunnel. For half a second, it seemed like the cry of some sort of great bird, but it prolonged into a howl, and as the sound lingered, it seemed more akin to the scream of a young child.

Charlotte felt every hair stand on end as the unnatural sound reverberated around her. It resonated in her chest, kickstarting her heart to pound so loudly she was certain it, too, added to the vibrations in the tunnel.

Two bright gleaming green gems peered up at her from the darkness. They had an unholy glow, and despite being the only illumination in the tunnel, Charlotte knew there was no comfort to be found in them. She felt a chill of terror run through her.

With the cry a now-distant echo, she was able to hear what sounded like a great flapping of wings… and the gems began to rise through the darkness toward her.

"Shit." Charlotte turned on her heel and planted her hand firmly against the brick wall, using it now to accelerate her speed as she climbed the darkened stairway as fast as she could.

The sound of the wings was getting closer, like leather cutting the air to hoist the creature further up, then over the rail of the stairs, where it crashed onto the ironwork with an earthshaking thud.

Charlotte stumbled up the stairs blindly, her mind pleading with her legs to go faster. She didn't dare look behind her. It would only slow her down.

Another unholy shriek and she could feel it heavily clamoring up the stairs, gaining speed and closing distance between them. Animalistic, focused. On the hunt.

Her heart pounded in her chest as her legs raced, her hands grabbing onto the rail as she felt the ironwork vibrate with the movement of her pursuer.

Must go faster, must go faster! She urged herself forward, but her legs were starting to burn. She felt again like she was moving through water, and every movement took twice the effort it should have.

The tunnel shook more, and the movement was starting to dislodge bricks. Misty morning light began to seep through in wisps of hope. But the creature was moving faster, and it was getting closer.

Another shriek and Charlotte raised her hands to cover her ears to shield them, hunching over with the movement as if she could get under the sound waves. It was so piercing she felt as if her ears might bleed from the decibel.

It was a brief relief.

The sound dislodged more bricks, and with her center of gravity compromised, Charlotte tripped over one of them. She removed her hands in time to catch herself before her face collided with the stairs, but her right leg and hip stung from the impact. Trembling, she pushed up to rise again, but the soft sound of claws slowly resting on the ironwork behind her made her pause.

Half in shadow, half obscured by the curling smoke of light seeping in from the hole in the brick wall beside them, stood a gargoyle-like creature. Large, clawed toes dug into the ironwork platform, supporting a digitigrade foot with another claw at the heel to help grip perches. The long limbs raised the creature well up to six feet, even in its hunched state. Emaciated, the skin clung to the bone and what lean muscle existed just around it. Its face, or what she could make of it, was gaunt and hollow, and long, jagged teeth unevenly met together in a way that seemed too large for its mouth. The gums had receded, and the lips had thinned and crabbed, unable to prevent thick saliva from sliding down its fangs and chin. But the moment she made eye-contact with the eerie glowing orbs set where its eyes should have been, Charlotte could see nothing else. Her heart stopped, her blood chilled, and her breath caught. She would die here.

Then it leapt on her.

Charlotte startled awake with a terrified gasp, her hands flailing toward where the creature had been only moments before in her nightmare, fingernails poised to do whatever she could to get it off her. As the details of her room came into focus, her hands relaxed, her eyes darting around to see evidence of the threat.

Nothing.

She reached to gingerly touch her face and examine her arms. No bites, no claw marks. Her hands raised to her ears. No bleeding.

Nothing.

She sighed in relief and rested a hand over her heart, feeling it pound against her ribcage. "Holy…" She hadn't had a nightmare that visceral since… She took a deep breath and concentrated on her breathing as she took in the room around her once more to confirm her reality. She was home, she was safe, she was in her bed. Yet somehow… some part of her still felt… not quite there.

She looked to her bedside clock.

It was only 1 a.m.

A few pieces of framed artwork from her mother's books were hung on her wall. One depicted large trees that stretched high above anything seen on Earth. Giants far older than humanity itself that it caused the population surrounding it to look no bigger than a fairy village. Another showed a beautiful fantasy castle, the spires shining white and opalescent where the sunlight hit the stone. It was the center jewel of a large bustling city. Charlotte had spent endless hours of her childhood imagining what it would be like to live in either place, and, even now as she looked on them, she couldn't help but feel inexplicably drawn to them.

School books were splayed out across her bedspread. She'd finished nearly all her homework the previous night.

It was calming… seeing the familiar things. And yet, it somehow seemed more dreamlike than the nightmare she'd been immersed in only moments before. She needed something more tangible than visuals or memories. She needed her mother.

She reached forward and closed the nearest textbook, moving it out of her way so she could slip out of bed.

The door to Alys' room was still open, and the bed was empty but unmade. Charlotte frowned and walked further down the hall to her mother's studio, the empty bedroom at the far end. Perhaps she hadn't been the only one who hadn't slept very well.

Alys was sitting on a stool at her easel, hunched over herself, but leaning away from the canvas itself, one foot pulled up to her chest, the other perched on one of the lower rungs. Charlotte couldn't tell if she was staring at the painting or past it.

"Mom?"

Alys startled, looking to the teenager hanging in the doorway. "Oh... hey, sweetie. Did I wake you?"

"No." Charlotte shook her head. "Nightmare." She wandered further in. "What about you?"

"Me, too." There was a weight to Alys' words that her daughter couldn't understand.

Charlotte gnawed on her lower lip, wondering if inquiring further would be prying too much. "What are you working on?"

"Puck," Alys answered simply. "Been giving me a great deal of trouble through this whole project. I wasn't... getting her nose right. Just couldn't picture it in my head. I think I'm forgetting..."

"*Her* nose?" Charlotte asked. "Puck is a she?"

"Puck has always been a *Sidhe*," Alys joked. "And I'm sure she's quite tickled that she's been such a source of frustration... Or she would be if..." She shook her head.

Charlotte came around to look at the canvas. The fae perched on a rock in the painting had a mischievous glint in her large green eyes. Her features were petite, perhaps borderline childlike, and the windswept outcrop of brown, red, and gold hair was styled much like Charlotte's. Two horns peeked out around her temples, mirroring the same two points of her ears that peeked out from her hair on either side of her head. "Any particular reason for the change?"

"Favor for a friend," Alys said wistfully, then smiled. "Plus, really, when you think about it, who's really more likely to give a man a literal ass head?"

Charlotte laughed. "You have a point."

Alys pulled her daughter to her into a hug. "What was your nightmare about?"

Charlotte shook her head. "I… don't even know."

"Do you want to talk about it?"

Charlotte thought a moment to consider this. How would she even begin to talk about that… *thing*? The sound of it screeching still resonated in her bones. She shivered and shook her head once more. "No. How are you doing?"

"Me?" Alys shrugged and released Charlotte. "Other than running on extraordinarily little sleep, and finally caught up on the pages I have to send Sherrie… I'm…" She looked back toward the canvas, and Charlotte thought she saw her mother's expression flinch. "Fine."

'Fine' had never been a word that carried any weight in the Carroll household. "Really bad nightmare?"

"No…" Alys' voice was notably softer. "It's just…" She puffed out her cheeks and debated on how to answer this question properly. "Been a *very* long time since I… encountered one."

Charlotte's brow furrowed. "How long?"

"Eighteen years," Alys breathed.

Charlotte stood a little straighter, her throat feeling tight. "Mom, what's wrong?"

Alys bobbed her shoulders upward in yet another shrug. "I don't know."

"People don't just have nightmares out of the blue for no reason. It's related to some kind of stressor, and since you've been late on a deadline many times before, I have to believe it's something else."

"So, what's your excuse?" Alys asked dryly.

"Stop dodging the question. *Something* happened."

"I'm sure something *did*." Alys bowed her head, her paint-stained fingers cradling the watch around her neck. "I just wish I knew what."

Charlotte examined the way the jewelry seemed to glimmer, even beneath paint covered fingers. Perhaps a different approach. "You know… you've never told me where you got your necklace. I don't think I can remember a day when you didn't have it."

Alys smiled; a strange, sad, nostalgic sort of smile. "…Your father gave this to me… actually."

Charlotte raised an eyebrow. Alys never mentioned Charlotte's father. While she hadn't spoken ill of the man, she had made a very pointed effort throughout Charlotte's life, for as long as she could recall, to not mention him at all. "He did?"

"When I was eighteen." A short laugh forced itself out of Alys in an abrupt exhale to inhale; a similar rhythm to catching your breath mid-sob. "First day we met… actually. Or the second… It's hard to remember, it was really a blur, to be honest. So much happening at once. He was sweet… and I… I suppose I was never one for first impressions."

"How did you meet?"

Alys closed her eyes tightly and laughed, somewhere between embarrassed and amused. "I nearly hit him with my car."

"You nearly ran him over?" Charlotte asked, her jaw dropping.

"Well, he shouldn't have been standing in the middle of the freeway like an idiot!" Alys defended, finally meeting her daughter's eyes again. "He's lucky I saw him in time. Don't know what would have happened if I…" She shook her head and dropped her gaze once more to the cherished pocket watch in her hands. "Well, anyway, I'm glad it didn't…" She ran her thumb along the intricate flower design, letting a silence fall between them.

Charlotte leaned against her mother's shoulder. "You never talk about him," she remarked softly.

"…I don't." Alys nodded, releasing the pocket watch so she could reach one arm around Charlotte, and the other up to wipe at her left eye. "And I am sorry about that. I'm sure you have questions… I'm sure you have *a lot* of questions. I would. I *did* when I was your age… I might have asked them if I'd felt safe to…" She took a deep breath. "It's hard… remembering what we don't have anymore. I know you haven't really lost anything like that yet, but... it sort of haunts you. The idea of what *might* have been if things were different. If you'd be happier." She took a deep breath and smiled at her daughter.

"*Would* you be happier?"

Alys hesitated. It was a loaded gun of a question. "Charlie, the truth of the matter is there isn't a day where I don't miss your father."

"Have you ever tried to find him?"

"I don't need to find him," Alys answered, gingerly smoothing down Charlotte's hair with her fingers. "I know exactly where he is and how to reach him. *I'm* the one who left."

Charlotte's eyebrows raised, surprised. "*You* left? Why?"

Alys rested her hands on Charlotte's shoulders, and visibly chose her words very carefully. "Because I love you very much. And I wouldn't trade you for anything."

Charlotte shook her head. "I don't understand... would you have had to give me up?"

"...I'm very certain I would have, yes."

Charlotte's eyes widened.

"And I couldn't do that. Not in a million years, not even before I knew what an amazing person you were going to grow up to be," Alys whispered. She pulled Charlotte into a tight embrace. "So, I left, and I never looked back. There may be things about that life and world that I miss, sweetheart, but I don't regret my decision for a second."

"Promise?" Charlotte whispered.

"I promise," Alys hugged her tighter. "One day I'll tell you the whole story. The whole improbable and complicated story."

Charlotte wondered on this, on what kind of man could be capable of loving her mother but would have made her give up their child. Was there financial issue? The intricate quality of the pocket watch Alys wore around her neck made her doubt that. Were they simply too young? Her mother had given birth to her at only 20 years old, but she had somehow done very well for herself as a single mother.

True, she had friends to help, she'd built connections that opened doors, doors that she utilized during the first few months of pregnancy when she pitched her first children's book: *Rhyme and Reason*, a strange love story between two people on opposing sides of logic and imagination. It had gone on to win a Newbery Medal and was found in nearly every library and bookstore. But then Charlotte wondered if that opportunity would not have been available had she stayed.

She had so many questions, but all were weighed down by the knowledge that she wasn't going to be getting any answers that night. But there was one now that nagged her more than anything, and she couldn't help herself. Pulling back enough to look at her, Charlotte asked, "…Does he know about me? Does he even know I exist?"

Alys' expression clouded over. It had the telltale signs that she'd been crying only moments before, and Charlotte wondered if there was at least one aspect of the situation, that Alys regretted after all. "No, love. He doesn't. But believe me that it's better that way."

"I don't... understand."

"I know." Alys held Charlotte's face in her hands. "And I don't expect you to. I promise, I'll explain it one day. You know I will... but for now I need you to just trust me. Right now, you're safer if you don't know about him, and he doesn't know about you."

Charlotte's brow furrowed. "Should I be worried?"

"No. The only thing you should be worried about is finishing your homework in time to go back to school on Thursday."

"I just have a math assignment to do," Charlotte answered. "I'll be done before dinner tomorrow night."

"Good." Alys stretched. "I'm done for the night. Think we should both turn in."

Charlotte hesitated. "Can I stay with you tonight?"

Alys smiled, taken aback with amusement. "Are we six again?"

"I just figured... since we both had a nightmare."

Alys' smile seemed to fade a notch before she forced it to expand. "Sure. Go on ahead of me. I need to clean up."

Charlotte nodded and kissed her mother's cheek before wrapping her arms around herself and heading toward the door. "Goodnight, Mom. Sweet dreams."

"Sweet dreams, Charlie."

The sun was out when Charlotte woke the next morning, but she was still the first one up. Her mother was hard asleep and cocooned in most of the comforters beside her, unaware of anything in the waking world.

Charlotte slipped from the bed, sneaking back to her own room to get ready for the day. She peeked in again after she was dressed and showered, but Alys hadn't moved. Dead asleep.

The teenager laughed to herself and ate breakfast before once again climbing the stairs to peek at her mother's room. Nope. Still asleep. It was still relatively early, so instead of bothering her, Charlotte decided she would finish her math homework.

And as the clock creeped closer to noon, Charlotte began to suspect her mother had in fact *not* gone to bed when she said she would last night.

Still, Alys had finished what she needed to the previous night, and Charlotte was fully capable of entertaining herself. She gathered her phone and wallet and wrote a note that she was going Geocaching and left it on the kitchen table.

It was exceptionally cold that morning, but the sky was clear. The ground was still wet from the downpour the day before, and Charlotte kicked up some of the rainwater from the pavement as she walked.

She'd found all the caches in her own neighborhood. She didn't even need her GPS to locate them now. It was a bit of a walk to the 44 bus, and mostly uphill, but it was refreshing. The city always felt better after a day of rain.

The brisk walk and fresh air helped clear her head of the strange nightmares, and so she could better focus on and sort last night's conversation with Alys.

Somewhere out there was the man her mother had loved. The man she *still* loved. And due to strange circumstances surrounding her own birth, they couldn't be together. It was like something out of a book. But the part that really lingered with her, the most *unnerving* part, was the suggestion that things were "safer" this way.

She wished she could tell someone about it, bounce ideas off them, so she could have a place to put them other than her own mind. It all felt muddled and mixed up—a complicated math problem with too many variables, and the more she thought about it, the more questions she had. Perhaps if she had a whiteboard to map the possibilities.

No logical scenario seemed a particularly comforting one. For a brief few minutes, she entertained the idea that her father was some kind of royalty. She indulged in the thought inspired by so many fantasy books—the long-lost daughter of a great king. Her mother had somehow encountered a prince from a place no one had ever heard of, and they fell in love. However, Alys, not being of noble blood, could not marry the prince, and so he would be forced to marry another. That would mean she would possibly be the first child, but still a bastard heir.

"Oh my god, I might be a princess," Charlotte whispered to herself in astonishment, her eyes growing wide as she realized that despite the absurdity of the notion, it certainly fit what few clues she had.

The woman sitting to the right of her on the bus gave her a funny look.

Charlotte smiled sheepishly and looked out the window.

No, that was a very fantastical and stupid answer. For all she knew, her real father was some kind of criminal who'd... murder her and Alys if he knew where they were.

Though she had a hard time imagining Alys loving anyone who would physically harm them.

She was starting to wish she hadn't asked. While she respected her mother's wishes, her mind had more questions now than ever.

Charlotte got off the bus on Market St., the smell of freshly roasted coffee beans wafting out of Ballard Coffee Works just down the block. She pulled out her phone and checked the Geocaching app. There was a cache entitled "The Upper Room" about an eight-minute walk from where she was standing.

However, she was feeling dangerously under-caffeinated, and it would have been a true crime as a resident Seattleite to not at least grab a quick cup of *something*.

The shop wasn't empty—not completely. Ballard Coffee Works always had the odd smattering of patrons, but as it was a Wednesday afternoon, it was quieter. And just beyond the espresso bar, working the counter on her own... was *Kimiko*.

Kimiko was a graduate student working toward her PhD in public administration at the University of Washington. When Charlotte had asked what exactly that meant, Kimiko had said it was "like a business degree" but she got to "retain her soul and had no expectation of making any money".

Kimiko had a sharp wit and did not suffer fools. She had a passion for sports but also found a strange joy in discussing the economic structure of Batman's Gotham city. Her sleek black hair faded into a purple ombre, and it was always pulled back in an effortless messy bun on her head. She was kind and compassionate, and Charlotte was certain that one day, she might singlehandedly save the world. Of course, not with capes or superpowers (though it was plausible Kimiko possessed both), but in that underappreciated way that volunteered time in outreach programs, went door to door to talk about the next voting cycle, and worked hard to make sure her own campus was a safe space for minorities.

Charlotte's heart skipped a beat as she fumbled for her wallet. "Hi."

Kimiko's expression brightened as she met Charlotte's eyes. "Oh my gosh, Charlie, hi! I almost didn't recognize you with the new hair. It looks great!"

"Oh," Charlotte blushed. "Thank you."

"What are you doing out of school on a Wednesday?" Kimiko handed a latte to a man waiting at the bar. "It's not winter break for you guys already, is it?"

Charlotte winced, remembering her current situation. "I… got suspended for three days."

Kimiko's dark eyes widened. "You? *You* got suspended? How is that even possible?"

Charlotte scuffed her feet. "I may have knocked a jock in the face."

"You didn't! Are you alright? Did he attack you?"

"He called Diana… well, I won't repeat it," Charlotte answered, shoving her hands in her pockets. "He's ignorant, stupid, and well-deserving the broken nose I gave him."

Kimiko looked at her in surprise and what almost seemed like admiration. "Is your mom around?"

"Nah, just me."

Kimiko reached out her fist for a bump of approval. "Good for you. There's not a single one of us who hasn't daydreamed about saying 'eff it' to the high road at least once in those situations."

Charlotte felt a surge of pride. "You ever get in a fight in high school?"

"There were many battles of wits, but sadly my opponents came woefully unarmed. So much I'm afraid they were unaware of the devastation I left them in. Tragic, really. My talents were so wasted." The barista leaned forward on the counter, languishing in the luxury of a friend at the register after the morning rush had rushed away. "I grew up in Spokane, which isn't really a terrible place, but it's like… It's *very* white. Not like, Ballard where it's like, very Norse, or Boston where it's very Irish, just like… like *white bread*, Stepford Wife white, very limited in its point of view, very…"

"Stupid?"

"*Different* from here."

Charlotte laughed.

"I mean, don't get me wrong—it wasn't like some places I've been, but the shit I heard at my school when I was your age?" Kimiko exhaled. "High Schoolers are assholes."

"They really are." Charlotte shook her head almost in wonder as she thought back on the event.

"Anyway." Kimiko shook her head and waved the subject off. "Enough about all that. What can I get you?"

"16-ounce vanilla latte, please."

"Alys not waiting for you outside?"

"Mom is still asleep at home."

"Still?"

"She had a late-night working."

Kimiko rung her up, and Charlotte circled around to the bar to watch her make the drink. She liked the way the barista's hands moved. It was like a dance: strong, with the effortless fluidity of motion acquired through repetition.

"So," the woman asked in that tone of voice that knows it's about to ask a trite question. "Do you know what *you* want to do after high school? Beyond inflicting sweet justice on bigots, that is."

"Not a clue," Charlotte answered with a laugh. "I mean, I'm doing well in all of my classes, but nothing really... *excites* me, I guess. It all just kind of blends together. It's just something I *have* to do, so I do it, you know?" She rested her palms on the counter. "What about you? Did you know?"

"Sort of," Kimiko admitted. "But I'm an exception, so don't get discouraged that you don't know yet. None of my friends knew at your age." She carefully poured the steamed milk into Charlotte's to-go cup. "Everything about my whole life up to that point kind of informed the basic gist of what I wanted to do. I wanted to make sure that regardless of economic background, everyone was afforded the same opportunities. And when I went into college, I realized the education system is where I wanted to focus my efforts." She smiled and slid the coffee cup to Charlotte. She'd made a heart design in the latte foam. "But you'll find your way, Charlie. Just keep your eyes peeled and mind open, and you'll find it."

"Thanks, Kimiko."

"Any time."

Charlotte grinned and expertly glided her cup over to bar with sugar packets, coffee stirrers, and most importantly, the tops to the to-go cups. She took a sip of the creamy foam before securing the lid. With her heart still fluttering from her coffee shop crush, she started off toward her bounty in "The Upper Room."

She read the blurb the owner had left. It was a large one, detailing a little history of the area.

> *Local legend said that Ballard's city fathers had been so concerned by the power of alcohol that they had passed a mandate stating, "a church for every bar." So, any time a saloon was built, a church also had to have been built. Though a search of city archives never found written ordinance of the law, from 1904 to when Ballard became part of Seattle in 1907, the number of bars to churches was equal. Apparently, upon examining the number of bars and churches within the city limits of old Ballard, there were 27 of each.*

Charlotte smiled, happily logging the information away, and followed her GPS to its coordinates: Amazing Grace Spiritual Center.

It was a happy soft custardy yellow with bright red windowpanes, kept clean and pristine with the kind of care to detail that only came from a labor of love. There were a few potted plants along the perimeter, the mailbox, and a green bench just below the porch that led to the entrance inside. She peeked around the area, checking for any prying eyes, and then dropped to each plant, carefully peeking in each and around the leafy branches of shrubs for the familiar sight of a small cache. Nothing.

She checked under the bench for anything velcroed to the underbelly. Still nothing. She did, however, find a rather unsightly mass of chewed gum. She sat up and pretended, to no one in particular, to simply be resting her legs as she eased up onto the bench and checked her phone.

The Upper Room. She read again. She chewed her lip and glanced up at the building behind her. Could they have hid the cache within the church itself? Was there some kind of attic that she would have to sneak into?

She double-checked the difficulty. No. It was a low-level cache. There was little chance someone would have marked something that required indoor espionage as a low-level cache. She wasn't entirely sure that kind of thing was legal in the first place.

Charlotte might have been rather obsessed with this relatively new hobby, but she was still a novice and not entirely clear on all the rules.

She was debating risking venturing inside when her eyes rested upon a birdhouse-like structure, sitting on a pole in the yard. It was green and amid the plants and shrubbery, she'd overlooked it.

Upon closer inspection, she recognized it as one of the free libraries that had popped up around town, filled with donated books that were to be borrowed and returned, or even replaced with something else. In a small window above the compartment itself sat a small, odd-looking black bird behind a triangle-shaped window inset into where the roof came to a peak.

Charlotte opened the door and carefully browsed through the limited selection. There was a bible and a few pamphlets about the center, as well as a battered copy of *The Boxcar Children* and a true crime novel. No cache though.

Her hand lightly touched the ceiling of the inside of the compartment, but there didn't appear to be any latches or hidden compartments.

Charlotte looked back at the bird thoughtfully. Really, if anything, that window was the upper room. She took hold of a pin that stuck out where the roof met the window. At first it looked simply like part of the design, but with a gentle pull, the triangle window pulled out, letting her get an uninhibited look at the small fake bird.

She didn't like the lifeless bead eyes that looked back at her. She crawled her fingers carefully around it and pulled out the small tube she found hiding in the dark behind it. The small film canister simply held a short pencil and a logbook.

Charlotte wrote her name and the date before replacing it. Then she updated the last found date on the app on her phone.

It always brought a nice sense of accomplishment, even if the rush did seem to fade too quickly, especially after an easier find. With the day waxing on to nearly

3 p.m., Charlotte made her way back to Market St., latte in hand.

It was 4 p.m. by the time she'd hopped off the bus and walked home, and as she got closer; she couldn't help but feel a little disappointed that she'd be trudging back into school the next day. There would likely be more repercussions—more taunting from the hyenas.

Charlotte wasn't sure she had the energy yet to ignore them. The mere thought was exhausting.

She reached into her coat pocket to retrieve her keys... but found nothing. She checked her jeans, which were rather useless in terms of pockets, and only found her phone. Her other coat pocket, her wallet. With a huff she circled around back to reach beneath the flowerpot and retrieve the spare key hidden there. "Idiot," she chided herself. She unlocked the back door and went inside. The lights were still off in the downstairs, and her note on the kitchen table seemed untouched.

Charlotte's brow furrowed, and she placed the spare key on the kitchen table beside the note. "Mom?" She called out to the house.

No answer.

Charlotte glanced outside the kitchen window. Alys' car was still in the driveway.

She skipped up the steps and peeked her head into her mother's studio, expecting to see Alys at her easel or laptop, headphones blaring away any outside sound from notice.

It was empty.

Charlotte smiled and shook her head, making her way to her mother's bedroom. She knocked and upon no answer, opened the door. "You are not seriously still in bed."

In a ball of covers, there she was, still blissfully sleeping.

"Mom, how late were you up? It's almost dinner time." Charlotte gently shook her mother's shoulder but with no response. She laughed and hopped onto the bed. "Wake uuuuup! Wake up, wake up, wake up!" She sang loudly.

Alys didn't so much as stir.

Charlotte felt a pit in her stomach, and the air around her seemed to tense as the uncomfortable notion that something was wrong began to set in. "Mom, this isn't funny." After still no response, she reached out and touched her mother's face. It was cold. "*Mom?*" Her voice cracked and she pulled back the covers. She looked very pale, but Charlotte could see a shallow rise and fall to her chest. Her mind spun with the news coverage she'd seen over the past few days, and her hands fumbled for the phone desperately, shaking.

"911, what's your emergency?"

5

THE REALITY NIGHTMARE

Charlotte sat, hunched over herself in the hospital waiting room, her knees bouncing nervously. Her folded arms tightened, and her teeth grit. She watched white coats and scrubs vanish in and out of the emergency room doors. She couldn't tell how much time had passed since they arrived, how long it had been since they'd rushed Alys out of sight. Ten minutes? An hour? Everything felt hazy.

She'd called Diana after she'd called the ambulance, but she wasn't entirely certain what she'd said. She'd been crying, she hadn't been able to stop crying since she'd first dialed 911. The only thing she really remembered saying was managing to choke out the word "hospital." Had she explained what was wrong? Had she managed to say *which* hospital? Her stomach lurched, and she was starting to feel ill.

Her fingers danced along her knees, and she stood to approach the nurse's station but detoured when she saw a frantic looking Diana walk through the door. "Diana!"

Diana shifted her trajectory to move to the smaller girl and pulled Charlotte into an abrupt embrace. "I came as fast as I could—do we know anything?"

Charlotte shook her head, which was difficult given how tightly Diana held her. "No, still waiting."

Diana released her just enough to take a step back to look at her. "What happened?"

"I don't know!" The words tumbled out of Charlotte's mouth, and she began to realize the depth of her panic. "She was fine just a few hours ago. She'd been up late finishing up some things for Sherrie—we talked for like half an hour. She was FINE."

"Deep breaths," Diana soothed.

Charlotte focused on her breathing. In for five, out for six. Repeat. Repeat. Repeat. She swallowed, trying to push the panic down or at least push past it, and when she spoke again, her voice was deliberately slow. "And then we went to bed, and she was still asleep when I got up, and I didn't think that was weird because she'd been working all night. But then I came home around 4 and she was still out, and she was cold and barely breathing, so I called the ambulance and they…" Tears were streaming down her cheeks and her voice finally caught. She tried to take another deep breath to continue but it broke down into a sob.

"Okay," Diana whispered, pulling her to her again in a comforting embrace. "It's going to be okay, baby, it's going to be okay."

"She wasn't moving," Charlotte choked. "I tried to shake her awake, and she didn't move."

Diana stroked Charlotte's hair, her brow furrowing. "She's going to be okay. You did the right thing."

"If I'd called sooner…"

"You couldn't have known."

"But if I'd called sooner—"

"Hey," Diana's grip tightened around her. "Your mother is going to be alright; *everything* is going to be alright. I promise you."

"You don't know that."

Diana frowned and gently guided Charlotte back to the chairs. "Sit down a minute. I'm going to let the nurse know I'm here."

Charlotte slowly released her and watched her walk up to the nurses' desk to introduce herself as Alyson Carroll's emergency contact. She sank back into her chair, her knees trembling. The noise around her muffled. Her focus sharpened on Diana, and everything else blurred. Her mind began to wander again, and with its departure from the present, even Diana faded from her vision.

Her mother was going to be okay. She *had* to be okay. There was no plausible way the situation could play out other than Alys making a recovery. Diana was sure of it; that meant it had to be true. Things like this… didn't happen. Or if they did, they happened to *other people*. People you heard about on the news, never anyone you knew, never…

Charlotte buried her face in her hands, giving into the new wave of sobs that shook her frame.

This couldn't be real. This was a dream. Another nightmare. Her mother could not be taken down by some strange illness, she'd… She'd always been so invincible up until now.

"*Save* her," a voice whispered close to her ear.

Charlotte raised her head abruptly, but there was no one near her. The cacophony of the emergency room flooded her ears once more, and people shifted back into focus. She looked nervously from side to side before facing front to see Diana's hand held out to her.

"The Doctor's ready to talk to us, honey."

Charlotte took her hand shakily, and they moved through the doors.

"You're Alyson Carroll's family?" a man in blue scrubs and a lab coat inquired, a chart tucked under his arm.

"Sister and daughter," Diana answered briskly. "How is she?"

"She's still unconscious, but her vitals are stable. We're moving her to a room."

"Already?" Diana asked. "That seems a bit soon. Isn't there risk?"

"Ms. Carroll—"

"*Mercer*," Diana corrected curtly. "Diana Mercer."

"Forgive my assumption. Ms. Mercer. It would be nearly impossible for you not to have seen the news coverage lately, so I'm not going to tiptoe around the situation. We believe your sister is suffering from encephalitis lethargica, sleepy sickness, as you probably know it… though this particular strain is unlike anything we've seen before. Every case seems to be severe."

"I don't understand," Diana shook her head.

"Historically, a patient would typically experience symptoms indicative of the common cold, headaches, fever, sore throat, delayed mental or physical reactions. In extreme cases, they might enter a coma-like state in that they would neither move nor speak but still often be capable of eye-movement. You had the sense they could still hear and see, even if they couldn't respond to you. Your sister, like a growing number of other patients, seems completely comatose. Her eyes won't open, her brain appears to be in REM as if asleep…"

"So, she's dreaming?" Diana asked. "There's consistent brain activity?"

"For now," the doctor answered gravely.

"What exactly does that mean?" Charlotte asked, feeling her heartbeat begin to accelerate again.

"We don't know." It was a cautious but blatantly honest statement. "Right now, all we can really do is observe. A few cases woke up in a few days, some people have been unconscious for weeks, and vitals have decreased over time…" He paused, deciding something, and continued. "I do need to ask… Does your sister have any history with breathing difficulty, circulation issues? Anything out of the ordinary she might have neglected to visit a doctor about?"

Diana shook her head. "No, Alys was always incredibly careful about of that sort of thing, for both her *and* Charlie."

He nodded and moved to the nurses' station to set down the chart, taking up a Post-it note and pen to scribble down a note. "We're running some tests as to what might have caused the severe temperature drop and shortness of breath. It's not consistent with any of the other patients' symptoms this early on. Until we get the results, however, I'm afraid all we can do is wait and keep an eye on her condition."

"Can I see her?" Charlotte asked quietly.

The doctor nodded. "We'll just need some time to get her settled."

Charlotte had never spent much time in hospitals, but that didn't stop her from having a deep-seated discomfort with them, no matter how kind the staff. She hung back in the doorway as Diana and the doctor entered. There was something ominous about crossing this threshold, something strangely powerful about that moment. She knew if she stepped through it, she'd be grounded in this reality. This would no longer be dismissible as a nightmare—as something she could possibly wake up from. Her mother would be lying in a hospital bed, and she would be unable to help her.

"Private room," Diana observed, looking back at Charlotte with a weak smile as if straining to find some silver lining in all of this.

"We've suspected that previous strains were the result of an immune reaction, so while it's not infectious, we feel it's best to keep patients isolated and away from any possible cross-contamination. Neither of you are sick, I take it?"

"No, of course not." Diana shook her head. She stared at Alys in the bed a moment, her brow furrowing, and when she spoke, she didn't dare look away. "Could you give us a moment?" She grabbed a chair and pulled it by Alys' bedside before easing down into the seat.

"I'll send a nurse by to check on you later." The doctor nodded respectfully and slunk past Charlotte.

Diana looked back to Alys, forcing a smile. "We got to stop meeting like this, Aly-cat." She reached out and took one of Alys' hands, giving it a gentle squeeze. "That was the deal, remember? I'd be your emergency contact, and you'd never give anyone reason to use it." She took a deep breath and exhaled a laugh. "At least this time when you wake up you won't have to buy a new car, right? She ever tell you that story?" She looked to her side, and, seeing no one, looked behind her to realize the teenager was still hovering outside. "Charlie?" She frowned sympathetically and beckoned her with a gentle tilt of her head. "Come on in, sweetie. It's okay."

Charlotte hesitated. Her mother looked so small and unreal in the bed. Her approach was tentative. She

129

was all too aware that with each rolling step on the hospital floor, the pit in her stomach grew larger and heavier. "It doesn't make sense, Diana… She was fine last night. No signs of anything out of the ordinary…"

Diana took her goddaughter's hand. "Let's try to stay positive, okay? The doctor said a few cases were awake and healthy again in just a few days."

"What if she doesn't wake up?"

"She's going to wake up." Diana's voice was firm.

"But what if she doesn't?" Charlotte felt the pit rising to her throat. "And why is she the only one who had breathing problems?"

"He didn't say she was the only one, he indicated that the other patients hadn't exhibited those symptoms this early on," Diana said calmly.

"But that's still a bad sign, right?"

"There's a lot we don't know right now, but more importantly, there's not a lot we can *do* right now, and getting worked up is certainly not going to help anything."

Charlotte couldn't believe what she was hearing. "How can you expect me to calm down. Aren't you upset? Aren't you worried about her?"

"Of course I am." Diana turned an almost stern gaze toward her. "But letting my imagination run away with me isn't going to help her, and it certainly isn't going to help *you*. Until your mother is back to health, *and there is no question that she will be*, I am in charge of your care." She brushed Charlotte's bangs from her forehead tenderly. "Now," she began smoothly. "Have you eaten?"

"Not since breakfast," Charlotte replied quietly.

"Okay." She stood slowly, a woman on a mission. "I'm going to secure us some dinner that's a little more appetizing than the hospital cafeteria. Do you want to come with me?"

Charlotte shook her head.

"I thought not. Wait here, don't get into any trouble, and I'll be back as soon as I can." Diana gripped Charlotte's shoulders firmly so that she could level her gaze with her goddaughter's one last time. "She's going to be *okay*, Charlotte. *Everything* is going to be okay." She kissed Charlotte's cheek and took her leave.

Charlotte listened to the precise click of Diana's heels until they faded away completely into the busy hum of the hospital wing's activity. She sunk down into the chair next to the bed, folding her arms on the mattress as she watched her mother sleep. They'd hooked her up to a breathing machine and a heart monitor. She couldn't really read anything, but the sound of the steady beep was mildly comforting. She exhaled slowly and rested her chin on her arms.

One hand took Alys' and ran her thumb over her knuckles. It was warmer than before, but still colder than it should be. She sat up slightly as she noticed they'd changed her into a hospital gown and wondered where her mother's pajamas had gone... or the necklace she wore. Her eyes darted around the room.

She located the clothes easily enough, folded on top of a dresser in the room. And when she stood to get a better look at them, she saw the pocket watch necklace sitting on top of it. She stood to pick it up, looking back at the sleeping woman, conflicted. It wasn't hers; she didn't feel right taking it from her mother's presence… but she didn't trust leaving it there unattended either. Not when anyone could walk in and snatch it. She considered putting it back on her mother but… they'd removed it for a reason. She could understand why the doctors weren't comfortable leaving jewelry around a patient's neck who was already having trouble breathing. Maybe if the chain were far more delicate and the watch less heavy. Or perhaps they wouldn't want anything around a patient's neck… just in case.

Charlotte clutched the watch to her heart indecisively a moment before raising the chain and putting it around her own neck, letting the watch fall to hit just above her belly button.

It felt strange wearing it—almost wrong, a heaviness of not belonging. She reached down, gingerly raising the pocket watch to look at it, turning it with her fingertips to examine it.

"Swimming and showers," Charlotte said aloud, looking back to Alys. "I think that's the only time I've seen you take this off." She made her way back to the bed to sit on the edge, cradling the watch in her hand. She was surprised at how natural speaking to her was, even knowing she couldn't hear. She kicked her feet a little and glanced from the watch to Alys and then back again, evaluating how to pursue this one-sided conversation, what she needed to say. "Now that I know where you got this, I have like… a zillion questions. Like… why did he give you a clock? Were you always late to meeting him? Did it have something to do with nearly hitting him with the car? Was it a family heirloom?"

Charlotte shrugged and appraised the watch, raising it to eye level. "I know I'm no expert on romance, but it seems like a weird gift." She lowered it back down, frowning in thought. "Or at least a gift with a story… You'll have to tell it to me when you wake up. No excuses."

Charlotte looked to Alys and tried to smile as if she was expecting an answer. Her finger traced the design etched into the metal of the front of the watch. "You'll also have to tell me what kind of flower this is, because it's really cool looking." Her thumb popped open the spring latch, and she gazed into the mirror on the inside opposite of the watch face.

"I remember looking into this when I was really little and would sit on your lap. I always thought it had a magical quality to it, like pure quicksilver… I don't know…" She stopped as she looked closer at the watch face itself. "This watch has too many hands… I never noticed that before."

The extra hand seemed stationary, longer than the others, and rather than being made of the same ornate black material as what she assumed was the hour, minute, and second hands, it was gold.

"Why does it have *four* hands?" She shifted in her sitting position and noticed that the hand moved slightly, as well. She paused and slowly stood, shifting from side to side on a hunch. Sure enough, the gold hand moved with her so that it continued to point in the direction toward the bathroom door. "Oooh, so it's a compass." She smiled, temporarily distracted by the quick resolution of the mystery. "That's kind of cute. Did he know you were terrible with directions?" She looked over her shoulder at Alys with the jab, and then remembered she would not be receiving a snarky response. Her grin faded, and she sighed, looking back down to the gold hand. "So, I guess this would be north?"

Charlotte looked at the bathroom door and frowned again. She blinked and looked to the window on the opposite side of the room. "But that can't be right..." She squinted at the dark outside, pressing her cheek against the cold glass to strain to see what was just out of her view. "Because I'm pretty sure that I-5 north is just over there." She leaned back on her heels and rubbed the cheek print off the window with her sleeve. "Maybe I just found the cause of your bad sense of direction... Is this broken? *Can* a compass be broken?" She looked back down at the open watch in her palm. "Or does it just point me to the nearest toilet?"

She giggled to herself and looked over her shoulder at Alys but of course the older woman wasn't laughing. She wasn't anything.

Charlotte's shoulders slumped. Her heart ached. "You would have found that hilarious, you know," she remarked almost judgmentally. "Or at least you would have given me a pity laugh… if you were awake." She closed the watch and trudged back to the chair. "You know… earlier today I was really wishing that I didn't have to go back to school tomorrow… Seems so stupid now, wanting to avoid bullies when you're laid up in a hospital… Though I suppose going back tomorrow is probably not happening anymore, so silver lining, I got my wish…" She gave a strangled sort of laugh that would have sounded suspiciously like an strained sob were anyone listening. She slumped down in the chair again and rested a hand over her chest, feeling the racing of her heart. Anxious. Anxious and guilty, and she couldn't shake the illogical thought that she was somehow responsible for all of this. "I want you to know this is not at all what I had in mind…"

Charlotte could feel a burning sensation in spots of the skin of some of her fingers. "I'll make you a deal…" She closed her eyes tightly and focused on inhaling and exhaling in slow and even counts of five and six, respectively. "I'll go to school tomorrow… if you wake up tomorrow. Okay? I'll even… apologize for breaking Danny's stupid nose… I'll…"

Charlotte had started crying, a fact that she'd been unaware of until a tear slid down her cheek. She opened her eyes, and more fell. She laughed in frustration and raised her fingers to wipe at her eyes. "Ugh, I guess that's something Diana and I can talk about when she gets back, isn't it? That'll be a fun practical talk…"

She leaned forward and took her mother's hand in her own. She ran her thumbs over the knuckles and thought how many times her mother must have sat by her bedside much the same. When she was sick, or simply just singing her to sleep when she was younger. "*Beautiful dreamer, wake unto me…*" Her voice cracked ever so slightly as she sang. She nestled down, resting her arms on the bed, and her chin on her arms. "*Starlight and dewdrops are waiting for thee…*" She watched the slow rise and fall of her mother's breathing. Her brow furrowed. The heart monitor ticked the minutes away, and she found herself squeezing Alys' hand a little tighter than she'd intended. "Don't die on me," she whispered, letting her grip relax. "Please…" Her eyes closed. "Just don't die."

Charlotte was beginning to become accustomed to a very particular kind of nightmare when she drifted off to sleep. It had a strange feeling akin to letting yourself sink below the surface when swimming. Down, and down, and down into the unending darkness until she felt the ground crunch softly beneath her feet to the forest floor. The air around her was frozen; frigid. A cold that hugged, enveloped, and swallowed you as you slipped into it. The warmth slowly draining out the top of her head until she was completely encased in the icy air.

She blinked slowly, and her eyes adjusted to the dark. They first caught sight of the snow drifting down from between cracks in the dark ceiling to coat the ground beneath her feet. The flakes caught the dim grey light that managed to seep in above her from outside.

Outside.

Which meant she was inside somewhere.

She blinked again and tried to orient herself. Was she *inside* the sky crack now?

A snowflake landed on her arm, and she jumped slightly, shocked by the cold and wet sensation that melted against her skin. Her brow furrowed.

This was not the same burning snow from the woods.

She looked to either side of her. As she adjusted to the faint light, she saw the trees around her were not trees at all but great shelves which rose rather organically from the ground as if they had grown into their shape rather than been crafted. And they were filled to the brim with books. Unending books.

"*Dreamless...*" A chorus of voices—no. One voice? The voice or voices held a similar quality, and yet did seem different pitches, different ages, and they were echoing over themselves as if whispering through an extremely resonant chamber. Despite whatever obstacle seemed to be in their way, they beckoned to her.

Charlotte startled and looked down the dimly lit but otherwise empty stack of books. "H—hello?" She sidestepped to another aisle and peered down that one as well.

"*Find her*," the voices urged.

Charlotte moved down the aisle, walking quickly to glance down each stack on either side of her, but every row was as empty as the last, until she caught sight of a faint glow just on the other side of one of the shelves.

Her brow relaxed in surprise, seeing that one of the volumes in the row... was glowing.

"*Save her*," the air trembled with the plea, and her hair and clothes waved gently as it rushed down the aisle past her like a great gust of wind. Even flecks of light pulled off the glowing volume as the wind vanished down and out the other side.

Curiously, Charlotte moved down the aisle after it toward the glowing book. She glanced to the other books to her side, but they didn't seem to have any titles. Or perhaps it was simply too dark to see them. Her heart began to pound in her chest as she approached, and the closer she got, the brighter the book seemed to glow. She squared with it, finding it rather hard to look at, the illumination starting to sting her vision. She turned her head slightly away, squinting.

Her hand tentatively reached out, fingers splaying out to grip it. Her fingers rested on the spine, and the book extinguished. Her eyes relaxed, and she turned back to the book, just in time to see what looked like a tangible and sentient darkness slip around from either side of the cover. She pulled her hand back quickly but not fast enough to avoid what felt like a sharp bite on her index finger.

"Shit!" Charlotte stumbled back, shaking her hand, her back slamming into the opposite shelf behind her. Her eyes were able to focus on the book's title, *Nightmares & Horrors*, before the darkness enveloped it completely from sight. As if by infection, it then swallowed every book on either side of it, rapidly devouring color and light amid a low and ominous rumbling sound.

Her eyes widened, and she instinctually scrambled out of the book stacks, staring down as the darkness hungrily draped itself through the library. Despite that the light still seemed to seep in through the fretwork of the ceiling, it was not strong enough to penetrate these new seemingly solid shadows.

Charlotte's finger began to feel cold and numb, and she looked back down to it. To her surprise, her fingers had elongated much like claws, the skin blackening to the same tangible darkness that was spreading like ink on paper up her palm, slowly now, but with no sign of stopping. "What the…"

"It's without constraint or government," a voice remarked, both new and familiar.

Charlotte looked to her left and saw the same grey figure in the dim light, leaning against what appeared to be a librarian's desk. Like before, she could not really make out his features, as if he were barely more solid than the mist that curled out past her lips with every breath.

In his hand he held something that seemed far more in focus: an orb of a perpetually shifting darkness, flecks of light intermixed in the ever-moving ether as if he had trapped a galaxy within. "Unchecked, it will devour everything."

Charlotte's brow furrowed. "What will?"

"The *Nothing*," the figure answered, and for a moment she almost thought she could see his face as it turned. Was it out of focus, or was she simply unable to remember it the moment she looked away? His voice was not one of the chorus. She could tell that at the very least.

Charlotte shrugged helplessly. "I… don't know what that is…" Now that she had a view of him from profile, she did notice something else odd about him, something that separated him from every other person she'd seen in her dreams thus far… "Why don't you have a cord?"

Another low, ominous rumble in the near distance—or was it a *rustle*?

"The Dreamers are dying, Charlie."

Charlotte's attention shifted back to him. "Dreamers?"

"And the Dreamless now stands without defense."

"*Find her. Save her,*" the voices begged over and over, carried on a wind that curved around them like a gentle cyclone.

"I don't understand," Charlotte admitted to them, and something about this gave her a sense of panic. They were trying to tell her something. Something important. And she wasn't getting it.

The figure raised his free hand as if to ask the voices for a moment, and with it the wind dissipated respectfully.

There was a crackling sound, like wood straining, as if about to splinter, not above them but somewhere down in the belly of the stacks of the great library.

The figure pushed off his perch on the desk, and though she could not see his face, she could feel the sense of urgency heighten. "They need your help, Charlotte. And so does your mother."

"My help?" Charlotte squeaked incredulously. "What could *I* possibly do?" She was about to raise her hand to her heart when she caught sight of it. The ink-black darkness had spread to her forearm now. "Oh my god—what is happening to me?"

He raised the orb to her eye-level, barely inches from her face, so it pulled her focus, and she found herself getting rather lost in the ever-shifting night within it. Blues, purples, swirling blacks, and bright tiny stars continuously swallowed and exposed again within a glass-like orb the size of a lime. "You're going to *need* this. Meet me *here*."

Charlotte pulled her gaze from the shifting galaxies within and tried to meet his eyes. Were they too grey or… was her mind desperately trying to fill in the blanks? "I don't even know who you are," she told him in frustration, then looking around. "Or where *here* even is. What *is* this place?" She looked back to him, and as her questions went unanswered, her voice raised in volume and frustration. "What the hell is *The Nothing*? Why can't you just tell me what's going on?!"

The rumbling was much louder now—much closer in response to her voice, and she could hear a scratching sound—something akin to branches against the window.

Charlotte felt a chill run through her. A hand grasped her wrist and finally she made clear and direct eye contact with pale silver irises—so pale they nearly blended into the whites of his eyes.

"We have to calm the tide, Charlotte. We have to bridge the rift."

The wind picked up once more. "*You have to save Alys.*"

He released her wrist. "It's time to stop running."

The bookstacks crashed over like great trees being clear-cut, each one collapsing into the one in front of it like dominoes. The sound was deafening, books tumbling about, being smashed and crushed around them. Each shelf shook the ground, and as the snow and errant pages began to flutter down to the ground, Charlotte had a clear view of what looked like a great tree.

Whatever this thing was, it was enormous, crafted from shadow and twisted branches. In the dim light she could see the jagged edges, the gnarled pieces that created its semblance of a face, broken sharpened sticks creating its shark-like mouth of teeth. If this was an Ent or talking tree from various folklore, it had found form from the very depths of every child's nightmare. It was the personification of branches that scratched against your window, of that thing you knew logically was just wind rustling the trees, but your imagination could not be convinced.

Charlotte's heart pounded in her chest, and she felt once more a small child reaching for her blankets to cover her head.

But she wasn't in bed. Her mother wasn't just down the hall.

So, Charlotte ran.

Charlotte startled awake again as Diana was setting down a bag of food on the bed. She looked wide-eyed and on edge, like a cat with its back arched and hair standing on end.

Diana startled herself from the jerky movement, and then laughed. "Sorry, kitten, didn't realize you were actually out. I thought you heard me come in and were just relaxing."

Charlotte just stared, then looked around, taking the hospital room in and reacquainting herself with her surroundings. It was warm, it was unnaturally sterile, and it was bathed in fluorescent light. And her mother.

Her heart sank. It had really happened. And despite the fantastical sights and sensations, the horrific creatures and mysterious vanishing figures that had haunted her dreams, reality seemed the real nightmare. She sat up, frowning as her eyes examined her mother's sleeping face.

No change.

She sighed heavily and looked to Diana, then slowly drew her attention to the take-out bag. "Thai 65," she read quietly.

"Yeah…" Diana answered, pulling up a chair next to her so she could sit and wrap an arm around her. "I know it was a you-and-her thing, but… it seemed you needed it. Bit of sunshine."

"Thank you…" Charlotte leaned on her godmother's shoulder as her thoughts returned to just before she'd drifted off. "What are we going to do?"

"Carry on, kitten," Diana answered softly. She took a deep breath and tried to smile. "Just like the British. Keep calm, and carry on."

"I'm supposed to go back to school tomorrow."

Diana took a moment to silently think on that. "… Is that something you feel emotionally prepared to do right now?"

Charlotte looked at her mother, then back at Diana, and shook her head. Of course it wasn't.

"The distraction might be good for you, keep your mind off of this while we wait to hear next steps."

Charlotte shook her head again. "I'll go on Friday, I promise, I just… I can't tomorrow. Not so soon after this. I can't."

Diana nodded and kissed her forehead. "Okay. I'll call in the morning. We can carry on, on Friday."

6

THROUGH THE LOOKING GLASS

They got home well past 10 p.m. that night. Diana promised she'd stay over, and the next day, and the next if she had to until Alys was back to health and home again.

Charlotte found the confidence with which her godmother spoke comforting. No faltering, no hesitation or doubt. It was nothing but *when* Alys woke up, and *when* she felt strong enough, and what they'd do *when* things calmed down again. Never *if*.

It quieted her anxieties. Made it easier to believe.

"I'm not really tired," Diana confessed, hanging up her coat on the rack by the door. "Are you?"

Charlotte shook her head.

"Should probably try…"

"Probably…"

Diana looked up the stairs; toward the bedroom she knew was now empty of the woman they'd left behind. "How about you get in your pjs, and we'll put something on 'til we pass out on the couch?"

Charlotte nodded. "Okay."

Diana wandered into the kitchen. "I'm going to see if your mom stocked any good snacks."

Charlotte clasped her hand around the pocket watch absently, stopping at the bottom of the stairs. She hesitated, her gaze moving up what now felt like a gauntlet to her room. She took the stairs one by one, half the speed she normally did, her free hand grappling the railing as if she were climbing a mountain. Her chest tightened; her breath caught.

The master bedroom was just to the left of the top of the stairs, and as she reached the summit, the wide-open door caught her attention.

Charlotte's fingers tightened on the railing, but her body instinctually leaned toward Alys' room, as if she were caught a current, afraid of being swept away if she let go.

The lights were still on.

One by one, her fingers released the rail, and she curiously peered through the doorway. She lingered a moment, gazing with the cautious reverence one might reserve for a crime scene. No one had died, and yet the room seemed haunted. The bed was bare save for the fitted sheet. The EMTs had dumped the covers over the edge before they'd moved Alys onto a stretcher. Charlotte took a wary step over the threshold to take in the remainder of the room which remained undisturbed by the afternoon's events.

The clothes in her closet hung, unknowingly abandoned, her shoes lined up and ready for use as if their owner hadn't been carted away without even slippers. The standing full-length mirror reflected the carnage of the bed but remained upright and untouched itself.

Charlotte exhaled heavily, realizing she'd been holding her breath. Inhale 5, exhale 6.

Repeat.

She moved to the closet thoughtfully.

When her mother woke up, she'd need clothes, they'd taken her away in her pajamas. She fingered the fabrics hung up with her right hand, her left still tightly gripped around the pocket watch.

Something cozy. Hospital gowns were stiff and uncomfortable.

She pulled a sweater from the closet and gently rubbed it against her cheek. It was then placed on the bare mattress. She returned to find jeans and laid those out beside it. Then a bra, then underwear. She did it one by one, because her left hand refused to release the watch, thus forcing her to complete her task one-handed. It wasn't practical, but the things that soothe our anxieties rarely are. There was a comfort in holding that familiar piece of jewelry, like a security blanket.

Socks were selected. Then shoes.

Charlotte stood back and appraised the outfit she'd selected before nodding slightly to herself. This seemed good. But perhaps…

She sat on the edge of the mattress and dipped her fingers into the small bowl of jewelry on top of the nightstand. A few necklaces and rings. She peered at them individually, picking through, deciding if any of these accessories would be welcome treats when her mother awoke.

Alys wouldn't wear them. She never wore them. But it was something to do.

Beside the bowl of jewelry was the book Alys had been reading before bed, and it was filled with what looked to be nearly a hundred small Post-it markers sticking out of the pages.

Charlotte ran her thumb over the markers and pushed it open carefully. She tilted her head and scanned over the tiny familiar scrawl of her mother's handwriting that filled the margins, the highlighted passages, and underlined quotations.

Her left hand relaxed, and she carefully took it in her right. She flexed her fingers, trying to ease the oncoming cramp. Her palm was indented from the watch's flower design, and seeing the red marks made her exhale a laugh through her nose.

Her attention then turned back to the watch itself. She tapped her thumb on the clasp to open it. She flinched at the sight of her own reflection in the small mirror. "You look like hell," she mused to herself before looking down at the clock face. She let it lay flat in her palm, turning it so the golden hand layered over the minute hand, both now pointing at 6.

She huffed a laugh, shaking her head. "Okay, now I *know* that's not north," Charlotte muttered, looking up to where the compass was pointing. Her breath caught in her throat.

The full-length mirror diagonally across from her in the corner, was *moving*.

"What the…" The pocket watch slipped from her fingers and she raised her hand to wipe her eyes. When she looked again, the mirror had solidified.

Charlotte blinked hard. Her feet slid to the floor, pushing her up to slowly make her approach the mirror. It *looked* normal. She tentatively tapped it with a black-lacquered fingernail. It *felt* normal. Her brow furrowed, and she leaned back on her heels, staring back at her reflection utterly bewildered. Had she imagined it? The dim light reflecting off the golden sheen of the watch caught her eye again, and she pursed her lips in thought.

"Charlie, I've found some salt-and-vinegar chips and am thinking about putting on *Singing in the Rain*. Sound good?" Diana called up the stairs

"Be down in a minute," Charlotte chimed distractedly, narrowing a hard focus on the watch's reflection as she took it in her hand again. She brought it slowly closer to her face, shifting focus from reflection to the object itself.

The clasp was still undone, and she carefully turned it over in her hand to look at the hands once more.

The mirror did nothing.

She took a deep breath and slowly turned the watch in her palm so that the golden hand layered over the 6 again.

In her peripheral vision, she could see the mirror shudder, and while she could feel her body minutely trembling, she tried to remain as still as possible as she slowly drew her gaze up to look at the mirror.

Her reflection was almost gone, and beyond the glass, which seemed no more than ripples on a pond, was a grand and lavish room of opulent marble and brocaded fabrics. She could see a crystal chandelier hanging from the ceiling and a bed so large...

Charlotte's eyes widened. She nervously glanced at the empty doorway, wondering if she should tell Diana...

Tell her *what*, exactly?

Her fingers cautiously touched the glass—it felt and reacted like water, but when she retracted her fingers, they weren't wet. The mirror itself rippled from her touch and calmed like the surface of a pond. "I must have fallen asleep again," she murmured, though she couldn't recall when that might have happened, or the last time she had been so sure while dreaming that she must be dreaming.

She stuck her hand farther in, watching it pass through while her body remained on the other side. Her arm retracted and, upon close examination, appeared no different and completely unharmed. But if books had taught Charlotte anything, it was not to stumble into mirror universes and unknown worlds all willy-nilly and without preparation.

She snuck in a foot, then a leg through. She seemed to be standing on solid ground. She could see her other half on the other side, and feeling that she had tested this enough, she held her breath, closed her eyes, plugged her nose, and stepped through completely.

Charlotte stood a moment before cracking her eyes slowly open.

White marble swirled with silver and opal below her boots, stretching across the grand floor, making up large pillars, as well as the walls and ceilings. She would expect that, being surrounded by marble, the room would have been chilly, but she found she didn't much notice the temperature of the air at all.

"Whoa…" Charlotte whispered, closing the pocket watch and letting it go to hang around her neck. "Where… the hell am I?"

Thankfully, there appeared to be no one around to answer her. And she wasn't entirely sure what they'd think of her if they had been.

Alys had never not worn this necklace. It stood to reason that Alys knew that this mirror and this pocket watch created a portal… was it just *that* mirror? Or was it *any* mirror? She zipped up her hoodie, shielding the watch from view. It was a subconscious act more than anything else. Another valuable book-inspired lesson: You didn't go waving around the rare magic artifact to just anyone. That always caused more trouble. That was, of course, assuming it *was* a rare magic artifact. Though, she suspected it must have been, otherwise she'd have been more accustomed to people just wandering in through her mother's bedroom mirror.

Bedroom mirror travel. That… And she'd had this watch the whole time? And it was… magic? What else could it be?

"Oooh, Lucy, you got some s'plainin' to do…" she whispered, her jaw dropping at the utter grandness of the room.

The bed was large enough that it probably could have swallowed five people easily, and it was covered with expensive-looking blankets neatly made. She took in a large closet, a sitting area and coffee table—which always struck her as odd. Who exactly was entertaining guests in their room around a coffee table? She imagined that if you had a room this large, you would undoubtedly have a million other rooms that didn't have a bed in them where you could conduct business and such.

She turned around to look behind her, and her reflection stared back from an extraordinarily large mirror, with no sign of her mother's bedroom or that it had been a door only moments before. "Huh…" She self-consciously adjusted her disheveled hair and wiped under her eyes where her eyeliner had smudged before walking around the room to explore.

Charlotte also thought it was a little strange that in a room this large, they had foregone any TVs or stereos. What in the world did one do with a room so big? No music for dancing, no TV for vegging… There were some bookshelves, but she didn't recognize any of the titles she looked at, and she could only confidently pronounce a handful of them. Out of paranoia, she checked for the title she'd seen in her dream. Nowhere to be seen. She wasn't sure if she found that comforting or not.

Where the hell was she? Some kind of castle? A castle where? And how did her mother get a hold of this item?

Wait, no, she knew that. She got it from Charlotte's father. But how did *he* get a hold of it? And did he know about its power?

There was a lot about the room that struck her as strange. She noticed that while the materials were fine, there didn't seem to be an excess to them. They were classy, not gaudy—and while this was not particularly remarkable on its own, Charlotte had never seen anything remotely so artistic. It was like something from a European museum. The lack of power outlets also seemed incredibly unusual, and once she noticed it, she realized she wasn't entirely sure if the chandelier above her was lit by electricity or something else. It seemed to glisten like starlight.

But the strangest thing of all was one of the paintings hung on the wall in the sitting alcove: a woman in a white gauzy gown, and her white hair was pinned up off her elegant sepia-toned neck, in cascading ringlets.

Atop her head sat a fantastical-looking crown of pearls, opals, and diamonds. Her face was both youthful and... alarmingly familiar. In fact, Charlotte could have almost mistaken the woman in the portrait to be an older and far more flatteringly elegant version of herself were it not for the piercing blue eyes that stared back at her.

As questions had been piling on questions, this painting seemed to help bring them to conclusion. Because the most notable thing about the painting, even more than her seemingly likely relation to the woman depicted, was that the painting itself was created by her mother.

The aesthetic itself was unmistakable—Alys' distinct artistic style had practically grown up alongside of Charlotte. She'd know it anywhere. And if she'd had any doubts, when she leaned up on her toes and stared at the lower right corner, she could see the characteristic flourish on the A of the artist's signature.

Charlotte took out the watch once more as if it could give her answers. "What were you doing over here?" She stared at the intricate flower etching, then slowly back up at the signature on the painting.

And while the particulars were still very fuzzy and unclear, one thing did seem very certain to Charlotte. This is where *he* lived.

It was why he gave Alys the watch. It was why... for whatever reason, they couldn't be together. Somewhere, on this side of the mirror, Charlotte knew in the core of her, without a doubt, she was going to find her father.

She swallowed and looked back at the mirror. Her reason reminded her of Alys' words about her safety—that it was better her father didn't know she existed. For both of them. Somehow.

She hesitated.

She was likely in danger on this side of the looking glass, and for a moment of cool intelligence, Charlotte considered going back through the mirror after all.

Diana *would* worry if she were gone much longer.

She took a hesitant step, then looked to the door that led out of the room.

Her father was *here*.

She gnawed on her lower lip.

Her *father*, the man Alys had kept her a secret from, someone whom she had the ability to see by just *stepping through her mirror*, was *here*.

She paused at that, thinking over her last conversation with her mother. Not a day went by that Alys didn't miss him. "You were this close, and still you somehow stayed away?" Her brow furrowed. "Just for me?"

She took another step toward the mirror.

If her mother had gone to *all* that trouble, resisted visiting even with that much temptation, with him that easily accessible, shouldn't she go back? Respect that wish?

Charlotte toyed with the pocket watch idly.

But... if her father had access to something like *this*—something that could make portals out of mirrors… perhaps… *perhaps* there was *something* on this side that could help wake her mother up. Something to *help* her.

Charlotte took a deep breath and made her decision. She tucked the pocket watch back beneath her sweatshirt and opened the door. She cautiously peeked her head out. The hallway was grand and decorated, and thankfully, just like the room she'd first entered, empty. She stepped into the hall, closing the door as silently as possible behind her as she took in the gold filigree along where the wall met the ceiling.

She paused to listen.

Only silence. It seemed strange that such a place would be so empty. Weren't places like this typically full of lords, or guards and… servants and… such? She expected to have to dodge around people, try to remain unseen, reenact one of the many video games she played where going unnoticed was key. Perhaps don a disguise from… some conveniently placed laundry room.

That she saw no one, and heard no one, set her more on edge. It made her heart pound. Was she dreaming after all? Was she going to turn this upcoming corner and come face to face with the gargoyle or monster tree or something else horrific that her mind concocted? She nervously glanced around the corner.

Nothing.

Charlotte exhaled in relief and made the turn, peering at the large portraits of people on the wall

she had to assume were important for some reason…
but she still had no real idea of who any of them were.
Or where she was. Her brow furrowed. Were any of
these her father? Her nose scrunched.

She scrutinized each, reading names but finding no real answer in them. There was one that was
labeled King Morpheus I, and she did linger on his
portrait for the pure novelty of his name. He was
not, however, played by Laurence Fishburne. Nor did
he seem much like the Greek myth—though she
supposed she had little to go on regarding that. He
stood stalwart like the others, but despite his heroic
stance, and the dragon-like head in one hand, his
sword in the other… he didn't look how she imagined
a legendary hero—or a god of dreams. He was not
imposing; he was almost mischievous. And instead of
bulging muscles, he was on the leaner side, perhaps
even a little scrawny… but his bone structure was
strong. As was his nose.

Then, as she looked over the rest of it, something
behind him caught her eye. She blinked and peered
at it. It was the crack in the sky! She was certain of it.
The same crack that had haunted her sleep and yet…
in this context… it almost looked like a tree.

She took a step back, confused, and raised a hand
to her head. So, she was dreaming. That stood to reason.
How could she have stumbled through a mirror into
an alternate world if she'd been awake? But if that
were true…

How long had she been asleep? What was dream and what was not?

Was *she* the one in a coma right now?

She turned as panic began to set in, and her eyes locked on the portrait directly ahead of her. Her breath caught, her eyes softened, her muscles relaxed. "Mom?" The need to walk quietly fell away. Her neck craned up as she closed the distance between her and the painting, trying to understand just exactly what she was looking at. This painting was not like the one in the bedroom, the style far more realistic than the wistful sort of fantasy her mother's work invoked, the artist's style in line with that of the other portraits in the hall…

Still, it had to be Alys, rather than mere coincidence. Her face was identical to her mother's. The young woman stood boldly, her shoulders back, feet planted and chest forward in a stance that showed no fear to the opponent not depicted.

Darkness swirled around in a mass behind her, textured shades of blue and black full of movement like a Van Gogh painting. Unlike the portrait of the woman in the bedroom, she was dressed in modern clothing, and Charlotte realized she recognized the light blue sweatshirt Alys still wore from time to time. In her hand she held a rapier more beautiful than any blade she'd ever seen. The hilt twisted around her hand, glittering with diamonds, but the pommel was a round stone that mirrored the twisting blackness behind her, and the blade itself seemed to be made of light. It was mesmerizing.

It was *familiar*.

Charlotte's eyes widened as she remembered the orb the grey figure held in front of her. It was the same pommel.

Set into the bottom center of the ornate gold frame around the painting was a simple plaque, like the others around it. Charlotte had to take a few steps forward to read it.

The Hero of Terra Mirum.

The King's Reason was strained. War was all about strategy, but strategy lost all meaning when the air itself seemed capable of corrupting and consuming your soldiers. So now Elan Vital was overrun with refugees. They had been discussing options for hours, and Basir was feeling cornered and helpless. He was a tall man with a strong bone structure and dark complexion. He and Robin had retired to their quarters for a moment of peace, of rest, but instead of finding his wife there as he thought, he'd found a nervous soldier with news that only increased his feeling of helplessness. "So, she left without telling me because she knew I would not agree with the idea." He removed the top hat from his head and tossed it onto the bed in frustration. "Brilliant."

"I tried to stop her, sir," the soldier protested softly.

"And a valiant effort, I am sure it was, but trust me, after being married to one for centuries, there is little use arguing with an Unseelie who has already made up her mind." He huffed through his nose and removed the high-collared coat of emerald and gold brocade. "Did it occur to her, by chance, that not informing me of her intention does not, in fact, improve her plan simply because I am not there to object to it?'

"Um—"

"It was a rhetorical question, private, stop sweating." The coat was thrown on the bed with similar fury.

"Right."

Basir sighed, thinking. "How long ago did she leave?"

"Not twenty minutes. If we hurry, we—"

"Would be lucky to even see her shadow in the distance. Fae are faster than Dreams, and Robin herself could probably circle the globe itself in a mere 40 minutes." He gave a heavy sigh as he felt the weight of his own sense of inadequacy. "Not to mention that any pursuit would require us to lower the barrier, which reminds me, how is it holding?"

"Strong, sir," Private Faris assured. "No signs of impending breach."

"Well, there is one comfort." Basir clasped his hands behind his back. "And when she did depart…?"

"She flew to the top of the barrier," Faris answered. "Passed right through without harming it, and that high up, there was no risk of letting any of the nightmares in."

"Good…" His brow furrowed, and he sank down onto the bed. "Good." His shoulders slumped. "Wonderful, reckless woman." His lips pursed, and he tapped his toe a moment before looking back to Faris. "Does the King know?"

"Not yet. Should I inform him?"

"No, no," Basir dismissed firmly. "I will." He stood up again, not sure if he was exhausted that he could not rest, or relieved that he at least had something productive to do. "The King will undoubtedly have questions that you will not be socially equipped to answer."

"Sir?"

"Robin is a member of court, Faris, and a man of your station would do best not to speak ill of nobility. I, on the other hand, am her loving husband and political equal, and am therefore perfectly within my rights to call her an idiot." Basir's shoulders hunched, and while he spoke with a tone so clipped it could have sheared off his companion's nose, his expression softened.

Faris reached up a hand to rest on the other man's arm, then thought better of it and dropped it awkwardly to his side. "I'm sure she'll be fine, sir. The Nightmares can't infect Unseelie blood, can they?"

"Turning you into one of them is not necessarily the worst thing they are capable of," Basir said lowly. He reached for his coat and paused, looking over the formal trappings. "She isn't invincible… no matter what she'd like to think." His brow furrowed. What even was the point of decorum now? He dismissed the thought with a brisk brush of his hands down his vest and straightened it by grasping the lower hem. "But you are right. I'm sure she'll be fine." He took a moment, still holding onto the fabric of his vest as he stared somewhere on the ground a foot or two in front of him. "She has to be fine."

Faris looked to either side, feeling uncomfortable in the silence that fell between them. "Do you think the Fae will send aid?"

"Without some sort of bribe being offered in return?" Basir huffed. "I very much doubt it. Oberon may have assisted us in the last war, but it was not without a high price. I shudder to think what such a man will demand of us now…" He looked up, then to the window in the general direction of Arden. "Or what she would offer up to keep us safe." He reached for his coat and put it back on, straightening his hems and cuffs as he turned to the mirror. "I will tell the King about Robin's… possibly misguided effort to reach Arden. Would you please return to the great hall and bring word of our ration supply? I'm sure he'll want an update on that, as well."

Faris nodded, bowed, and scuttled off.

Basir took a deep breath and replaced his hat, taking in his visage for a long moment. He practiced his smile and took a moment to push back his shoulders and relax the visibly tense muscles. He took one last look, decisively nodded to his reflection, and made his way to the throne room. His pace was confidant, determined, and in complete opposition of the tempest within him. There would be time for worry after. There would be a place to address his panic in the privacy of his quarters. For now, people needed him, they… Basir stopped short as he rounded the corner and caught sight of a strange figure standing in front of the portrait of Alys.

She was short, with wild windswept white hair, and entirely unfamiliar.

"Pardon me, miss," Basir began carefully. "I do not mean to be rude, but for your safety, it would be best if you stayed downstairs with the rest of the villagers."

Charlotte felt a hard pit in her stomach, like a child being caught with her hand in the cookie jar. She slowly turned to look at the man addressing her, sheepish expression fading as she met his eyes, and her jaw slightly slackened in surprise. She was looking upon the living incarnation of one of her mother's creations. As clear as day, the man before her seemed to have stepped out of the very pages of her mother's first children's book, from his top hat to the spats visible beneath his perfectly tailored pants. "Reason?" she whispered breathlessly. Now she knew she was dreaming.

Basir was also taken aback by the teenager before him, and his breath caught as he stared upon what seemed like a ghost. The face was the same, her hair— it was as if he'd been transported back through time and now the image of the White Queen herself stood before him. "Your Majesty?" He answered in disbelief.

Charlotte's expression contorted into a scowl. "What? No."

Basir shook himself and took a step back, for the first time acknowledging her clothing and general appearance. He slowly looked from the black hoodie around her to the white skull tank top, skinny jeans, and large knee-high boots. Two things became certain to him in that moment. First, this was not a vision of young Aislynn, and second, this was not someone native to Terra Mirum. "*Who* are you?"

Charlotte's eyes widened slightly as the man before her went from taken aback to authoritative—even, she dare admit, intimidating. "Charlie Carroll," she answered quietly. Then, regaining a flicker of defiance and courage. "*Who* are you?"

Basir looked bewildered only a moment before realization dawned on him and his gaze shifted to the painting behind her. "Very. *VERY*. Disappointed."

7

HEAVY IS THE HEAD

It was well past the witching hour, or whatever hour it was that the mind melted into a useless dew. It weighed heavily upon the occupants of the war room. Each had become well acquainted with this time of morning for the past few nights, yet still, they all refused to sit. It was possible this stubbornness was born of the knowledge that if they did allow themselves even the smallest of reprieve, they would find themselves drifting off to sleep.

The table was strewn with maps and parchments, letters, and reports. Markers had been placed along the maps indicating areas that had been lost to the Nightmares, whether by voluntary evacuation... or worse.

Three decorated soldiers had removed their coats and flung them on the chairs behind them, and at the head of the table stood a man in white and gold brocade.

The White King had not had an easy reign. After losing both his parents in the last war against the nightmares, he ascended the throne with only Rhyme and Reason to guide him. He had not aged much in appearance, but there was a weariness to his eyes now that seemed to weigh on his entire being. Two wars between Dream and Nightmare in just his lifetime. It was exhausting. And even more terrible, they were not likely to receive the same aid they were so fortunate to find the last time. He had sent Robin and Basir, both, to rest, as the exhaustion was starting to wear too thin on either advisor. But his generals had insisted on continuing without them.

One general, a Dream of a muscular build, sleeves undone and rolled up to the forearms, was leaning across the table, fixating a hard glare at the man across from them. "How," they began carefully, the irritation showing in the way their jaw tightened, "can we *possibly* hope to combat a foe whose mere presence is toxic to our people? The armies of Arden are our only hope."

The second general tilted his chin, with its neatly trimmed beard, slightly upward, his own arms folded as he seemed to ground his heels further into his opinion. "We cannot rely on our past allies to save us."

"Then what *good* are they?" The first scoffed, pushing off the table in disgust at their colleague.

Oswin sighed, as it was becoming apparent he would have to attempt to calm the war breaking out within his walls as well as outside them. "Oberon's support has come at a very high price in the past," he gently reminded the first.

"Does he have nothing to lose, as well, if Elan Vital falls?" The third spoke up, her brows knitting together as she looked over the parchments near her for what seemed to be the millionth time. She knew there must be something, something she simply missed that would help them.

"Perhaps," Oswin permitted.

"What other choice do we have?" the first prompted, having yet to receive a satisfying answer to any question they'd posed that evening on the matter.

Among the papers, the third general found the treaty between the two nations, and her eyes scanned it, but found nothing. "What of Titania?" she asked, looking up again to her king. "The Red Court has been known to take up arms in the past when dire circumstances called for it. I cannot think of a more dire circumstance than now. Half of Terra Mirum is overrun."

The second general growled in frustration as if he saw this as a personal offense. "Is there *nothing* we can do to fight this ourselves? Truly no weapon we can craft?"

The first sighed heavily, answering the question they had been prompted to give answer to many times in the past two days. "We have alchemists and mages at work, but nothing substantial of use at this time, Toulouse."

"Galen," Oswin addressed, "Has anyone been able to reach The Librarian?"

The first general shook their head. "No, I'm afraid the Phrontistery has fallen, Your Highness. The entire

Forest of Thought is infested with Nightmares, and what inhabitants survived have evacuated."

Oswin swallowed, hard. "...Do we know if she made it to safety?"

Galen shook their head regretfully. "Reports were inconclusive. She hasn't been seen."

Oswin's head hung, and he leaned his palms against the table. "Dammit."

"What of The Hero?" the third general asked cautiously.

She was answered with a tense silence, but she noticed the king's shoulders relax, and though his head didn't raise, it did seem to tilt ever so slightly, as if he were inclining an ear toward her.

At last, Toulouse broke the silence with a roll of his eyes and the same disdain that had been overgenerously lathered over every word he spoke that night. "The *Hero*, Malon."

Her back straightened. She was a lithe woman, but not without presence. Her short brown hair curled almost cherub-like around her face, but her eyes were sharp. She reached down to undo the button at her right wrist and fold her sleeve upward, giving in to the stifling quality of the room and opting for relief. The adjustment of her garment partially revealed the heavily detailed bronze-and-silver clockwork cogs tattooed from her wrist to beyond her elbow. "During next high noon, it should be bright enough for us to open a portal through the barrier. A small scouting party from my battalion could wend a path to the waking world. Attempt to find her."

Oswin's breath caught.

Toulouse rolled his eyes once more and Galen rather wondered if they might be done with it and just roll out of his head already. "Unlikely they'd manage to survive the journey."

"So, we shouldn't try?" Galen concluded incredulously. "Because… it may risk the lives of those who vowed to risk their lives for Terra Mirum?"

"I am saying we should not be risking them needlessly and carelessly," Toulouse argued.

"Carelessly?" Galen repeated, moss green eyes narrowing at the accusation. "Is that what you believe? That we are merely throwing lives away on a whim? That we have no faith in any of these plans, that we aren't at the end of our rope?"

"Haven't we lost enough already?" Toulouse growled.

"We will lose more if we don't do something *soon*," Malon said levelly.

"Supposing you *did* find her—what then?" Toulouse demanded. "Are you suggesting we bring a Dreamer back over our borders? We may owe her our lives, but we cannot ignore the overwhelming danger she herself presented just by being here."

Malon's shoulders shifted back, but her voice remained unnervingly calm. "She was invaluable in our last battle with the Nightmares, the Jabberwock may never have been discovered without her, and she is the only known living person who can wield the vorpal blade."

"A weapon which lies in *Oberon's* possession," said Toulouse.

"Perhaps you could attempt devising some solutions of your own rather than pointing out the perceived problems in everyone else's," Galen commented dryly.

Toulouse sniffed. "Forgive me, General Galen, but in light of Basir's current absence, someone has to point out the inevitable failures of these so-called strategies."

Malon's hand twitched, and she undid the button of her other wrist and folded back that sleeve, as well, in slow controlled movements. "The King's Reason knows how vital The Hero was to our survival in those days."

"The King's *Reason* would still agree that knowingly bringing a Dreamer across our borders is a fool's errand at best, if not a warrant for our own destruction," Toulouse dismissed.

"What other choice have we?" Galen demanded.

"It's the principle of the thing—"

"DAMN your principle. I hope you choke on it!"

"I think," Oswin finally interjected, and his voice eased the tension building between one side of the table and the other. "While Toulouse's concerns are valid, Galen makes an unfortunate point."

Toulouse's jaw slackened in shock and Oswin elaborated quickly.

"We may no longer have the luxury of cautious strategy or playing it safe." The king swallowed; his throat felt dry. Seeing her again. "Perhaps reaching out to Alys is an avenue... worth exploring." His heart quickened at the thought.

"It should be taken into account, Your Highness, there have also been reports of *something* inside the train tunnel... making any travel through it quite an impossible task," Toulouse slid a small stack of papers across the table toward the King.

Oswin's brow furrowed, his eyes scanning over each report but gleaning little information from them. He read them again and wasn't sure if his mind was too exhausted to take in words or if they were truly as generic in their description of the creature as they seemed. "What *something*?"

"No one has been able to get close enough to say for certain. When we were able to send out scouts, nearly half the party vanished without a trace." Toulouse picked a piece of lint from his shirt sleeve. "Not to mention, if we did manage to bypass the monstrous thing, whatever it may be, we have no guarantee The *Hero* hasn't also been taken under like so many of the rest of them."

The idea struck Oswin like cold water to the face, and he straightened up, his head finally raising. He frowned, feeling his heart ache, and subconsciously he massaged the muscle above it with his fingertips. "No," he said, his voice now unusually soft. "That is the one thing we can be certain will not be a problem."

The three generals looked to each other, bewildered by this sentence.

Galen spoke cautiously, "...Your Highness?"

There was a characteristic knock from the guards posted outside the doors, which prompted the two posted within to take hold of the handles and pull them inward, revealing The King's Reason himself standing in the doorway. His posture seemed even more rigid than usual, his shoulders square, his back straight—even his jaw was tight. His clothing, while impeccable as always, seemed a tad askew, as if he had taken slightly less care to put on his jacket, or some unforeseen jostling had knocked off his hat, which was now gripped by the brim in his right hand. In his left hand was a short and hooded person, gripped at the bicep but doing their best to petulantly lean away from him, trying to create as much distance between them as possible.

Oswin was startled both by Basir's abrupt return and the tension that accompanied him. "Basir... I thought you were going to retire for a few hours."

"Forgive the interruption, Your Highness, but I must beg a moment of privacy with you. It is of the utmost importance." His voice was level, deeper than his typical timbre, but level—and calm.

Despite this, from their vantage point closest to the door, Galen noted Basir's tight grip around the smaller figure's arm and how it made the tendons of his hand far more prominent.

Oswin felt his stomach lurch as he prepared himself for the worst. "What happened? Is Robin alright?"

Basir cursed under his breath as the reality of his wife's current location flooded back to him, and he gritted his teeth. He was a man of poise and precision, but even he had his emotional limits. "No. I am afraid *that* is another conversation entirely that I must also speak with you about."

Oswin did not find any comfort in the manner his question was dismissed, and his advisor's reluctance to even speak of what might be the issue with others present made him even more wary. Something was wrong. Something was very wrong. He glanced to the figure so tightly clasped by the arm, then to the soldiers standing about the table. "Let's retire for now. We will come back in a few hours with fresh eyes and minds less addled by sleep deprivation."

The three generals nodded respectfully, and each turned to fetch their coats from the seats behind them, filing out one by one past Basir, whose gaze was so fixated on the king they did not dare to drag their feet or even linger for a moment.

Oswin shifted his weight uncomfortably and moved from behind the table to get a better look at the two. He tilted his head to the side, noticing the strange but familiar style of clothing the smaller figure wore. "This…" His heart began to beat faster. "Who is this?" he asked softly.

Basir waited a moment, listening for the clear and decisive click of the door shutting and sealing behind him before he spoke his own question. "Am I not the King's Reason?"

Oswin blinked. He stood up straighter. "You know you are."

Basir nodded, his lips pursing tightly together as he finally broke their eye contact, the hand that held his top hat moving to carefully replace it atop his head. "Your mother was the first to award that title, because her trust in me was integral to her triumph in the Battle of Arden, which ultimately won us the war against the Fae. She herself said things would have gone differently had I not been there."

Confusion battled with the rising anxiety inside of him that Oswin could not quite explain nor soothe. "I am well aware of your value as an advisor," he stated simply.

"In my years of knowing *you*, I had come to believe that my advice and point of view was also seen as an asset to you." Basir returned his gaze to the White King, his words very deliberate and staccato to underline his point. "Well received. Well *respected*."

"So it is, old friend." Oswin was feeling unnerved now. It felt like watching a cat decide if it was going to pounce on you or not.

"*Is* it?" The taller man seethed, his decorum slipping as his anger found its way to his voice. "That being the case, I find it curious that perhaps the most important, the most *imperative* counsel I have ever given you has been so callously ignored."

"I… I'm afraid I'm not following you." It was the slight breach in propriety, the speaking to his king in a manner Basir would have normally found unacceptable, that told Oswin something was deeply wrong. His mind raced. He looked to the figure beside Basir, noticing how he could not see her face. Her height and how she was dressed not very unlike the woman who had stumbled into his life not so long ago, and he could hear his heartbeat in his ears as he asked again the still unanswered question. "Who *is* this?"

"*This*, Your Highness," Basir's throat sounded tight as he reached to yank down the hood of the figure so awkwardly attempting to hide, "is your *daughter*."

Charlotte's eyes were closed tight as she felt the shelter of the hood pulled from her head. She heard nothing, and so very slowly, her eyes opened, first the right, then the left. She took in the floor first. Real wood, deep mahogany, and waxed so expertly it reflected her face back up at her. Then she took in a pair of men's chocolate brown dress boots. They were clean and reached to about his knee, where camel fall-front trousers had been tucked neatly into them. Over these trousers he wore a double-breasted vest of gold and white brocade, which complimented the white shirt beneath. He'd rolled up the sleeves, and all in all, despite his disheveled nature, he looked rather regal. A quality she felt no familiarity with. But as she dared look further and examine his face, she saw the similarity in their features that could not be denied.

Oswin didn't dare blink. He didn't dare breathe. Surely... he hadn't heard Basir correctly. "M-my..." He swallowed, hard, before he struggled to tear his attention back to Basir. "My *what*?"

"Your daughter." Basir repeated the word with enough weight that Oswin could practically feel it settle somewhere heavy in his chest. "At least," the King's reason continued, the strain in his voice audible. "I feel that is safe to assume, given that she looks *exactly* like you and she claims her name is Charlie Carroll."

Charlotte shot Basir a glare. "It *is* my name."

Oswin stumbled back slightly. "Charlie... *Carroll*?" His head was spinning, and he found himself struggling to breathe, as if all the air had suddenly been sucked from the room.

Charlotte stared back at him with an unimpressed expression. This was the man her mother kept her from? He seemed so... harmless. What about being separated from him was keeping her safe? "Why does he call you Highness?"

Oswin's looked at the hair on her head—it was *his* hair, his skin, his eyebrows... *her* eyes. He felt the muscles in his face relax. Alys' eyes. Honey intermixed with flecks of gold and ochre... It had been what felt like centuries since he'd seen those eyes. His heart tugged painfully, and he breathed something that mingled a joyful realization and a pained exhalation. He took a step toward her, then stopped, thinking better of it as he tried to process this. "Alys is your mother," he said hoarsely. Of course she was. Even now, the expression she had fixated on him, the pure skepticism—it was as if he were looking back on the very first day he'd met her.

"Changelings are *dangerous*, Your Highness. I cannot believe how many times this has been stressed to you—to *both* of you, even," Basir spoke almost as if he were scolding a child, and it snapped Oswin back to his senses. He was tired and at his wit's end. He was clinging to protocol. Barely. "The risks it puts on both our world, and the waking realm—not to mention the mother."

Charlotte, irritated at being ignored, turned to look at Basir. "Is he some kind of a king?"

Oswin swallowed. "Basir, I swear to you, I had no idea Alys was pregnant." *This* was what she wouldn't tell him, what she had been hiding, what she had been *lying* about.

"And yet you still pursued a relationship in the first place," Basir accused.

And this was *why*. "A course of action *you* of all people can hardly pass judgement on, old *friend*," Oswin volleyed the accusation back with a mirthless smile.

"Robin is not a Dreamer!" Basir's voice raised. "Let us not pretend our circumstances are the same. Though, even if they were, we clearly exercised leagues of more caution than you two attempted, given our present circumstance."

The two men glared at one another as a tense silence settled between them.

Charlotte looked from Basir to Oswin, then back again, as no one spoke. "Do you two need to like… hug this out?"

Finally, the adults looked toward the teenager as if, despite her presence being the exact point of contention, they'd completely forgotten it.

Basir released her arm, realizing that regardless of his feelings about her existence, this was, for lack of a better term, the only living heir to the White Throne… and as such probably should not have been manhandled.

Oswin cleared his throat. "Where is your mother?" His voice was softer, gentler. Hopeful. "Is she with you?"

"How did you even get here?" Basir asked in bewilderment, folding his arms as he looked down at her. He sized her up but saw nothing particularly impressive or formidable. "No one has even been able to get remotely close to the tunnel, and even then, you'd have to get past the barrier, so how could you possibly have managed to…" As the realization dawned on him, he looked to Oswin, who, seeming to guess his thoughts, returned a challenging gaze. "You gave Alys the Coleridge Clock," he concluded incredulously.

Oswin's chin raised slightly.

"You literally *handed* a human access to our world."

"You *severed* her!" Oswin spat the words that had been burning within him unspoken for years. "You cut her off from *everything*. Do you know what that's like for someone like Alys? What hell that is? To be adrift, to lose that part of you and no longer feel that connection? To be *Dreamless*?"

Charlotte's breath caught at the word.

"Robin did what she had to so Alys could go on living her life as normal, so this would be nothing more than a faded memory. We did what we thought was best for her," Basir defended.

"Without her consent!" Oswin could feel anger far too long unexpressed boiling over now. "You altered her very perception and relationship with the world around her without so much as a warning."

"We were perfectly upfront about protecting her from the Nightmares."

"Bullshit, you were protecting her," Oswin growled. "Nightmares may be a threat to us, Basir, but it's *different* for Dreamers. Yes, they're manifestations of fear, but they're still a part of them. And you took that away from her. You took away a piece of her! And you took that away because you were afraid of what she could be capable of, not for her protection. *Don't* insult me with that lie."

"She *was* a danger to us—we did what *had* to be done," Basir tried to reason as he closed the distance between him and Oswin, "what was *best* for Terra Mirum, a concern you yourself have clearly neglected and forgone for your own selfish desires." His brow furrowed, and he fixed a look of betrayal on the younger man. "How could you let this even be a possibility? How could you bring her back here?"

"Because she didn't *want* it to be just a dream," Oswin pleaded, his voice simultaneously exasperated and desperate. "Because *we* didn't want it to be some faded memory, and regardless of what you believe, neither you nor Robin had the right to take that away from us."

"You acted without Rhyme or Reason and put your own needs before that of your people—of your kingdom."

"And the only person it hurt, Basir, was *me*," Oswin answered. His voice broke, and Basir was visibly taken aback. "Just me." The man felt his body shake. He'd never spoken it aloud before. It gave the pain an overwhelming reality, and for a moment he just stood there, breathing through it. Basir merely stared back at him, not speaking, and so Oswin continued. "Despite what you may think, my people were not harmed by their King falling in love with a human." His chest felt tighter. "And before you continue this self-righteous crusade of yours, you should know I haven't seen Alys in years." He bit his lower lip in a rueful smile and shrugged. He knew he hadn't made the smartest decision… but he also knew he wouldn't have done anything differently. He took a deep breath, resolved. "I certainly didn't intend to bring a child into her world, let alone ours, but it certainly has nothing to do with the war we face now."

Basir thought a moment, tapping his fingers softly but rapidly on the table before he asked the question, he knew he had to. "…Do you know that?"

Oswin's eyes sharpened. "What?"

"Do you know for a fact it is not related?" Basir elaborated, knowing he was walking on extremely dangerous ground. But it had to be tread. "Have you any remote idea what she is even capable of?"

"She's a child," Oswin whispered incredulously.

"She's a changeling."

Oswin felt his hand ball into a fist and cock backward before slamming it down onto the table. "SO IS SYLAS!" His voice resonated against the walls in the room.

Basir didn't move. It was such an uncharacteristic outburst; he didn't even dare breathe.

Oswin exhaled and spoke again at a more level volume, but the intensity remained. "And the world has yet to fall around our heads simply because he lives in it. So, perhaps you might consider that your fears around the matter might actually be more misguided superstition than fact."

The King's Reason swallowed, and then spoke against his better judgement. "Your Highness, a union between Dream and Dreamer—"

"Has never happened." Oswin sighed heavily and seemed to deflate. "I know."

"And the coincidence of her arrival time," Basir cautiously explained.

Oswin covered his face with his other hand, rubbing his forehead, eyes, and cheeks with his fingers as his fist relaxed. Another heavily labored sigh.

It was Charlotte who finally broke the silence. "Could... someone tell me what exactly... is going on here? What is this place? What... is a changeling?"

Oswin looked to the small girl, his expression softening as he remembered her rather immediate presence again. He frowned but spoke quietly. "Your mother never told you?"

Charlotte shook her head.

Oswin's heart twinged, but he nodded at the logic of the decision. "Right. Of course she didn't. She wouldn't have... not after..." He looked to Basir a moment, thinking, shook his head, and then looked back to Charlotte. "Terra Mirum. Where you're from would know it as the Dream World."

Charlotte blinked. "I'm where?"

"When you sleep, your mind comes here. But, certain kinds of people—like your mother—have the ability—the gift, really—to travel here physically, to come here when they are not sleeping. Does... does that make sense to you?"

Charlotte mulled this over a little. "Dreamers?"

Oswin nodded.

"And mom... *was* one?"

Another nod. "When she first came here—the first time she came here, she—"

"Saved everyone?"

Oswin blinked, surprised.

"I found her by The Hero of Terra Mirum portrait in the upstairs hall," Basir explained.

The King looked from his Reason to his daughter. "Ah. Yes, that's… that's pretty much exactly what she did."

"And now it's all gone wrong again?" Charlotte's brow furrowed.

"In a manner of speaking, yes."

"And you think it's because of me?"

"No!" Oswin answered far too quickly.

Basir averted his eyes.

"No," Oswin repeated in the direction of his advisor. "Though we… had possibly hoped to enlist Alys' aid again." He swallowed. His throat felt dry. "Did she come with you?" The hope was back in his voice.

The surrealness of the moment was overcome by Charlotte's own reality, how she had discovered this place—how she had come to be in possession of the clock that opened a door through the mirror. "No…" She practically whispered the word, and the fire in her eyes seemed to extinguish. "She's sick."

Oswin's heart stopped. "Sick?"

Basir's attention riveted on the girl.

"Back home there's this… sickness, this disease going around. People go to sleep, and they don't wake up. Falling into comas… Mom…" Charlotte's throat felt tight, and she dug her fingernails into her palms. "Mom's in the hospital. She can't wake up. The doctor said her symptoms were stronger than most cases this early... I don't know what's going on." She was not going to cry. Not here. Not now.

The room felt so much colder to Oswin as he took an unsteady step back, half easing down, half collapsing into a chair. The room was spinning, and everything seemed so... silent. He could hear his own heartbeat. "It's not a disease." He leaned over himself, his head in his hands.

Charlotte looked to him uncertainty. "Then... what is it?"

"The Door to the Nothing has opened," said Basir.

The words were familiar, but the voice was not the same as from her dreams. Neither man was the voice from her dreams. She didn't know why, or even how, but what was becoming clearer as she listened to them was that what had been plaguing her sleep the past few days was not merely nightmares. "What *is* The Nothing?"

"The realm where everything does and doesn't exist. Where all matter and myth are formed, and where Nightmares are born and held at bay. Centuries ago, it was the core of our world, an epicenter of Chaos until the first King of Elan Vital created the Door and sealed it away safely in its own dimension."

Charlotte squinted. Her head was starting to hurt trying to wrap around this. "O...kay, so why not just close the door?"

"It's unfortunately not that simple." Oswin raised his head with the weariness of man facing down the same problem for countless days of sleepless nights.

"The Nightmares have infested almost all of Terra Mirum, and the more Dreamers they feed off of in this unending sleep, the more powerful they grow."

"My mother is being *fed* off of?" Charlotte choked on the words.

"I don't understand how this is even possible." Oswin stood again so he could pace across the hardwood floor. "They shouldn't have been able to do this. Not to her. They shouldn't have even been able to reach her."

"What do you mean?" Charlotte asked.

Basir shook his head subtly, but Oswin ignored him, "After Alys left our world, she was severed from it; her connection to Terra Miram destroyed before you were even born so that the Nightmares that plagued her sleep could never haunt her again…"

"The Dreamless…" Charlotte remembered her nightmare, and how disturbed her mother had been the last time they spoke about having a nightmare of her own. The discomfort, the worry… "Then why is she like this? How is this happening?"

"Because *something* reconnected her…" Basir explained. "Something powerful that re-established that link, perhaps not a very strong connection, perhaps an unstable connection, but a connection back to our world and The Nothing nonetheless."

Charlotte remembered the tattered and frayed silvery cord she'd seen attached to her mother—merely threads. Her stomach churned. "What… could be that powerful?"

Basir looked to Oswin pointedly, and the young king began to realize what his advisor had already figured out, why the man had shaken his head, attempted to stop them from reaching this moment.

"Giving birth to a changeling child..." Oswin answered numbly.

Charlotte felt cold panic spiderweb outward at her chest and over her lungs. She took a step back. "So... this really *is* because of me? I'm the reason any of this happened?"

"No, of course not," Oswin tried to soothe.

Charlotte took another step backward. "But they *did* get to her because of me? They were able to find her?" She looked to Oswin, who averted his eyes, and so she spoke to Basir. "What will they do to her?"

Oswin shot a warning glare at Basir, who stared back at him almost blankly before looking to Charlotte to answer her. "The Nightmares will use her life force to feed them until she becomes too weak to keep sustaining them. Then they will move on to another."

Breathing was getting difficult for Charlotte. "So, it will *kill* her?"

"Yes."

Charlotte startled as her back hit the wall and she realized she had been continuing her retreat subconsciously. "Then," she searched for words of action but found no experience to give her really any authority to speak on the matter. "Then we have to do *SOMETHING*!" she declared as the panic began to take over. "We can't just let this thing eat her—or any of the others who have fallen sick."

"We're trying to figure that out," Oswin assured.

"What is to figure out?" Charlotte demanded. "Go. GET. HER."

"If it were possible, I would, but we cannot merely charge into The Nothing."

"Why not?" Charlotte squeaked. "You're a king, aren't you? Don't you have an army?" She gestured to the maps and markers on the table.

Oswin exhaled through his teeth. "It isn't that simple. An army of Dreams would be immediately corrupted into Nightmares the moment they set foot into The Forest of Thought—assuming they even got that far."

That took Charlotte off guard. "They can do that?"

"They can, and they have," Oswin confirmed grimly. "The casualties thus far have been… staggering."

"Well over 150,000 souls so far that we know of, roughly estimating based on the cities that we know had no time to evacuate, and units that have not returned from missions."

"…You are facing an enemy you literally cannot fight because if you try straightforward regular methods… you'll become one of them?"

"Correct," said Basir.

Charlotte's mind was racing. "But… there must be *something* we can do."

No one answered her.

"You have a huge painting memorializing her as this great hero. I don't know what she did, but I'm assuming she put her life on the line for all of yours. You're telling me you won't even attempt the same?"

"We already have attempted the same," Oswin said, his brow furrowed. "Countless times, nothing we have tried has worked. Alys was human. She could have stood a fair chance against the Nightmares; she couldn't be corrupted. For my army to continue to march against the Nightmares—to march into The Nothing without some sort of defense—would be pure suicide."

"I'm human," Charlotte said.

Both men stared at her.

"Send me," came the desperate offer.

"Completely out of the question," Oswin dismissed.

Charlotte felt an anger wash over her. "Why?"

"We don't even know for sure if you'd be immune. You may be your mother's daughter, but apparently you're also mine."

"Meaning?" Charlotte spat.

"Meaning you're possibly just as susceptible to corruption," said Basir.

"*Meaning* I am also responsible for your safety," Oswin corrected.

Charlotte wanted to throw something at him. *Now* he wanted to play father? A mere half hour ago he didn't know she existed and *now* he wanted to pretend he knew best? When her mother was in trouble?

"Maybe you can just stand around while my mother is in danger, but I *can't*."

"I'm not just standing—you'd get yourself killed the moment you stepped out there!" Oswin said, flustered.

"At least I'd be trying something!" Charlotte accused.

"What good are you to her dead?" Oswin asked condescendingly.

"No worse than you are alive, apparently!" Charlotte shot back. "You think you're the first person to fight a war? Reach out to allies—to ENEMIES if you have to—fight dirty, use illegal weapons—do whatever you have to do to stop this and put everything *right* again!"

"It's not—"

"*Don't* tell me it's not that simple!" The teenage girl started at him in a rage. "You're just sitting here, arguing among yourselves, not even *DOING* anything. People are in danger. My *mother* is in danger. Doesn't that mean anything to you?"

"It's *everything* to me!" Oswin roared at her, startling both Charlotte and Basir back a few steps. "Do you think this is easy? That I haven't done everything in my power? You're a *child*. You know *nothing* of war, or loss or pain!"

A silence fell in the room again, the air humming with the lingering resonance of the King's fury. The anger on his face slowly softened, and he raised a shaking hand to rest over his heart before looking to the guards still stoically standing at the door.

"Escort our guest downstairs and keep an eye on her until we have a better understanding of how to proceed."

"What?" Charlotte's eyes widened.

Dutifully, both guards moved forward in a practiced unison, and each took hold of Charlotte's arms.

"Back home you might be as self-sufficient as your mother, but here, you are a potential danger, both to us and to yourself," Oswin explained coldly.

"Are you *serious*?" Charlotte demanded, trying to pull her arms away from the guards.

Oswin turned his back to her, walking to slowly circle around back to his place at the table.

"You can't arrest me, I want a lawyer!"

He heard the door close behind them as they left and he leaned over the maps, eyes looking over the fallen regions, the reports of missing soldiers… He gripped his heart with one hand while the other slammed angrily down onto the surface of the table.

"…Your Highness?"

Oswin looked up to see The King's Reason still standing in the room, albeit looking rather bewildered. He sighed. "With all due respect, Basir, I do not need an advisor at this moment."

Basir nodded, turned to go, then hesitated. "… What about a friend?"

Oswin's face crumpled, and he slumped down into his chair. He picked up one of the reports Malon had given him but didn't read it so much as already know every word within it because he'd practically memorized them all at this point. "...I don't know what else to do," he admitted softly. "We charge, and they overwhelm us. We have attempted multiple calculated attacks, and they overwhelm us. Our resources have been drained, our people destroyed—I... I can't keep sending people to their deaths, Basir. I do not know what else to do." He rubbed his face with his free hand, feeling his eyes sting. "It's insanity, but my *one* comfort in all of this madness had been that at least... she wasn't caught up in all this, that she might have been severed, but at least this *thing* couldn't get to her." He laughed bitterly as a tear fell, and he wiped at it blindly. "I'm well aware of how selfish that is, so if you could spare me the lecture..."

"I wasn't going to lecture," Basir said gently.

Oswin stared blankly at the report before setting it down gingerly in front of him. "She said we had to be practical," he mused.

"Malon?"

"Alys. The last time I saw her. She said she had to be practical. That she had to live her life..." Oswin sniffed and exhaled slowly, calming himself. "I knew she was lying. I didn't know *why* but..." A small, fond smile pulled at his lips. "She makes too much eye contact whenever she lies. Like she's daring you to call her on it." He shrugged. "But she wasn't wrong, even if it was a lie. We couldn't keep existing in this state of in-between... and since then I've managed to at least content myself with this notion that she was living her life. Happy. Safe." His smile fell completely as he looked back to Basir. "Now I won't even have that, will I? I really am going to lose her."

Basir shook his head. "You will not."

"You don't know that."

Basir conceded. *Slightly.* "I do not. I would not even dare to say I know Alys. But *you* do. And you know she is not one to back down easily... am I correct?"

"Without question, the bravest, strongest, most infuriatingly stubborn person I have ever met," Oswin breathed a laugh.

Basir gave a small encouraging nod. "There. Do not give up hope just yet."

"Hope is all I have left at this point," Oswin answered, "hope that something will turn the tide, that some discovery or help... Without Arden's aid, I am... nothing. Useless."

Basir sighed and moved to sit in the chair beside him. "That, I am afraid, was the other matter I needed to speak to you about. Robin left."

Oswin sat up slightly. "Left?"

"For Arden," Basir clarified. "To help plead our case. Or threaten it, I suppose. I have a hard time picturing her *pleading* with anyone." He forced a smile, but it faltered and fell rather instantaneously.

Oswin began cautiously. "Are you..."

"I'm fine," the taller man answered too quickly. Then, realizing this, he added. "I'm... She will be fine."

"Basir…"

"Our options are very limited these days, Your Highness. You can hardly fault her for leaning into the immediacy of the situation," Basir said practically. He was sitting more rigid, he was busying himself with straightening his coat. He was the picture of a carefully put-together man desperately trying to not fall apart.

"I'm not faulting her for anything," Oswin assured softly, watching his friend carefully.

"Good…" Basir reached up and adjusted his hat. "Good."

Oswin reached out, resting a hand on the other man's arm. "She will come back, old friend. She always does."

Basir's face fell, and he nodded. "And yet my heart has not been able to return to its natural pace since I found out…" He sighed. "Love has very little to do with reason," he admitted, looking to Oswin with a defeated sort of smile. "Even now, I find myself still ill-equipped for it." He studied the younger man's face, the furrowed brow, and heaviness that had settled in some time ago. He'd never been able to fully under-stand that unplaceable melancholy. Until now. "You weren't… entirely wrong before."

Oswin tilted his head quizzically.

"If Robin had been a Dreamer… I would not have done anything differently." It was a weighty admission, and Basir made sure Oswin fully understood exactly what he was admitting to before he continued. "I would still love her, logic be damned… And honestly, though I wish I could deny it, I do not think I would be able to look at anyone the same if they had done to Robin what had happened to… what *we* did to Alys." He pursed his lips thoughtfully a moment, his eyes wandering in thought. "I do not regret what we did. It had to be done. I do believe that… but I would not blame you if you hated me."

"I don't hate you," Oswin said.

"No?" Basir was genuinely surprised. "For a moment there, I was certain you might strike me."

Oswin gave a strained laugh. "So did I." He rubbed his face with his hand. "Fates, what a mess…" He raked his hands through his hair. "Why didn't she just tell me?"

Basir followed his gaze. "Charlie?"

"Alys. About Charlie. Why didn't she just *tell* me… that we had…" Oswin sighed heavily and shook his head. His mind was spinning, and he was too exhausted to attempt to slow it. "I understand it would have been difficult, and the intricacies of changeling biology are full of unknown factors and variables, but… we still could have made those decisions together." He rested his chin on his hand, his elbow propped on the arm of the chair. His eyes stung again, but he wasn't sure if it was from tears or if his eyes were now just watering from the sleep deprivation. "She didn't have to do this alone. *I* didn't have to do this…" His voice broke. "Alone."

Basir's brow furrowed. "Oswin…"

"That was the day *I* became dreamless…" Oswin admitted darkly. He looked up and caught Basir's worried expression, which caused him to sigh heavily again. "Forgive me, old friend. I am tired, and I… think I need some time alone."

8

GROUNDED

Oswin was not entirely sure how long he'd taken to himself. He certainly hadn't been looking at a clock when Basir left him, so when he looked at it now, it was entirely useless information. All it told him is that it was late. Or early, depending how one chose to look at it. And he was exhausted.

Still, he found himself, hands in his pockets, his jacket forgotten in the war room, his hair tousled from running his hands in it far too many times, and his eyes a little puffy around the edges for reasons he'd never publicly admit to, walking down the winding steps that led down to the dungeon.

His stomach churned, and his heart felt like it stumbled as he took a few rhythmic steps down. He halted, frowned, and placed a hand over his heart, uncomfortable with the sense memory the action had triggered. He took the next few steps quickly, then the one after slower. His breathing was purposefully awkward and arrhythmic, and his walking attempted the same sort of disjointed pace until he reached the bottom where he shook himself and attempted to smooth down his clothing.

There were things even time could not erase, and the discomfort that came from a constant mechanical rhythm would always be one of them for the White King.

He nodded to the guards at their posts and murmured for them to wait at the end of the hall, taking the keys from them as he passed by. His pace slowed as he approached the cell door, and he wasn't entirely sure if it was the guilt of his action or a sick kind of reverie that took hold of him in that instant. He shook his head once more and cleared his throat, raising his hand, hesitating, and knocking on the thick wooden door. "Charlie?"

"Fuck off," came the brooding answer.

Oswin blinked, then felt that flicker of anger returning. "Excuse you? What kind of language is that to talk with the…"? He wasn't her king. "To talk to your…" It seemed unwise to pull the parent card given he hadn't been aware of her until a few mere hours ago. "To me. To talk to me."

"*You* locked me in a dungeon," Charlotte answered with an incredulous, even exasperated sigh.

She had a point. Oswin knew she had a point. He even flinched as if the point could quite literally pierce him. "Not my… finest moment, I'll admit. I…" His mouth hung open a moment, trying to find the words.

"I'm sorry." It was always the best place to start. "You sort of caught me at… War does take its toll on even strategists, and I… Look, I wasn't expecting… I've never had…" He sighed. He was no good at this. "I'm sorry. I'm truly, so deeply sorry."

"You *locked me* in a dungeon," Charlotte repeated.

Oswin rubbed the back of his neck. "On the bright side, it is dry and remarkably clean in there, wouldn't you say? You should have seen the place years ago."

There was a moment of silence. He heard her inhale. "You. Locked me. In a DUNGEON!"

Oswin was certain if she had something to throw, she would have done so in that moment. "I did say I was sorry."

"Leave me alone!"

"I thought you might like to spend the night in an actual bed," Oswin offered. "Unless, of course, you'd prefer to stay locked in a dungeon."

"You sure I can be trusted?" Charlotte asked bitterly, but at a much more controlled volume.

Oswin shrugged and leaned against the door. "If you think it would be smarter to leave you here, then I can hardly argue against your judgement on the matter."

Charlotte rolled her eyes. She could hear the smile in this man's voice, and it irritated her. What right did he have to be playful? To be happy? "I can be trusted," she muttered half under her breath.

Oswin theatrically tilted his head toward the door for an audience of just himself. "What was that?"

"I can be trusted!" Charlotte snapped back in exasperation.

"Good." Oswin smiled, feeling a sense of triumph that he could not quite place. It almost felt smug, which under normal circumstances would have also made him feel rather uncomfortable. But there was something about this… kind of interaction, this not quite hostile back-and-forth, that he'd really missed, that he genuinely hadn't felt since… since Alys. His heart tugged a little, and he placed the key in the lock and opened the heavy wooden door.

Charlotte emerged from the dark with eyes ablaze with fury. She glared up at him from her rather unimpressive height, and Oswin saw even more of Alys in her.

He felt a strange surge of pride simultaneously with a pang in his heart. Subconsciously he raised a hand and pressed his fingertips into the muscle just below his collarbone. He gestured with his head for her to follow him. "Let's find you a place to rest for the night, shall we?"

"Begging your pardon, your Royal Highness, but it is nearly dawn," one of the guards commented with a stoop of his head.

"Is it?" Oswin asked in realization. He blinked a moment. "Well… then…" He looked between the two. "One of you is dismissed to find your replacements, the other will follow until they arrive." He took a few steps, paused, and turned around. "My mother's former quarters, I think."

The guards nodded, and one broke off from the other without much conference, walking briskly ahead of them and out of site, while the other followed behind at a respectful distance.

Oswin strode leisurely with Charlotte beside him, his hands clasped behind his back as he did so, attempting some sort of posture of ease.

He was not at ease.

Charlotte too was attempting a sort of air of nonchalance, and though she was far more successful in her parroting of the appearance, she herself could feel her heart pounding. Her father. Her. Father. She glanced sideways at him, feeling her eyes narrow involuntarily. "What exactly do I call you?"

Oswin's brow furrowed, and he looked to her, then realized he had not actually given his name. His mouth opened, hung there for a moment, then closed. He stared straight ahead as he fumbled over this seemingly innocent question, a question that, were it asked by anyone else, would have been a great deal easier to answer. "I suppose 'Father' is out of the question." It was more statement than genuinely checking in, based on her attitude toward him and… admittedly, his own discomfort with the word. It was still such a strange and new concept to him. Father? And most fathers had the luxury of being able to ease into the title, when the child was still small and unable to talk back with any acuity.

Charlotte was, for all intents and purposes, a rather fully formed individual, who had very clearly fully formed her opinion of him, judging by the way she rolled her eyes. "Hard pass."

His brow furrowed. It didn't seem entirely fair that she should already have a fully formed opinion of him, especially as it did not seem to be based on any manner of intel, whether fictitious or factual. "I am the King of Terra Mirum," he offered awkwardly, which, again, under normal circumstances, would have been the only appropriate address.

"I'm not calling you Your Highness, or any other form of it," Charlotte answered with another eye roll.

Perhaps it was his lack of experience with teenagers, but Oswin was certain most did not roll their eyes this much. It did, however, by proxy, somewhat color his opinion of General Toulouse, as he also seemed to engage in the action far too often. He took a deep breath and fidgeted his fingers behind his back uncomfortably. "You can call me Oswin." It seemed a sensible, albeit awkward, compromise, not so formal that they were driving a further rift between them, but not so intimate as to belie a familial camaraderie that had not yet any time to develop.

"Oswin," Charlotte repeated, but whether it was simply to get acquainted with the name or to disdain it, wasn't clear.

The sound of their steps on the floor filled the silence for a few moments.

"What about you?" He asked tentatively.

Charlotte glanced at him with what he assumed was contempt. "You know my name."

"No, I mean…" Oswin sighed, not sure how he could make so many missteps with one person in such a short time. "I imagine you were named after your mother's childhood friend, but… is Charlie short for something?"

Charlotte weighed this information in her mind. Her mother didn't speak about Charlie easily. She was very protective of his memory, so if she'd bothered to share it with this man… She dismissed the thought with a sharp exhale through her nose. "Charlotte."

"Charlotte," Oswin repeated warmly, a smile creeping into his eyes. It wasn't much, but it was progress—small snippets of information he did not previously have about his daughter. His *daughter*. His mind kept hitting snags every time it tripped along that fact. He dared to glance at her. "Do you have a middle name? I remember your mother was very particular about middle names," he allowed himself to chuckle a little.

Charlotte's mouth quirked slightly despite herself at the sound and the memory of one of many rants Alys had gone off on such things. "Well, she didn't like not having one. She said it felt like her name was incomplete."

"Did she ever tell you why?"

"Lucy was furious about not being given the epidural, so when the nurse came in with the paperwork, she just said, 'Just put YOUR name,' and when she was asked about the middle name, 'Ugh, I have to think of

ANOTHER one, too?' Apparently, they still talk about it in the hospital from time to time."

Oswin shook his head. He'd heard the story before, and it never ceased to baffle him that anyone could treat a baby so contemptuously. "Piece of work, that woman."

"She had nine months, nine months to think up something, and she couldn't be bothered to give me *anything*?" Charlotte repeated, mimicking her mother recounting the tale.

Oswin chuckled again. "Amazing Alys turned out the way she did. From what I've heard, I count myself lucky to have never had the unfortunate circumstance of encountering Lucy Carroll."

"Me, too," Charlotte allowed herself a giggle, and her heart felt infinitely lighter from the small release. She looked at him appraisingly again, with perhaps a little less animosity. "Aislynn."

Oswin's eyebrows raised in surprise, and he looked back to her, unable to repress the large smile which spread across his face from that information.

Charlotte's smile faded slightly, aware that something had transpired in that moment she was not aware of. "What?"

"That was *my* mother's name."

"…Oh." Charlotte blinked, stunned by this information. How had she never known that? She'd been carrying a piece of this other part of who she was all this time, and yet… she'd just assumed someone had simply misheard her mother say 'Alyson.' She averted her eyes. "We're not bonding right now, you know."

Oswin's back straightened slightly, and his smile fell. "Oh. Yes. No, I know that."

"Good," Charlotte answered in a clipped tone, and their footsteps continued the conversation again without them for a few long moments. She chewed her lower lip, unable to shrug off this new information about her name. Having had no relationship with her mother's mother and hearing only horror stories… Curiosity won over the desire to shun him. Curiosity was a dangerous drug in the Carroll household… "She's the woman mom painted for you, isn't she? Your mother?"

Oswin's brows raised slightly, then relaxed. Of course she'd seen it. She would have come through the door in Alys' room, which… He nodded a little. "Yes, she is."

A breath of a hesitation. "What was she like?"

"Brave," Oswin answered without missing a beat. "Not fearless, mind you, but very brave. And impossibly clever. I don't think Oberon has ever quite forgiven our family line because of how clever she was during the war. Only person to ever have outsmarted him, so he says…"

"Oberon?" Charlotte asked.

"Oberon," Oswin confirmed.

"What, jealous Oberon—Fairies skip hence, I have forsworn his bed and company—*that* Oberon?" Charlotte's excitement grew. Could it be *he* was real too?

"The very same."

Charlotte blinked, finding herself stopping quite literally in her tracks before she rushed to catch up with him again. "Don't tell me, Shakespeare encountered him years ago and ended up getting an ass' head for his trouble."

Oswin looked back at her, confused. "I thought you said your mother didn't tell you about any of this."

Charlotte ran her fingers through her hair, bewildered as she shook her head. "I… guess I just wasn't listening hard enough…" She looked to Oswin. "So that means there are other fairies, right?"

"Yes."

Charlotte made a somewhat undignified squeak of suppressed excitement, which caused Oswin to look at her and Charlotte to look away and clear her throat.

Oswin's mouth hinted at another smile. "We've sent word to them, actually, requesting aid. It was a rather heated point of argument when you and Basir came in."

"Why?"

"Well," Oswin began carefully. "General Toulouse feels that relying on the help of our allies makes us appear weak, and that we should find a way to stand against this beast on our own. Whereas Galen and Malon feel this is an unrealistic expectation."

Charlotte chewed the inside of her cheek thoughtfully. "What do *you* think?" It was a question that surprised even her.

"I… think there are too many lives at stake to not reach out to our strongest ally, though I feel ally is a rather loose term with the Unseelie Court, always has been." Oswin frowned as he thought about it. "And the last time we asked for their aid, it came at an exceedingly high price… I do not know what he will ask of us this time, should he even entertain the idea." He looked to Charlotte; his brow furrowed. "I do love her, you know. All of this? It isn't because I don't care. Of course I care."

Charlotte, as if only then remembering what she'd accused him of before she'd been sent away, bowed her head and stared at her feet.

"Fates, I was ready to risk *everything* for her… Disobey natural law, as it were…" He exhaled a laugh through his nose. "Well, I *did*, in the end, it would seem…"

Charlotte's nose scrunched. "I don't really understand what the big deal is. Or that word he called me. Changeling? What even is that? Why am I such a problem?"

"Ah… Well," Oswin teetered on how to explain the answer for a moment. He pursed his lips. "When Alys first came to us, she was a Dreamer—someone who shares a very strong connection to our world, in so much that they have a kind of power in it."

"Like a superpower?"

"Mmm, not quite—for instance, when you fall asleep, your subconscious connects with what we call

The Nothing. It creates, it formulates, and on some occasions, I've been told, you're aware you're dreaming and you're able to control it."

"Right," Charlotte followed the explanation easily enough. "But mom didn't dream herself here, right? She... walked in through whatever tunnel that guy mentioned?"

"Basir," Oswin filled in for her. "And yes, she did."

"And that's extra bad because..."

"She still had that power."

"Oh." Charlotte's brows raised.

"And, while unknowingly, she possessed it over things beyond the creation of her subconscious."

"Oh!" Charlotte exclaimed in realization. "Wait, so if I'm understanding you..."

"It's an incredibly powerful form of magic," Oswin continued for her, "but impossible to control, and exceedingly volatile in nature, and outside of The Nothing, it could very possibly destroy our world as we know it. You see, Charlie, a Dreamer entering our world physically is like... Well, do you read like your mother?"

"You mean obsessively?"

Oswin laughed. "Yes."

Charlotte shrugged with a nod. "I guess so."

"You're familiar with... Greek Mythology?"

"Pretty familiar."

"A Dreamer entering Terra Mirum would be somewhat akin to a god descending from Mt. Olympus to the mortal realm."

Charlotte was struck by this. That kind of raw and epic power… her mother had wielded that? It was dumbfounding. Still, her humor got the better of her. "Cursing people for being prettier or more talented than them, and/or having sex with everyone while possibly in the shape of an animal?"

Oswin blinked, opened his mouth to answer, closed it, and looked back at the young girl.

She returned the gaze as if she were entirely serious. He might have even believed she was serious if that expression were not so burned into his memory as the look you'd see when Alys Carroll was joyfully messing with you.

"…You got your mother's wit, I'll give you that," he mused.

Charlotte smiled.

Oswin returned to the matter at hand. "We knew a lot less about specifics back then, to be honest. But what we did know was a myriad of emotions or thoughts could possibly cause a Dreamer's mind to shift and turn, and with it, the very matter that surrounded them."

"Okay… but *I'm* not a Dreamer, right? I'm a Changeling… whatever that is—wait, wait, does that make me sort of like a demigod?"

Oswin was about to deny this, paused, and then realized the analogy did translate rather well. "Not… so unlike, I suppose. Changeling was a term coined to refer to a child born between worlds, a being created from mixed magics… and until recently, there had only ever been one recorded in history. Sylas. He's a shapeshifter who... serves the Fae Courts of Arden."

"I can shapeshift here?" Charlotte gasped.

"*Even* if you shared similar parentage, *which you don't*, there is no guarantee your abilities would manifest in the same way... And even so, the point still stands... You have different parentage. His father was a Dreamer and his mother a Fae. There's really no telling how your own... powers, if you'll permit the word, will manifest."

Charlotte squinted at him. "Surely *someone* over the thousands of years has had someone like me. I can't really be the *only one* in all of history."

"Only one we know of," Oswin answered. "If there were others, they were kept secret. *Very* secret."

"Okay..." Charlotte mulled this over as they started to slow to a stop in front of a large door. "Let's say I have powers of *some* kind. I could use those to help Mom, right? And the others!"

"No, you couldn't."

"It might not even bend anything unnatural. You don't know! Maybe I can just do things like shape shift," she tried to reason.

"Maybe you can, maybe you can't. Maybe you split reality in two or cause the world to implode on itself." There was something to Oswin's voice that almost had an air of experience to it.

"Maybe you're being a bit over-dramatic."

"Maybe, regardless of ability, you're also still just a child."

Charlotte look struck by this accusation. She looked the older man dead in the eye. "I'm *sixteen*."

Oswin looked back at her and blinked, unimpressed. "Forgive me. You are truly battle-worn in your years and unmatched in combat prowess," he stated flatly.

Charlotte glared at him.

Oswin held her stare and reached over to the door, turning the knob and giving just enough of a push that it opened. "This will be your room. There are plenty of books to keep you occupied until we figure out what to do with you."

"What to *do* with me?"

Oswin's back straightened and he gathered back what sense of authority he could. "Your mother is no longer able to care for you, so that duty falls to me until she is recovered."

That glare burned into a fury. "I *have* a legal guardian in the case of her being unable. Diana has been my mom's friend for ages. *She* takes care of me.

"*If* she can, that is *if* it comes to that, yes, she will. But we need to figure out how your biology has manifested before I can allow that to happen."

"Why?" Charlotte demanded.

Oswin wasn't sure how to explain. "There could be... complications going back."

"What *kind* of complications?"

"We don't *know* yet. That's why we're doing this, for your own safety. At least until we've had a doctor and... fates know who else might be qualified to look at you."

"I can't just sit here while my mother is in trouble!"

"I'm afraid you can, and you will," Oswin said firmly.

"She's my *mom*!" Charlotte pleaded desperately, for once feeling like the child they all insisted she was. "She's literally the only family I have. I can't wait for someone I barely know to decide if her life is worth saving—I already know the answer: Yes! Of course she's worth saving. I'd risk everything to save her, so just let me go save her!"

Oswin felt his heart wince, but he held firmer to his resolve. "Alys may have kept your birth a secret, but now that I know you exist, Charlie, I'm not letting you out of my sight. Maybe, after all of this is through, I can't save her. But I can save *you.*"

Charlotte could feel her eyes pricking with tears, which just made her angrier. "So, you're going to what, lock me in my room?"

"I want you as far away from this war as possible."

"This is just going from one dungeon to another," Charlotte said bitterly.

"I believe in your world it's called *grounding*," Oswin answered in the tone adults often employed when they felt a teenager was being overdramatic, and Charlotte was not happy about it. "Now. The Coleridge Clock… Do you still have it on you?"

Charlotte looked him dead in the eye. "No."

Oswin stared back and sighed. "You bluff like your mother too," he muttered, then turned to the guard. "Remove the mirror, won't you?"

The guard stepped inside ahead of them to do so, but Charlotte took this into account. This meant it worked with all mirrors, not just those she traveled through.

"This is bullshit," Charlie grumbled as the guard exited carrying a large full-length mirror.

It was then the two guards sent to relieve him arrived.

"Charlie," Oswin began, dropping to one knee and taking her hands in his. "I've sent word to Arden, *begging* Oberon for aid if that's what it takes. We have people researching and working night and day to find *something* that will enable our armies to fight them back. I'm tapping every resource available, and I'm going to continue to do everything in my power to save Alys— to save all of them. You have my word."

Charlotte looked down at their hands. There was comfort there, a comfort she didn't want to admit to. Then she looked to his eyes, and despite never having met him before today, there was something undeniably familiar about his face. Her heart ached, and some lost feeling inside her wanted nothing more than to throw her arms around him and break down crying. And she resented him for it. "What good is that?" she spat, yanking her hands away as she turned to vanish into the room, slamming the door behind her.

Oswin hung his head a little and sighed heavily, his hands pressing into his thigh to push up into a standing position again. "Goodnight, Charlie… Get some rest," he said to no one. Then, to the two guards remaining, "I want two men posted here at all times. Her safety is of the utmost importance, understood?"

Tears streaked down Charlotte's face as she leaned her back against the other side of the heavy oak door. "Dammit," she cursed under her breath. She took in the room. It was fine like the rest, but though it had been maintained very well, she got the sense it had been some time since it had been truly occupied. A large bookshelf full of both books and a few decorative pieces, a bed, and a door that Charlotte assumed led to a bathroom of some sort. Did people here use plumbing? God, she hoped so. Great windows gave way to the dim light from the rising sun, the beams diffusing from long gauzy curtains. She wiped at her eyes with the back of her hand and moved to push back one of the curtains and look down below, where she took in an expansive garden courtyard. She could see a round platform, which looked like it would serve as a nice stage for musicians or even a small play performed for the royal court. The white marble was surrounded by a ring of deep-blood-red roses.

Charlotte wasn't sure why, but there was something about them that made her stomach churn a little. It was inexplicably unsettling.

The courtyard was a small part of a large labyrinth of hedges, which seemed to surround the castle and potentially lead into town.

Charlotte dejectedly rested her forehead on the glass, looking down at was directly below the window.

It looked like a balcony. Her eyes widened, and she craned her neck. She pressed her cheek against the cool glass, straining to look downward. It was... and it had stairs down to the courtyard. She peered around on either side, then pulled back to look around at the room itself. She looked to the bed. There were more than enough blankets to safely close the gap. It really wasn't that far down at all. She moved to the great bookshelf and examined it. It had no backing, leaving the shelves open cubbies on either side. She wrapped her arms around the cubby and gave it a hefty heave.

It didn't move. It was sturdy wood—far stronger than the IKEA furniture that filled most of her home. If it wasn't secured to the floor, the books that sat on it were heavy enough to keep it from moving.

She moved back to the windows to examine the frame. Her shoulders slumped. Just glass. No way to open them? She ran her hands around the large panes, verifying her suspicion. There was no contraption to open or even crack them enough for airflow. They were meant to remain closed. Her lips purse in irritation. "Talk about a fire code violation..." She tapped her fingers on the glass surface thoughtfully... and her eyes rested on the reflection of a large encyclopedic book sitting atop a writing desk near the door. She smiled. "Ah, silly man. Like I'm *not* gonna break a window," she mused to herself.

But first, she moved to the desk and pulled it, with great effort, toward the doors. She was hoping since she hadn't heard much on the other side, they wouldn't hear her. Much like the doors, the desk was heavy oak, and were it not for the smooth floor, she wouldn't have been able to move it at all. Unfortunately, it did cause a sharp squeak from time to time as it barely slid across the marble.

Charlotte would pause, tentatively look toward the doors, and upon seeing that she hadn't alerted anyone, begin trying to move the desk again. Finally, she scooted it in front of the doors. It wouldn't prevent anyone from entering, likely, but it would buy her time.

Then she set about to dismantling the bed. Sheets were twisted with great effort—she tightly wound them together as best she could. It was a skill that had been acquired through a particularly sugar-fueled film night with her mother during an '80s and '90s movie marathon. After seeing three separate characters in three separate films all use bedsheets to climb out of windows, Alys and Charlotte had set about researching how to do such a thing. And since Charlotte didn't have scissors, the twist and tie method would have to suffice. She paused in her work as a disquieting thought hit her; a pang at the realization that if she failed at this… they'd never have a movie night like that again. They'd never do *anything* like that again.

Charlotte glared toward the door, and, more determined than ever, she twisted and made multiple knots in the sheets, both to keep them from untwisting and to better hold when she tied them together. Then she pushed books out from the bottom shelf of the book-case enough to tie the sheet securely around it. She paused, examining that this took a good five feet or so of rope away and, pressing herself against the glass again, she hoped it would be enough to at least make the drop harmless.

She swallowed, took a deep breath, and picked up the large book sitting on the desk. She hefted it in her hands and mused to herself as she positioned herself in front of the window, "In case of emergency, break glass." She threw it with all her might against the window.

It smacked against the crystal-clear surface, mess-ily fluttered to the ground and landed with a loud "THWAP" on the marble floor.

Charlotte blinked. "Well, that was anticlimactic," she commented to no one. She set about looking for a larger book. She found another of comparable size, but the hardbound cover seemed to have sharper edges. Heft. Strategic positioning so it would fly corner first. Throw.

It opened midair, the pages split against the glass and it also fell uselessly to the floor.

Charlotte huffed air upward, blowing the hair around her eyes straight up in the process. "What the hell…"

She searched for anything heavier… and when she found it, it was of course on the top shelf: between a few decorative vases and a clock too high for anyway to be able to read it, sat a stone bust stoically gazing out into nothing.

She could climb the shelf… but there was no guarantee she wouldn't drop the bust or fall in trying to carry it down. It was then back to the bed, where she began the task of yanking the large pillowy mattress from the frame.

This was a Herculean effort. The beds, while extremely downy, were far less formed than the mattresses at home. And she found herself yanking and pulling with great frustration as she wrenched it free from the bed itself before dragging it awkwardly to the other side of the bookshelf.

Charlotte eyed this a moment before also collecting the leftover pillows and comforters in order to make more cushion, as well as a sort of soft barrier in case the bust tried to bounce off the mattress and onto the floor.

Then, with a deep breath, she carefully positioned her foot in one cubby of the shelf, gripping the other tightly with her fingertips. A few books fell out the other side as she pulled herself up. She took a deep breath and scaled another cubby hole, then finally the last she needed to reach the sculpture.

It was surprisingly lacking dust, despite that she didn't imagine many people would have been up that high, but then again, she had to remember she was in a literal palace. Who'd have thought her wild guess would have been even remotely…

"Focus, Charlie, focus," she muttered to herself with a shake of the head. She reached out and began to bat at the bust with her fingers, carefully scooting it closer and closer until finally it dropped over the edge toward the mattress. Charlotte had pulled away to avoid being hit and in doing so lost her grip.

She dropped to the floor feet first, her knees cushioning her fall and her hands slapping against the surface as she collapsed forward. She was okay. Her hands and feet hurt a little... but she was okay. She stood, a little achy, rolled her ankles and wrists a few times before slightly limping to retrieve her new projectile.

Unlike her, the bust was completely unscathed.

Charlotte flexed her fingers. She stretched a little, working out any lingering shock from her fall. If this worked, she'd have to make swift work of it. She squatted down and took hold of the bust, awkwardly positioning herself in front of the window. She swung it between her legs like a kid with a bowling ball. "One... two... Sorry about this... three!" She released the bust into the window where it shattered through the glass pane. "YES!" Charlotte cheered, her hands raising in victory as the glass came crashing down.

That alerted the guards, and she could hear a muffled shouting on the other side of the door. "Princess?" A hurried unlocking and then a thump as the door collided with the desk, not opening more than a crack.

Charlotte kicked some of the glass still obstructing her way with the thick soles of her boots, grabbed her makeshift rope and leaped through the opening to the platform below.

She managed to clear the glass around the frame but the jerk of the blankets holding was an abrupt one, which caused her to swing and her shoulder to slam into the building.

Still, the blankets *did* hold, and she wasn't *dead*. It was the small victories at this point.

She slid down the blankets, which were indeed too short to fully reach the balcony, but the drop was manageable. It wasn't the most graceful of landings, but she didn't slip on the glass she landed on, and by pure *miracle*, she didn't cut her hand when she set it down for balance.

There was a moment of relief until she heard a pounding above her head which was undoubtedly the guards breaking through her makeshift barrier. She took off down the stairs and through the labyrinth at a dead run, hoping that between the desk and their armor, the guards wouldn't be able to catch up to her.

Oswin had taken away the mirrors. Which meant the mirror in her mother's room wasn't particularly special—that somehow, with the clock, *any* mirror could be used for travel between the worlds. Charlotte just had to find a mirror. Then she could get home and tell Diana what was going on. If Diana would believe her.

There was time to worry about that later.

She could hear distant shouting behind her.

Charlotte made a wrong turn and found herself at a dead end. She doubled-back and went the other way— but by now she could hear there were other people in the maze. She cursed under her breath and prayed that she would find the way out. Desperation was starting to grip her. *Don't let them catch me. Please let this be the right way. Let this be the right way.*

As she rounded another corner, she nearly ran directly into a guard.

She screamed in surprise and leaped back, bringing her arms up to protect herself, and in that moment the hedge *moved.* It curled away from her right side, rapidly growing in and blocking the space between her and her pursuers, leaving an open gap to the floral hallway that had been one lane over and led to the hedge maze exit.

Had she done that?

Charlotte stared in disbelief, with no time or mental capacity to truly mull over the questions swimming in her head. She broke through the exit, which led in a path down to the city below.

All she had to do was find one mirror big enough to climb through.

Charlotte stumbled onto the stone roads of the city. She stopped rather abruptly, taking in the surroundings of the strangely dressed people who all looked like they'd stepped out of time. A few stopped to give her a strange look, and knowing how out of place her clothing was, Charlotte felt the urge to adjust the hem of her sweatshirt. As if this helped.

She weaved through the crowds as best she could—and it occurred to her how strange it was to see so many people up and about at what she was certain was still so early. But it would provide cover. The moment she could, she turned down an alleyway, and barely dodged a strange steam-powered contraption that chugged its way down the lane, picking up any litter it found as it went. She continued down the smaller and less crowded corridor, hoping to find anything that might be of use to her. She pulled up her hood and shoved her hands in her pockets, and as she wandered out onto another overly crowded street, she caught sight of what looked to be some sort of restaurant. People were moving in and out at a bit of a bustle, bringing out food with them. Perhaps a makeshift soup kitchen?

She'd remembered something Basir had said about villagers... The city and castle had undoubtedly taken in refugees from the areas that had been overtaken by nightmares.

Charlotte fought like a salmon swimming upstream to make her way through the current of people moving about their day to pull herself onto the building's stoop and enter through the front door, slipping past the line.

The host was a tall, prim sort of man, who locked eyes with Charlotte. He carried himself in a way that suggested before the war time he might have been akin to throwing people like her out. However, during this time of crisis in the Kingdom, he was not about to send anyone away. "May I help you? The line starts—"

"Bathroom?" Charlotte asked with hope, her throat feeling tight.

Begrudgingly, the man pointed toward the lavatories, and Charlotte set off, determined.

She ducked into one and locked the door behind her. It briefly occurred to her that this would cause trouble when she was gone—they wouldn't be able to open the door after her... but that was a small worry in the grand scheme of things, and her escape was a matter of life and death.

Charlotte turned around abruptly to examine the room she'd closed herself in and found it not terribly different from her own world. There were copper pipes, the toilet appeared as if no one had ever sat on it in its life, and there was a rather elegant-looking sink made of porcelain, but the greatest relief was that above the sink hung a large, gilded mirror.

"Okay," Charlotte pulled the Coleridge clock out from her sweatshirt and opened it. "How did I do this?" The extra hand was pointing toward the mirror, but nothing seemed to be happening. On a hunch, she moved the clock from side to side, but the hand remained pointed at the mirror. "So *that's* what you do. You're not a compass pointing north, you point out the nearest exit..." She smiled. "Crafty..." But the mirror wasn't changing.

Charlotte thought a moment. She had moved the clock in her hand so that the hand had pointed towards the 6, and so she repeated her actions. Due to the construction of the watch, she realized that in doing this, the mirror that sat opposite of the clock face was forced to point directly at the mirror she was trying to travel through. She watched the mirrored images reflect each other to what seemed like forever, which caused the space around it to ripple outward.

"Cool," Charlotte whispered to herself. She dropped the watch to back around her neck to climb onto the sink. But the mirror had re-solidified. "Right…" She frowned and awkwardly crouched in the bowl of the sink, nearly falling more than once as she did so. She opened the watch again and pointed the mirror toward the other. "I must have to keep these connected to keep the doorway open."

As the ripples calmed to soft waves, she could see a darkened bathroom on the other side of the mirror. She took a deep breath and carefully put her feet through first, resting on what felt and looked like another sink. "Here goes nothing." She slipped through the mirror completely.

9

UNFAMILIAR BATHROOMS

When Charlotte stepped through to the other side of the mirror, there were two things she knew with absolute certainty. The first was that she was back on Earth because she'd nearly slipped on a flat iron. The second was that she did not even remotely recognize this bathroom. She was in someone else's house. And it was late—or early enough—to still be dark outside.

Her heartbeat quickened. There was no explanation of how and why she had gotten there that would satisfy any policeman that would inevitably be called were she to be found, and so she took extra care to be quiet. She breathed through her mouth slowly, easing herself down to the floor. The ground creaked quietly, and her heart stopped for a few moments, her hearing sharpening. Had she been heard? Was this it?

There was nothing.

She allowed herself to relax ever so slightly. She looked out the window first, and judging by what little she could see beyond the tree that mostly blocked her view, she appeared to be on the second floor of a house or condo.

As the bathroom door was open, she was able to soundlessly peek out into the hallway. All the other doors on the floor were closed.

She tiptoed her way along the carpet toward the stairs and stopped. On the landing below was a fluffy, snuffling, sleeping husky.

Charlotte bit her lower lip. Even if she risked that the dog was friendly, it was still likely to bark and wake the house. Rushing past it was also rather out of the question—it could then see her as a threat and chase her down. She tiptoed backward into the bathroom and silently closed the door behind her.

Deep breath, fists resting on her hips. Think, Charlotte, think.

She couldn't go back through the mirror; the guards would have likely tracked down her location by then.

Her eyes rested on the small window curiously. She reached forward and raised up the blinds. She judged the size of it, then unlocked the latch and pushed open the window and gave it a look over again.

She could fit through that. And as she looked at the way the tree reached out towards the house, obstructing most of the window's view, she also knew if she was *very* careful... she'd be able to reach a sturdier branch.

Charlotte knew this was a stupid idea. She also knew she had little choice in the matter.

She climbed up on the toilet so she could sit on the windowsill, ducking her head outside while her legs dangled within. Her heart fluttered nervously. She reached up and grasped a branch, pulling down a little to see if it would support her weight. It would, but not without bending. She swallowed and used it for balance as she shakily stood up on the windowsill, then reached out her foot to find another branch, still holding onto the top one for dear life. "Oh please... oh please..." She whispered to herself as she removed her foot from the windowsill. She could feel the branches sag beneath her weight, but they did not break. She could feel the relief exhale from her in that moment.

She monkeyed her way from the outer branches downward, taking her time to pick the strongest and sturdiest of the bunch. As she reached the main trunk, it became a different matter of trying to feel with her feet as she traversed downward until she was safe enough to drop. She didn't get a chance to make that call, however, because just as she was looking over her shoulder to judge the drop height, the branch beneath her supporting foot snapped and she fell to the ground. She landed on her feet first as before, but then crumpled backward to lie flat on her back.

Charlotte lie there, disoriented, doing her best not to cry out or even just cry as the dull pain shot through her. She held her breath and slowly exhaled. She looked up, pained, trying to get an idea of where she was. It hadn't occurred to her that she wouldn't be put back almost exactly where she'd left. It also hadn't occurred to her that she might not even be in Seattle anymore—or Washington, for that matter.

Slowly, she rolled over to her stomach. Then she didn't move for a full minute or so as she felt both sore and mildly nauseated. At last, she pushed herself up with a wince into a child's pose position.

That felt... *good* was not the word, but it at least helped her achy limbs. From there she reached out to gingerly press against the tree base, using it as an aid to stand. The world wavered, and she raised her free hand to her head and trudged to the sidewalk, picking a direction to walk until something started to look familiar.

Thankfully, she didn't have far to go. She was in Greenlake, which, comparatively, wasn't that far from home. After a little limping, she was even able to find the bus to take her back to the University district.

She'd never been so relieved to see a bus before in her life—or that she had her wallet and thus bus pass on her.

What Charlotte hadn't considered was that she didn't have her *keys* on her. So, when she approached the house, she was set to a dilemma: how to get in?

She tried knocking, but no one answered. She tried again, and nothing stirred. Either Diana had gone home or was too dead asleep to hear her. Or was she out looking for her? She checked the driveway but didn't see Diana's car.

Charlotte wondered how long she'd been gone. She knew it only felt like a matter of hours, but... it was possible that time didn't exactly work the way it should on the other side of the looking glass. Not much else seemed to, so time didn't seem like it should be any different.

She walked around to the back and checked under the flowerpot where they kept the spare house key. It, too, was of course missing.

Charlotte remembered placing the spare key on the kitchen table. Stupidly, in all the fuss, she had NOT remembered to put it back. She pursed her lips and huffed. "Okay..."

She tried the first-floor windows—all of them were locked.

Charlotte sniffed, wiped her nose, and circled around the house, looking up at the top floor for any point of entry. There wasn't.

She briefly considered breaking another window... but she was certain even if by miracle the cops weren't called on her, both Diana and her mother would tan her hide thereafter.

Charlotte would have to trek to the nearest public phone.

With a heavy but determined sigh, she trudged toward University Way. It was the street most likely to still be populated this late at night. She had expected to find one of the corner stores, or even a bar, open. Her brow furrowed, however, when she saw the streets rather bustling, and even at a few blocks away Starbucks was open—and still well populated. When she and Diana had returned from the hospital, it had been 10 p.m. By a simple guess of time, it should have been past midnight by now, yet the coffee shop she was certain closed at 11 was still crowded as ever.

Was it… even the same day?

The thought chilled her as she made her way toward the coffee shop, so much that she didn't notice Shelby Ferris among the gaggle of girls she passed until one of them called out to her.

"Hey!"

Charlotte turned to catch sight of the snow-white face of her teenage tormenter and bit back a sneer.

"I love your hair; did you get that done locally?"

Charlotte suddenly remembered her shorter hair, the gum that had been shoved into it that had caused her ridiculous mistake of cutting at it, and the repairs Diana had been forced to do. Her eyes narrowed, and she shoved her hands in her pockets. "Bite me," she growled and continued down the block.

The girls left her alone, but not without a few surprised whispers and Shelby's very pointed use of the word "bitch" in Charlotte's direction.

Charlotte had half a mind to turn back around and go off on the other girl. Shelby had picked the exact wrong day to reappear in her life, or to make any sort of judgmental remark. But she had more important things to do. She had to find Diana… and figure out how long she'd been gone.

Charlotte pulled her hoodie tighter around her and wandered inside. There were too many people; it was almost assaulting. She stood in a long line to get to the register. She must have looked like a miserable puppy judging from the face the cashier gave her.

"Bad day?"

"Yeah," Charlotte answered, pulling her wallet from her back pocket. "Can I get a venti no-water chai? And… if it's not too much trouble, can I borrow your phone? I'm locked out of my house, and I need to call my aunt to come let me in with the spare."

"Oh gosh, yeah, of course, kid. One second." He shook his head at her wallet as he pulled out the phone from under the counter. "Don't worry about it. This one's on us."

"Thanks… Oh. What time is it?"

"Quarter to 9. Name for the cup?"

"Charlie. Thanks…" Charlotte took the cordless phone and stepped off toward the corner to get as much privacy and silence as she could. Had she been away an entire day? She dialed the number to Diana's cell. "She's going to kill me," she muttered to herself, listening to it ring.

"Hello?"

"Hi. It's me. I'm okay—long story. I promise I'll explain, but… I locked myself out of the house, so I'm holed up in a Starbucks on The Ave and unable to get in."

There was a long silence. "I'm sorry, who is this?"

Charlotte winced. "I know I probably worried you sick by disappearing like that, but I promise I will explain everything, I just need you to come save my butt. It's just... not something I should really talk about on the phone."

"No, I'm sorry, the number is unknown, and I don't recognize your voice. Who is this?"

Charlotte laughed a little in disbelief. "Come on, stop fooling around... it's Charlie."

There was another long silence. "I'm sorry, sweetheart, I don't know anyone by that name anymore. I think you have the wrong number."

"W-what?"

"Good luck." She hung up.

Charlotte slowly lowered the phone from her ear and stared at it. "...What?"

"No-water chai for Charlie!" The barista at the bar called out, setting her drink on the counter.

Charlotte picked up the to-go cup and set the phone down in its place. She sighed, still trying to wrap her brain around the phone conversation before easing down into an empty chair by the window. What was going on? Did Diana seriously not know who she was? It wasn't a wrong number, she'd recognize her godmother's voice anywhere. Her eyes widened slightly. Did she DIE? Diana had said she didn't know anyone with that name *anymore*.

Her heart fluttered in a panic and she nervously sipped her tea. She stopped and looked at her tea quizzically. No. If she were dead, the barista wouldn't have been able to take her order or give her the phone.

And Diana had claimed not to recognize her voice—which in itself was ridiculous because Diana had known her voice on the phone since Charlotte had learned to dial as a child.

Anymore.

There was, of course, the Charlie she had been named for, a man who'd died long before her own birth but had been very dear to both her mother and godmother. She'd heard stories. So many stories…

And then she took up that mantle. Yet, despite having 16 years under her belt being called that name by both women… here she was. Forgotten.

It was like she had somehow been selectively erased, which… she couldn't decide if it hurt or confused her more. "This doesn't make any sense."

None of that day had made any sense.

"Maybe, I'm like… dreaming and just need to wake up." Charlotte dropped her head into her arms.

"Excuse me?" a familiar voice asked.

Charlotte looked up, and her eyes met a friendly face. "Kimiko!"

The girl hesitated, looking a little uncertain. "Do we know each other?"

Charlotte's heart sank to the pit of her stomach. "Charlie Carroll? My mom and I visit the coffee shop you work at least every weekend?"

"Oh! Riiight, Charlie *Carroll*," Kimiko said, in that unconvincing tone someone used whenever they were feigning remembrance. "Right, sorry, I just… we're in the middle of a big project, so my brain is a little fuzzy." She looked down at her hands, which were settled on the chair. "Um… can we borrow this? We've got a study group going and we need one more."

Charlotte nodded numbly. "Yeah, sure…"

"Thanks!" Kimiko lifted the chair and carried it over to a table where a group of people had gathered around piles of books.

Charlotte watched her retreat, her mind swimming. Kimiko had looked at her like an absolute stranger. "What… is going on?"

Had she used the clock wrong? Had she traveled to some parallel universe where she'd never been born in some strange *It's A Wonderful Life*-like scenario? As her mind raked over possibilities, her stomach churned… and then landed very heavily on something Oswin had said.

There could be… complications going back.

Was… this what he meant? Her very existence being erased? Had Shelby Ferris thought she was complimenting and inquiring about a stranger's hair rather than taking an opportunity to rub the gum incident in her face?

And if her existence had somehow been erased… did that mean her mother was possibly *not* in the hospital? If she'd never been born, then her mother never

236

would have been reconnected to the Dream World and then…

But where did that leave *her*? Sixteen and homeless?

It was too late for visiting hours at the hospital, but she couldn't wait at home with no way to get in. And the coffee shop *would* be closing in a matter of hours.

Charlotte reached back into her pocket and pondered her bus pass. It was solid enough. It wasn't fading like the photo in Back to the Future. So at least *that* existed, which meant she could use it to get where she needed to go.

And right now, she needed Beth's coffee. A lot of it.

Beth's was another bus ride away, but it was the only 24-hour restaurant she knew of that she could justify hiding out in for multiple hours. On a weekday she had the luxury of being able to not annoy the waiters by sustaining a night-long stay with just small orders of coffee or food every few hours.

The emergency credit card her mother had given her not only was also still in existence and working, but it also had never been *given* so much work.

It took what seemed like an eternity, and Charlotte was hunched over what must have been her 20th cup of coffee that night. Her eyes were starting to feel bloodshot from sleep deprivation. She'd tried to draw the tree or gargoyle monster on about five of the many pieces of paper made available to her, but she found crayons didn't much do either monster from her nightmares justice.

It wasn't really the sort of thing that felt appropriate to hang alongside the other doodles diners of the past had tacked up along the interior of the restaurant. She tried to look at them now—they covered every available space of wall, and most were cheery or funny and gave the greasy spoon that sort of homey touch of a house full of small children.

If her mother was at the hospital—what did that mean? Or if she wasn't, would she be back at the house? And if she had never gotten sick… would she also look at Charlotte with that vacant expression of no recognition Kimiko had given her?

Her stomach churned, possibly from too much caffeine on a relatively empty stomach, or from the thought of her own mother not knowing her.

"It's 7 a.m., honey," the waitress on shift told her as she refilled her coffee. "They said you'd want to know."

"Oh, thank you…" Charlotte mumbled, handing her the credit card. "Could you be so kind as to cash me out?"

"Course."

Charlotte numbly took a drink, looking down at the many pieces of paper she'd drawn on with crayons the restaurant had provided. Among the nightmares were pictures of the great hall, the library, and even her own home, which had deteriorated in swirls that she'd gone over with another crayon. Bunch of garbage.

At last, she simply took a large blue crayon and wrote on a blank scrap: Charlie was here, before tucking it beside a drawing of Godzilla singing into the space needle like a microphone. It wasn't much, but the small reassurance of physical evidence made her feel a little better.

She was starting to get sick of the bus. Or possibly she was starting to get sick on the bus; it was hard to tell. She should have skipped that last cup of coffee. She felt jittery, and despite the number of eggs and hash browns she'd consumed, almost achingly hungry. She also had a sneaking suspicion that she needed a shower. She watched the dreary-looking landscape as she rode her way back to the hospital that had admitted her mother days earlier. She wasn't sure what she'd find.

How long had she really been gone? She should have checked a newspaper. And how did no one remember her?

It did occur to her that if no one could remember her, she couldn't possibly be in trouble for missing any more school. Her suspension was technically meaning-less, too. In a strange way, that was a sort of silver lining.

She could even, potentially, get revenge on the flock of morons who attacked her in the first place. Considering they wouldn't know who she was and therefore couldn't expect any malicious intent, she was practically spy status. She tried to daydream about that for a moment but realized rather quickly she couldn't think of any remotely realistic forms of revenge. It also occurred to her that there were so many often pushed around by that group of goons that not remembering who she was really didn't give her much of an edge. They probably didn't remember most of the people they shoved into lockers or verbally harassed.

Charlotte sighed and slumped down in her seat. She was so tired. She wasn't sure if it was the traveling between worlds, the running from the guards, the stress of her mother being in the hospital, or all the above, but her body felt like it had been up for a week.

"Who knew encountering alternate dimensions would be a tad more strenuous than cramming for the PSAT?"

The bus's brakes, desperately in need of care, cried out in a gargoyle-like screech as they slowed to a halt, jarring Charlotte back to the present. She winced and shook off the nails-on-chalkboard uneasiness as she stood and trudged off into the misty morning.

She was lucky she didn't need to talk to the nurse. It was possible she needed to check in, but if she had learned anything from Alys, it was that if you simply look like you know where you're going, that you are supposed to be going there, no one questions you. Because no one was usually really paying attention to you anyway.

As Charlotte approached what had been her mother's room, Diana emerged, her steps full of intent and her eyes intense. It was such a relief to see her she almost called out to her, but stopped herself, remembering Diana's confusion on the phone. She found her own walk slowing to a halt awkwardly, unsure what to do.

Diana, looking like an Amazonian pin-up model, passed her with a tight but polite smile and quiet, "Hi."

There was no familiarity to it, no recognition in her eyes, and it left Charlotte feeling cold and empty.

She watched her Godmother walk down the hall to the nurse's station.

If Diana truly didn't recognize her... then she didn't have much time. She ducked into her mother's room, closing the door behind her for extra insurance.

Alys was lying in bed just as before; asleep and unaware of the chaos that surrounded her. She looked paler than Charlotte remembered.

"Hey," Charlotte whispered awkwardly. "So... I met dad..." She tapped her fingers awkwardly on the bed. "And I know you said you'd tell me everything later... I just... I'm kinda curious when you thought the best time for that... was gonna be. Is that like a graduation kind of secret or... on my wedding day?" She laughed a little, strained. "Hey honey, turns out you're part... Dream? Like what is that even?" A beat. "And am I technically a princess? Because they called me princess... So that's... really weird." She sighed deeply. "I really wish you could talk to me... I feel like I've never needed your help so much... in my life."

"I'm going to fix this. *Somehow*. I promise. As soon as I figure out how exactly to do that... I'm..." Charlotte's voice broke, and she paused again to focus on her breathing. "I'm going to save you. You're going to be okay. *We're* gonna be okay."

The sound of Diana's heels approaching warned Charlotte she'd run out of time. "I love you," she whispered, ducking into the bathroom and locking the door behind her. She tried to slow her breathing as the door opened.

"Look, I don't understand anything about this, but this doesn't look how it did yesterday," Diana insisted. Charlotte could hear her clear as day through the door.

The nurse's response was much softer, and Charlotte couldn't make it out.

"Well, if they're dropping, then shouldn't you be doing something?"

Again, the response was a soft murmur. Whatever they were discussing, Charlotte knew it couldn't be good.

Doctors couldn't help her mother. No medicine they administered would help wake her.

Alys' salvation and the answers to Charlotte's questions could only be found in one place.

Charlotte took a deep breath and opened the pocket watch again, pointing it as she had before at the bathroom mirror above the sink.

The glass rippled out like a stone tossed into a pond, her own reflection darkening and fading away until all she could see was endless black.

Charlotte climbed onto the sink and peered through, trying to make out anything she could. But whatever was on the other side, there was no light on to give her clues.

The doorknob jiggled suddenly. "Is someone in there?"

Charlotte startled and pursed her lips together to keep from making any noise.

The knob jiggled again, accompanied by a knock. "Hello?"

Charlotte closed her eyes, took a deep breath, and pushed into the endless darkness of the looking glass.

10

THE POOL OF TEARS

At first Charlotte felt like she might have tumbled into space itself. She couldn't see, she felt like she was floating, and she was absolutely freezing. Then a more logical thought came to mind as her eyes adjusted.

She was under water. Saltwater. It burned her eyes.

A few startled bubbles escaped her as she took in her surroundings. It was very, very dark, but Charlotte could make out the broken ruins of what might have once been beautiful quarters of a fine ship, including the barnacle-covered mirror she'd escaped through.

I'm going to drown. Charlotte panicked and she swam toward a broken opening, hoping to find a way out. *I'm going to drown before I ever get close to helping mom.*

She used pieces of the ship to pull her along, the broken wood long covered in seaweed and barnacles from ages of exposure to the deep. It was speeding her movement, but how long could she hold her breath?

I can't die here.

She could see the open ocean just beyond a shattered and cracked piece of the hull. It was likely what drew the ship down, but the space was too small for her to fit through, increasing her desperation. She leveraged against a fallen beam and kicked her boot around the edges, causing more air to escape out her nose.

I cannot. Die. Here.

Another vicious kick, this time it broke off some of the hole. Her legs were starting to ache, and she kicked harder.

I refuse to die here.

A large piece collapsed beneath her foot and she lost her balance against the beam. She twisted in the water, flipping around so she could carefully swim through the jagged hole.

I'm going to find her. I will save her.

She crouched on the hull of the boat, angling her body upward where she could see the distant light of the sun penetrating through the waters. She took a moment to rest her legs, forgetting that logically she should have been out of air.

Perhaps there was no time for logic. Simply gratitude for what she still had.

She launched herself upward, leaving the ocean floor at a pace that seemed too fast to be humanly possible. She was starting to get that notion that she was in a dream, a dream under her control.

Charlotte broke the surface of the waves, gasping for the air her lungs had been convinced they didn't need only seconds before.

A piece of wood she'd kicked free from the ship had also bubbled to the top with her, and she clung onto it best she could.

The sun was bright overhead, leaving everything awash in a bright blinding light.

It was the kind of sun a place like Seattle would never know, and she squinted against the rays and reflection to gaze out to an endless ocean on either side. No land, no ships. Nothing.

"You have got… to be kidding me." She took a deep breath and adjusted her grip on the chunk of ship. It wasn't big enough for her to climb on, but it would hold her head above water.

She used it to paddle a ways, but stopped. Unsure if she was heading towards land or away from it. Was there a way to tell? Could she decipher by the tide? She tried to scan the sky for seagulls or any kind of bird but saw nothing. Not even a cloud.

Charlotte rested her chin on her own arm. She began to ponder how little school had prepared her for anything real—not that this world matched any concept of reality she'd previously had. Admittedly, the thought of being prepared for the possibility of getting shipwrecked in the middle of the ocean would have also seemed like useless information at the time, but even if she wasn't currently stranded, that knowledge would still seemed more useful than how to find the square root of X.

Not that the square root of X wasn't valuable to *someone*. Charlotte just had a hard time picturing how it would be valuable to her beyond graduation.

If only she had a flare or some way to signal to somewhere or someone that she was out there and in need of help. Or even if she had a notion of what direction land might be, she could maybe attempt to swim toward it.

In any survival novel she'd read, the hero had been at least equipped with *some* kind of *tool*. Even Brian Robeson in *Hatchet* had... well, a *hatchet*. Every character she'd read or seen had been at least remotely prepared for the wilderness. Well, except in *Lord of the Flies*, but Charlotte rather thought that book was a load of rubbish. She then spent far too much time reminiscing on how she didn't agree with Golding's perspective on the fragility of human decency, how much she'd cried when Simon died, and how she still wasn't entirely sure of the correct pronunciation of a "conch shell." Fixating on petty things helped her ignore the panic-inducing facts around the reality of her own helplessness.

Charlotte's eyelids were starting to feel heavy, and she felt herself slowly drifting toward a state of unconsciousness that would undoubtedly prove dangerous in her current situation.

She fought to keep her eyes open, but the sun was so bright that her eyes grew tired from squinting so often. It was a relief to close them.

I'm going to die here, she thought hazily, *and no one will even notice.*

Her heart ached painfully, and she felt her eyes prickling with tears.

"No, come on, not here..." she sniffled as she felt the saltwater from her eyes make its rapid descent toward the ocean around her. Her grip around the floating piece of ship made it rather impossible to properly wipe her cheeks.

She wondered if her father remembered her... or if the memory of her had been erased as well when she traversed back home. Was it possible Alys had once told him after all and she'd just simply been wiped from all recollection? Was that why it was safer neither knew of each other?

She was going to die. Forgotten. And alone.

The heat was starting to get the better of her, and she felt her stomach churning with nausea.

She closed her eyes tighter and began to wonder what sort of eulogy was given for a body found with no known relations. She remembered learning about Dia de Los Muertos, and how families decorated altars to show the dead they were not forgotten.

But she was forgotten. So, what then? What happened if she died? Would she just... cease to be? Was there anything for those who were forgotten?

She dimly hoped that she died of exposure before a shark tried to eat her.

The air was starting to smell funny. The stale scent of seaweed and saltwater was still apparent but now the light breeze brought the smell of something new, something different, something… familiar and nauseating.

It almost smelled like… diesel?

Charlotte's eyes shot open and she tried to push up to get a better view, but the wood beneath her shifted farther under the water with the effort. She craned her neck either way until she finally swung around completely, seeing a dark shape on the horizon approaching. She wouldn't say it was moving fast, per se. It did not move toward her like a speed boat, but it certainly moved at a pace she didn't expect from a world that seemed to have no concept of electricity or any other modern technology.

Was she imagining it? It seemed plausible she'd be hallucinating at this point.

Then the ship became two, and then two became three, until Charlotte could see it was an entire fleet of at least ten small steamboats. At least, they *looked* steam powered. And while she was certain the faint diesel smell was coming from that direction; she could not decipher why.

As she pondered the logistics of the boats that were now close enough that she could make out some detail, it finally occurred to her that she should attempt to get their attention.

"Hey!" She croaked blindly at them. Then, realizing that gave little context of where to look, she adjusted to, "Help!" She flailed with one arm while the other gripped the piece of ship tighter to try to keep afloat. "SOS! DROWNING GIRL!"

She was beginning to fear they'd never hear her over the roar of the engines and she'd likely get run over by the entire fleet of tiny boats. Yet, as the ships approached, not only were they almost disturbingly silent, but they also turned gracefully like swans, coming up alongside her and resting a mere 100 feet away.

"Help! Please! Help!"

No one spoke to her, but she could see figures, silhouetted by the sun, which was now at the most unfortunate angle to let her see anything that wasn't at the same level as her face. She could see shadows leaping from small rope bridges that connected the boats. She was rather certain one made the jump without any assistance at all. They seemed to congregate on the lead and closest boat, likely discussing her predicament.

This discussion… took a while. Or at least it *seemed* to take a while. Being half-drowned and dehydrated made the mind's perception of minutes slur into hours.

Charlotte's throat reminded her that the only water for miles that she had access to was the sort that would eventually kill her. The heat on her skin reminded her that genetics could only protect her skin so much, she could almost hear it sizzle. "Help," Charlotte whispered miserably. "Preferably while I'm still alive.

One of the shadows separated from the group and dove rather gracefully into the water.

Charlotte's heart leapt with relief. She wasn't going to die lost at sea! It occurred to her that she simply might have traded that death for one by murderous pirates or even scurvy, but it wouldn't be today!

Probably.

Charlotte noticed the diver hadn't come up for air yet to swim toward her, and that seemed curious... or worrisome.

Then something hooked around her waist and dragged her up out of the water and into the air.

The pressure of being yanked out so abruptly was initially enough to literally take her breath away, but as Charlotte watched the water get farther and farther away from her, she found it hard to breathe for other reasons. They were flying. *How* were they flying?

She didn't dare move in case this thing or person who now carried her in midair high above the ocean surface decided to drop her. Her feet dangled, water weighing her clothes down and dripping in their wake. They rose above the first ship and then dropped.

Charlotte screamed.

Then, as if a parachute had launched only ten feet above the deck, they caught in the air before slowly descending to the floor.

Charlotte's knees crumbled beneath her, and her palms pressed into the wood. She was so grateful to be out of the ocean she could have kissed it. Instead, she simply rested her forehead on it. There was less judgement to be had with that action.

"I told you she wasn't a siren," a warm voice said, rather amused by the notion.

"Doesn't look infected either," reasoned another. Someone nudged Charlotte with their foot, and she lazily reached out to bat at them.

"But not a Fae at all—is she a Dream?" Asked a third.

"This leaves more questions than answers then, doesn't it?" grumbled a fourth.

"What's that around her neck?" A fifth asked, excited, and Charlotte heard what sounded like a hand being slapped away from her.

"Don't touch it," said the third voice.

"*I'll* be the one looking at any potential treasure if there is any to be had, you hear?" said the grumbly voice.

"Yes, Captain," said the formerly excited voice.

A rough and large hand gently reached to untangle something heavy and metal from Charlotte's neck.

"We should get her out of the sun," said the first voice. Charlotte would remember thinking it had a kind resonant melodic quality. "She doesn't look at all well."

There was a long, tense pause before the grumbly voice of the Captain spoke again. "Let her rest in my quarters, Thorn. There may be more treasure in this girl than all the gold in Terra Mirum…"

"I don't have anything," Charlotte managed to whisper.

"Once she's had time to regain her strength, I'm going to have a lot of questions that will be needing answers," the captain said gravely.

Charlotte could feel the same arms that had plucked her from the sea carefully untangle her form and pull her up into their arms again, but opening her eyes seemed impossible at this point. She was barely clinging to consciousness. "But I don't…" she protested with a weary mumble. "I don't know anything…"

A hand cradled her head to their chest, and the warm voice soothed, "I know, Treasure, I know.

Charlotte's entire body sighed, finding comfort that she could finally let her body rest without risking drowning, and her body grew limp in the arms that carried her.

It would be the first completely dreamless sleep Charlie Carroll ever had.

It made rest feel disconcerting and brief, like she'd merely blinked, but when she opened her eyes again, it was nearly sunset. She could see the oppressively glowing orange orb making its decent toward the horizon from the large window she was lying beside. She blinked a few moments, disoriented and groggy. Her throat was parched, and every muscle in her body ached.

She flinched as she pushed up from her place curled up on a plush bed-like window seat, and her head complained at the movement. Her hand raised to her forehead, and she exhaled grumpily. Her hair felt… crunchy. *Everything* felt crunchy.

Ah, that's right, she'd been pulled out of the ocean.

Charlotte rubbed at her eyes and stared out the window, half-asleep, and half-exhausted. Her jeans were still damp, as were the socks in her boots, and as she became more and more aware of her current state, the more certain she was that she would be incredibly grateful for a change of clothes. And a bath. And a rather large glass of water.

She slipped from the bed, and as her feet connected with the floor, she could feel the way the ship slowly rocked on the waves before she took in the room.

It was simple enough—the real bed not far from the window, and a closet-like sliding door seeming to lead to a bathroom of sorts. A dresser, a table with maps strewn over it, and a large mirror that unkindly revealed how much her appearance had reduced to that of a drowned rat.

Charlotte approached it and tried to salvage the mess of eyeliner that remained, giving her a far more zombie-like appearance than she would have preferred. Or a raccoon. Or a zombie raccoon. Either way, she knew it wasn't cute. She wiped at her eyes, but it was a fruitless effort.

That was when she noticed the Coleridge Clock was missing.

Her hands flew to her neck, grasping about for the chain. Nothing.

She stumbled back toward the makeshift bed and searched through the blankets. Again, nothing.

She could feel panic sweep through her, the moment of reprieve vanishing as the one tool she had in her favor in saving her mother was now gone. *GONE.*

She stopped as a vague memory of someone pulling a weight from her neck filtered back through her mind.

Not gone. Stolen. Someone on this ship had stolen her mother's clock—and her only way home.

Angrily, Charlotte turned on her heel and marched to the door, fully intending on giving whomever a piece of her damn mind, but as her hand grasped the handle, it didn't move. She blinked, looked down at it, and tried again.

It didn't budge.

She was locked in. Again.

"Ugh!" Charlotte gave the door a frustrated kick and nearly fell over as the force of it knocked her off balance.

The door opened almost immediately after, and Charlotte found herself face to face with perhaps the most beautiful person she'd ever seen in her life.

Androgynous and athletic in their form, their skin was light but golden, and flawless save for the pale barbed crisscrossing scars along her exposed arms and shoulders. Moss green eyes fixated on her warmly, and she could see the circle of gold that wrapped around the pupil and seeped into the iris, like sun breaking through the leaves on a summer day. She was so entranced by every little detail, and that everything about them seemed saturated with warm color—that she almost didn't notice the pointed ears that stuck out from beneath the asymmetrical layered strands of deep-crimson-colored hair.

Charlotte forgot every word in every language, and her breath caught.

"Well," they said warmly, and she recognized their voice as the person who'd carried her from the deck. "You look like hell."

Charlotte huffed, her arms folding over her chest. "Yeah, well you're not so... Shut up."

They gave her a friendly smile, and irritatingly, it seemed to make them look more captivating. It was almost as if they glowed. "Would you like a proper bath, maybe? Clean clothes? The Captain would like a few words with you when you can, but as we've decided you're very unlikely to be a threat, we figured you might want to be comfortable."

Charlotte blinked. "I..."

"Forgive us for leaving you sleeping in wet clothes, but..." They shrugged. "What were we supposed to do? Change you ourselves without so much as a nod of the head that you were alright with us doing that?"

Charlotte remembered the clock. "My necklace was stolen."

"Captain has it," they said simply. "Not to worry—it will be returned to you. He has no intention of keeping it. Just needed to have The Librarian look at it."

Charlotte's headache was starting to complain louder. "Librarian?" What did pirates need with a librarian? What did any seafaring folk need with a librarian?

They took a step toward her, hands reaching out. "May I? I promise I won't touch you."

Charlotte, uncertain of what exactly they *were* going to do, simply nodded, eyes moving suspiciously back and forth between each hand.

The sailor stood close enough to properly size her up, measuring where her head came on them in height (to about their sternum), and their hands measured her shoulders and width in approximation to their own. They paused a moment thoughtfully, then held up a finger before heading out the door again. "I'll be right back."

Charlotte's eyes widened as they turned around. Unmistakably, folded down on their back like a cape, were translucent, iridescent wings.

Fairy.

Had she stumbled upon one of Oberon's fleets? Is that where she was?

She peered around the room once more and decided this could not in fact be the case. While she knew nothing of what the King of Shadows was *actually* like, she had a feeling if he had a fleet of ships, they would not be so humbly decorated or outfitted.

She tried the door again, but it had locked behind the uncomfortably attractive fairy, and so she grumbled and wandered around the room. She found a simple wooden goblet and a pitcher of water, and eagerly, she poured herself a glass, and then another, as the first was downed in nearly an instant.

The door opened again, and the fairy had returned, carrying an armful of clothing and setting it down on the plush window-seat cushion. "I'm Thorn, by the way." They turned and winked at her. "I'm the one who pulled you out of The Pool."

Charlotte wasn't sure if she'd misheard. "The *pool*?"

Thorn stepped through the closet-like door to where the bathtub was. "The Pool of Tears," they explained. "The sea we found you half-drowned in—don't you remember?"

Charlotte slowly moved to watch, hovering awkwardly in the doorway. "I'm... not really from around here," she deflected. "Odd name for an ocean, isn't it?"

Thorn gave a shrug. "The main river that feeds into it falls off a large rock face that vaguely resembles that of a crying girl." They looked back at her curiously. "I thought everyone knew that." They turned a faucet on the bathtub, and hot steaming water began to pour from it, filling the large basin.

Charlotte smiled nervously, but it faded slowly as curiosity about the bathtub took over. "That's... weird."

Thorn looked from her to the tub and back again. "What is?"

"Well... honestly, I didn't expect there to be plumbing on this ship at all, and second, I've never seen it come out immediately steaming like that."

Thorn paused. "Did... you want a cold bath?"

"No," Charlotte shook her head. "I... I'm just used to having to wait for it to warm up."

"Isn't that a waste of time and water?"

Charlotte opened her mouth, closed it, and just nodded. "Yeah, I guess... I guess it is." Come to think of it, she'd never had a dream where she'd had to bother with things as mundane as waiting for water to warm up. Now she wasn't so sure if it was because her brain didn't bother to think of it, or because Terra Mirum simply worked differently.

"Where exactly *are* you from?"

Charlotte looked at the fairy to her side, realizing their face was rather close to her own now—or at least as close as it could be without leaning up on her toes. "That's... really a discussion I'd prefer to have when I'm not soaked through to my underwear," she said quietly.

Thorn smiled lopsidedly and leaned in slightly, in a manner that made Charlotte think they might plant a kiss on her forehead, but instead they winked. "Fair enough. I'll leave you to it, then." They moved passed Charlotte toward the door, stopping to gesture to the clothing. "There's a few different things in that pile... I wasn't entirely sure of your exact size or preference, but... you should be able to find something in there to your liking."

Charlotte nodded. "Sure."

"Just knock when you're done, I'll take you to see the Captain."

Her heart stopped. "You're... going to be right outside the door?"

"Well, *relatively* right outside the door."

"Can you like... *hear* me out there?"

Thorn smiled, raising a quizzical eyebrow. "That depends… what exactly are you planning on doing?"

"Nothing! Wash up, get dressed. Nothing weird! I just—privacy! Concerns. Concerns about privacy. Why—what did it sound like? What did you think?" Charlotte felt the words spill out of her and she shifted on her feet, suddenly unsure what to do with her hands. They rested on her hips, then she folded her arms. She tried to gesture to make her point and then finally pinned them behind her by clasping her hands behind her back to keep from fidgeting.

Thorn exhaled a laugh. "No, I can't hear you on the other side of the door."

"Great," Charlotte squeaked, giving a weak thumbs up. "That was all…"

Thorn nodded and turned to go again.

"Charlie," Charlotte blurted out, causing Thorn to once again pause and look back at her. She cleared her throat. "*My name*… is Charlie."

Their smile widened to a grin, and Charlotte felt an unnerving sensation of butterflies release inside her ribcage. "Pleasure to meet you… Charlie." They tipped an imaginary hat, took a low bow and closed the door behind them.

Charlotte felt her face burn before she buried it in her hands. "Oh my god… what is *wrong* with me?"

11

PLAYING WITH FIRE

None of the pants had fit right, so Charlotte had opted for the dress. As it turned out, measuring someone by their approximation to you wasn't the best form of tailoring.

It had laces, thankfully, and she tried not to linger on the thought of who it had belonged to before her. She knew she'd been given no reason to think any foul play was afoot… but she'd also read far too many stories where getting rescued from drowning was just hopping into another frying pan. The door *had* been locked when she woke, after all.

It was an empire waist, which Charlotte frankly didn't care for, but since beggars couldn't be choosers, she decided to make do. The silk material of the skirt was a subtle ombre that transitioned from a sky blue to a deep cerulean. It tapered down around her knees in a handkerchief hem that raised as far as mid-thigh. The bodice of the dress was thicker and made of a fabric with white-and-blue vertical stripes and was held in place by two delicate straps.

Being Seattle-born, Charlotte was accustomed to layers, and so she also took a white under-bust vest which covered her bare shoulder blades and forced the fabric to conform to a more hourglass shape. Then, after fidgeting with some matching striped socks, she put on her own boots. They were a little wet still, but the thick socks made it impossible to notice for the time being.

Charlotte twirled in the mirror, looking critically at herself. She had to blend in. And she had to get the clock back. They didn't know how she got there, and she wasn't about to let them in on it. Satisfied with her current appearance, she gave the door a confidant knock.

The door opened, and Thorn smiled approvingly, but it faded slightly as their eyes moved downward. "You've forgotten trousers."

Charlotte felt immediately self-conscious and defensive. "No, I didn't, I'm wearing a dress."

Thorn's lips pursed to stifle a snicker, which just melted into a lopsided grin. It was still infuriatingly charming. "No, I'm afraid you're not. At least, it wasn't a dress for the original owner... Though you *are* considerably shorter than she is."

Charlotte felt her cheeks burn, and she looked down at her skirt, brushing it with her fingers. When was she going to stop making a fool of herself in front of this person? "Well, most of what you gave me didn't fit."

"My apologies. We'll find you something else if you'd like."

"No," Charlotte said decisively. There were more important things, more pressing things than embarrassment. "I'm ready to meet the Captain."

Thorn nodded and extended their elbow to her.

Charlotte looked down at it, confused a moment before it dawned on her they were offering for her to take it. Sheepishly she did, feeling goosebumps rise along her arms as she felt her companion's body heat seep into her skin.

Thorn, on the other hand, seemed rather unaffected by the contact, leading her up the stairs and onto the deck where the sky itself seemed on fire with the setting sun.

Charlotte felt her jaw slacken, her lips parting in awe as she took in the steamship—far larger than she'd first thought—about the size of one of the ferries she'd taken to the islands around Seattle, but their size was all that was similar. Wood and steel intertwined in perfect unison as if the ship had grown together in such a fashion instead of painstakingly crafted. Giant steam stacks towered above them.

Up on deck, she caught the scent of diesel again, and as they turned to walk up another flight of stairs to the upper deck, she saw people lighting great torches. Gas lanterns—that was what the smell was from.

Charlotte pointed to them with her free hand. "What are those for?"

"Night lights. They keep the Nightmares at bay."

Charlotte giggled before realizing Thorn wasn't joking. "...Seriously?"

"The darkness pushes out further every day since The Door opened. Many people were driven from their homes and have retreated to the sea until the land is habitable again. Nightmares don't like the light. We burn it all through the night in case any of them get daring enough to cross the ocean."

Charlotte considered the fae beside her a moment. "Were you driven from your home?"

Thorn looked taken aback by this question, and they studied Charlotte's face and posture a moment before answering. "Yes, I suppose I was... though long before the Nightmares invaded."

Charlotte's brow furrowed.

"Joined Captain Lory's crew a few years ago. They were slow to trust, but I proved my worth."

"How?"

The fae's smile stretched to a broad grin, which made Charlotte's heart flutter and a sense of unease creep into her mind. "I'm resourceful," is all they said, before releasing Charlotte so they could open the door to the bridge.

Charlotte entered the room situated at the very topmost level of ship. Each side was more window than wall, but what little space existed between was plastered with maps. She noticed marks indicating which coasts were safe to harbor. There weren't many. The others were marked with deep red Xs crossing out entire shores, ports, and cities.

"After all that, and this is what walks in? Well… can't all be gold, I suppose…" a gruff voice remarked, and Charlotte's attention shifted to the only other person standing in the room. It was strange she hadn't noticed the strong-looking man before, but she blamed the amount of bright orange light pouring in from the windows, as it washed everything with the same hue, including the man's clothing. As he stepped from the direct light, she was able to better see the bold and bright colors he adorned himself in. He looked akin to a parrot, from the bright blue feather plume in his hat to his maroon silk shirt and the large green velvet captain's coat. "Close the door, Thorn," the Captain ordered.

Charlotte felt the hair on the back of her neck stand up with the snap of the door shutting behind them.

"I wasn't sure what to make of you at first when we pulled you on board," Captain Lory admitted, turning to face her. "I knew you weren't a Nightmare; but that didn't mean you weren't a threat." He reached in his pocket and produced the Coleridge clock, which glistened in the light. "And then I saw *this*."

Charlotte's breath caught, but she tried, unsuccessfully to look undaunted. "It's a clock— so what? Pirates don't keep time?"

"Not with a *Coleridge Clock*, we don't."

A moment of hesitation. "Well with all those catchy shanties, why would you?"

Thorn chuffed.

Lory glared at the fae, before returning to Charlotte. "Well, you don't have the mouth of a princess, I'll give you that."

"I'm not a princess," Charlotte spat out.

"No?" Captain Lory asked condescendingly. "Then I suppose this is absolutely stolen property, isn't it?" He dangled the pocket watch high above her head. "And given that we've just saved your pathetic little life, we're within our rights to claim it as payment for service."

Charlotte could feel her heartbeat quickening, but she clenched her fists at her sides. "You can't do that—it's mine!"

"Artifact this rare might fetch a high price with our buyers—or perhaps a reward for returning it. What do you think, Thorn?" Lory asked.

"Returning a cherished relic *and* bringing the thief intact for Oberon to deal with personally? I believe we'd be heroes, sir," said Thorn flatly.

"I didn't steal it!"

"Then how'd you get your hands on something like this, guttersnipe? Passed down in the family, was it? Present from your dear dead mum?"

Her mother. Her *mother*. Her mother who was still in danger, who was somewhere out there, who *needed* her. Charlotte's eyes narrowed, and though her body trembled from panicked nerves, something stronger surged through her, something *terribly angry*. She spoke in a low staccato growl. "Give. Me. Back. My. Necklace."

The Captain shifted back on his hip, raising his chin as he looked down at the small girl tauntingly. "Or you'll what?"

Charlotte's skin felt hot again, as if she were beneath the direct sunlight once more. Her teeth gritted and body shook as her focus narrowed on the captain. Her fingertips tingled, and she felt her right hand start to raise toward him without a thought.

A hand rested gently on her shoulder. "That's enough," Thorn said to the Captain.

Charlotte blinked hard and looked toward Thorn, and as she did, she saw the faint hint of illumination from her skin extinguish. Her brow furrowed.

"Forgive me, Your Majesty," the Captain apologized, his tone far softer, far kinder now. "I had to be sure."

Charlotte looked back to him, bewildered. "Sure of what?"

"Of what you are," the man said gravely, and Charlotte felt her stomach churn. "Though it does explain why you were lit up like a lighthouse when we pulled you from the water."

Like a… "I was what?"

"It's how we found you," Thorn explained, tapping their fingers on Charlotte's shoulder. "There was this great pillar of light coming from your location, like a star in the ocean."

"Half the crew were convinced you were some sort of treasure," the Captain mused.

"They weren't entirely wrong," Thorn pointed out.

The Captain snorted softly and took a step toward Charlotte to remove his hat with his free hand and take a deep flourishing bow. "Captain Jonathan Lorinaee of the *Brass Gryphon*, at your service. It's an honor to have royalty aboard my ship, and I promise you won't find any Changeling prejudice nonsense here." He righted himself and replaced his hat once more. "As long as you are under my care, you will be safe here." Then, remembering, he held out the Coleridge Clock to her. "And it would do best to keep this hidden, as well. We are in times of trouble. The panicked are never predictable creatures. Best they don't know they're among royalty."

Charlotte felt relief flood through her as the clock landed back into her palm. She held it to her heart. "… How did you know?"

"You're the spitting image of our beloved late Queen and in possession of a Coleridge Clock. It's not the longest voyage to connect those dots."

Charlotte flinched in embarrassment. "Call me Charlie."

Thorn inhaled sharply through their teeth. "Well…"

Lorinaee looked to them and remembered. "Ah, right. In all the excitement, I've forgotten myself. No one goes by their given name here. So, I'd appreciate if you kept mine to yourself. It began as a safety measure just for my crew… but we've sort of instituted it on the entire flotilla."

"I don't understand," Charlotte admitted.

"You don't want a Nightmare to have access to the name your heart answers to," Thorn explained.

"Call me Captain Lory. Like the bird. Easy enough to remember for my crew. You already know Thorn's, and… well you'll want to think of one for yourself, too."

Charlotte was only half listening. What happened if a Nightmare got a hold of your name? And if Alys had been so instrumental in the last war against Nightmares… "Could a Nightmare have gotten hold of my mother's name?" she asked barely above a whisper.

Uncomfortable silence answered her.

"Your mother?" Thorn asked.

Charlotte nodded. "That's why I'm here. She was pulled under with the other Dreamers. She won't wake up… I need to get to The Nothing. I have to help her."

"The Hero of Terra Mirum has been dragged into The Nothing." Lory was in disbelief.

Charlotte nodded numbly.

Lory took a moment, as if this information had physically struck him. He raised a hand and uncomfortably rubbed his chest just over his heart. His eyes averted. "I'm sorry, child. There's nothing you can do for her."

Charlotte couldn't breathe for a moment. She felt dizzy and sick. She stumbled into Thorn. "Excuse me?"

"If the Hero of Terra Mirum has been lost to the realm of the Nightmares, you have no hope to save her now," Lory said gravely.

Her eyes stung with tears, and though the absolute certainty in his voice made her ill, she tried to deny it. "There has to be something I can do."

The captain leveled his gaze with hers. "The Nothing is a violent and dangerous place for anyone. Its sole existence is destruction and consumption—it would have swallowed all of Terra Mirum had it never been sealed away. *No one* has ever traversed through and survived."

"But," Charlotte protested, feeling the panic rising in her throat again, "that doesn't mean no one could."

"I'm afraid it does."

"You don't know that!" cried Charlotte, pushing herself away from Thorn to stand on her own feet again. "And if you aren't going to help me, *fine*, but I have to try." She turned on her heel to exit the bridge, hiding the tears about to fall.

She hadn't realized Thorn had followed her until she heard their voice beside her. "Where are you going?"

"I'm getting off this ship," Charlotte spat.

"Going to take a walk back to the shore, are you?" came the teasing reply.

"There's a mirror in the Captain's quarters, I'm going to go through it, and then I'm going to find my way to my mother." Determinedly she walked down the first set of stairs.

"Do you even know where it goes?"

"I'm going to find out."

"Is that how you ended up in the middle of the ocean?"

Charlotte stopped. She looked at the fae beside her with uncertainty. They had a point, but she wasn't ready to concede to it. "I'll figure out how to control it this time."

"You can't. That's not how it works," Thorn dismissed.

The sureness of their tone annoyed her. "How would *you* know?"

"The Coleridge Clock was made using Seelie magic, and I'd wager I know a great deal more about that than you would, hmm?"

Charlotte looked down at the clock, her lips pursing thoughtfully, then back to them hopefully. "Can... *you* control it?"

"That's not how it works, Treasure," Thorn said gently.

"Then how the hell *does* it work?"

The fae sighed and gently took the hand that held the Coleridge Clock. "It opens doors, *not* portals."

Charlotte held her glare while admitting, "I don't know what that means."

Thorn raised their other hand and traced along the floral design of the clock with their finger. There was something... sad, or nostalgic, about the look in their eyes in that moment. "Portals can go from any point to any other point. A door, however, no matter how many times you open it, will always go to the same place." Their eyes flickered up to meet Charlotte's. "I've heard that multiple doors sometimes open to the same room, but I've never personally experienced it, so I have no idea how to utilize it—or if it *can* be utilized without splitting someone in two…" They closed their hand around both Charlotte's and the clock. "You can't keep jumping from place to place not knowing where you're going to land. You have no idea what it could do."

Charlotte's brow relaxed. "…Why do you care?"

Thorn smiled crookedly. "It's my personal creed to not let cute girls rush unprepared into danger."

Charlotte pursed her lips. "What about non-cute girls?"

Their hand raised to gently cradle her chin with their curled index finger. "I don't see how that applies here."

Her heart thumped, and her cheeks felt warm. She felt lost in their eyes, suddenly aware of how easy it would be to just lean up to kiss them. It was… unnerving how strong that urge was. She blinked. "You're… trying to distract me," she accused in a whisper.

Thorn's smile expanded to a grin. "Is it working?"

"I…" She swallowed. "No."

Thorn took a step back, and Charlotte found it so much easier to breathe. Even the air felt cooler. "Let's go for a walk, get some food."

Charlotte blinked. "Why?"

Thorn extended their hand to her. "Because when was the last time you ate?"

"I..." Charlotte flustered. They had a point. And it irritated her. "*Fine.* Dinner."

Thorn flashed a grin. "It's a date."

Charlotte pointed authoritatively. "But *then* I'm leaving."

Thorn nodded sensibly. "Oh, of course. I wouldn't dream of keeping you from your demise." They took her hand and began to lead her out toward the deck. "Just one dinner, dancing, a kiss goodnight, and then you can head off to your doom."

"You're not funny."

"I know you're just saying hurtful things because you're scared."

"I'm not scared.

"You know," Thorn remarked thoughtfully. "There's a few people here you might want to talk to before you leave. Could have some useful information."

Charlotte was curious. "Like what?"

"Liiiike how to fight a Nightmare when you see one." Thorn eyed her suspiciously. "Or were you just planning on glowing at it?"

Charlotte pursed her lips. "I don't even know how I did that."

Thorn clicked their tongue, winked, and pointed to her. "Might be a good idea to figure that out first then at least, wouldn't it?"

"How do you suggest I do that? I can't even ask someone—we're forbidden. From what I hear, I'm like... one of *two* Changelings to ever even exist."

"I'd start with talking to the Librarian," Thorn offered.

"You got a library on this floating pirate isle?"

"She used to be the sole caretaker of the Phrontistery within the Forest of Thought. We weren't always a flotilla. The *Brass Gryphon* was just... *this* ship," Thorn explained. "But when the Nightmares came, people fled to take to the water..."

"You tied all the boats together," Charlotte concluded.

"Safety in numbers," Thorn chimed.

"Did this Librarian bring any useful books with her, by chance?"

"No idea. But the Phrontistery houses every fathomable form of knowledge—formally recorded or not—so I don't think it would hurt to ask. Maybe she can help."

"And if she can't?" Charlotte asked miserably.

Thorn stopped to turn to face her completely, lifting her chin again with their fingertips. "If she can't, I will personally tell you how to find the only other known Changeling."

Charlotte's eyebrows raised. "You know them?"

Thorn nodded. "He's sort of... family."

Charlotte's brow lowered, and her eyes narrowed. "You're bluffing," she accused.

"I'm not," swore Thorn.

"*Family?*" she asked skeptically.

"Have you ever seen a game of Bennu ball?" the fae asked abruptly, turning to lead her to the rail of the upper deck.

"Bennu... No, what does that have to do with—oh my god, what is THAT?!" Charlotte leaned over the rail to peer at the deck below, where a long metal pole that had once been a flagpole hung a spherical wire cage from a chain. Within the cage was a ball of literal fire. She could see it being smacked back and forth between two players standing on either side of the pole with what looked to be metal rackets. Every time metal met metal, sparks and embers flew, briefly granting a flash of more illumination on those playing, but from this vantage point, she couldn't see much more detail.

"Life on the high seas has some... less than eventful nights. You get bored. You find things to do," Thorn explained in amusement.

"That is the coolest thing I have ever seen," Charlotte awed, leaning over the railing slightly to get a better look.

Thorn looked from the game below to their companion and gently nudged her with their arm. "You wanna play?"

Charlotte hesitated. "I... shouldn't."

"C'mon," Thorn urged. "When is the next time you'll be able to play something like this?"

Charlotte pursed her lips.

Thorn leaned in, resting the bridge of their nose against Charlotte's cheekbone. "You know you want to."

"*One* game. Dinner. Librarian. *Then* we go."

Thorn grinned against her cheek. "Deal." They pulled back to tug her down the stairs to the lower deck. "Think you can beat me?"

Charlotte rolled her eyes. "Think I care enough if I do or not?"

"Oh, come on," Thorn teased. "Where's your sense of competition?"

"It died with third-grade relay races."

The fae looked back at her quizzically. "Third-grade... what?"

The teenager shrugged noncommittally. "Human thing, not worth explaining."

"Hey Mouse, mind if we cut in for the next game? We're on a schedule." Thorn released Charlotte to place a friendly hand on a small wiry looking boy holding a battered-looking book where he seemed to be keeping some sort of score.

Mouse blinked his unusually large dark brown eyes first at Thorn and then at Charlotte before squinting, and Charlotte began to wonder if he didn't possibly need glasses but had no ability to equip them stuck out here. "Alright," he finally agreed after far too much thought. "Just one game." He wiped a hand across a soot-smudged face before nodding back to a pile of things behind him. "Gear up, we'll get you in after."

Thorn led Charlotte to the pile of gear, handing her a hat, goggles, and a coat. They were all more than a little too big for her, but given that this was clearly protective gear, she didn't much complain. "Rules are pretty basic. You will be given a racket; you'll use that to hit the fire ball. You cannot touch the chain, and the goal is to get it wrapped around the pole so that there is no chain left."

"...So, it's tetherball."

"It's what?"

"It's like tetherball," Charlotte reasoned, then paused as she looked back at it. "But on fire."

"Sure?"

The coat smelled vaguely like gasoline, not so much that she was particularly worried about being flammable, but it was clear that these garments didn't get much wash between games.

Thorn handed her gloves. These were also too big. "You're trying to get it wrapped around in the direction to YOUR left. That's important. We'll be on opposing sides, so you don't want to let me get it wrapped to MY left. For you that will be counterclockwise. You want it to go clockwise, always."

Charlotte nodded and dismissively waved her hand as she pulled on her gloves. "Yeah, yeah, I get it."

Thorn eyed her a moment, amused by something they chose not to voice. They handed her a stick with a metal wire racket on either side that might have once been some sort of fishing cage, and its center handle had been wrapped in heat-protective cloth to stop it from overheating. "You don't care for competition for competition's sake?" They asked, watching her as carefully as Charlotte watched the current ongoing game.

"Just doesn't interest me," Charlotte just shrugged. "Seems kind of stupid."

Thorn nodded and watched the flaming cage make its final wrap around the metal pole, extinguishing upon the impact. "So perhaps we make it something that does interest you."

"Oh yeah?" Charlotte mused distractedly, feeling her nerves begin to rile up as the players shook hands, making motion for Thorn and Charlotte to take their place on the court. "And how do you suppose we do that?"

"How about a kiss to the winner?" Thorn grinned impishly.

"What?" Charlotte startled, feeling the blood burn in her cheeks. "I don't... I... what?"

Thorn laughed, their natural bright aura seeming to glow a bit more in that moment. "It's just so easy to fluster you."

Charlotte's eyes narrowed.

"You both understand the rules?" Mouse asked, reaching up to untangle the round wire cage from the pole with a long wooden stick with a hook on the end.

Both players grunted in agreement.

Mouse climbed up on top of a large crate, suspending the wire cage in the air with his long-hooked tool. He fumbled about in his pocket and produced a long-nosed lighter which he stuck through the round cage, igniting the coal-black matter within. "Don't touch the pole, don't touch the chain, no wings, no magic, and first person to wrap it clockwise from their direction wins." He squinted his enormous dark eyes at the two of them. "Ready?"

Thorn winked at Charlotte.

Charlotte nodded and pulled down the goggles over her eyes. "Bring it on, sparkles," she growled to herself.

Mouse shifted to release the hook from the flaming cage.

It was like watching a falling star descend from its high arc.

Years of being told NOT to play with fire made Charlotte hesitate a moment. But that moment was all it took.

She heard a metal thwack accompanied by what seemed like the flash of an explosion, and the strangely loud sound of fire blazing past her face registered before the reason for the bright light. She took a quick and startled step backward in time to register Thorn hitting the star-like ball again to accelerate its trajectory toward her.

Charlotte took a step to the right, using it to propel herself up and to the left to smack the cage back around the other way. It was still louder than she thought it would be. Sparks flew—MORE than sparks, flaming embers that died before they reached the ground.

Thorn volleyed it back.

Charlotte didn't let them gain ground. Easily flustered. Her? She… she'd never been easily flustered.

Thwack!

Anxious, yes, but flustered?

Thwack!

It made her genuinely irritated at the accusation.
Thwack!

She was calm.

THWACK.

Cool.

THWACK, THWACK!

Relatively collected.

She was barely flinching at a flaming fireball that was swung repeatedly toward her head. She was LEAPING to hit it with a metal racket.

THWACK!

Just because (THWACK!) some shiny (THWACK!) sparkly (THWACK!) DISTURBINGLY BEAUTIFUL PERSON (THWACK!) was pretending to flirt with her (THWACK!) caught her off guard. (THWACK!) Didn't mean a THING!

THWACK!

Loud cheers.

Charlotte blinked. She looked up at the now extinguished and tangled ball at the top of the metal pole. She squinted up at the dark. Was it wrapped… clockwise? From *her* perspective? "I… won?" She hadn't been expecting that. Her mouth pulled into a disbelieving grin. "I *won*," she stated, bringing her gaze down to see Thorn, who looked equally surprised. "Oh, and that would mean you *lost*, wouldn't it?" She pointed the racket at Thorn. "You thought you could fluster her, you thought you could get in her head. You thought wrooooong!" She crowed happily and held the racket above her head triumphantly, throwing her head back. "I am QUEEN of this game!" She cheered to the sounds of the crowd around them, doing a turn, and as she lowered her arms, her feet bringing her forward again, she nearly took a step directly into the fae who was now right in front of her.

"You won," Thorn acknowledged graciously, taking Charlotte's face in their hands. "A deal is a deal…"

Charlotte's breath caught. She could feel goosebumps rush down her arms and her eyes widened, as she could catch the scent of pine and petrichor as Thorn leaned closer.

The fae gently pressed their lips against Charlotte's forehead and it sent a rush of warmth from the place of contact to the very tips of her toes, leaving a strange tingling sensation in its wake. When they pulled back, Charlotte said nothing, and so they smiled at her. "Let's get you some dinner."

12

THORN

Time as a concept had become rather meaning-less since Charlotte's first excursion back home through the Looking Glass. She wasn't sure how much time had transpired between when she left and when she returned, and after falling asleep in the *Brass Gryphon*, she wasn't sure how much time had passed since she first stepped through again.

Still, she had slept, and now that she was fed (with more baked fish than she thought possible to stomach), she was starting to feel more like herself again. She'd been convinced to walk around the flotilla with Thorn, "just until her stomach settled." It was also reasoned to her that everyone was having dinner, and it was best not to assault The Librarian with questions while she was trying to eat.

It had sounded logical, at least at the time, but now in the cool brisk air felt like another delay tactic. "Tell me more about the clock."

The fae shrugged noncommittally, far more interested in the stars on the horizon than any of their companion's questions. "What's left to tell?"

"You're right, a pocket watch that has the capability of turning mirrors into doors is completely self-explanatory. What a silly question for me to ask," Charlotte huffed. She rested her elbows on the rail next to Thorn's and purposefully bumped against them. "*Why* is it called a Coleridge Clock?"

"The first was made so a man called Coleridge and a fae of Titania's order could meet in secret." It was said so casually Charlotte was starting to think world-hopping clocks were rather commonplace in Terra Mirum, despite that she knew the contrary.

"Why in secret?"

"Cavorting with mortals is rather frowned upon nowadays."

"*Why?*"

"I don't know. Those who do know are forbidden to speak about it."

Charlotte frowned. "No one's let even a little slip? You never asked?"

"You misunderstand me. They literally cannot speak on it. Their tongues are bound by magic. Whatever happened back then, a spell forbids them to ever talk of it—or allude to it. Dark magic, binding. Immensely powerful."

Charlotte shuddered. "Who would do something like that?"

"Oberon," there was no love lost in the name.

"What could be so horrible that a King would forbid his people from even speaking of it?"

Thorn looked to her, taking her in a moment before remembering that this was someone who knew little of their world, who had no basis of comparison for what sort of character or creature Oberon could be. "If I had to hazard a guess? Because he wants the memory of it to die. Likely because whatever part he had in it is one of the very few things he truly regrets, and the King of Shadows *does not* regret easily. He's cruel and calculating, but he would rather hide his shame than face it. So, whatever happened back then… you can bet he had a key hand in it."

Charlotte took a moment to consider this, and she looked down at the clock around her neck. "Could it have had something to do with my mother?"

Thorn looked at her, surprised. "Alys? No. It was well before your mother crossed our borders. And despite our laws, your mother is remembered rather fondly in Arden. My mother even spoke of her from time to time."

Charlotte's eyes lit up. "Really? What do they say?"

"Talk of her bravery—the Dreamer who rallied Fae and Dream together…" Thorn's mouth quirked to the side. "But mostly about how her tongue was about as sharp as the vorpal blade itself."

Charlotte beamed and nestled down on her perch on the rail. "Sounds like mom."

"You inherit that?"

"Her wit? Hardly," Charlotte played with the chain of the Coleridge Clock absently. "She'd have probably already fixed all of this by now if our roles were reversed."

"You shouldn't be so hard on yourself," Thorn nudged her.

"There's a lot of things I shouldn't be," Charlotte answered, her attention focusing harder on the clock itself. The design on the outside, the craftsmanship, the metal... "You said the first one was made... Does that mean there are more now?"

"Not many," said Thorn. "A handful."

"But cavorting with humans is frowned upon? Do they get much use these days?"

Thorn shrugged.

"You said you knew more about it!" Charlotte laughed in exasperation.

"When?"

"Back there, before dinner, after the talk with Captain Lory."

"No, I said I knew more about Seelie magick than you."

Charlotte blinked. Why did that sound familiar? "Seelie?"

"The Seelie Court—even old folklore had record of us—don't they teach you anything about anything in those human schools nowadays?" Thorn teased. They took a moment to ponder how best to summarize it. "There are two courts within Arden, Seelie and Unseelie,

Titania's and Oberon's, Dawn and Dusk, Summer and Winter, Rebirth and Death."

Charlotte took a moment to let this sink in, piecing together the snippets of information she'd been gathering over the past few... days? Hours? Who even knew anymore? Time was irrelevant in exact measure, and all that mattered was it was scarce. "So... this was created by the... Summer court? Life Fairies?"

"Fae," Thorn corrected.

"That's what I said."

"You said *fairies.*"

"I don't under..." Charlotte's brows furrowed. "What's the difference?"

"Well, I've *seen* the things your kind associates with the word 'fairy'—the art, the stories, the strange little figurines you put in your gardens—with all due respect, I am not like that and would prefer to not be associated with such."

"Small, kinda stupid, and so temperamental they're only capable of one emotion at a time?"

Thorn tapped the tip of Charlotte's nose with their index finger. "We've many names in your languages, some less kind than others, but that's personally my least favorite."

"Your least fae-vorite?" Charlotte joked.

"You think you're funny, don't you?"

"Fae-tally."

Thorn rolled their eyes dramatically with a short exhale that Charlotte suspected might have been a suppressed laugh.

Her gaze lingered on the Fae beside her, mulling on this idea of what their kind was or wasn't. She looked beyond the initial sparkle and shine and considered the scars along their arms. They almost looked like they'd tangled with a briar patch and barely escaped to tell the tale. Strangely, it was perhaps the most imperfect thing about them, and Charlotte couldn't help but think it was also the most beautiful. She liked that they made no real effort to hide them either. She resisted the urge to trace a fingertip along one of the long, twisted lines and forced her attention back to their face—the light freckles she could faintly see along their cheeks when standing this close. She smiled to herself, content that while her attention was so riveted on Thorn, Thorn's attention seemed rather pointedly on the horizon. "So," she finally, but coyly, broke the silence. "What *are* you like?"

Thorn smiled but did not look at her. "As you see," they responded anticlimactically.

Charlotte rolled her eyes. "*Other* than bioluminescent."

Thorn's smile cracked to a chuckle. "I also once belonged to the Seelie court."

Charlotte leaned in slightly. "Until?"

"Until I didn't."

Her shoulders slumped. "Oh, come on."

Thorn glanced at her sideways. "You don't *really* want to know all this," they said dismissively.

"I do," Charlotte insisted. "That's why I asked. People tend to ask questions because they want to know the answers."

"People tend to speak to fill the space because they are uncomfortable with silence."

"I think you're uncomfortable with the question," Charlotte mused.

"Uncomfortable with—" Thorn looked genuinely indignant a moment, met Charlotte's eyes, and huffed so that air blew the hair in their eyes straight upward. "This won't get you to your mother, you know. It's completely useless information."

"I think I'll decide what I do and do not consider to be useless information, thanks," Charlotte answered.

Thorn exhaled heavily, clearly frustrated with either accepting that they were uncomfortable answering or having to answer. They drummed their fingers on the railing of the ship a moment, chewing the inside of their cheek. "I belonged to the Seelie court until I ran away from home."

"Why?" came the soft but instantaneous question.

"Why does anyone run away?" Thorn asked in exasperation. They briefly met Charlotte's eyes and then averted their gaze back to the horizon. "They're unhappy with their life, with the life they *would* have had if they stayed."

"You're dodging again."

Thorn's attention snapped back to her, their voice pitching much higher than their regular tenor. "I do not dodge."

"Was it because of…" Charlotte frowned, realizing she was very clumsily approaching a likely sensitive subject. "I'm... sorry, I'm not actually sure how you identify."

Thorn blinked. "How do you mean?"

"Your... pronouns? He/She/They?"

"Ah," Thorn took a moment to consider this. "They, I suppose. We have... a few different ways, but that will probably be easiest for you to remember."

"It's not really about what's easiest for *me* though," Charlotte commented.

Thorn smiled slightly at her, pleasantly surprised. "I'd... forgotten how focused on that sort of thing your world was."

Charlotte cocked her head to the side.

"Gender. It's... very rigid there, oddly black-and-white, one or the other, no room for real identity, just some boxes to shove yourself into."

Charlotte couldn't really argue with that, but she did attempt to lamely add, "I mean, we're getting a little better about..." She thought about the encounter regarding Diana and her suspension. "Is it not like that here at all?"

Thorn glanced at her sideways, then gestured to themselves pointedly as evidence. They were effort-lessly breathtaking and androgynous. They had both aspects that one would consider handsome and those that could be described as beautiful.

It occurred to Charlotte there had likely been no room for the more toxic ideas around the masculine and feminine in their life... especially if everyone sparkled quite so much as they did. She cleared her throat. "So… if not *that*, why did you run away then?"

"You're a very curious thing, you know that?" It wasn't entirely clear if Thorn was annoyed or endeared by this fact. They turned to lean their elbows and back against the railing of the ship. "My step-father had a lot to do with it. He wasn't too keen on my general existence. Overbearing, abusive, narcissistic creature, and fates help you if you ever crossed him. He would make you regret it… whether it was your fault or not." Their brow furrowed. "I can't say he hated me—I was left living, so I suppose that's proof I did manage to garner some of his compassion, if you can call it that, but he certainly treated me like a burden. Never called me by my real name, just as the 'thorn in his side.'"

"Is that where you got the name?"

Thorn took a moment, their composure shifting. "Well, I've never really seen any bad in the idea of thorns. They protect beautiful things." They smiled at Charlotte. "What's not to like about that?"

Charlotte could feel her cheeks burn slightly, but she held the Fae's gaze. She was not going to be flattered out of getting a straight answer again.

And then it came. "But, I suppose, all things considered… yes. Seemed both a badge of honor and a sort of jab at him…"

Charlotte smiled softly. "What's your real name?"

Thorn pushed off from the railing to begin walking down the ship, keeping to just along the railing so they could retain some semblance of privacy from the rest of the flotilla's occupants. "Ah, that I can't tell you."

"You know mine," Charlotte reasoned, following.

"That was your mistake," Thorn mused.

Charlotte huffed, exasperated. "Come on, tell me."

Thorn stopped to playfully bat around the idea of it. "Hmmm... how about you start guessing, and I'll tell you when you're getting warmer."

"What's the harm in telling me?" Charlotte asked, stopping beside them.

Thorn reached out, gently stroking fingers along the side of Charlotte's face, gliding beneath her jaw to raise her chin ever so slightly toward them. "The things one can do with the name your heart answers to, Charlie," they whispered with a smile.

Charlotte felt her heartbeat stutter. "...I'm not a nightmare," she said quietly.

"But I've still yet to decide if being under your thrall wouldn't be just as dangerous," Thorn lightly traced their thumb over Charlotte's lower lip, closely admiring the flecks of gold in her eyes.

Charlotte could feel her temperature rise, goosebumps spread out across her skin, but she swallowed and somehow found her voice without it shaking. "Does this impossibly charming act come naturally or is it just a defense mechanism when you feel you're at risk of being too vulnerable?"

Thorn blinked and took a self-conscious step back, their hand falling from Charlotte's face.

Charlotte smiled. "Am I getting warmer?"

Thorn simply stared back at her, as if seeing something for the first time, not just in Charlotte, but almost as if they were literally perceiving something they had never truly witnessed before.

Charlotte turned on her heel, feeling a little smug at this small triumph, and continued her line of questioning. "So. Ran away from home to get away from your asshole step-father... what about your mother?"

Thorn felt disoriented enough by the moment prior and the shift in conversation, they didn't much think about the answer before speaking. "She's nothing like him. Their marriage is... It's more one of necessity than affection." Their hands slipped into their pockets for comfort. "I do miss her. Most days. But I think she probably understands. I was feeling suffocated by that life—she could see it—everyone could see it. It wasn't me, honestly. I know I was born into it, but I wasn't made for it—it wasn't the life I wanted. I was never going to be that person, or any sort of person who would have been happy there. And I'm sure my step-father wouldn't have permitted it even if I did manage to find happiness there."

"What kind of life would make you feel *that* trapped and unhappy?" Charlotte asked.

"What about *your* mother," Thorn asked abruptly. "The whole reason you're here, yes? I know she's the famed Hero of Terra Mirum, but what's that to you? You weren't even alive then. Neither of us were. So why is she so special, hmm? Why are you willing to trudge through hell just for a slim chance you might save her?"

Charlotte was dumbfounded by this. "Are you serious?"

"Completely."

"She's... she's my *mother*," Charlotte answered incredulously.

Thorn nodded a little, turning their wrist to illustrate moving past what they saw as simple logic. "Yes, she birthed you, she raised you, for that you are grateful, but you don't owe her the very real possibility of repaying that life as a cost of attempting a rescue."

Charlotte could not wrap her head around this questioning. This was her mother. That seemed logic and reason enough to mount a rescue no matter the cost. "She'd do the same for me."

"She's a mother, it's her duty to protect her child— that's what mothers do," Thorn said simply.

"And this is what *I* do," Charlotte explained. "I *love* her. She's more than just the woman who gave birth to me. She's my best friend, she's my world! I will do anything and everything I can to help her—to bring her back. I can't just abandon her. She's my only family."

Thorn tilted their head slightly to the side. "Last I checked your father was yet still living."

"That doesn't make him family."

Thorn's eyebrows raised. "Touché."

They walked in a few moments of silence, which settled between them unusually comfortably. Thorn's hands folded behind their back; Charlotte fiddled with the pocket watch around her neck.

"Thorn?"

"Hm?"

The question gnawed at Charlotte, and she in turn gnawed at her lower lip. "Can... Can the Coleridge Clock... *erase* people?"

They looked genuinely perplexed by this question. "What?"

"You said I couldn't keep jumping from place to place," Charlotte reasoned. "And before I got here, I sort of... That's exactly what I was doing. Could that erase me? Like from existence?"

Thorn stopped walking, concerned, and gently took hold of Charlotte's arms just above the elbows to turn her towards them. "Do you feel like you're disappearing?"

Charlotte considered the sincerity of the fae. She studied the faint freckles on their cheeks, the soft glow of their skin, and the bright burst of sunshine that surrounded their pupil. She swallowed. "No one knew who I was back home. I went back and even my own godmother didn't recognize me. Not even a little."

Thorn's eyes widened ever so slightly in realization. "Oh, Charlie..."

"*No one* seemed to know who I was, my friends, the jerks from school. I don't... I don't know why. It was like some horrible nightmare where I'd never even existed."

"You're part Dream," Thorn said softly.

"So?"

"You're part Dream and you returned back to the world of dreams. You crossed over to this world... and those who had known you consequently woke from the dream of you."

Charlotte blinked. "What?"

"No more yielding but a dream," Thorn explained rather remorsefully. "Because of what you are, they aren't able to hold the memory of you when you leave their world. The memory faded as if you had been like any other dream."

Charlotte blinked, not daring to move. Had she heard right? So, it wasn't some fluke? She had truly been forgotten, by her friends, by her school... by Diana? And if that were the case, then did that mean... Her mouth felt dry. "So... there's a very real possibility my own mother won't even remember me after I find her?"

Thorn spoke very, *very* softly: "I don't know."

Charlotte's eyes narrowed, searchingly. They were telling the truth. She took a deep breath. "Take me to the Librarian."

"Charlie—"

"You promised," Charlotte growled forcefully.

Thorn was taken aback at first but slowly released Charlotte's arms, then nodded. "You're right. I promised." They nodded down the walkway. "Follow me."

Charlotte followed in silence, down to the lower deck to cross from one ship over a platform to another.

They made their way along the flotilla carefully, and as they began to reach one of the far ships, they could hear music.

Two women were the center of a small group's attention, one playing a lute, the other singing.

The lute player's short purple hair was tousled by the wind, her coloring complimented by the blues that made up her costuming. Around her neck, a snake was happily nestled, keeping warm between the body heat and the scarf loosely draped around her.

The singer was adorned in crimson, black, and gold, and her long hair was an unusually deep blue. As they walked past her, Charlotte could see what looked to be a slight iridescent coloration around the temples of her skin. Her voice was clear, and rich, and for a moment, as she listened, Charlotte forgot what she'd been so worried about moments before. She felt soothed. Safe.

Thorn gently took her hand then and continued to lead her. "Come on, Treasure, focus. We've no time for siren calls."

Charlotte blinked and shook her head slightly, her free hand raising to gently touch her own temple. "S-sorry."

"Don't be. Lark has that effect on people." They led her a little away from the crowd around the two musicians, where another woman was sitting in a nest of books.

She was dressed a great deal more properly than the others. Tweed slacks and a sensible brown vest, and while her blouse was ruffled at the collar, creating an almost ascot-like effect, the sleeves were rolled up to the elbow. Her hair had been swept into a tight bun at the base of her neck, but the winds of the ocean had clearly been tugging at it, as the many small intricate braids that made up the bun were starting to slip out one by one.

Thorn cleared their throat. "Pardon us, Alexandria."

The woman looked up from the book she'd been deeply engrossed in. She blinked and adjusted the spectacles that sat on the bridge of her nose and comically exaggerated her eyes with their magnification when just the right angle was achieved. "Ah, Thorn, how can I…" She looked to Charlotte. "You're very far from home."

Charlotte was surprised but nodded. "I am."

"Did you come for a story?" The Librarian looked about the stack of books around her regretfully. "I'm afraid I do not have quite as many as I used to."

Thorn shook their head. "No, Charlie here needed to ask you a few questions."

Charlotte nervously extended her hand. "Charlotte Carroll… though I suspect you… already know that?"

Alexandria nodded and shook Charlotte's hand gently. "I knew your mother some."

Charlotte's eyes widened. "You did?"

"Our paths crossed." She paused. "I believe they will again."

Charlotte felt a leap of hope in that moment. "You do? Even though she's…"

"Perhaps not in this life," Alexandria mused, "but they will."

Charlotte's shoulders slumped. "My mother is in trouble. She's been dragged into The Nothing."

Alexandria did not react to this news, and Charlotte suspected it was because inexplicably, she already knew this, as well.

"I need to help her."

Nothing.

Charlotte bit her lower lip. "How… do I do that?"

Alexandria blinked. She looked toward an extremely large volume titled *The History of Ever,* but its volume number was so many tiny Roman Numerals Charlotte couldn't see them clearly enough to count them. "That hasn't been written yet."

Charlotte didn't quite understand her meaning. "Is there perhaps knowledge from your library that could assist me in defeating whatever opened the door to The Nothing? Or how to fight a Nightmare? How to tap into my magic as a Changeling?"

Alexandria squinted at her a moment and adjusted her spectacles. "No."

"No?" Charlotte repeated, her eyes widening slightly.

"What you're looking for… It's in the Phrontistery… but it's not a book. You won't find it in any pages."

Anxiety and anger fought their way up Charlotte's throat. "What. Is it?"

Alexandria shook her head. "That I don't know."

Charlotte pursed her lips. "Isn't there anything you can tell me?"

Alexandria squinted again. "Nightmares and fear are inescapably bonded."

Charlotte took a deep breath. "Seriously?" She ran her tongue along her canine, suppressing her frustration. "That's all? You can't help me anymore than that?"

The Librarian shrugged.

Charlotte abruptly walked away, feeling the anger bubbling up inside her. She walked without purpose or direction. She just walked. Quickly. And she continued walking across the deck, over one platform to another until her travels across the flotilla hit a rail that blocked her path to the open sea, and she could walk no further. She fumed, staring off onto the horizon dimly lit by the half moon. Her hands gripped the railing, her nails biting against the metal. "Fuck this!" She yelled off into the horizon.

"...Charlie?" Thorn cautiously approached.

She turned abruptly to face the fae behind her. She focused intensely on them, unable to find a proper channel for the swirling emotions trapped inside her. "If I don't do something *soon*, my mother is going to *die*. Do none of you get that?"

Thorn looked away.

"The one person who has been there for me every step of the way, who fought back *my* nightmares at every turn, and now that I have the chance to literally do the same for her, I can't!" She turned back toward the rail, not sure if she felt sick or if she just felt more balanced when she focused on the horizon. "At least, I can't do it on my own." She shook her head and wiped at her eyes with the back of her hand. "I'm out of my depth, I don't know what I'm doing, and no one, *not even my long-lost father*, the king of Dreamland or whatever, is willing to HELP me!" She slammed the side of her fist down on the railing before letting herself crumple over it.

Thorn calmly leaned their back against the rail beside her, their elbows shifting to rest on the rail itself. They pursed their lips thoughtfully before speaking. "… If you're going to take on The Nothing, you're going to need an army."

Charlotte choked on a laugh. "Great, know where I can get one?" she asked miserably.

Thorn looked down at their boots. "…I might."

Charlotte looked up from her crumpled posture.

"Do you know if your father reached out to Arden?"

"He's not… He mentioned sending word—they hadn't heard back. He didn't seem terribly optimistic about it."

Thorn spit out a laugh. "No, I imagine he wouldn't—he's not a fool, and Oberon isn't known for his generosity of heart. He'd want… *something* in return."

"What sort of something?" Charlotte asked.

"The last time his aid was bought with a life debt."

"A life debt?"

Thorn reluctantly met her eyes. "It's a kinder way of outlining a lifetime of servitude to someone."

Charlotte's eyes widened in recognition, taking in what that meant. Or if it even mattered what it meant. "Okay."

Thorn stared at her. "What? *No.*"

"If it saves my mother—"

"Charlie, you don't know what you're saying—"

"Stop it," Charlotte snapped. "*Please.* I'm tired of being told that I don't know. That something isn't as simple as I'm making it out to be. That I'm just a child, I'm naive. *You* don't know what *I'm* saying, okay? My *world* is crumbling, everything I have ever known, and if I can save even a *shard* of it, even if she doesn't remember me, *if I can save her*, I don't care about anything else."

Thorn was taken aback by the smaller girl before them—the passion in her, the sincerity, the absolute certainty about what she was doing. They raised a hand to their heart subconsciously. "This... really means that much to you?"

"Yes," Charlotte breathed without hesitation.

Thorn calculated, staring off into the horizon, chewing the inside of their cheek before at last nodding decisively and taking Charlotte's hand. "Come with me."

"Where?"

"We're going to steal a boat."

13

SIRENS

They'd snuck back to the galley and packed a bag of food. Thorn had grabbed some spare clothes and retrieved their cutlass—which was the only supply Charlotte took issue with, not that Thorn *had* a weapon, but that *she* did not.

"Do you know how to use a sword?" Thorn asked doubtfully, climbing carefully into the lifeboat.

"What does that matter?" Had been Charlotte's petulant reply.

"A great deal, I assure you," Thorn laughed quietly to themselves. "You might accidentally stab yourself."

"I might accidentally stab myself with a sword?" Charlotte asked in a skeptic whisper. "How would one even do that? It's longer than my arm."

Thorn winked as they took a bag from Charlotte and gingerly placed it in the boat. "How about we get you one of the Bennu ball rackets? You seemed pretty handy with that."

"Great, then I can smack you in the face with it," Charlotte grumbled.

"You know," a new voice purred. "Most people wait to get in a lifeboat *after* the main ship starts sinking. Do you know something we don't?"

Charlotte looked up and caught the gold eyes of the siren from earlier.

The turquoise-haired woman raised a knowing eyebrow at them.

"Are we sinking?" The singer's purple-haired companion peeked around the shorter woman.

"No, Adder, they're stealing a boat."

"*Liberating* a boat," Thorn argued. "Borrowing it, really. We fully intend on bringing it back."

"Don't make me sing the truth out of you, Thorn. Lying does not become you." A part of Charlotte knew this was some kind of threat, yet the longer she listened to Lark's voice, the more she felt her own anxiety dissipating.

"Did you sabotage the flotilla?" Adder queried with a squint. Though a head taller, she was the far less intimidating of the pair.

Lark sighed. "My darling, no one did anything to the ships. I was being facetious."

Adder nodded decisively, then jabbed a finger at Thorn's chest. "Where are you going, hmm? Hmm?"

"Home."

All mirth vanished from Thorn's crewmates. Lark and Adder looked at each other, then to Charlotte, then finally back to Thorn.

"…Why?" was all Adder could manage.

"Because war is devouring the world," Thorn answered. "And as dramatic irony would have it, it seems the only ones who may be able to help us... are the last people I ever hoped to see." They took a deep breath. "So, I'm taking Charlotte to them, and with any luck, we'll survive to see each other again."

Lark focused gold eyes on Charlotte thoughtfully. "You're the one we pulled from the water..."

Charlotte felt a light pull at her neck. She whipped around to see Adder suddenly at her side, the Coleridge Clock shining in the pirate's hand. Her own fingers flew to her collarbone, confirming the necklace was gone.

"Symbol of the Summer court," Adder flashed the clock's design to her companion.

Lark appeared directly before Charlotte—or perhaps Charlotte simply hadn't noticed her move because she found herself unable to look away from the siren's eyes. A hand firmly gripped Charlotte's chin, keeping her gaze from straying away once more, but when the siren spoke, the melody of her voice was so relaxing and soothing, the rough manner in which she was being held captive faded from her notice. "Are you an Emissary? Did they send you here to steal Thorn back?"

"No," the honest answer felt pulled from her tongue more than volunteered. Charlotte wasn't entirely sure who "they" were in this instance, but she couldn't manage to straighten her thoughts out enough to ask.

"Lark, please," Thorn stepped carefully back onto the deck.

The siren turned her gaze to Thorn. She began to sing, though if the tune had words, Charlotte did not recognize the language enough to discern them as such.

A haunting lullaby that incited frisson across her body, and her vision to double and blur, the song seemed to take on harmonies, as if several voices came together to weave a chorus of unseen singers.

Through the haze Charlotte could see Thorn's form, unmoving and frozen in time. Her vision obscured and shifted as if viewing everything through a lens of restless water.

"She's not a threat to us!" Thorn's voice called above waves before a crash on the shore drowned all sound but sea and song.

Charlotte struggled to keep her eyes open. Everything sloshing and out of focus, her body heavy and sluggish. She couldn't remember what she'd been doing.

"Who sent you?" The question was more felt than heard. As if being asked in her own voice, her own mind.

"No one," Charlotte confessed as if it were no more than breathing. "I came on my own."

"What are you?"

Charlotte hesitated, and she could almost feel the answer hit the back of her teeth as she clamped her mouth shut. There was something Captain Lory said she was supposed to do. Or not do. Something she couldn't remember.

Her teeth hurt. Painfully. She could feel every one of them rotting from the word she kept inside her. They felt loose. Were they loose?

"*What. Are. You?*"

The question burned in her heart and exhaled in her ears as the song reached a crescendo and the waves crashed. There were gulls overhead and she was sinking into the sand of the shore. With each breath of the waves, the sand pulled from beneath her, pushing back to build beside and pile on top of her. The beach began to swallow her, shoulders deep in sand as the shore continued to wash over her. Waves crashed against her neck, but she could not bring herself to move, to try to climb free. Everything felt numb and relaxed, content to drown and be buried.

At last, both song and seawater overwhelmed her, filling her lungs with a sting unlike any she'd ever felt. It took hold of the answer the question demanded and ripped it from her.

"Changeling!" the word coughed out of Charlotte violently, and Lark startled into silence. She was back on the boat, standing on wooden blanks and far above the sea water.

The siren recoiled from Charlotte and retreated to Adder, who took this as cue to unplug her fingers from her ears.

Charlotte coughed again; her body still convinced it had been drowning but moments before. She felt dizzy and she teetered, stumbling back against the rail.

Thorn, unhindered now by the siren's magic, was quickly at Charlotte's side, wrapping their arms around her. "I've got you."

"Did… she say what I think she did?" Adder breathed.

"A changeling?" Lark could not bring herself to speak above a whisper.

Thorn brought a hand up to cradle Charlotte's head to their chest. "If you'd given me a moment, I might have explained as much."

"Don't patronize me, Thorn, not now," Lark's voice broke ever so slightly. "Tell us what's going on."

Thorn sighed in defeat. "Charlotte is the daughter of The Hero of Terra Mirum…"

"And the White King," Lark concluded softly, her eyes widening. She looked to the Coleridge Clock still in Adder's hand before meeting the other woman's eyes.

Something unspoken passed between them, and Adder gently kissed Lark's brow in understanding before she offered the pocket watch back to Thorn. "So, you really are leaving of your own free will?"

Thorn nodded and held Charlotte a little tighter. "I am."

Charlotte blinked, finding herself again, the world no longer waving and her stomach settling to a place safely away from the nausea that had set in.

"My people sang songs of you," Lark spoke in an awed whisper, removing the dangling earring of crystal beads and golden feathers from her right ear. "The bridge between mind and matter…" She knelt and took Charlotte's hand in her own reverently. "You are not your mother, daughter of the fearless. Remember that. You were not chosen; you *chose* to act." She closed Charlotte's hand around the earring. "That will be your greatest strength."

Charlotte stared at the siren, speechless. She glanced down at her hand, then back to the unnervingly bright gold eyes that shined so kindly on her now. "…Thank you."

"You should get going," Lark stood with the help of Adder, who was at her side again, "before someone else sees you."

"Agreed." Thorn helped Charlotte into the lifeboat. "You'll delay our departure's discovery as long as possible?"

Adder took hold of the pulley to lower the boat to the water. "Oh, I wouldn't worry about that. We can be *very* distracting."

Thorn snorted and settled in. "Try not to drive Captain too crazy while I'm gone, Adder."

"Nonsense," Adder dismissed. "Captain loves me." She grinned at her companion. "Right Lark?"

The siren smiled cryptically. "Be careful, you two…"

As they descended to the water, they could still hear Adder asking repetitions of the same unanswered question. "I am right, though? Captain loves me. Right? Lark? Right?"

14

SAUDADE

It wasn't until the *Brass Gryphon* and its flotilla was long out of sight that Charlotte dared to speak. She absently turned the feathered earring Lark had gifted her hands. "Do you know what she meant by that? That her people sang songs of me? I mean how is that even possible?"

Thorn looked up in contemplation. "Every culture has their own lore around Changelings. I don't see why sirens would be any different. Human myth, I believe, now has them painted as things fae put in the place of stolen children… which to me sounds like the sort of lie you tell when you don't want to take full responsibility for rotten offspring." When Charlotte didn't laugh at this joke, Thorn smiled encouragingly. "I wouldn't take too much stock in it. You don't need the pressure of legends on your shoulders."

Charlotte nodded, turning the feather over and over in her fingers so that it caught the moonlight.

"You were not chosen, you chose to act," she repeated thoughtfully. "That will be your greatest strength…"

"Well," Thorn reasoned. "There's truth to that at least."

"How do you figure?"

"Nothing brought you here, Charlie. You stormed through the looking glass on your own. You didn't have to come back. You don't *have* to rally an army against The Nothing. You don't *have* to try to save your mother."

Charlotte blinked. "Don't be stupid. Of course, I have to. She's my mother, I love her."

"But no one is forcing you to help her."

"I… well no."

"You chose to," Thorn pointed out.

"I… yes?"

"You don't know much about Alys' time here, do you?" Thorn mused.

"Not really."

"Alys stumbled upon us much the same way you did, as I've heard it told. But she was rather tricked into lending her aid."

"Tricked?" Charlotte asked.

"Let's just say if you wander into any strange offices, and a kindly bespectacled man happens upon you— don't answer any questions. He means well, but it will end very badly for all," Thorn explained, and Charlotte did not quite understand but chose to not push the matter further. "Alys, of course, was seen for what she was—a Dreamer, the ultimate weapon against a

Nightmare and her army. She was a gift of fate. She was chosen. She helped because she had to—and she was never going to leave our world if she didn't. But you…" Thorn produced the Coleridge Clock and offered it. "You could leave any time you wanted."

Charlotte carefully took the pocket watch in hand, examining the broken chain from where Adder had somehow quickly and almost imperceptibly cut it from her. "No one knows me back home anymore—where would I go?" She carefully pried open one of the other links with her fingers to reconnect them again. It hurt, but it was doable.

"Wherever you wanted," Thorn reasoned. "You could easily survive on the other side. And any time you got into too much trouble, you could hop back and forth, and no one would remember you. Clean slate every time."

Charlotte's stomach churned at the thought. "I couldn't do that. It'd be taking advantage of people."

Thorn hummed in amusement. "Oh, Treasure," they smiled. "You would make a truly wretched pirate…"

Charlotte quirked her mouth to the side. "So, you say…" She replaced one of her own earrings with the dangling golden feathers. "But don't I look the part?"

Thorn squinted. "No, not really…" They returned to the compass. "Rather surprised she parted with that, to be honest. Gryphon feathers are not easily come by."

Charlotte's eyes widened. "Gryphon?"

"Well, when you're romancing a siren, what more wondrous thing can you give her than a gift from the sky?" They smiled. "Some legends say they can cure blindness…"

Charlotte frowned. "I'm not blind."

Thorn shrugged. "Well, Lark's a funny thing sometimes. Perhaps she thought it wouldn't hurt if you could see things a little clearer."

She looked at them a moment. Perhaps it was the feather's touch, perhaps it was merely the idea of it, but Thorn seemed a bit less surreal now—more human. "Would your family have really sent someone for you? To drag you back there?"

Thorn shrugged, focused on the horizon. "Possibly. I can't say it hasn't been a fear of mine… that they'd somehow find where I was. When I first saw your clock, it even crossed my mind they might have sent you, at least until I got a better look at you."

Charlotte's brow furrowed. "Adder said this was the symbol of the summer court," she pointed to the engraved flower.

"It is."

"Why would your family be sending an emissary bearing the seal of the summer court?"

Thorn paused. Noticeably. "My family is of the summer court."

"Yeah, but… I'm *of* Seattle. That doesn't mean the mayor sends out a personal search party if I go missing."

Thorn shrugged dismissively. "I wouldn't know the difference in your customs from mine."

"Thorn," Charlotte began skeptically.

"I can see the outline of the shore in the distance," Thorn commented. "We should wait here until the sun rises. Don't want to get too close while it's still night. It will be safer to travel during the day. You should try to get some rest."

The sky was a soft hazy purple when they came ashore. Thorn hopped out into the shallow water to pull the boat further onto the sand, beaching it, before offering a hand to help Charlotte out.

Solid ground felt strange beneath her feet. There was no sway, no bobbing. Just earth. She hadn't realized how much she missed it until she felt her whole-body exhale in relief. "Do you know where we are?"

Thorn peered around at the abandoned beach, then to the rock face along the shore. "Ah!" They pointed to an odd formation in the distance that cascaded water-falls into the ocean. It looked rather like a girl collapsed into tears. "See? I told you." They smiled to themselves, as they oriented their surroundings to a location in their mind. "That means we're… very north of Arden… but still walk-able. Or fly-able, depending, I suppose."

"You know the way?"

"Roughly," Thorn said, shouldering the backpack and bringing out their compass again, "a lot better than you, anyway. We should be able to find our way without too much trouble. Assuming we aren't terribly murdered on the way."

Charlotte exhaled. "Ugh. Brillig."

Thorn blinked. "What did you just say?"

Charlotte felt unsure of herself. "B… brillig?"

A hard stare of confusion. "That's an old fae term. It used to refer to the start of things—the very beginning—when everything was in chaos and mayhem. It doesn't really have a common tongue translation, but it's typically used as a curse these days."

"My mom used to say it."

"Ah."

"…Am I using it wrong?"

"No, no… it's just… it's odd hearing it from an *outsider*."

"Outsider?" Charlotte huffed.

"Those not of the kinfolk," Thorn corrected. "Don't get offended; it's not an insult." They began walking inland, Thorn leading the way.

"Why did you decide to come with me?"

"Would you have preferred I had stayed on the flotilla?"

"No, of course not, but you'd said—"

"So, you're glad I'm here," Thorn glanced over their shoulder.

"I… yes?" Charlotte felt clumsy in her answers.

"You would have missed me if I had stayed behind?" Thorn's voice had lowered to a silken murmur as they took a step toward her, and Charlotte subconsciously reached up to lightly stroke her fingers along the golden feathers hanging from her ear.

"Why won't you answer my question?"

Thorn's smile faded, and their eyes averted. "I have a creed, remember? Don't let cute girls run unprepared into danger." They turned to continue leading through the forest.

"You were just going to *tell me* where I could find the other Changeling. At the time, at least, it seemed rather clear that you weren't going to come with me."

"I saw you play Bennu ball. I became concerned for the general welfare of the Nightmares."

Charlotte rolled her eyes and bumped her shoulder against their arm. "Tell me."

Thorn exhaled through their nose stubbornly, taking a moment to fume about being called out. "It was the way you spoke about your mother."

"How so?"

"I've never heard *anyone* speak so fiercely on behalf of the welfare of someone else. I don't know if you're insane or…"

"Or…?"

"I don't have a word for it, but it… you made me want to help you—if just to understand that kind of loyalty; see it with my own eyes, confirm it can exist. Perhaps help you save it. If I can. I mean, I think I *can*, it's just…" Thorn winced. "Charlotte, there's something I should probably tell you before we reach—"

A low guttural croak drew their attention, a strange sound that generated from the back of the throat. *Jub–jub.*

Thorn froze and instinctively reached for Charlotte's hand, pulling her behind them. "Brillig," they muttered under their breath. "Bloody brillig."

Jub–jub.

Charlotte's eyes darted about, trying to find the source of the sound that had clearly distressed Thorn, and finally looked up.

Sitting on a tree branch, its long legs bent behind it so it could nestle over its strange talon-like feet, was what looked like, to Charlotte, the Shoebill stork from hell. Its enormous black bill resembled an elongated shoe tree, save for the tip, which curved to a sharp point. When the light hit it, it had a gasoline-like sheen, and looking closer, she could see the very edge of the bill where the two halves met was serrated on either side. It fixated on them with milky white eyes. It's raven-like feathers fanned out smoothly along its great head, only to stick up in the back in a feral manner. It loomed, raising its neck just enough to tilt down curiously at them. Its wings expanded a moment, stretching out to show they, too, were terrifying, if there was any doubt. Its throat undulated and croaked out another unsettling *jub–jub.*

"What... is... *that*?" Charlotte whispered.

"Jub-jub bird," Thorn's throat sounded tight as they held Charlotte close to them, almost as if they were preparing for a waltz. "Do me a favor? Think of something happy."

"What?"

"Jub-jub birds feast on tragedy. I don't want it focusing in on you."

Jub-jub. Another eerie and curious head tilt.

Charlotte swallowed. It was as if every happy thought she'd ever had completely vanished from her. Her mother... Even if she survived, she was likely going to be an orphan after all of this...

"*Charlie,*" Thorn warned softly as the bird started to raise up on its legs.

"You just think lovely, wonderful thoughts," Charlotte recited from Peter and Wendy nervously. "And they lift you up in the air."

"What?" asked Thorn.

Charlotte continued to the best of her memory, focusing on reading books and singing songs with her mother beneath the canopy of a blanket fort constructed in the living room. "Beautiful dreamer, wake unto me, starlight and dewdrops are waiting for thee..." Reciting the lyrics to the song shifted to singing. "Sounds of the rude world, heard in the day..."

The bird almost seemed irritated, and it folded its wings back and began to settle down once more.

"Lull'd by the moonlight have all passed away."

"Well, that's one way to keep a jub-jub at bay," said the fae, impressed.

"How would you have done it?" Charlotte couldn't help but feel a little judged.

"Well, I certainly wouldn't have broke into song," Thorn teased, their form visibly relaxing. The pair began to make their way down the path to put more distance between them and the disconcerting avian.

"I just saved our butts through musical intervention—"

"You're right! Crisis averted. Thank you. Truly." Despite their lop-sided smile, Thorn did sound sincere. They gestured behind them with a thumb. "Don't see too many of those around. *Never* good when you do."

"What do you think happened there?" Charlotte asked.

"Hard to say," Thorn said. "They're as peculiar as they are unnerving. They not only linger where a great tragedy has been, but they can also sense where one is to come."

"So… literally emotional vultures."

Thorn bobbed their head. "And it's never clear if they're feeding off what has been… or if you're about to have a very, *very* bad day."

Jub-jub.

Another bird was perched on the low side of a worn wooden sign that had come partially unhinged and sagged to the ground on the bottom right corner. The faded letters read, "Saudade," indicating the name of the town some fifty feet behind it.

Thorn froze, the hair on the back of their neck standing up. They glanced over their shoulder toward the tree and confirmed that the bird they'd encountered before was still there. "Two birds…"

"If we play this right, we should only need one stone," Charlotte joked.

Thorn looked at her, bewildered, didn't know if her levity was out of ignorance of the severity of the situation or if she was trying to maintain the lighter mood as instructed.

Charlotte didn't know either.

Jub-jub.

"This is bad. This is very bad. They don't travel in flocks—it's rare to see two so close together."

"Oh."

"Yeah."

"So… how bad would things have to be for that to happen?" Charlotte pointed past Thorn to the town beyond the sign. Where on every rooftop, countless great jub-jubs perched. The sheer weight of the creatures causing some structures to sag.

"Fates…" Thorn gripped Charlotte's hand tighter.

"What is this place?"

"Somewhere we should leave. We need to get through as fast as possible. If they catch hold of us, we may never leave. Just swallowed by our own personal tragedies until death finally releases us. And even then it will still give them something to feed off of for probably years."

"Tell me something happy."

"What?" Thorn flustered.

"Tell me something happy," Charlotte repeated firmly.

"Charlie, I don't really have…"

"Well, that's bullshit," Charlotte huffed.

"I can't *think* of anything right now."

Charlotte tugged their hand to get them to face her. "Hey." Her free hand pointed from Thorn's eyes to her own. "Eyes on me, focus." She thought a moment, humming "Beautiful Dreamer" to herself again as her mind raced for ideas. Then she stopped humming. Then started again, her hand counting the rhythm. It *sounded* like ¾ time—at least she was pretty sure she could change it to ¾ time even if it wasn't. "Can you dance?"

"What sort of dance?"

"Can you *waltz?*"

They squinted at her doubtfully. "Can *you* waltz?"

"Oh, not a step," Charlotte laughed, and in turn Thorn laughed, almost forgetting the imposing creatures that sat not far from them, let alone the battalion that populated the otherwise seemingly abandoned city of Saudade. "But if you lead, that doesn't seem like it will matter too much for our purposes."

Thorn's mouth quirked in a strange lopsided smile and adjusted their hold around Charlotte, one hand resting at her lower back, the other taking her hand out to the starting position of the dance.

Charlotte's heart fluttered. "Ahem. I'm really sorry if I step on your feet."

"If we get out of here alive, I'll find it in me to forgive you," Thorn commented wryly. "Besides, it will make me laugh, and that only works in our favor."

Charlotte nodded and began to sing again. "Beautiful dreamer, wake unto me."

And Thorn led them toward the entrance of the town, twirling to the rhythm of Charlotte's voice.

"I think you're off-beat," Thorn suggested gently.

"Probably am, but what can I say?" Charlotte sang along her reply to the tune. "Who cares if it keeps the nightmares away?"

Thorn snerked. Thankfully they were much better at dancing than Charlotte was at keeping rhythm and in spite of everything, they were able to keep to a count in their own head.

It created a blur of the world around them save for the town exit through the main street, which served as their focus for spotting as they turned. The danger seemed to melt away into a mess of color. There was no town, there were no birds of prey, there was only spinning and song and lyrics and—

The ridiculousness of the situation began to strike Charlotte, and her singing broke with laughter; giggles interrupting her words so that the actual melody was scarcely recognizable as they spun. It dissolved into loud trumpet like "la da da"s and a mix of lyrics that in the haze she was starting to forget despite having it repeated so often in childhood.

"Something and something, and other words here…"

Her laughter was infectious, Thorn catching it not long after it had begun. It was boisterous, joyful, and delightfully unrefined. "If we're together, there's nothing to fear."

Charlotte smiled at this addition, and despite that neither were singing in that moment, she could have sworn she'd heard music.

Had the two been able to see the great mass of birds, they'd have caught an avian disgust cross each one of them, as if beholding something rather unpalatable. And as the couple danced through the main street, they created a wave of jub-jub birds slowly turning their backs to them, being forced to look away to keep the nausea from taking hold.

At last, after Charlotte was certain she had accidentally stumbled over Thorn's poor feet for the millionth time, they broke past the last building and stumbled into the woods. Their laughter subsided to wheezes. But though their pace slowed, the waltz itself continued forward even after its necessity was over.

"That was bizarrely fun," Thorn admitted, glancing at the dilapidated town.

"I didn't know you could cover so much ground that way—I'm surprised people don't do waltzing races for the Olympics," Charlotte sighed as her adrenaline dissipated.

Thorn smiled. "That was... absolutely brilliant. Thank you."

Charlotte giggled sheepishly. "Thank Louis Armstrong."

"I don't know who that is."

"This world has truly failed you," Charlotte deadpanned.

"What?" Thorn laughed.

Charlotte released them so they could walk side by side. "Lois Armstrong, phenomenal Trumpet player, iconic voice, literally one of the most influential figures in Jazz." Thorn's expression showed no sign of recognition, so she added, "...and a powerful Dreamer if I had to guess."

"We don't catalogue all Dreamers over here," Thorn mused, "just the ones who somehow manage to make it past our borders."

"Shame," Charlotte tsked. "Missing out."

"You're a fan of his work, I take it?"

"Mom is. She said his voice may not be typical for crooning, but she always thought it had a kind of magic to it. It could 'take you there', whatever that means. But the song has been around since like... the 1800s? Been recorded by a lot of the greats... But mom liked Louis."

"It's an oddly...fitting song," Thorn remarked carefully.

"Feels a little ironic," Charlotte acknowledged. "She used to sing it to me when I was little to get me to sleep... There's a music box in my room that plays it, even. Beautiful Dreamer, wake unto me... I wish it were that easy."

"We should try not to linger on that," said Thorn. "At least until we're sure those damn birds are far behind us."

Charlotte glanced back at Saudade. "What do you think happened there? Or *is* going to happen there?"

327

"That many jub-jub birds in one location and not a person in sight?" Thorn asked. "It would have had to be some kind of massacre..."

"The Nightmares?"

"No... something worse. People have been gone for a long time, yet so many birds still have something to feast on. Though how something so horrible could happen and no one know about it, I'm not sure."

"Maybe they've been magically forbidden to speak about it."

"Magical bans aren't that commonplace, Charlie," Thorn dismissed with a playful hand squeeze.

"I'm not suggesting it's a different one," Charlotte insisted conspiratorially. "Entire town gets massacred... that'd certainly be something you'd want to shut people up about, right?"

"Why would Oberon want to cover up the massacre of an entire town of Dreams? That's at best an act of malicious negligence on Terra Mirum—it violates the treaty. It could start another war."

"The reason you said," Charlotte said excitedly. "Because he had a key hand in it, and he wants to hide his shame rather than admit he did something wrong! You said he doesn't regret easily—if hundreds of people died because of him, that seems like something big enough to get even your King of Shadows to feel regret."

"He's not *my* King of Shadows," Thorn said rather abruptly. "And he may be a right narcissistic and selfish

328

asshole, but he wouldn't slaughter hordes of helpless people."

"Well, maybe not directly," Charlotte pointed out.

"No. Not even indirectly. He's… He's terrible, but he's not a murderer."

"Fine." Charlotte chewed the inside of her cheek thoughtfully. "I guess we'll never know…"

The trees were starting to change as they walked. There were more autumnal leaves on the ground, and as the sunlight hit them, they seemed to glow and glitter.

"The Amber Groves," Thorn breathed in recognition. "We're getting closer to the outskirts."

"Of what?"

"Arden. Which means our Changeling friend should be nearby."

Charlotte ran her fingers over her thumb in slow soothing circles, starting with the index and moving down to the pinky and back again. "Are you nervous to go back?"

Thorn touched one of the trees, then examined a large hole beside it where someone had uprooted one. They peered around and took note of a few similar holes, some of which had been covered over with dirt, but not enough to fully raise the divot. "They've been moving the trees."

"Why would they do that?"

"They absorb sunlight and glow throughout the night. Arden must be fortifying its walls with light sources that won't strain resources. That's good."

"Because it means it will be a safe place for us?"

"Because it means they're scared," Thorn said. "The key to getting help from Arden will be convincing Oberon it's in his best interest to join with your father again against the Nightmares. Compassion, the man doesn't much understand, but self-preservation? That's his native language." Thorn patted one of the trees thoughtfully. They drew their sword, calculating. Every now and then they would stop, examine a smaller branch, and whisper something to the tree before using their blade to cut it off.

"So, when I speak to Oberon, the thing to focus on is *him*?"

"Always." Thorn handed a branch to Charlotte. "Don't talk about your mom, don't talk about the other Dreamers, or even Terra Mirum—make it clear why *he personally* should want to help you. How *he'll* be in danger if he doesn't." Three more branches were passed to Charlotte's arms.

"That almost sounds like a threat."

Thorn shrugged, not really arguing with this assessment, and cut a fourth branch to pile on. "At all costs, avoid wording it as a threat... but that's essentially what it is." They sheathed their blade.

"So, don't *threaten* him, but threaten him."

"More or less."

"Great," Charlotte looked at the softly glowing branches in her hands and held them up. She was mesmerized briefly, a smile curling involuntarily. "What are these for?"

"They hold their abilities for a few days after being severed. We can make circlets out of them. A little added protection from the night."

"Ah…" Charlotte looked from the branches in her arms to Thorn curiously. "You never answered my earlier question."

"Which?"

"Are you nervous about going home?"

"Ah. Yes. That was intentional."

"I thought you didn't dodge," Charlotte tried to wheedle.

"No, I *said* I didn't dodge. There's a difference," Thorn clarified.

"What difference?"

"One is an act, the other is a lie."

Charlotte huffed. "I tell you things."

"That's your choice."

"I just saved your life."

Thorn pursed their lips and sighed, turning back to her. "Yes, alright? Yes, I am nervous." Admitting it out loud caused anger to spur them on. "I am absolutely terrified if I step foot into Arden, I'm never going to be able to leave again. I nearly died the last time I clawed my way out of there, and I'm not looking forward to the idea that if I am forced to do it all again, I may not actually make it."

Charlotte's brow furrowed, and she felt a pit forming in her stomach. She took a hesitant step toward them. "I'm sorry, I didn't…" She shifted the branches to one arm so she could reach out to take their hand. "I won't let any of that happen, I promise."

Thorn's lopsided smile half-heartedly returned. "I appreciate the sentiment, Treasure, but I'm afraid there wouldn't be much you could do about it."

Charlotte stood a little straighter. "In what I *think* are the past 48 hours, I've hopped through worlds, committed breaking and entering, been locked in a dungeon, survived a shipwreck, smashed a window using what I can only imagine is priceless art, and evaded palace guards. There's no telling what I might be capable of."

Thorn guffawed. "Alright, you're a loose cannon."

"I get it. I'm off the force. I'll turn in my badge and my gun."

Thorn blinked. "You are a strange one, Charlie Carroll."

"If you were from my side, you'd be able to appreciate how hilarious I am."

"I'll take your word on it—ah." Thorn pointed ahead to a cozy cottage nestled into the trees. "There we are."

"…That's Arden?"

Thorn laughed and shook their head. "No. It's my brother's house. Well, step-brother."

"Is your step-father here?"

"Fates, no, I'm actually happy to be *here*." They squeezed Charlotte's hand and pulled her toward the house. "We'll be safe here. Nothing to worry about just yet." They knocked on the door.

But the woman who answered was not whom Thorn was expecting, and clearly, *they* were not whom *she* was expecting. She was small in frame, almost boyish in her litheness, but her face was beautiful and sprite-like. But despite that Charlotte could see she was also fae, she did not carry the same unearthly glow about her that Thorn did. Her hair was a mix of browns, golds, and reds, but in this light, the strands had an almost orange hue. Two small horns poked out of either side of her head, and it took Charlotte a moment to realize she *knew* who this was. She could hear Alys' words in her head, and the wistful way she had said, "favor for a friend."

Charlotte's eyes widened, and her heart quickened.

"Princess?" Puck gasped from the doorway.

Thorn shot a look to Charlotte and back again. "Heeeey… Robin, I didn't know you'd be…" They awkwardly cleared their throat. "Is Smoke home?"

15

FRIENDS OF THE FAMILY

Robin nodded vaguely in response to the question but seemed still rather stumped by their mere presence. "Why are you… *How* are you—"

"We would be doing better if we were permitted to come inside out of the soon-to-be Nightmare-infested forest," Thorn pointed out kindly.

Robin blinked, then awkwardly stepped aside to allow them to pass. "Of course, forgive me…"

Thorn gestured with their head for Charlotte to follow them inside. "Thank you."

Robin bowed her head out of habit, then paused. "I don't understand—how did you get here? Where have you been? Does your mother know you're here?"

Thorn flinched. "No, but not to worry—she will soon enough."

Robin's attention finally moved to Charlotte, and there it stopped dead as if she'd just laid eyes upon a ghost. "You…"

"So, you and Charlie have already met?" Thorn asked.

Robin's head snapped to Thorn. "Charlie?" Then to Charlotte. "Charlie."

"Hi," Charlotte greeted meekly.

"Your name… is *Charlie*?" Robin looked Charlotte up and down so intensely, Charlotte thought a hole might burn through her.

"Yes?"

"Charlie," Robin repeated for clarity, the name almost growling out of her now at this point.

"Charlotte, but Charlie…" Charlotte offered helpfully. Her mother had called her a friend, or at least *alluded* that Robin had been a friend… "I think you knew my mother?"

Robin's face fell with the confirmation, and she sighed with a shake of the head. "That's what I was afraid of."

Thorn cleared their throat. "I'm confused."

"So am I," Robin said hopelessly. She shook her head and finally closed the door. "Fates, this does complicate things."

Thorn's eyes widened. "Oh. You *didn't* know."

"No," Robin slowly turned back to face them. "I did not."

"Nobody knew," Charlotte both offered and explained.

"*Nobody* knew," Robin scoffed.

"My mother kept it a secret, even my father didn't know I existed until… a day ago? A few days ago?"

"Does *your mother* know where you are?" Robin asked exasperated.

Charlotte's face fell.

"Alys is sick like the rest of them," Thorn explained gently.

"How is that even possible?" Robin asked without thinking. "Nothing from this side should be able to touch her—"

"She had a changeling," explained Charlotte. "It's *my* fault."

"Robin, I heard the door… Is someone…" The rustling of brocade stopped as Rosalind paused in the doorway to take them all in. The Duchess paused, confused at the newcomers. She was a tall, willowy woman, her hair left natural and wild, gold wisps intermingled with the dark curls that dangled just above her collarbones. She was briefly taken aback by the sight of Charlotte, a hand raising to rest on her chest. "Aislynn?"

Charlotte's gaze shifted sharply to face Rosalind at the name. Her middle name—no, her *grandmother's* name.

Rosalind's glossy eyes dried, and she shook her head as she got a better look at her guest. "Forgive me. At first you looked just like… It must be the light."

"Or the blood," Robin answered dryly.

Rosalind's brow furrowed, and she looked from Robin to Charlotte, her expression relaxing in a sort of amused realization. "It's getting dark. I suggest we all retire to the firelight. There is clearly much to discuss."

Charlotte swallowed, feeling a sense of anxiety come over her as the elegant woman departed. Were they also going to attempt to send her back? Could they even do that? They hadn't asked about the Coleridge Clock. Perhaps if she kept it hidden...

Thorn nudged her knuckle with their own, and she looked down at their hands before she accepted theirs, linking their fingers tightly. "It's alright," they whispered. "You're going to be safe here."

Charlotte wasn't particularly concerned with her own safety. She had neglected to explain to Thorn that she had already been in a safe location, that she had fled the castle in favor of rescuing her mother.

As they traveled down the hall, Charlotte realized the lights that came from the sconces weren't candle-light at all but rather clipped branches and leaves like the ones cradled in her arms.

It was a short walk, but to Charlotte, the uncertainty made it feel like a gauntlet. She glanced from Thorn to Robin, but neither said anything more until they stepped through the large open archway into a den filled with bookshelves. It was lined with branches, giving it a warm and protected feeling of illumination, a hundred nightlights against the darkness. Could this be the same library from her dream? No, it was far too comforting. The look of it coaxed a smile from Charlotte, drawing her attention upward along the large shelves so much that she barely heard Thorn speak her name.

"Charlie, this is Smoke, my brother. Well, sort of."

"In all ways that actually matter," Smoke assured Thorn. He was a tall man, but despite his clearly corporeal form, there was something about him that seemed insubstantial, as if she couldn't quite focus on him. Perhaps it was how he was backlit by the roaring fireplace behind him, or that something about the room was stinging her eyes. He handed a small bundle cradled in his arms to Rosalind. He was a wash of grey, from his hair to his clothing. Even his eyes were a piercing pale steely grey that made her feel on edge.

Charlotte took a self-conscious step backward. Was this... the man from her dream?

"You would be Charlie?"

Charlotte released Thorn's hand, holding the bundle of branches to her chest protectively. Neither he nor the elegant woman beside him had been present for her name. "Y-yes?"

Smoke took a few careful strides toward her and dropped to his knee to get a better look at her. "You look just like her."

"The late Queen?" Charlotte asked.

"Your mother," Smoke answered warmly, and the genuine admiration in his eyes was so disarming that Charlotte felt the tightness in her chest release.

"You knew her?"

"Very well."

"Did... did she tell you about me?" Charlotte asked hesitantly, wondering if she had finally met someone on this side that her mother had felt safe to confide in.

Smoke shook his head with a sad smile. "Not in so many words, but... I knew."

"You *knew*?" Robin asked, infuriated.

"You're starting to sound like your husband with all that indignation, Goodfellow."

"Smoke, I swear—" Robin started.

"What would you have had me do, Robin?" Smoke asked gently. "I owe my love and my life to that woman—*as do we all.*" He let that point hang in the air a moment. "What in this world do I have any right to deny her if it harms no others?"

"It *does* harm others," Robin protested, and Charlotte flinched at her vehemence. "Allowing a Dreamer into Terra Mirum—"

"Was our *only hope* last time, if you recall," Smoke said calmly.

Robin's lips pursed. "Last time we got lucky."

Smoke ignored her. "Tell me, Charlie, are there any other of your mother's traits you happen to share? Her particularly strong talents in The Dreaming, by chance?"

Charlotte shrugged, feeling like she was somehow simultaneously tempting fate and letting people down. "I really don't know."

"Think," Smoke encouraged. "Has anything unusual happened since you came to Terra Mirum?"

Charlotte squinted at him. "…You're kidding, right?"

"Beyond what is natural to *this* world. It could be the smallest thing. Something you barely noticed at the time, but if you *really* thought about it, it wouldn't quite add up." Smoke's eyes narrowed on her, and Charlotte felt uncomfortable with the palpable scrutiny. "You would have been desperate for an outcome, so desperate that when you got it, you were too grateful to question that perhaps you *shouldn't* have received it."

Charlotte remembered the hedge. Had she moved it? Or was there something about that place? She had thought in the moment that it seemed to move very coincidentally with her fear to keep from getting caught. And then there was her second entrance into Terra Mirum, submerged so deep in the Pool of Tears. How did her air never run out? She had been down there far too long to last on one breath—especially as she had never been particularly adept at such a thing. "I... think I breathed underwater?"

Robin was visibly worried, but the other three seemed intrigued.

"I was stuck in this... sunken ship in the Pool of Tears. I had to break myself out, but... I hadn't even had a chance to take a deep breath—I hadn't been prepared to end up underwater. But I had the energy and strength to break out and get to the surface." The words spilled out of Charlotte's mouth as the realization dawned on her. "In fact, I'm certain at one point when I was kicking a hole to escape, I breathed *in*." Her eyes widened. "Did I do that? Is that... Is that my power? Or can most people breathe underwater here like you do when you're dreaming?"

"Dreamers can breathe underwater when they're dreaming," Smoke corrected. "To us who live in Terra Mirum, it is no different than how you experience water in your world. Well, unless you're born with gills, or water magic."

"Don't forget you also glowed when we found you," Thorn reminded, and Smoke puzzled at this. "Like a beacon. Big pillar of light from the sky. Led us right to her. Found her half-drowned and dehydrated."

Smoke looked back to Charlotte, impressed. "You sent out a distress signal…"

Charlotte's head felt light and spinning. "What… else can I do?"

"Let's not explore that, shall we?" Robin interrupted.

Smoke waved a dismissive hand. "The thing to remember, Charlie, is while you're here, this may not be *your* dream, but it is *a* dream. If you can convince yourself of something, you can make it happen."

"Smoke," Robin warned.

"There are, of course, *consequences*, so the bigger your wish, so to speak, the bigger impact you could have on our entire ecosystem and way of life," the man in grey winked.

"Stop it!" Robin snapped.

The bundle in Rosalind's arms began to cry.

Everyone grew still as Rosalind calmly moved closer to the fire to rock and coo.

"What is wrong with you?" Smoke snapped at Robin in a hushed tone.

"We don't know the extent of her powers, Smoke," Robin warned. "You don't know what she could do."

"Excuse me?" Charlotte folded her arms.

"Dream magic is *volatile*. It's unpredictable—it… it requires an incredible level of discipline we can't even begin to fathom. Even the smallest spell could have a ripple effect."

Smoke clicked his tongue. "You know something you aren't telling me."

"I know a *lot* of things," Robin seethed. "Whether I can speak them or not, it would be in your best interest to heed my warnings."

The man paused, took a deep breath, and considered this, before speaking with a more level, gentle tone. "Robin, I, too, have a Dreamer in my parentage, if you have not forgotten…"

"Your father and Alys are two very different Dreamers, Smoke."

"Be that as it may—"

"It *broke* him."

"And Alys remains intact, despite the crown's efforts to stifle her."

Robin looked scolded. "We did what we had to."

"I'm not arguing the practical facts of preserving millions of lives, old friend, merely making a point that the whole picture not be ignored," Smoke intoned. "She's strong—there is no debating that. Perhaps that strength has been passed down. Perhaps I could teach Charlie how to use it, how to harness her power—not be a danger to herself or those around her. To *help* us."

Robin shook her head. "It's too risky."

"Now is the *time* to be risky."

Robin turned to Charlotte. "Does the King know where you are?"

Charlotte's gaze dropped, her stomach churning. "I sort of… ran away."

Robin scoffed. "I won't have lost all respect for him, then."

"Robin—" but the fae silenced Smoke with a raise of her hand.

"What exactly were you expecting to accomplish?" Robin demanded of Charlotte.

The young girl tightened her hold on the branches in her arms. "To convince the Fae Courts to fight against the Nightmares?"

Robin rapped her fingers against her own arm. "Not the most idiotic of plans, considering, but the bar is rather low." Robin shot a glare at Smoke. "And how did you propose to convince The King of Shadows that it would be worth the effort?"

"I would explain what's going on," said Charlotte.

"There is no possible way he doesn't know what is going on already. What will you bargain with?"

Charlotte blinked. "Doesn't he stand to lose as well if he doesn't help Terra Mirum?"

Robin shrugged. "Perhaps. Fae born aren't susceptible to corruption in the same way Dreams are. Perhaps he's still sore about losing so many years ago. It would be one way of expanding his kingdom—to wait for the Nightmares to wipe out the Dreams first." Her tone was so light, so easy, so callous.

Charlotte whispered, "How could he?"

"Because he's a bitter creature still sore that humanity has all but pushed Fae back into the Dream for good," Robin spat. "As your civilization grew, it pushed through the forests; the wilderness that Oberon feels belongs to the Fae and the Fae alone—because Dreams denied him his conquest of Terra Mirum."

"Wouldn't that be a violation of their treaty?" Charlotte looked to Thorn for confirmation. "Malicious neglect at best?"

"Hard to hold someone accountable for a treaty if you're all dead," Smoke offered gravely.

"…He would let this world die just to claim more land?" Charlotte asked incredulously.

"Pride makes great fools of us all," Robin growled.

Smoke coughed in a cadence that suspiciously sounded like, "You're one to talk."

Charlotte looked from person to person, feeling her glimmer of hope being snuffed out. "How did my mother do it?"

"Partly by pointing out his own precarious situation, partly by essentially selling my soul," Smoke explained. His fingers splayed in the air, and in a plume of mist, a cigarette formed between them.

"It's you!" Charlotte pointed squarely at Smoke's nose, causing him to look cross-eyed. "The life debt— you're the one Thorn was talking about!"

Smoke looked to Thorn. "Darling, were you talking of me?" He preened, running his hand through his hair vainly. "Whatever they said, I can assure you it's all slander and lies…or absolute fact and understated." He frowned and glanced sidelong at Thorn. "Wait, what did you say?"

Thorn smiled mirthlessly through gritted teeth. "She was going to sell her life to Oberon to save her mother—what did you expect me to say? You were my cautionary tale."

"…How disappointing," Smoke deflated. "And entirely lacking in poetry and gravitas." He took a long drag of his cigarette.

"Is this life so bad?" Charlotte gestured to the cottage. "You seem happy here."

"Here, yes. But so little of me *is* here," said Smoke.

"Oaths are dangerous things, child—especially those to Oberon," snarled Robin.

"You said I needed something to bargain with. What have I got to lose?" Charlotte demanded.

"More than you can possibly imagine," said Robin.

"The only thing I *have* to lose will *be* lost," countered Charlotte. "Without her, I have nothing!"

"And yet still, Oberon will take more from you!" Robin scolded. "When you are hollowed out and lost, and have become *Nothing*, still he will take. And take. And TAKE."

"You're not listening to me!" Charlotte cried.

"Nor should we. You do not know what you invoke."

"Don't talk down to me like I'm a child!" Hot tears were streaming down Charlotte's face. Her chest was tight. Burning.

"YOU ARE A CHILD!"

"SHUT UP!" The branches in Charlotte's arms burst into flames as she let out a feral wail halfway mixed between rage and despair.

The others shielded their eyes from the brightly glowing embodiment of fury that stood in Charlotte's place.

The baby's wailing joined Charlotte's howls of helplessness.

"It's okay, it's okay, Imani. Hush, little one... She's simply scared. It will be okay," Rosalind attempted to soothe her infant.

Hearing a mother's assurances extinguished Charlotte's flame. The light was gone as quickly as it had come, and embarrassment took its place. Her eyes wet, cheeks stained with tears, she looked to Robin. "Please. I have to help her."

"Smoke," said Robin, stonefaced.

Smoke shook himself, struggling to regain his composure. "I'm alright." He patted down his sleeves as if expecting to find embers.

"You have one day," Robin warned. "Don't waste it."

Charlotte wiped at her eyes. "What happens after one day?"

Robin closed in on the girl. "*Don't*. Waste it."

16

TRUST

Charlotte was curled up on the window seat on the first floor. The fire was still roaring, and she was wrapped in blankets, surrounded by pillows. She closed her eyes but could still see the light through her eyelids. She rolled on her side and pulled the blanket over her head, but that was too warm. She pulled the blankets back in a fluster. Nothing felt right.

"Now I know how Goldilocks felt." Her eyes focused on the woodgrains of the ceiling above her and the way the light danced off them. Her brow relaxed. It vaguely reminded her of drifting off while watching movies on the couch, seeing the different colored lights play against the walls and ceiling. She bit her lower lip and tried to focus on her breathing. Inhaling for five, exhaling for 6. Inhale, one, two, three, four, five. Exhale, one, two, three, four, five, six…

It wasn't helping, and she sat up once more to look out the window. If there was anything out there, she couldn't see it. And that made her so much more nervous. Should she be so close to the window? Was it dangerous? Her eyes adjusted to focus on her own reflection in the black glass.

"I'd have thought you'd be passed out by now," Thorn mused from the entrance into the hall. "You've had quite a day."

"It's too bright."

"Protective measure." Thorn sat by her legs on the edge of the window seat. She could see their faint reflection in the window.

Charlotte sat up further and drew her knees closer to her chest. "From whatever might be lurking in the shadows?"

"It could be anything out there."

"Then who's to say it's bad?" Charlotte finally looked from their reflection to their form. "It could be *anything*."

"So, you think, what? This whole invasion of Nightmares is just a big misunderstanding?"

Charlotte shrugged. "Maybe."

"Were the world so sweet, Treasure," wished Thorn.

"Have a little hope, Highness," Charlotte urged.

Thorn's gaze whipped to her, and Charlotte thought she saw a hint of fear in their eyes. "What did you…? How did you… How long have you known?"

"Robin didn't know who I was," Charlotte said softly.

Thorn looked even more puzzled.

"When she opened the door, she said 'Princess'— but she didn't even see me until we'd gone inside—so she couldn't have meant me. Then I met Smoke, and the way you both talked about Oberon—quick to slander and distance yourselves, yet also defend his character—that kind of polarizing loyalty can only mean family." She shrugged with a small smile. "It's not the longest voyage to connect those dots."

Thorn rubbed the back of their neck sheepishly.

"I take it Robin hadn't seen you in a while."

"I'm going to have to be more careful what I say around you. You actually *listen*."

"I'm not an idiot."

"I never thought you were."

Charlotte glared doubtfully.

"Not wanting you to sell yourself into bondage has nothing to do with my opinion on your intelligence," Thorn grumbled.

"If it helps my mother—"

"Yes, I know," Thorn sighed. "And it would. But perhaps we should consider less eternally damning solutions before resigning ourselves, hmm? Quick solutions are rarely the best."

Charlotte's expression crumpled.

"I know you blame yourself for your mother's current predicament, Charlie, but throwing yourself to the wolves isn't going to make you feel any better about it."

The young girl folded her arms and slumped back to stare out the window again. "If something happens to her, I'll never forgive myself."

"It will be okay."

"You don't know that."

Thorn shrugged. "You'll just have to trust me."

"Bit of a double standard, don't you think?" Charlotte asked.

They sighed. "Then you *are* angry with me." They bobbed their head in resignation. That's fair, I deserve that."

"I'm not angry."

"I was going to tell you."

Charlotte rolled her eyes.

"I was! There just wasn't… a lot of… time?"

"Yes, the hours of rowing through an empty ocean were particularly bereft of reprieve," she sarcastically agreed.

"It's not who I am anymore—it didn't seem relevant."

"Not relevant that our plea for aide was going to be a really awkward family reunion? Or were you going to skip out on that?"

"I wasn't going to abandon you," Thorn said firmly. "Not to Oberon, not to anyone." They raked their fingers through their hair and sighed. "I'm sorry." They rested a hand on Charlotte's knee. "I was scared, and I let that be my compass."

Charlotte layered her own hand over theirs and met their eyes. "Me too."

"No more secrets," Thorn promised.

She chuffed a laugh.

Thorn studied their hands a moment, mulling something over in their mind. They swallowed before offering, "Learic. My real name is Learic."

Charlotte blinked, genuinely taken aback by this offering.

"You're worth trusting, Charlie," they explained, giving her hand a little squeeze. "I hope you'll feel the same about me and believe me when I say we can get through this with all of our personal freedoms intact." The glint in their eyes danced in the soft glow of the firelight.

Charlotte sucked on the inside of her cheek a moment before sighing and nodding in agreement. "I trust you... *Learic.*"

Thorn glowed a little brighter. "There. See? Now we're a little closer, and a little stronger."

"Would you prefer I call you it?"

"Treasure, you may call me whatever your heart desires."

Charlotte coughed. "No—I mean—is it—are you *comfortable* with that name? I mean, you haven't gone by it since you left, right?"

Thorn outright laughed as they flustered and ran a hand suavely through their hair. "I like Learic. It suits me. It has music. I just prefer most people don't use it. It feels too..."

"Formal?"

"Intimate."

Charlotte swallowed. She needed a glass of water. "I'll just... stick to Thorn then," her voice cracked.

"As you wish." They winked and reached past Charlotte, their arm grazing her cheek.

"…What are you…"

"This should help you sleep." Thorn sat back, showing the sash that had pinned back the curtains. They carefully tied it around her eyes like a blindfold.

"Oh…" Charlotte felt her face burn as she nestled back down. "Thank you."

A kiss gently pressed to her forehead. "Goodnight, Charlie."

"Goodnight," Charlotte echoed, listening to their retreating footsteps. "…Learic."

17

PERSONAL GROWTH

Charlotte awoke the next morning long after the sun had risen. She'd slept soundly for perhaps the first time since before she could remember without the aid of sleep deprivation and near dehydration. The sun was happily filtering through the window she'd curled up against, casting rays on her eyes so intensely she could no longer ignore them. It was a strangely peaceful way to wake and seemed a stark contrast against the threat that had lurked in the dark unseen the night before.

Charlotte found she was the last to rise, and Robin had left at first light. She nibbled a little on some bread before Smoke promptly took her by the crook of her elbow and led her outside with Thorn not long behind.

"But I haven't had breakfast," Charlotte complained.

"Breakfast is for people who rise early enough to eat it," Smoke dismissed. "We've already wasted hours. You can eat when we've made progress."

Charlotte glowered at him. "A bit strict, aren't we?"

"While you are untrained, Charlotte, you are a literal danger to yourself and those around you. Leniency is really not a concern of mine at this time."

Charlotte was a little taken aback. "But last night you were defending me."

"And then you nearly burned my home down." Smoke smoothed down the front of his tunic. "You should be given a chance to prove yourself. That does not, however, make Robin's cautions any less valid or troubling." He paused. "Just don't told her I said so." The lanky grey-toned man stood at his full height and examined Charlotte, taking a deep breath. He spoke more to himself than to either of the teenagers in his company. "Now… the first thing we should determine is your limitations…"

"My limitations?" Charlotte echoed with a furrowed brow.

Smoke nodded, tapping his knuckle to his chin thoughtfully. "For instance, my magic is fairly self-contained. I can manipulate my own shape, but not anything around me."

Charlotte's head cocked to the side. "What about the cigarette?"

Smoke shook his head and gave a dismissive fluid wave of his hand. "That's an illusion."

"So… it's not real?"

"Not at all. It's rather akin to chewing one's nails."

"So, it's a *nervous* habit?"

Smoke paused, raising an eyebrow almost indignantly. "Nervous?"

"Something you do when you're feeling on edge." Charlotte looked skeptical. "You're telling me you *never* get nervous? Ever?"

Smoke slowly squinted at the small girl, his lips pursing. "Are you always this irritatingly perceptive?"

"*Yes*," Thorn blurted out, startling the other two's attention to them.

Smoke rolled his shoulders back with some authority and cleared his throat. "Point being, it's an extension of myself of sorts—it's not really an object appearing out of thin air—it is air, and only I could interact with it. By that same right, I cannot shift the shape of anything but myself. I cannot make something out of nothing. *You* said you breathed underwater. That would also be an instance where your power was limited to be within yourself. Kicking the ship would be a matter of strength that perhaps your powers also could have aided."

"And the *fire*?" Thorn asked.

"Trust me, I haven't forgotten the fire." Smoke cleared his throat again. "All of these are fortifying you—reactive, and protective, but remain within you rather than manipulating anything outside of your form. Yes, the branches caught fire, but because *you* caught fire. So, it would stand to reason you might have the similar limitations, as I do—which, undoubtedly, will be a relief to Robin."

Charlotte remembered the hedge maze and felt a prickling in her stomach. "...*Well*..."

"Well?" Smoke prompted warily.

"I don't know if I really did it," Charlotte dismissed, feeling hot spots along her skin as her anxiety spiked, like a sunburn that wasn't there.

"Did what?" Smoke urged.

"It could have been a coincidence," Charlie took a step back with a shrug and awkward laugh.

"Did *what*, Charlie?" Smoke demanded quietly.

"I moved a hedge!" Charlotte threw her hands up defensively. Then, she shrunk a little and spoke softer. "Maybe. *I think*. I don't know."

Smoke blinked.

"I was being chased through the castle grounds, and I almost got caught in the hedge maze, and the hedge just... moved."

Thorn whistled. "Unless that hedge is the friendly cousin of the brambles that surround Arden's castle..."

"Trust me," Smoke began, his voice low and without any sign of the mirth it seemed to normally carry. "It isn't. Quite mundane in terms of plant life, I'm afraid..." He gave Charlotte a hard stare. "You say it *moved*. How did it move? Could it have been the wind?"

"A whole panel shifted. It blocked off one of the guards from reaching me and gave me access to the exit."

Another low whistle from Thorn. "Definitely not the wind."

"Do you remember what you were feeling?" The tall man inquired quietly.

"Scared they'd catch me."

"And when you escaped the sunken ship?"

\   "Scared I was going to drown."

Smoke's lips were pressed so tightly together they vanished entirely into a mere thin line before he spoke again. "And right before you were rescued by Thorn's ship? When you... *glowed*?"

Charlotte swallowed. "Scared I was going to die..."

"And last night you were scared you weren't going to be able to save your mother."

"I was angry, no one was listening."

"You were scared."

Charlotte's eyes averted. "Maybe."

"Does fear always play such a pivotal role in everything you do?"

Charlotte's nervousness melted into anger. "Excuse me?"

"Your mother also used to have a rather unnervingly strong relationship with fear... The Nightmares could smell it on her," Smoke said quietly.

Charlotte remembered Lark's words. "...I've heard some refer to my Mother as The Fearless."

"A title not easily gained. She overcame those fears and found her true strength. Every time *you've* been able to tap into your talents, you've been motivated by fear. It's been purely reactive, a supernatural manifestation of self-preservation."

Charlotte felt her chin tilt upward and her shoulders roll back. "So?"

"So that's not terribly sustainable. Not to mention incredibly unfocused and volatile." The man looked distant a moment as he mulled over variables. "Given the right circumstances, or more aptly, the absolute *wrong* circumstances, you could become the exact world-shattering problem Robin is terrified you will be."

That sunburned feeling spread to Charlotte's face, and she self-consciously touched her cheek with her fingertips to ensure her own anxiety wasn't manifesting sensation into reality once more. "What absolute wrong circumstances?"

"An army of creatures that feed off of fear, for instance," Smoke said pointedly.

A pit was forming in her stomach. "Oh." Still… surely there had to be a way she could use this to help her mother. "…What would it take for it to *become* sustainable?"

"Control. Not just in regard to summoning it but being able to hold it back. An ability to suppress it—direct it."

Charlotte puffed her cheeks out. "But how do I do that?"

"Summoning is simple. You have to want something, and then go get it."

Charlotte blinked, but Smoke was sincere. "You make it sound like grocery shopping."

"Would you focus, please?"

"Can't I just wax a car or paint a fence or something? Play Eye of the Tiger? Run up some steps? Do a montage?"

"Do you *dream*, Charlie?" Smoke asked in a severe tone.

"…Yes." Charlotte squeaked quietly

"And have you ever found yourself somewhat in control of that dream?"

Charlotte thought for a moment. She had control over her own actions but… "No," she admitted dejectedly.

Smoke sighed and ran a hand through his hair. "Perhaps Robin is right."

"You're really going to give up on me that easily?" Charlotte challenged, folding her arms.

He looked at her. He must have seen something, something that softened his gaze, and the hand in his hair dropped to his side with another exasperated sigh. "Fine. But no more sarcasm."

"No promises."

Pale grey eyes hardened a stare at her.

"I'll try," Charlotte amended with a sheepish smile.

"Good." Smoke looked about the yard and pointed to a branch that had fallen to the ground a foot or so away from Charlotte. "Pick that up."

Charlotte did.

"Now, how did you manage that?"

"Manage what?"

"How did you pick up that branch?"

Charlotte's face scrunched and she looked back at Thorn who just shrugged. "You… just saw me do it."

"Explain it to me."

Charlotte stared at him, but again, he was sincere. "I just... You asked, pointed it out, I saw it, reached for it, then picked it up. That's all."

"That's summoning."

Charlotte was skeptical. "Picking up a branch is summoning?"

Smoke gave her a warning look.

"That was doubt, not sarcasm!" Charlotte protested.

"Well doubt quieter," Smoke grumbled. He looked around again and pointed to a tree not twenty feet away. "Get me a leaf from that tree."

Charlotte took one step before Smoke's stern tone stopped her.

"*Without* moving your feet."

Charlotte looked down at her feet, then to Smoke again. "Like... hop?"

"Like *summoning*," the man said simply. "I want you to see what I point out, reach for it, and pick it up."

Charlotte shook her head in disbelief and looked toward the tree. "I..." She reached her arms out but was nowhere near it, and so she simply grasped air. "It's too far."

"*Reach*, dammit," Smoke demanded.

Charlotte tried to imagine focusing on the leaves. She strained her fingertips and imagined magic in movies or having the power of the force and the leaf would come to her like a lightsaber to a jedi. But nothing. She exhaled. "I can't."

"You won't," came Smoke's immediate reply.

"I *can't*," Charlotte insisted, glaring back at him.

"If you can move an entire hedge, Charlie, you can fetch a single leaf." His tone was condescending.

"Well, it's not working, so maybe you're just a shitty teacher."

"Fates, child, would you just…" Smoke growled in exasperation, meeting the girl's gaze. His frustration dissipated in a half-amused sigh. "You are your mother's daughter…" He rubbed his brow, pinched the bridge of his nose, then paused, his eyes rising over his hand to stare at the horizon in thought. He turned to the rather amused Thorn, who was sitting on the stone wall that circled the cottage. "In the kitchen, you'll find some plants hanging above the window, if you are *facing* the window, the second to the end on the left—that's on the *left*—will have some very vibrant green leaves. Bring me one, would you?"

Thorn hopped off the wall and began to walk back toward the cottage.

"Oh," Smoke called to them. "And just to be on the safe side, you should probably bring a little of the plant to the right of it, as well."

Thorn looked a little bewildered but nodded. "As you wish."

"So, *they* don't have to summon it?" Charlotte sassed.

"For starters, *they* aren't able to do what you can," Smoke explained. "And summoning is clearly too complicated, so we're going to start smaller. I'm going to shrink you."

"You're what?"

"Shifting size is a fairly simple task," Smoke explained. "It's one of the first things I learned. The plant Thorn is fetching will shrink you, and you'll be able to get a feel for it. Then, fates willing, you'll be able to mimic it."

"The *plant* will *shrink* me?" Charlotte continued to doubt.

"Yes, Charlie, keep up. At this point, plants altering your size upon consumption should be commonplace by now."

Charlotte considered her time in Terra Mirum thus far. He had a point. "Fair enough… How *much* is it going to shrink me?"

"A foot or so, I'd say," Smoke answered noncommittally.

"I'm going to lose an entire foot?" Charlotte asked incredulously. "I don't have a lot of height to begin with!"

"No, you'll still have both feet," Smoke deadpanned.

"You know what I meant."

"And here I thought you had a sense of humor. My dear girl, you're going to shrink to *about* a foot or so. And the other plant will restore you to normal should you fail to make the shift back yourself."

Charlotte looked around nervously. "What if I don't want to shrink?"

"Why don't you want to shrink?"

"The grass is already up to my knees here."

"Are you afraid you'll get lost?" Smoke asked with a wide grin, his white teeth flashing in the sunlight.

"No." She lied.

"Remember, Charlie, your mother is known as The Fearless in our world…"

"I'm not my mother."

"No…" Smoke answered cryptically. "You're not."

Charlotte subconsciously touched the feathered earring as Thorn returned with the items Smoke had requested. She was not chosen. She *chose* to be there. That made her mighty. That was her strength… If only it felt like a strength and not foolhardiness.

Smoke took both plants from Thorn but only held out one to Charlie, very deliberately. "Ingest this. Should take but a moment, but I recommend closing your eyes. The first time can be a bit dizzying. Wouldn't want you getting sick, no matter how small the mess would be."

Charlotte took the leaf cautiously, examining it. It looked relatively harmless. "Does it taste weird?"

"I find it rather pleasant to be honest," Smoke answered.

Charlotte squinted at it. "Why do you even have this."

Smoke shrugged. "You never know when it will come in handy. And look," he smiled a bit smugly. "It has."

Charlotte took a deep breath and closed her eyes. She resisted the urge to plug her nose as she opened her mouth to chew the leaf. It… was not an unpleasant taste—a rather surprisingly strong herb flavor that was almost… familiar. She swallowed. She didn't feel any different… but she was terrified to open her eyes. She could already see the blades of grass in her mind, and self-consciously she reached out to grasp one. Her eyes opened. Sure enough, she was about only a foot tall, the grass towering just a little over her head. "Oh… wow…" The sensation was… dizzying. She was smaller. She was literally the size of a doll. It was unnerving, but she found her anxiety was far more relaxed with processing this than she thought it would be. After walking around a bit, she finally was able to see Smoke. She looked up at him and shrugged. She hadn't really felt anything, so she wasn't sure what she was supposed to mimic. "Now what?"

Smoke looked at her expectantly, the other plant still in his hand. "Now grow."

Charlotte looked down at herself then back up at him. "How?"

"I'd try working backward from how you shrunk. Think big thoughts."

Charlotte frowned. "Very funny."

"I've already told you how, Charlie. Want it, then get it. Become it. Pick up the damn branch."

Charlotte stretched her arms up. She jumped up and down a few times. She stood on her tip toes and even tried to imagine what a growing potion might taste like. Nothing. "I can't do this."

"You can."

"Maybe I'm a broken Changeling," Charlotte offered.

"Maybe you're a lazy Changeling who isn't trying hard enough."

"Just give me the other plant."

"Not until you try."

"I *am* trying!" Charlotte stomped her foot in anger.

"Not hard enough," Smoke tsked. "If this is how you plan to save Alys, Charlie, I am afraid nothing will come of it."

"Shut up!"

"Don't you want to save your mother?"

"Give me the other plant!" Charlotte demanded.

"If you want it, come get it," Smoke raised it above his head.

Charlotte leapt at his left leg, startling him. She dug her fingers into the fabric of his pant leg, reaching up, and up.

"What are you doing?" Smoke asked, startled.

"Saving my mother," Charlotte growled to herself. She reached, stretching to catch a pocket, then a button. Climbing higher, her fingers moved quickly. She'd climb up his entire arm to reach the plant if she had to. She was not going to be held back by some snarky, smug, know-it-all who didn't know a thing about her if he thought not being able to change height was going to keep her from helping her mother. She grasped his sleeve and snatched the plant from his fingertips. "Aha!" She looked back down toward Smoke and puzzled. He was considerably farther down than just an arm's length. And then she realized she wasn't climbing his form at all, but standing on her own two feet, nearly two feet taller than him.

"Aha indeed," Smoke said, pleased.

Charlotte blinked and felt herself relax back to her natural height, like a rubber band releasing in slow motion. She stared at the plant still in her hands and then looked back to Smoke. "I... I did it."

Smoke laughed. "Of course, you did. You'd already done it by shrinking."

Again, Charlotte blinked. "I... what?"

Smoke plucked the plant from her fingers. "This plant can't do anything, Charlie. You just had to believe it did so you could accept it was going to happen. Same trick worked on your mother years ago. Didn't have time to explain Dreamer magic to her. Never thought that trick would work twice on the same family, yet here we are..."

Charlotte smacked her tongue against the roof of her mouth, remembering the taste of the leaf she'd eaten and feeling suddenly very thirsty. "What exactly did I eat?"

Smoke tossed the plant piece in his hand over his shoulder. "Basil. Speaking of, are you hungry? I think it's time for lunch."

18

THE SLITHY TOVES

Charlotte had improved after lunch. She still struggled with shifting her shape—changing herself seemed far more difficult a task than any other sort of magic, no matter what Smoke said. But she *did* figure out how to summon things, through rather childish means, in fact.

It took a lot of concentration, but she found that if she squinted with one eye and reached her hand out for the thing she was retrieving, she could pick things up and move them using an amusingly similar method to pretending to squish people's heads between one's fingertips. It was a matter of ignoring depth perception—not moving an object to her but rather picking it up, regardless of the distance between them.

She was practicing with a house plant inside the den as the sun began to set.

Charlotte would squint, reach out her right hand and pluck it between her fingertips, carefully move it to the other side of the room, and repeat. Sometimes she would bring it just close enough that she could properly grasp it with her left hand, then replace it somewhere in the room again. The novelty of this trick was so bewildering she'd gone about it for hours on end. She felt light; giddy.

Then Robin returned.

The Fae was breathless, flustered and windblown. She pulled the goggles off her eyes to pin the wind-swept locks of auburn, gold, and red out of her face. "I'm back!" She called up the stairs before running her hands rapidly back and forth over her arms to attempt to warm them up.

Smoke took the stairs down two at a time. "You made it! The others were starting to worry something had happened."

"You weren't worried?"

"I know I'm not so lucky as to be rid of your criticism so easily."

Robin pursed her lips. "You're not charming enough for me to ignore that."

"You're not convincing enough for me to believe that," Smoke quipped.

Thorn, who had finished carrying the last of the logs into the den, poked their head in. "You're alright, thank the Fates."

Robin smoothed down the front of her tunic. "Where's Charlie?"

Thorn stuck their thumb out over their shoulder.

"Your majesty," Robin strode into the den.

Charlotte startled, dropping the plant, which tipped over and spilled soil all over the floor.

Robin blinked, cleared her throat, and began again. "Your Majesty, I have been entrusted with the task of bringing you home."

Charlotte felt cold. "But no one remembers me there."

Robin paused, then corrected herself. "Forgive me—what I mean is, the king has requested I bring you back to the safety of the castle first thing tomorrow morning."

Charlotte's fear contorted into a scowl. "Well, you'll have to send my apologies to the king." She leaned back against the wall again and focused on turning the plant back upright. "I'm afraid I can't be attending any tea parties at this time. I'm far too swamped with saving the world."

"I don't think you quite understand what a royal request is."

"A request is an act of politely or formally asking for something. Asking means the answer is dependent upon the person being asked, not the person doing the asking," Charlotte recited.

"*You* weren't being asked."

Smoke languidly leaned against the doorway. "Rough estimate... How much more precious time will we be wasting on useless trips back and forth do you think?"

Robin bristled, and every shadow in the room trembled. "Tell me, Silas, if it were *your daughter* volunteering to take a literal army of Nightmares head on, how would you feel about it?"

Smoke's lip curled slightly. "Imani is a baby."

Robin pointedly raised her eyebrows.

"Let's not get ugly about this," Thorn stepped in. "Can't we just have a simple discussion?"

"There's nothing to discuss," Robin dismissed. "I'm taking her back to Elan Vital; I have my orders."

"And regardless of what Charlotte ends up doing, your orders are a foolish waste of our time and resources," Smoke snapped.

"Don't I get a say about this?" Charlotte asked tentatively.

"No," Robin and Smoke answered in unison, never breaking eye contact with each other.

Thorn watched Charlotte wrap her arms around the pot of the plant protectively, hugging it to her for comfort like a teddy bear. "We're barely a thirty-minute walk from Arden. We've come all this way already. Can't she at least stay long enough to help you plead Terra Mirum's case on her father's behalf?"

Smoke looked to Robin and twirled his arm in presentation toward Thorn as if to give further weight the reasoned argument.

Robin's sighed, frustrated, but she did seem conflicted. "I gave my word I would bring her back safely."

"And so, you shall," Thorn reasoned. "*After* negotiations."

"We don't know how long those will take—"

"I imagine our case would be a great deal stronger if it were actually made by a member of the royal bloodline," Smoke opined.

Robin sighed. "*Fine*," she agreed in a hiss. "Tomorrow, we will leave for Arden first thing and meet with Oberon and Titania. *Then* I will be taking the princess back to Elan Vital."

"As you wish," Smoke agreed, but upon looking to Charlotte, gave the minutest shake of the head.

Charlotte wanted to find hope in that one small acknowledgement, but her heart ached. Maybe Robin's mind could be changed, but the fear that control was slipping through her fingers was inescapable.

"But if *anyone* so much as *breathes* the word Changeling while we're there, I swear to the Fates above and below, I will—"

A loud crash of broken glass interrupted them from above, and Imani began to cry.

"Silas!" Rosalind's voice had barely called for aid when the adult changeling was gone like smoke on the air, out the room and up the stairs.

Thorn and Robin drew their swords.

"Stay with the princess," Robin ordered. A flutter of wings, and she, too, was gone as quickly.

Thorn closed the distance to Charlotte. They wrapped an arm around her, pulling her close which squeezed the house plant askew and caused more dirt to spill.

There were crashes, yelling, and a string of curses from Robin that did not sound like they were in English, even with the sound as muffled as it was.

"What's going on?" Charlotte whispered.

"Something got in…" Thorn answered gravely.

Something that sounded… very… *hissy*.

"Is it getting closer?" Charlotte asked, but she could still hear them struggling upstairs.

Thorn's grip around her tightened as they realized the source of the noise was not coming from upstairs at all, but down the chimney. "No… there's more of them." They pivoted toward the fireplace and raised their arm from around Charlotte to gently guide her to stand behind them.

They saw the tongue first. It flicked out from the fireplace almost like a periscope, tasting the air like a snake might. The long wriggling thing dripped with bluish-black ooze, drops falling onto the unlit wood below with a sizzle.

If the thing *had* eyes, Charlotte couldn't see them, merely the row of bright silver teeth that caught every hint of light in the dimly lit room. It landed on top of the firewood with a crack. Its spindly arms bent, while its long lizard-like body wriggled free of the chimney. Darkness spilled out around it like water breaking through a dam; it poured in the room, swallowing any light it touched.

Charlotte could feel a biting cold wind slide past her ankles.

The creature raised its head, and focused its attention on Charlotte and Thorn.

Thorn was motionless, but Charlotte could feel it was not out of fear. They were gauging this thing's movement and senses. Even their breathing seemed more still. "Throw the plant," they whispered, tilting their head toward the right of the room.

Charlotte raised the poor house plant above her head and chucked it to the right of Thorn's sword, where it loudly thumped against the wall of books, causing a few to fall from their shelves.

The creature's attention shifted to the sound, its body turning to pounce on it, and in turn Thorn lunged, thrusting their sword into where Charlotte imagined its ribs would be.

The thing screeched a sound Charlotte would have been glad to have died without ever hearing.

Thorn retracted their blade to thrust into it again. "We need more light!"

Charlotte looked around the room frantically and caught sight of one of the lanterns. She squinted one eye, her heart racing as she raised her hand up. She opened the small door to see the lit candle inside. Her hand was trembling as she reached for the candle within. She quickly brought it to the fireplace, but the wind from the rapid movement extinguished the flame. "Shit." She dropped it and looked to another lantern.

Loud sizzles as more black saliva dripped down the chimney.

"There's more coming!" Thorn barely dodged the acid-slathered tongue.

"I'm trying, I'm trying," Charlotte answered hurriedly, looking to another lantern. She squinted and opened the door.

A screech on the second floor followed by another crash of glass. Thumps and thuds. Something coming down the stairs—quickly.

"Come on, come on," Charlotte urged herself, careful to remove the candle slower this time. She moved more deliberately, even raised her left hand to shield the air currents away from the flame as best she could. Both hands were trembling. She set it to the wood in the fireplace. Her breathing shuddered. She needed the wood to catch flame.

Charlotte's left hand was pulled away by a whip made of wasp stings. She dropped the candle, and it extinguished uselessly in the fireplace.

One of the creatures was crouched around the doorway, its tongue now wrapped around her wrist and fingers.

She screamed and tried to pull her hand back to no avail.

The thing began to drag her toward it.

Charlotte flailed, grabbing on to a bookshelf. Her hand was on fire. She could feel it swelling and about to burst into flame. Her fingers slipped, and she fell to her side, sliding along the floor.

"Charlie!" Thorn retreated toward her quickly, keeping their eyes trained on the chimney as another slithering thing crawled down and into the room. "Get OFF her!" They angrily severed the stretched appendage.

One half of the tongue retracted into the creature with a whimper, while the other slid off Charlotte's hand and to the ground beside her with a sickening damp thud.

The creature bared its razor teeth, screeched and reared back.

Charlotte squinted, and her right hand flew out, pinching the creature's head between her index and fore-finger, holding it in place from coming farther forward.

The thing screeched again angrily, its front legs flailing uselessly, unable to touch the floor.

Charlotte's hand trembled. Just squish it. Like a bug. That's all this is. Her eyes teared up as she focused on the thing caught between her fingers.

Thorn glanced between her and the creature that had now pulled itself from the chimney and was moving toward them. "What are you waiting for?"

"Just a bug," Charlotte whispered to herself, her fingers tightening slightly.

The thing whimpered again. A sad pitiful sound that made her heart ache.

"It's just a bug…"

"Charlie!" Thorn urged.

"Just a…"

A blur with a blade landed on the creature's back, sinking her sword tip into its prone skull.

The young girl gasped and released it, stumbling back a step.

Robin looked to the others as black ichor spread out from the body beneath her feet. "We have to run."

Thorn needed no further encouragement, scooping an arm around Charlotte. "Hold onto me tight and close your eyes."

Using the pommel of their blade, they shattered the large bay window Charlotte had fallen asleep beside only the night before. They gave some of the shards a kick before leaping up and through, more glass breaking as they shot up into the night.

Charlotte didn't open her eyes again until the cool night air was consistently whipping past them. She looked down and felt dizzy. She could see spots of light in the near distance. The replanted trees from the Amber Grove surrounded a great mist. She could feel Thorn's heart beating strongly against their chest.

"We'll land soon," Thorn assured, and they dove toward the grove.

Charlotte's stomach lurched.

As they neared the tops of the trees again, their descent became more careful, like a parachute, wings flapping just enough to adjust their positioning before allowing them to fall slightly, catch, then fall again until they safely reached the ground amid the brightly glowing trees.

Robin followed shortly after, cradling a crying bundle in her arms. She looked toward the other two. "Are you two alright?"

Charlotte finally looked at her left hand and fingers. The pain had dulled to nothing sometime during their flight, but more remarkably, the skin remained unblemished. "I think so?"

"Where's the others?" Thorn asked.

As if on cue, Rosalind arrived riding a giant panther-like cat. She dismounted quickly, giving a glance behind them.

"Are they following?" Robin asked.

"No," Rosalind dismissed. "We'll be the least of their concerns now." She looked to Robin and reached her arms out to take the baby into her arms again. "Thankfully for us. It would be impossible for us to outrun an entire pack of toves." She carefully began bouncing the wailing bundle. "Shhh, we're okay now…"

The panther shifted from vapor to Smoke, who dusted himself off. "Forgive me, darling, I'm afraid your homes catching on fire is starting to become an unintentional tradition of these wars."

"Let's be sure to make that our chief argument of why we need to stop having them," Rosalind teased, carefully untucking the blanket around Imani enough to look at her. "At least we're all…" Her face dropped. She looked up tentatively. "Silas?" Her voice was hushed. Hoarse.

Smoke moved to his wife, joined by Robin. His brow furrowed. He could see a disconcertingly shadowed spot on the baby's arm, a color much like the shade of the tove's skin.

"She's been infected," gasped Robin.

Rosalind pulled the bundle in her arms closer and walked a few paces away from the group. "No..." She looked down at the baby in her arms who only cried harder, tears streaming down her cheeks as the spot began to spread like ink on paper. "No, Imani, no tears. You must fight, okay? You have to *fight*."

Robin looked from the retreating Duchess to Smoke and back again. "Your Grace," she started tentatively.

"Shut up," Rosalind growled before going back to cooing to Imani.

"She's too young to fight off the infection," Robin tried to reason.

"Shut up!" Rosalind barked at Robin.

Robin looked helplessly to Smoke, who looked frozen. He was staring off at nothing, his mind racing for an answer. "Silas, she'll infect all of us if we don't—"

"There has to be some way," Smoke insisted.

"There isn't," Robin pleaded. "You *know* there isn't."

"Dammit, Robin."

"We can't afford to be optimistic. If we don't leave her now—"

"She'll die."

"She already has."

Smoke stared at her, his face contorting. He wanted to argue, but compassion seldom stood chance against fact. His eyes shined in the autumn glow, and his mouth formed a thin line before he turned to his wife. "Rosalind..." He spoke softly, barely audible.

"*Lady Clara Vere de Vere, was eight years old, she said: Every ringlet, lightly shaken, ran itself in golden thread,*" Rosalind sang softly to the baby in her arms, rocking her gently back and forth.

The wailing continued.

Smoke reached out to set a hand on Rosalind's shoulder, but she shrugged him off. "Darling... I'm so sorry... I know I can't ask you to do this."

"*She took her little porringer: Of me she shall not win renown...*"

"But if I don't, I *will* lose you both," Smoke's voice broke. "Please, beloved..."

Rosalind shook her head and took another step away, pivoting so she could see him. Tears were streaming down her own cheeks. "*For the baseness of its nature shall have strength to drag her down.*"

"*Please* listen to me," Smoke beseeched, the fear bubbling up in his throat. "We *have* to..." He stopped. "We..." He couldn't bring himself to form the words. "If you don't let go, she's going to infect you as well..."

The small visible baby fingers had elongated to claws, and her skin shifted from a beautiful umber to a black as dark as pitch—shadow-made matter.

"*Sisters and brothers, little Maid?*" Rosalind slowly sunk to her knees as she rocked the nightmare child in her arms, sobs tightening her voice, but still she sang. "*There stands the Inspector at thy door: Like a dog, he hunts for boys who know not two and two are four.*"

Smoke's voice was weak, broken, and sounded so foreign coming from a man who never seemed shaken by anything. "Please, love, I'm begging you… There is nothing we can do now." He crouched and extended his hand to her.

Charlotte felt a chill run up her spine as they watched the thing in Rosalind's arms shift now to resemble nothing like a baby at all. Claws and teeth and disturbingly bright yellow eyes.

Rosalind slowly shook her head and looked at the creature in her arms. Her hold tightened as it struggled against her. "*Kind words are more than coronets…*" The woman's form shook with sobs as she looked up to her husband.

"Rosalind," Smoke met her eyes, tears falling from his own now. "Take my hand. Come with me. We have to leave, love. Now."

Rosalind shook her head and instead of reaching for his hand with her own, she closed her eyes and leaned her cheek into his palm.

She held the nightmare creature to her tighter, but it freed a clawed hand and scratched at her, bit her, drew blood and yet she never dropped it. The only sign that she even felt the wounds inflicted was a slight flinch in her eyes. She pressed a kiss into Smoke's palm before opening her eyes to look at him. "Go," she whispered. "Just go."

The bite and scratch marks greyed the skin before it too rotted of color to the same ashen darkness. It spread far more rapidly in the blood of a full Dream.

"No, Rosalind, please," Smoke begged.

Robin stepped forward to grab Smoke by the elbow and yank him away. "We have to go."

"We love you," Rosalind whispered before crumpling over the bundle in her arms as the darkness spread up her neck and began to distort her once beautiful features. Her nose, fingers, and teeth sharpened. Her dark skin lost its warm luster, becoming charred and infected. Her eyes darkened entirely as if hollowed out.

"NO!" The word howled out of Smoke like an animal in pain that echoed through the woods as Robin and Thorn roughly yanked him away.

They only dragged him a few steps before the man ran with them, and the smaller group fast approached Arden's gates now visible in the distance.

Charlotte looked back only once, catching glimpse of something that no longer resembled the beautiful and kind woman who had sheltered her. Instead, there was a shrieking thing, zombie-like, that shirked from the light, followed by a skittering crab-like creature that only reached about a foot off the ground in height.

Then both were gone.

Arden's great gates were framed by the roots of giant trees that raised from the ground to create an archway where large doors were inset and walls were built off from. Charlotte could see the delicate craftsmanship and care that went into every detail as their pace began to slow.

The strained creak of sinews pulling tight caught Robin's ear, and she broke from the group to fly up and shield her companions. "Fates above, hold your fire!"

Several fae stepped out from their places unseen on the wall, lowering crossbows.

Two other fae seemed to appear out of nowhere, standing against the gate, sheathing their swords.

"Puck?" A voice called, full of relief. "Aren't you a sight for sore eyes."

"We have to stop meeting like this, Moth," Robin agreed with a nervous smile.

The captain of Arden's guard dropped down from the wall, her wings softening the landing. She was dressed in dark armor, and she did have a strangely moth-like quality to her from the soft quality of her wings to the almost fluffy texture of her hair. She looked to Smoke. "You look like hell."

"We've seen it," Thorn breathed heavily.

Moth's attention shifted again, and she looked dumbstruck. "Your Majesty—"

Thorn waved a dismissive hand. "*Please*, Moth, we need shelter and possibly medical attention."

"O-of course... Come with me."

They entered through a much smaller hidden door to the right of the gates. "Medic, I need medics!"

Thorn took Charlotte's hand and held it out to the approaching healers. "Tangled with a tove, check for signs of infection."

One healer immediately raised up a lantern while another examined her hand closely. "What happened?"

Thorn looked torn to explain without betraying Charlotte's origins. "Not sure, just looked like she got close to it."

Charlotte, on the other hand, was craning her neck to try to see and overhear what was going on between Smoke and Robin.

"Smoke..." Robin struggled for words.

"*Don't*," the man growled, pulling his arm away from her. "Just *don't*."

"There was nothing you could do."

"No, Robin, there's nothing I can do *now*." Smoke violently slashed at the air as a healer approached him. "Don't touch me."

The healer paused awkwardly. "But your wounds—"

"Go to hell!"

Robin flinched, and Smoke walked away.

"Miss?" The healer holding Charlotte's hand squeezed it slightly, bringing her back to the moment.

"Sorry. I... Did you ask something?"

"Do you feel any different? Any pains or aches?"

"Oh..." Charlotte looked down to her hands and flexed them. Just poor circulation. Cold as always. "No, I'm fine."

The healers nodded and stepped back. "She's clear."

Charlotte looked to Robin, who hadn't moved since Smoke departed.

Her wings folded neatly down her back like a cape. Her neck moved like she'd swallowed a bitter pill and with that undulation her posture straightened one vertebra at a time. She exhaled and turned to face Charlotte and Thorn, her face still and emotionless.

"It's too late to request an audience with Oberon... but I think I know a place where we can stay the night."

19

NIGHT AND SILENCE

Charlotte was still staring up at the ceiling.

They were crowded into one room: Robin sleeping on the floor, Thorn and Charlotte sharing the bed. The two fae had drifted off hours ago.

She was mentally tracing the woodgrains above her, but every time she got to a certain point, it would be too dark to fully make it out, so she'd lose the line and start over. Her mind kept wandering back to the way the shadows had taken over Rosalind, twisting her features. It replayed over and over in her mind. It made her stomach churn.

Haunting.

Familiar.

The same sort of horrific alterations she had seen contort her own hand in her nightmare just days before.

Charlotte raised her left hand parallel to her face to look at the fingertips. The memory of the burning pain that had shot through them was fuzzy but still unnerving.

In the dim moonlight pouring in through the small window, shadows were cast about her fingertips, and her mind imagined them growing down her arm. She shivered and strained to raise her hand to bathe in the cold light.

No shadows.

She flexed her fingers and brought her hand back to rest on her stomach just above the arm Thorn had thrown over her in their sleep.

Charlotte exhaled slowly and looked at her sleeping companion.

Thorn, much like Robin, had been too exhausted by the day's events to be kept awake by such anxieties.

Or did fae simply not dream the same way humans did? Perhaps they didn't share the same fears. Did they even fear at all? Her companions certainly had seemed rather fearless in the time she'd spent with them.

Fearless like her mother.

Charlotte's chest felt hot.

She carefully slipped her feet down the side of the bed until they found the floor. Awkwardly, she shifted, trying her best to not disturb Thorn as she slinked out from under their arm. She tiptoed around the mattress Robin lay nestled on, padding to the door.

The knob turned soundlessly, and she snuck through a crack of an opening and into the hallway.

Charlotte exhaled silently in relief and walked down the stairs into the main room of the little inn they'd found.

All was silent.

She could see the streets of Arden outside were illuminated by jar lanterns and repotted trees from the amber groves. But it too was empty.

Charlotte slipped outside and breathed in the air. It was brisk, but still far warmer than she'd expect it to be.

The city seemed a rather large metropolis, and yet... not a soul in sight. She marveled at the great buildings, which had seemingly grown from the trees they were set into. She shook her head as she took it all in. Just as her mother had painted...

"It's almost like having you with me again... walking where you walked."

The flicker of the lamplight caught Charlotte's eye, and she looked up at one of the jar lanterns. There weren't candles inside at all, but rather two butter-fly-like insects fluttering about, seemingly made of flame. They danced together, intertwining, and when they did land, the flames licked the air, constantly moving even in the stillest moments.

Charlotte couldn't help but smile a little to her-self at the "fireflies" before she continued down the grass, her bare feet surprisingly comfortable on the ground. She let the breeze guide her through the empty streets, wandering like a ghost haunting a long-forgotten city.

If her dream about being infected had some truth to it, surely the rest had to have some truth to it, which meant there really was a grey man waiting for her in a library... She considered the trees above her and remembered the organic fretwork from her dream.

Was it here?

And was it Smoke? It certainly seemed like it could be him. But by now the voice from her dream had become muddled with time, like a tune she couldn't quite remember. And Smoke had done little to indicate any knowledge of a clandestine meeting.

Almost as if she had summoned him, following the breeze had led Charlotte to Smoke himself.

He was sitting in a nook between the large roots of the side of one of the buildings, staring almost wide-eyed into some unseen void. He seemed unaware of the world around him, and yet as she came to a stop, he spoke to her. "You should be asleep."

Charlotte looked around to confirm that she was in fact the only one in the vicinity before she felt comfortable answering. "Tried." She shrugged helplessly. "Can't."

Smoke exhaled heavily, his lips pulling slightly at what looked like a grimace and he leaned his head back against the root. "Well, that makes two of us..."

Charlotte chewed her lower lip, waiting, but he didn't continue. She rocked back and forth on her feet awkwardly, pigeon-toed and flexing her arches. Why wasn't he saying anything? Should *she* say something? Should she leave? She should leave.

"Every time I close my eyes..." Smoke confessed, his voice trailing off into the air. He shook his head and pressed the heel of his palms into his sockets with a sharp inhale. He remained like that a moment: breathless and still.

The silence wept with him.

He exhaled, his hands rotating ever so slightly to rub his eyes. "How will I ever…" His hands dropped to his lap, and he shook his head.

Charlotte wrung her hands as she thought. If she was going to prove herself to him… "I know I'm not Alys… but I *do* have the blood of a Dreamer in me."

He scoffed quietly.

"I know that's not the most reassuring thing I could say," Charlotte admitted quickly, trembling. "But… I promise I will do everything I can to make this right again."

Smoke's brow was furrowed in anger, but it relaxed upon looking at her. "You're just a child."

Charlotte's jaw tightened. "So was she."

"That was different," Smoke dismissed.

"How?" Charlotte demanded.

"Now is not really the time to talk about this," the man pushed himself into a stand, moving to put more distance between them.

"Time isn't really on our side," Charlotte insisted, following a few paces behind.

"Charlie—"

"*Maybe* I can help."

"How could you possibly—"

"If you would just give me a chance—"

"I wasn't a father back then!" Smoke barked, startling Charlotte back a step. His shoulders slumped, and he sighed, frustrated. "When I met your mother, it was easier to focus. I was more selfish back then—or less selfish, I suppose, depending how you look at it."

"I don't understand," Charlotte admitted softly.

Smoke ran his hands through hair, gripping the roots a moment in thought. "I don't think I would be able to do what I did back then if it were to have happened now. Do you understand? I couldn't be that callous again."

Charlotte could feel that pit in her stomach begin to grow again. "...What did you do?"

"What had to be done," Smoke answered reflexively. He paused and let his hands drop to his sides. "Or at least what I had decided had to be done..." His chest sunk inward, and he shoved his hands into his pockets, feeling his discomfort rising. "And to my credit, that gamble did mostly pay off, and your mother *did* save Terra Mirum... But just because you *can* do something, Charlie, doesn't mean you should. The end doesn't always justify the means."

Charlotte felt her teeth grind together, her eyes narrowing. "What. Did. You. Do?" She demanded lowly.

Smoke looked at her. He saw so much of the same scared girl in her that he'd met so many years ago. He frowned, torn between the necessity of honesty and the pain it would cause. "I erased her memories."

Charlotte's breath caught, and she felt cold. "...Why?"

Smoke couldn't meet her eyes. "We were facing down a Queen of Nightmares, and Alys was a magnet for them. The Nothing called to that part of her so strongly it nearly swallowed her whole when we'd first met. I thought if I removed the trauma that created those nightmares—her friend's death, her mother's abuse, maybe she could become the hero we needed."

Charlotte blinked in confusion, feeling a shred of hope. "But... Mom *does* remember those things."

"Yes, well," Smoke rubbed the back of his neck with a palm. "What I didn't anticipate was whose nightmares exactly that Queen belonged to." He blew air past his lips. "It all came back. And we nearly lost her to it."

"But she *made* it," Charlotte reminded, hoping that her mother's perseverance would stand as evidence for her own case.

"In *spite* of my foolhardy precautions," Smoke muttered. He thought a moment and corrected himself. "It wasn't useless, and it wasn't done out of malice. Without those memories, she had the strength to help us, to stand up to Oberon, to lead us into battle, to make it to that moment before it fell apart... And I'd like to believe it helped her realize later she had that strength within her if she could just get past that damn poison it had pumped through her veins for so long... But that doesn't excuse what I did. There were other ways. Other ways that wouldn't have violated her trust. I know that *now*. I know what weight I put on a *child's* shoulders. And I can't do that again—no matter how noble the goal."

Charlotte's brow furrowed, and she looked around helplessly. "Then... why did you teach me all of that stuff?"

"Because ignorance never helped anyone, and at the very least, I wanted you to be able to defend yourself."

"But I can do *more* than that."

Smoke sighed. "You don't know what kind of monsters you're up against. Those *creatures* we ran from? They will be the least of our future troubles. The things that took my family from me are the *tamest* of the terrors that make up their legion, do you understand?"

Charlotte didn't answer.

"I have seen Nightmares twist kings and soldiers into demons that your worst fear could not even hope to imagine—all in pursuit of doing *the right thing*. What do you think they'll do to you?"

Charlotte wanted to retort, say something witty, something clever, something confident, but all she managed was a stutter. "I... I..."

"Tomorrow we will implore Oberon for aid. And then you will return to your father. Safely." he waved a dismissive hand.

"Smoke—"

"I lost my daughter and the love of my life today, Charlotte," Smoke lamented. "Fates willing, I can spare Oswin from at least one of those same tragedies."

Charlotte shook her head; she could feel tears welling up in her eyes. "Please... I can help," she insisted. "My powers could be invaluable—"

"We will find another way," came the soft interruption.

"But my mother—"

"Is the strongest person I have ever met. She's a fighter. She *will* survive this."

"But—"

"And when she does," Smoke slowly dropped to a knee, his hands resting on her arms. "It will be with her memory *intact*."

Hot tears poured down Charlotte's cheeks. She turned her head away in a poor attempt to hide them.

"Look at how far you've come so far. How could anyone forget someone like you?"

Charlotte tried to pull away. "Because she's…"

"Your *mother*."

It was the sincerity in his voice that made her look back to him.

"Charlotte, the moment Imani was infected; I knew I had lost them both. Because that's the kind of person Rosalind is…" Smoke flinched. "*Was*." He swallowed and took a breath, shaking his head. "No matter how I begged, she was never going to abandon her. And had Robin and Thorn not been there to drag me away, I would have stayed with them. Because that's what it means to be a parent. I know Alys didn't have much of a role model in that department, but I have no such concerns for you…" He tentatively raised a hand to wipe one of her tears from her cheek. "And that's why it's different."

Charlotte felt something in her sink. "So, you never intended me to save everyone?"

Smoke looked at her in bewilderment, rising to a stand. "You're 16, Charlie." He embraced her to him, the lanky form towering over her. "The world doesn't rest on your shoulders." He pulled back with an exhausted look about him. "Now, go to bed."

Charlotte frowned but turned back toward the inn, feeling more lost than when she had started. If Smoke wasn't the man from her dream… who was? And how was she going to find him now?

20

A CRASH COURSE IN
COURT & CROWNS

Charlotte was back in her own bed. The warmth of the down comforter weighing on her. She could hear the rain on her window and feel the dim light of an overcast Seattle morning pour in on her face.

She could hear her mother moving around outside her door, shuffling about in the hallway. She snuggled further into the warmth of her bed, smiling as a wave of relief and contentment washed over her.

She was home. She was safe.

Everything was alright.

A bright light bounced off her eyes, jolting her out of her pleasant haze.

Charlotte squinted, the small room coming into focus. There was some rain against the window, but the dim light from outside was due to the fact it was barely past dawn. She looked around and caught sight of Robin, whose wings were fully extended to stretch. As the fae moved about, the translucent material of her wings cast rainbow beams around the room, and occasionally, directly over Charlotte's eyes.

When it happened again, Charlotte groaned, turning her face away from the technicolor beam and into a pillow.

"Oh good, you're awake," Robin commented, half-amused, rolling up her mattress.

"You did that on purpose," came the muffled accusation from Charlotte.

"I'm appalled by the suggestion," Robin answered, but Charlotte could hear the sly smile in her voice. "But since you're up, you might as well start getting ready."

"Both of you are talking far too loudly in your sleep," Thorn protested.

"I'm going to go find Smoke and ensure we can arrange an audience with the court," Robin announced, moving about the room at a pace that was far too lively for dawn.

"That's nice," Thorn yawned. "Now shut up."

"When I get back," Robin continued, walking over to steal away the pillow from under Thorn's head, which was answered by a less-than-pleased grunt. "I expect to find you both awake and washed."

"Expect away," Charlotte buried her head in her arms.

Robin sighed like a perturbed parent. She moved around to the bottom of the bed and snatched away the blanket, as well.

The two shuddered, their legs recoiling toward their bodies for warmth, accompanied by involuntary tired whimpers.

"Come on. Up we go. We've got narcissists to win over, wars to win, and people to save," Robin said cheerfully as she made her way toward the door. "I'll be back in an hour. Be up and ready, or there will be hell to pay." She said it all far too pleasantly, which made it unnervingly clear that she meant every word before the door closed behind her and she was gone.

"You're a mean, mean lady!" Charlotte called after her.

They could hear a distant cackle.

Charlotte slumped, bleary-eyed. "It's barely morning."

"You're a princess," Thorn answered grumpily. "Can't you make a decree or something?"

"Make a decree?" Charlotte asked skeptically.

"Wave your hand, shake a scepter… off with her head, that lot."

"Aren't *you* royalty?"

"Barely—lest we forget, I am a bastard."

"Oh, I won't be forgetting that any time soon," Charlotte mused, sitting up a little drowsily.

Thorn laughed and threw a lazy arm around her shoulders as they sat up. "Oh… you think you're funny," they mused through a smile before pressing a kiss to her cheekbone.

"I know I'm funny," Charlotte mumbled in response. She rubbed her eyes and looked about the room with a bleary gaze. It wasn't home. It was barely even vaguely familiar. She felt a sinking feeling as she looked around. "Are you coming with me today?"

"Do you not want me to?"

"I thought—I mean I want you to, I just—I figured you wouldn't want to see—you wouldn't want them knowing you're here."

"I re-entered Arden, Charlotte," Thorn reminded. "Trust me, they *know* I'm here."

"Are you worried?"

Thorn scooted off the bed, massaging their right shoulder. "I have more important things to worry about than seeing my parents again."

Charlotte squinted at them, and Thorn sighed.

"Terrified."

"About what?"

"That they'll make me stay. That this time if I try to escape, I won't make it out alive."

Charlotte's eyebrows raised. "Can they do that?"

"It wouldn't be the first time Oberon tried," Thorn admitted, running a finger along one of the scars that scattered up and down their arms.

"What about Titania? Doesn't she have a say in any of this?"

"You would think," Thorn answered, and Charlotte could hear what sounded like a twinge of bitterness. "But at the end of the day, before she is my mother, she is the Queen of the Seelie, and keeping the peace between our clans is her priority. It's an unpleasant lesson, but one I learned at a very young age."

"Why did you come this far? Why risk it?"

"Some things are worth facing your fears for."

Charlotte smiled despite her previously furrowed brow. She felt a flourish of warmth in her chest, and she sat up a little straighter. "Like me?"

"…Eh, you're alright."

"Do not, under any circumstance, bring up that you're a Changeling," scolded Robin.

"I *know*!" Charlotte flustered with the garments Robin had brought her.

"And if he asks, lie. Lie your damn head off."

Charlotte peeked her head out of the dress. It was made of a white, gauzy, chiffon-like fabric, layered in pleats to make an asymmetrical skirt. The dress itself was simple, cinched by a large light-brown leather belt. "So, is it to be death by ruffle?"

"It will be easier to believe you are Oswin's secret heir if you don't look like you've been fished out of the gutter."

"Oswin's secret heir…" Charlotte repeated. "Sounds like a plot twist on a soap opera."

"If you're going to be a princess, you have to look the part."

"What if I don't want to be a princess?"

"Then you have no business requesting an audience with the King and Queen of the Fae," Robin replied.

Charlotte glared and looked at her reflection, examining the thick brocade of the drop-waist bodice. She tilted her head slightly to the side. The wet hair and her general face didn't seem to quite go with this clothing. It was too fine, too elegant-feeling. "What if I can't do this?"

"Are you dressed?"

"Yes."

Robin turned around and took in her image critically. "We'll have to do something about that hair."

"And my face."

"Listen to me," Robin said firmly, getting the teenager's attention. "You are the daughter of one of the most amazing human beings I have ever had the honor of knowing. And I have known some impressive human beings in my time. Do you understand?"

"If my mother's stories are true, you turned one of them into an ass."

"Shakespeare was already an ass; I merely gave him the face to match," Robin scoffed, taking Charlotte's hand in her own. "Your grandmother was *revered* throughout the kingdoms for her wisdom and kindness. Your father not only helped end a war that we had never seen the like of, but more importantly, he was instrumental in Terra Mirum's restoration after the threat was gone."

Charlotte's expression crumpled.

Robin gently lifted Charlotte's chin. "Do you want to know who you are, Charlotte Carroll? You are the product of a history of greatness and strength." She smiled reassuringly. "And if anyone should feel anxious about this meeting, it's them, not you."

Charlotte exhaled shakily, feeling the butterflies escape from her stomach to her chest. "Then why am I so scared?"

"Everybody feels scared from time to time, sometimes about the most mundane things." Robin gently tapped Charlotte's nose before picking up a hairbrush. "It's how we respond to fear that truly defines us."

Charlotte let the brush run through her hair, watching as it seemed to magically dry with each stroke.

Robin flicked her wrist at the end of the strands, and Charlotte's hair held the shape as if it had been curled and sprayed.

Charlotte missed Diana. She could almost hear how *delighted* the beautician with such a magical item. "So... how do *you* respond to fear?"

"Inappropriately timed humor."

The answer came so quickly, Charlotte laughed.

"I'm serious," Robin smiled. "You'd be amazed what a laugh can do to release tension—regardless of how ill-advised it may be in the moment. Laughter is like... *armor* against fear."

"And fear *is* the mind-killer," Charlotte quoted *Dune*, but Robin just nodded as if this were merely a great truth.

"Now that you look somewhat presentable..." She reached into a large pouch on her hip and produced a circlet made of white gold and opals so beautiful Charlotte's breath caught when she saw it. "This belonged to your grandmother."

Charlotte's eyes moved with uncertainty from the circlet to Robin's expression. "Why do you have this?"

"Your father gave it to me."

"When?"

"When I went to tell him where you were."

Charlotte frowned. "Why?"

"He thought you should have it."

"But you said he wanted me brought straight home."

"I didn't say he believed it would work."

Charlotte smiled.

"You are your mother's daughter," Robin mused. She raised the circlet and carefully placed it on Charlotte's head, pinning it in place and wrapping a few curled strands around the sides. "Now. Take a breath. And exhale. You are the heir to the White Throne, and all of Terra Mirum. You bow down to no one. Keep your back straight, your head high, and your chin parallel with the ground."

Thorn was waiting for them in the public room below, accompanied by Smoke who was taking seemingly endless drag after drag of the cigarette that Charlotte knew was not actually a cigarette.

Nervous habit. Nervous wreck.

The man had not much improved in his disposition since Charlotte had seen him since the night before, though that was to be suspected. She couldn't imagine being able to sleep after witnessing what he had with his wife and child.

She couldn't really imagine ever sleeping again after watching such a thing happen to your own family.

Smoke looked up to meet Robin's eyes and took their presence as enough clearance for them to get going because he stood immediately and walked out the door without so much as a word.

Robin sighed inwardly to herself but nodded to Thorn before following him.

Thorn was the only one who really gave pause for Charlotte. They smiled broadly and bowed their head respectfully before offering the crook of their arm to her. "You look beautiful. Just like a princess."

Charlotte gave a tight smile. "God willing, they won't be able to see right through me."

Thorn tsked and reached with their free hand to run a fingertip along the golden gryphon earring dangling from Charlotte's right ear as if to remind her of its rumored magic. "I think quite the opposite. They better be wary *you* don't see through *them*."

Charlotte smiled crookedly and shook her head, allowing Thorn to lead the way. As they trailed behind Smoke and Robin, she whispered to her companion. "So, I take it he's still angry with you both?"

Thorn shrugged. "Smoke needs someone to be mad at right now. I suspect he knows we're not really to blame, but right now if it's what helps him get through the day, I have no qualms with it. So long as he doesn't do anything terribly stupid."

Charlotte looked at them quizzically, but they just shrugged.

"Grief and logic do not often walk hand in hand."

The walk to Castle Arden's gates was a long one—or perhaps it seemed that way because there were so many things to look at that were rushed by with barely a moment to glance. There was no time to give things a proper look and take it all in... and yet...

"My mother painted this place... a few times, actually. I had one of them in my room."

"It's a beautiful city," Thorn offered stoically.

"Is it strange being back?"

"Unnerving," Thorn corrected. "Like my skin wants to crawl off my bones."

"Gross?"

"Indeed."

The castle itself was a network of trees growing together and twisting heavenward, each trunk wider and taller than the next. And surrounding its base was an impossibly tall briar-like hedge that shifted back and forth in the wind.

However, as they drew closer, Charlotte could see the rose-thorn branches undulating like layers of tangled snakes, interweaving through each other—very much alive, and moving on their own. "Oh..."

Thorn's lips pressed together in a thin line and subconsciously they pulled Charlotte closer as they made their approach.

"What... is that?" Charlotte whispered.

"My namesake," Thorn answered grimly.

Charlotte's eyes widened slightly, and she looked from the hedge they were approaching, then back to the scars along Thorn's arms and back again. "So that's…"

"Yes."

"How long ago—"

"Long enough." There was a clipped finality to the statement that made the hair on the back of Charlotte's neck stand up.

Smoke stopped just in front of the hedge, a few feet back so the grasping thorns could not reach him. Shoulders back, he raised up his palm to the hedge and the thorns recoiled from him suddenly. The briars pulled back and twisted around themselves, creating an opening large enough for a carriage to pass through.

Robin nodded to Charlotte and Thorn to follow her and walked ahead of Smoke who remained standing still in place until they passed safely through to the other side.

"How did he do that?" Charlotte whispered.

"Old magic, but simple enough," Thorn answered. "Certain members of the court are given an enchanted item, or sometimes even a mark that restrains the hedge." Their eyes narrowed slightly. "I've never actually asked which it was in Smoke's case, but given Oberon's rather possessive nature, I can guess."

"That's awful…"

"That's Oberon," Thorn muttered distastefully.

Smoke stepped through the gateway himself and as he got passed the perimeter, the thorn covered branches of the briar hedge reached out with long dangerous fingers towards each other as he stepped away.

Charlotte's brow furrowed as she watched the briar weave back together, intertwining and tangling to once again make the seamless hedge it had first been. "Why weren't you given an item?" She looked back to the scars she could see on Thorn's visible skin.

"You mean so I could come and go as I pleased? That privilege was *revoked*," Thorn answered with a tight throat.

Charlotte's nose scrunched slightly. "Why?"

"This really isn't the best time to get into this, Charlie." It was a gentle sort of dismissal, careful to ensure Charlotte that they weren't angry with her, just uncomfortable with the specifics. "The short of it is that keeping me under his thumb made Oberon feel strong and in control. It helped him forget I was physical proof his marriage to Titania was for alliance purposes only, and that they still had yet to produce an heir of their own."

"Couldn't he just pretend you were his?"

Thorn laughed despite themselves, and instead of answering they just pressed a kiss to Charlotte's fingers and a silence fell between them.

Smoke led them through the large doors into a great hall and Charlotte found herself looking up at the ceiling expecting to see the ornate fretwork from her dream, but what she saw instead was countless flowers growing wild.

Vibrantly colored blooms that stretched over the ceiling and climbed with vines along the trees. As they passed by ones closer to the eye she took in the purple to red ombre that blossomed from the center to the tips of the flower, the petals forming what looked like a many pointed star.

Charlotte reached beneath her dress to pull out the Coleridge Clock with her free hand. She stopped to hold it up next to one of the closer vines and found herself smiling as she realized the etching she'd admired for years was of the foreign flower she looked on now.

Thorn looked back at her quizzically before making the connection of what she was looking at, their expression melting into a smile. "It's called Nymphea. My mother uses it as the symbol of the Seelie Court."

"To think I was looking at proof of this place my whole life…" Charlotte shook her head. "I always thought it was just some kind of lily…"

Thorn shrugged. "I suppose it sort of is… It just grows differently here."

Charlotte looked at them skeptically. "Seriously?"

"Our worlds have been connected since the dawn of time itself, Charlie. Don't you think in all those years, especially with the fae coming and going as they pleased, a little cross-pollination would come about? Different habitats, different colorings, different growth patterns…"

Charlotte squinted slightly, evaluating if Thorn was just pulling her leg before looking back up at the flowers, deciding they were sincere. "That's so cool…"

"Hey," Robin called to them. "Come on, you two. Don't fall behind, the throne room is just ahead."

Charlotte tucked the Coleridge Clock out of sight once more and Thorn gently tugged her arm to lead her back towards Robin and Smoke. For a moment, she'd almost forgotten her reason for being in that strange place, and her anxiety began to return. Her grip on Thorn's arm tightened slightly.

They approached yet another impossibly large door and Charlotte was starting to wonder if the size of the doors were to fit what she'd heard about Oberon's ego.

Robin turned back to face them and Thorn released her and took a step away. The shorter fae rolled her neck and exhaled, taking a moment to ground herself before looking Charlotte in the eye. "Alright, shoulders back, back straight, chin parallel with the floor."

Charlotte attempted to follow these instructions, her heart racing.

"If they meet your gaze, do not be the first to break it especially Oberon. It's about dominance, and he will want to make you feel uncomfortable, to put you off balance. Don't let him. Do not look at your feet, do not let your eyes wander, and try not to shake."

"This isn't helping me feel less scared, Robin," Charlotte whispered.

"Just don't let them see that either," Robin smiled mirthlessly.

"You can do this," Thorn assured.

Charlotte looked to them doubtfully and they reached out a hand to squeeze her shoulder.

"You can." It was said more firmly this time.

Smoke finally spoke up, but there was something about him that felt distant, like he was miles away and this apparition of him was relaying a message. "Wait here a moment, I will announce you." He paused and looked at Thorn and seemed briefly more present, albeit out of his depth. "Should… I let them know you're here?"

"I would be shocked if they don't already know," Thorn answered coldly.

Smoke nodded and hesitated again. "Would you care to…" He gestured towards the door as if Thorn should join him.

Thorn's eyes narrowed stubbornly. "I think I'm exactly right where I'm needed at the present time."

"Very well." Smoke looked to Charlotte. "I will not be able to speak on your behalf while in court. I will…" His jaw tightened. "Have to hold my tongue." And with that, one of the guards opened the door just enough to allow the man to slip inside.

"Deep breath," Robin reminded quietly.

"Deep breath," Charlotte repeated. She inhaled for five seconds and exhaled for six. And again. And again, but it would not stop the pounding of her heartbeat in her ears. It would not force her eyes to focus, and everything felt in a blur. It did not cease the string of panicked curse words that played on an endless scrolling marquee in her mind.

Thorn's hand slipped from Charlotte's shoulder with one last whispered. "I believe in you."

Smoke's voice uttered one terrifying sentence. "The Court will see you now."

21

PRINCESS CHARLOTTE

The doors opened and sunlight seemed to swallow her, and the world for Charlotte seemed utterly and completely silent save for the pulsing in her ears. There was a bitter taste in her mouth and a burning in her throat and nose that smelled somewhere between copper and ammonia. One hand felt burning spots, the other felt chill, and her chest felt so tight she began to wonder if her deep breaths were going to crack her ribs.

A mixture of the smell of lilies and a crisp winter morning wafted to their noses as they stepped inside. A raised runway-like path led up to steps which led up to a dais that allowed those sitting in the thrones atop have an uncomfortably high advantage point to look down at whomever approached.

On either side of the path, stairs led down to two deeply recessed sections where each monarch's court stood as audience. By the virtue of architecture alone, those on either court were about at waist height of those seeking audience, and at the feet of the king and queen.

To the left stood the Seelie. A sea of people who all shared the same warm glow about them as Thorn. Glittering and golden. They were sunlight personified, quietly looking on with jewel-toned eyes, and hair and skin of every color imaginable.

To the right were the Unseelie, shadows born from moonless nights. While they did not give the same spark of anxiety felt around nightmares, there was a kind of darkness about them. And while they also varied in a wide variety of shades, they seemed a cooler hue. They were still and hauntingly beautiful. Like a clear night sky in the dead of winter.

Upon the dais itself was Titania and Oberon.

Titania looked so much like the flowers that adorned her court. Her gown consisted of deep vibrant reds, lined with gold that glittered in the light. Her endless curls looped around her golden crown and she sat almost languidly in her throne, looking at them with curious golden eyes. There were strong resemblances between Titania and her child, and in some respects save for their eyes, Thorn was rather the spitting image.

Titania's husband sat to her left with a far different posture. He was perched forward, looking at them like a falcon regards its dinner before swooping downward. Oberon's sharp features and near black irises increased his bird-like quality and wherever his body made contact with his throne, frost formed in his wake.

Charlotte could just make them out in her anxiety haze, but they were more shape and color than beings. Her heartbeat in her ears, she felt she might throw up.

"His Royal Highness, Oberon, The Black King of Shadows," Smoke announced with a surprising weight of respect, his voice filling the large hall and rising over the muffled din of Charlotte's awareness. "And Her Majesty Titania, The Red Queen of the Morning."

Robin took a low and sweeping bow before them. "Our highest regards to the royal courts of Arden." She sidestepped to make way between Charlotte and the dais. "May I present, Her Majesty, Princess Charlotte, Heir to the White Throne of Terra Mirum."

Titania sat up from her languid position and she and Oberon shared a noticeable look between them before proper decorum struck her. She placed one hand on her collarbone and used the other to subconsciously check that her crown had not shifted by the abrupt movement. "Forgive our shock, child. I was not aware King Oswin had produced an heir."

"Nor I," Oberon commented darkly, shifting in a manner that seemed like a falcon about to swoop down on prey. He looked at Charlotte carefully as if sizing her up for a meal. "And such things do not pass my notice."

"Yet here I stand," Charlotte answered flatly, and everything around her came into focus all at once. Perhaps it was simply returning to a familiar place of badgering authority figures, but her anxiety dispersed like dandelion seeds.

Oberon's eyes narrowed and he huffed through his nose. His attention shifted to Thorn. "And with our own royal runaway in tow. How thoughtful of you to return them." His tone dripped with condescension and so Charlotte answered in kind.

"How careless of you to have lost them," came her immediate reply.

Oberon grew very still. His jaw tight.

Yet Charlotte continued. "I do hope the growing infection of Nightmares hasn't also passed your notice—I trust not by the manner we were greeted last night." She thought she heard Robin choke. Was her chin still parallel with the floor? It was hard to keep track of these things while simultaneously calling out a being that was eons older than you. "Yet, with such a threat posed at your door, I do have to wonder why a barrier and guard post is all that we did see."

Oberon's head turned to focus on the impertinent princess, deliberately meeting her gaze and daring her to continue. "I beg your pardon?"

Charlotte was never particularly good at turning down a dare. "My people are poised for war, Your Highness, yet yours appear to be contented with merely guarding the door." Her gaze did not waver. He was a bully—she could see that so easily now. Oberon was just a bully in a place of power, and while Charlotte had no experience being a princess, she certainly had ample past experience in putting bullies in their place.

Oberon's chest swelled and his body shifted so that his full attention was focused on the small girl standing before his throne. "I am acting in the best interest of my kingdom." But Charlotte noticed the way the corner of his mouth curled up and it set a fury through her.

"You are acting in the best interest of conquest," she spat.

There was an audible intake of breath from either court, followed by a silence so palpable one could choke on it.

Charlotte held her ground, and Oberon's piercing stare. "Are you hoping we'll die first? Are you hoping that because you both rely on the Shadows, that you will be able to tame the blight?" Every question made her angrier, made her remember the horrible screams of those being sucked into The Nothing. Remembering Rosalind and Imani. "Let me save you the trouble in wondering. You can't. You couldn't during the first war, and you won't now."

"Not only does she exist, my dear, she is apparently an expert on Nightmares," Oberon commented mirthlessly to his wife, though he did not look to her.

"If you consider listening to reason the credentials for being an expert, then yes, I suppose I am." Charlotte held her shoulders back so tightly her collarbone felt sore.

Oberon huffed and waved a hand and leaned back in his chair, dismissing her as not being worth the effort of intimidation. He lazily crossed an ankle over his knee. "I am sorry to hear your little kingdom is experiencing so much hardship, princess, but it would seem the nightmares have rather ignored Arden."

"A matter of time."

"Is it?" Oberon was picking at his nails now.

"They've already broken through to the human world," Charlotte's passion shook her voice ever so slightly.

"Good, I've been meaning to reclaim our lands there as well."

"Do not be so foolish to think they will not grow hungry enough to storm your gates as well!" Something in Charlotte broke with his carelessness. So many humans had been taken already her mother had been taken already. She felt a fire within herself, she growled at him. "You, King of Shadows, are not so powerful to withstand a force that can swallow entire nations."

"Do not be so foolish to underestimate my power, child," Oberon warned.

"Why have you ignored the King Oswin's call for aid?"

"What do I gain in aiding your sad little kingdom? Nothing. No, princess, I think we will take our chances with the Nightmares. Long after you and the humans are gone, Fae will retake our rightful place as rulers over this world." He waved them off. "I am done with you."

Robin reached for Charlotte's shoulder, but Charlotte pulled away. "You helped us before!"

"Yes, and what good did that do, hmm?" Oberon mused over this. "Not even a quarter of a century later and you find yourselves in nearly the same predicament."

"The Door to the Nothing was opened!" Charlotte protested.

"Doors are *meant* to be opened, Princess, that's what they do. Perhaps Terra Mirum should have prepared itself for that possibility. Or employed better locks." The condescension dripped from each word before pooling into outright disdain. "Your alliance has proven too taxing to maintain, and Arden will not be anchored down by such helpless creatures. You and your pathetic Hero have done nothing to preserve Terra Mirum, only put it in further danger."

"You will not speak of my mother that way!" Charlotte barked

Oberon stopped cold. "...Mother?"

Charlotte felt the fire in her extinguish. The thing she had been told she absolutely must not do. She felt off balance and the scent of ammonia burned the back of her nose and throat again. "Um..." She took a step backward.

"You are the child of The White King... and the Dreamer?" Oberon concluded as the mystery around this sudden heir came to light. He smiled a wide, unnervingly toothy grin. "A human changeling...." He steepled his hands and leaned back in his throne. "I'll make you a deal, Changeling. I'll lend you my army, if you swear yourself into my service."

Thorn took a threatening step towards the dais, but Charlotte raised a hand. "What you're suggesting is slavery," she accused.

"That's a rather ugly thing to say," tsked Oberon.

"The truth often is," said Charlotte.

"Indeed," Oberon conceded. "So, let me present you with another ugly truth." He leaned forward again to meet her gaze once more. "Your kingdom will fall. Long before mine."

"You can't be serious about this," Thorn said incredulously. "She's only a child. Surely another accord can be reached."

"Perhaps," Oberon shrugged. "When this card wasn't on the table."

"With all due respect to royalty present," Robin spoke up, knowing she was out of turn, but saw no other way. "In accordance with the treaty between our courts, forcing either side to deprive itself of an heir to the throne would be considered an act of aggression or war. Which as you know would be a violation of the peace between our people."

Oberon looked undaunted, glancing at her with an unimpressed shrug. "Is that so?"

"And without that peace, the portals between our cities may find themselves open to let the Nightmares through directly," Robin confirmed curtly.

Charlotte smiled slightly at Robin who gave her an encouraging nod before she turned back to Oberon. "Could you withstand their attacks if they happened within your own walls, your highness? Is the peace between us something you're that willing to lose at this time? Perhaps you can make amends on such an offensive breach by lending your aid in the war."

Oberon huffed and leaned back in his throne once more. "Or perhaps one could argue my actions are in response to you kidnapping one of our own heirs."

"What?" Thorn and Charlotte asked simultaneously.

"Our beloved favorite goes missing, only to magically turn up again in your company." Oberon looked from Thorn to Robin to Charlotte. "How am I to believe you did not kidnap them in the first place?"

"Don't pretend you have any affection for me now," Thorn shook their head.

"I know I've always been hard on you, but I wanted to see you grow. I've been so worried."

"Bullshit," Thorn accused.

Oberon smiled his uncomfortably satisfied grin. "Can you prove it?"

Thorn looked to Titania in disbelief at her silence. "Will you say nothing to this?"

Titania's eyes averted. "Oberon is acting in the best interest of our people, Learic. You need to respect that."

"You cannot be serious. Mother—"

"What do you say to those accusations, Your Majesty?" Oberon leveled at Charlotte.

"There may be things more slimy than a tove after all," Charlotte muttered.

"Return our heir, and perhaps offer something of equal worth, and we may consider forgiving you for such an affront on our good will." There was a regal smugness to Oberon's tone that grinded against Charlotte's patience so intensely, she wanted nothing more than to punch him square in the nose.

"If you manage to *find* your good will, your highness, I will consider trying to appease it," said Charlotte.

"What would you have me do, princess?" Oberon asked. "Bow my court to the demands of an insolent child with no experience, knowledge or power to stand against *me*, let alone an army of nightmares?"

Her jaw felt tight. Anger had overridden anxiety. "Will you not even lend us my mother's blade?"

"The vorpal blade? The sword of the fearless? The very weapon that will protect us against the dark tide?" Oberon pretended to be aghast at the very suggestion. "Even if you could wield it, you scared little thing, do you dare suggest we be left defenseless as well deprived of our prized heir? Is there no end to the assaults you heave against the courts of Arden?"

"You will not help us, but you will stand in the way of helping ourselves. I thought you were arrogant, but in truth you're just a violent liar. To sit on your throne and pretend you aren't even the slightest bit afraid of what they will do to you when—"

"I AM AFRAID OF NOTHING!" Oberon boomed, standing up to his full height to glower down at them from the dais. He was an imposing figure and the room seemed to tremble by the sound of his voice. He motioned to Smoke with an angry swipe of his hand. "Remove them from my sight, I no longer find this diversion beneficial or entertaining."

Smoke moved to escort Robin and Charlotte from the room and Thorn walked after them.

"Learic," Titania called to them. They looked back at her for only a moment, shook their head, and exited out the doors as well.

The doors closed behind them, and Smoke exhaled so heavily it seemed almost as if he had been holding his breath the entire time. "Well, that went well," he commented dryly.

"He can't be serious about this ploy," Robin muttered, her brow furrowed in thought. "This is some kind of game he's playing; I just wish I knew the rules. And why."

"To not even surrender the blade," Smoke shook his head. "Something isn't right here."

"Another changeling and he's mad with power," Thorn exclaimed in frustration.

"It must be more than that," Robin tapped her chin thoughtfully.

"He… really didn't like me suggesting he was afraid," Charlotte suggested but none of the other three seemed to be paying much attention to her.

"Titania was absurdly quiet," said Robin, looking from Thorn to Smoke. "Is that a new development?"

"Very," Smoke confirmed. "I can't say I've ever seen her so tight lipped, especially when Oberon was making a right ass of himself."

"She wouldn't even really look at me," Thorn added.

"Yes, something is very wrong here," Robin concluded.

"Nightmares?" Charlotte suggested.

"We don't really have time to speculate, unfortunately... I should report back to Elan Vital. And I do need to return the princess to her father."

Charlotte felt the blood drain from her face, and she nervously reached up to play with the golden feather earring. "I can't possibly go back now."

"We had a deal," Robin reminded.

"Things have rather changed since that arrangement, wouldn't you agree?" Thorn asked. "Is it even safe to make that trip back?"

"We're running out of time, Robin."

"I know that!" Robin snapped.

Charlotte stroked the gryphon feather between her fingertips and she glanced away just in time to catch sight of two very harried-looking medics hurrying down the hallway. She glanced back at the rest of the party who was continuing to argue. They had not noticed the fleeing fae. Nor did they seem to be noticing her.

Charlotte took a few small steps away from the small group, then another until she was around the corner and out of their eye-line. She turned and moved quickly down the hallway. She paused, not sure where the medics had gone, but she got the notion she should turn right down another corridor. She was moving away from the finery of the grand halls. This hallway was simpler. No less beautiful but lacking the rather excessive opulence that seemed to adorn Arden's court. She peeked around, feeling the individual strands of the feather. Then as she turned down another corner… she heard it.

Someone was *screaming*.

It was not like the sound she'd heard in either dream. It was not animalistic, but it was tortured. And as she moved down the hall the sound grew louder and louder. And she could make out voices.

"Dammit, Surin, I said hold him down."

"I'm trying!"

"HER EYES. FATES, HER EYES."

"You're safe now, Phin, calm down."

"I'M NOT SAFE, NONE OF US ARE SAFE, DON'T YOU GET THAT?"

"Fates, Surin, if you don't hold him down so I can administer the sedative, I swear by the void itself—there!"

Charlotte hovered around the corner of the infirmary door, listening intently.

"We're going to change." The screaming voice had quieted but had not lost its urgency. "We're all going to change. Greedy, hoarding things…"

"At least he's not yelling anymore."

"I want to check the blood samples we took," the same two medics exited the infirmary and walked across the hall to vanish inside another door.

Charlotte watched the door they exited before looking back at the infirmary door. It seemed quiet now. She glanced back and forth to ensure the coast was clear, and snuck through.

The infirmary was warm stained wood walls and white cloth that could be easily bleached and cleaned. A single patient, presumably Phin, was tucked tightly into a bed, strapped beneath the covers to keep him from thrashing. He was bandaged, gauze covering his right eye. It had been newly changed by the looks of it. He had an athletic sort of look about him, a no-nonsense haircut and what little she could see of him between the bandages and blankets were layered in years of varying scars.

Charlotte looked over her shoulder and cautiously took a step forward. The man was muttering to himself.

"Couldn't keep it safe. Nothing safe, nothing safe…" He rocked his head back and forth.

"Couldn't keep what safe?" Charlotte gently prodded with a soft voice.

"Any of us. Dreamer's blade. Gone. Just gone. Like it didn't even matter. Like *we* didn't even matter."

Charlotte's brow furrowed. The vorpal blade? "Gone how?"

"Snatched," Phin gasped. "Snatched from the King. Bam, gone. Hear it sing, hear it sing… it screams when it's close to you."

Charlotte paused. It sounded like the same creature from her nightmare. "It stole the vorpal blade from Oberon?"

"Stare into the void and it will swallow you. Hollow you. Make you hungry for what no longer fills you." Phin tried to raise his hands to look at them but couldn't. "Killed the squad, took the blade. An I for an eye… All gone, all gone. She's gone."

Charlotte felt an uneasy pit in her stomach. "Who's she?"

"She's not. Not anymore. It became her. Swallowed her. Twisted bones and sharpened teeth. All teeth, all hunger. Gone. Gone. Gone."

Charlotte swallowed hard as she began to put the pieces of his shattered speech together.

So there was something Oberon was afraid of after all.

22

FEAR ITSELF

Charlotte did not flee the infirmary so much as storm from it. She walked with such purpose and speed it created a wind through her hair. Her fingers tensed at her side in anger, and the energy of the air seemed to crackle in her wake as if lightning would strike at any minute.

Thorn and Robin were arguing, Smoke nowhere to be seen.

It as the electricity of Charlotte's presence that caught Robin so off-guard that it took her some time to ask what she and the others had been arguing about moments before. "Where have you been?"

Charlotte strode past them and braced both hands against the hefty doors.

Thorn's heart stopped. "What are you—"

"*Doors are meant to be opened.*" Charlotte shoved the doors open, and they banged loudly against the walls on the other side.

The court startled into silence.

Charlotte could feel hundreds of eyes on her, but her own narrowed on Oberon.

He had briefly paused in his actions, but that was the only sign of alarm. Once he saw the cause of the great noise, he languished back into his seat like a pleased cat. "It's rude to barge in unannounced and unwanted, Your Majesty. You will have to learn decorum if you're going to join my court."

Charlotte continued her determined walk to stand before the dais but said nothing, merely glared at him, unfaltering.

Oberon frowned. "Well, if you're going to bluster in here, you might as well say your peace. Come on, child, out with it."

Charlotte's jaw tightened, the hard stare burning into him. She was so angry she was almost worried if she spoke now it would just come out in screams.

It was uncomfortable, even for Oberon.

He flustered and broke their gaze, playing off his unease as boredom. "What *are* you looking at?"

"A coward," Charlotte spat.

The word echoed.

Oberon's disposition shifted, and the silent grace in which he leaned forward had an eerie quality that sent a shiver through his court. Ice sprawled in spider-web-like patterns along the throne and floor from his hands and feet. Icicles dangled off the dais, and the frost curled out off the edge off the platform, causing a few of the Unseelie to take wary steps back. "I beg your pardon?"

"You're a coward." Charlotte felt her hands shaking at her sides, and so she clenched them into fists. "That's why you won't answer my father's request for aid," she accused, only realizing the temperature in the room had dropped drastically when her breath curled into mist past her lips. The adrenaline kept her warm and drove her onward. "That's why you've shut yourselves into Arden, not because it's what's best for your kingdom. It's not even because you want to reclaim your land. It's because you're absolutely terrified of what lies beyond your gates and you're *praying* once it has gorged itself on all of Terra Mirum, it will be content."

Oberon's eyes were piercing. She could see by the way his upper lip curled back that his pearl-white teeth held an almost fang-like quality. "That," he spat. "Is a bold claim for a trembling—"

"I *know* about the vorpal blade," Charlotte interrupted.

There was a breath of hesitation, the minutest of flinches in his eyes, and a slight twitch at the corner of his lips. "What about it?"

"You don't have it."

Oberon's muscles visibly tensed as if the growing frost around him was now freezing him in place, as well.

Charlotte could see he was calculating, trying to read her in that moment and deduce how much she knew, and how much damage she could do with it. "You can't give it over because you don't even know where it is. It was *stolen* out of your own hands."

"That's impossible," Moth spoke up angrily. "The vorpal blade *cannot* be stolen. It protects those who wield it, and it can only be wielded by—"

"The *fearless*, yes, as your good King was so kind to remind me…" Charlotte looked back to Oberon.

His shoulders were back, his muscles rigid—he now looked more like a frightened cat than a predator.

"But you're not fearless, are you?" Her voice was unusually soft. "You stared directly into the eyes of what you're afraid of."

Titania wordlessly rested a hand over her husband's, and he gripped it tightly, gratefully.

"You saw one of your own twist and shift into something terrible. You saw in those hungry eyes what even *you* could become." Charlotte's brow furrowed.

Robin turned to Moth. "We saw no patrol outside of the gates on our way to your city."

"After our last one didn't return. We sent out a search—the King himself led it." Her voice trailed off slightly. "Only a handful returned. So, patrols ceased."

"Were you going to warn them?" Charlotte asked, feeling Thorn join her at her side. "What could happen? What fae are capable of becoming?"

"I will not answer to the judgement of an ignorant child," Oberon growled.

"Then you will answer to your people and your conscience," Charlotte challenged.

There was a brief pause, and Oberon looked out to the court. The facade was crumbling, and there seemed to be a hint of desperation about him. He stood to his full height, his hand waving her away like he was clearing air. "This... is the wild imagination of a desperate princess." The less calm he seemed; the easier Charlotte found it to feel grounded in the moment. "If your father wants Arden's aid, he will have to do better than this."

"Is that what you tell yourself when you close your eyes?" Charlotte catechized, "that it was just your wild imagination? That you could not possibly have truly witnessed what you did?"

Perhaps it was the inexplicable lack of mocking in her voice that gave Oberon pause, that prompted him to look at her and sincerely ask his next question without the same dismissal he'd given her countless times before. "What would you know of such things?"

"I've seen it." The longer they held each other's gaze, the more Oberon's god-like façade broke, and she saw the haunted man who had become recently aware of his own fragile existence.

"We cannot risk turning into that *thing*," Oberon's voice broke.

The court inhaled sharply at this confirmation.

"What she had become..." The King shook his head, his shoulders slumping. "I do not fear death, Changeling. *Death* is a beginning as much as it is an end. It is a beat; a rest." He sucked in sharply through his teeth, wiping his eyes with his arm. "*They* are unending. They are insatiable. Always hungry, always needing, always *hunting*. They are forever in ways eternity was never meant to be. You do not understand. You could not possibly understand—"

"I understand my mother and others like her are *dying* while you are hiding your head under the covers!"

Oberon flinched. "We cannot fight it," he whispered helplessly.

"We can, and we will. You stood with my father before. You beat back the threat."

"It wasn't like this," Oberon answered.

"Wasn't it?" Thorn piped up. They looked to Charlotte for courage and continued. "Haven't we always been at risk of something like this? The only thing that's shifted is our ignorance. We're aware we're vulnerable."

Charlotte felt a swell of pride warm her chest. "Is the knowledge that you have something to risk all it takes to crumble your resolve? Is your courage so brittle?"

Oberon's lips formed a thin line as they pursed together, his eyes narrowing. "You really are just like your mother."

Charlotte felt her back straighten a little proudly. "Thank you."

"Yes, normally that would sound like a compliment, wouldn't it?" Oberon sighed and reached to Titania, helping her rise to her feet. The two conferred quietly, foreheads resting against each other's, their fingers intertwined. It was a tender affection rarely seen in public between the King and Queen.

Titania gave her husband a reassuring smile. "Robin, give word to King Oswin that Arden will answer his call and add our might and magic to the strength of Terra Mirum's army.

Titania addressed the Seelie. "We must start preparations immediately. Notify the smiths. We have much work to do."

Oberon gestured to the Unseelie, and they, too, departed.

The King and Queen of Arden descended the dais, looking somewhat shaken but determined.

"Your parents would be proud of you," Titania told Charlotte. "You were unyielding. Wild and in need of molding—but the makings of a future queen."

Charlotte smiled a little awkwardly, and she felt both Robin and Thorn step up beside her.

"Without the vorpal blade, we *will* be at a disadvantage," Oberon muttered.

"I wouldn't worry too much about that," Charlotte answered. "I'm pretty sure I know where we could find it."

"You do?" Robin was wary.

"I had a dream about it before I came here. I didn't really understand what it was until now, but… I'm fairly sure I know where to find it."

"A changeling born from Dream and Dreamer…" Titania marveled quietly.

"Do any of you know where you'd find a vast brick tunnel? You can traverse down it by way of a wrought iron staircase? Possibly somewhere in the middle of the woods?" She looked at the faces around her. They ranged from bemused to worried. "Potentially referred to simply as 'the train tunnel'?"

"You had a dream the vorpal blade is there?" Robin asked.

"Well, no, I had a nightmare about the creature that attacked Oberon living in that tunnel, so…"

"So, you don't *know* the vorpal blade is there," Robin answered.

"It's the logical conclusion?" Charlotte offered.

"That's far too risky to send a group of soldiers there," Robin dismissed. "We have no guarantee, and we need every able-bodied soldier we can get."

Charlotte shrugged. "I could go get it?"

The stares on Charlotte seemed to intensify.

"That creature took out an entire search party of trained soldiers!" Robin growled incredulously. "It'd be an absolute suicide mission, and for what? *One* sword?"

"One very important sword—"Thorn tried to reason.

"We can fight this war without the vorpal blade," Robin growled at them. She looked back to Charlotte. "You have done far more than I imagine your father would have ever anticipated or even wanted. When the sun rises tomorrow, we are both heading back to Elan Vital. No more delays." She looked to Oberon, Titania, and Thorn and took a low bow. "Elan Vital's greatest thanks to the courts of Arden, with our strengths combined, we shall not fail." She grabbed Charlotte by the arm and pulled her out the door.

"But Robin—"

"You have done all you can, Charlie—*more* than you can," Robin hissed under her breath and pulled her out the doors.

"I can do *more*!" Charlotte insisted.

"Enough," Robin demanded. Her voice was low, commanding, and abrupt. A reminder that the woman who held her may be in the service of her father, but she was formidable herself and had run out of patience. "You have been *lucky* up until this point, do you understand? You can't keep putting yourself on the line like this. That luck is *going* to run out. And I will not explain that to *either* of your parents." She released her with a deep sigh. "Meet me back at our rooms. I have to brief the generals as best I can before we leave tomorrow."

Charlotte watched the fae leave and bit her lower lip.

Her anxiety was rising again. Her stomach felt sick. She knew without a doubt that if she went back to Elan Vital, she'd never find her mother. Or the man from her dreams.

If the creature was real… then surely, he was too?

He told her to meet him. But *where*? And how would she get there with the guards not letting anyone out, and Robin so determined to take her back?

The Coleridge Clock, as if to answer, weighed on her neck.

23

ESCAPE TO SOMEWHERE

Charlotte decided to be more methodical than the last time she'd fled a castle by way of clock by investigating what lay behind each mirror first. This, however, was proving increasingly difficult, as, unlike before, there seemed to always be people everywhere. Despite preparing for war, Arden's court was far more populated than that of Terra Mirum, or at least in a more concentrated space.

She managed to check one of the large hallway mirrors for a brief second, giving her a view of a quiet looking bedroom mid-day before the rapidly clicking heels of a group of Seelie nobles forced her to close the connection. She huffed to herself and let them pass. She could overhear the clamor of concern regarding this new development around a Fae's possible fate against the Nightmares, the oncoming war...

And then another group of fae, Unseelie this time, smaller in number, but Charlotte could see out of the corner of her eye that they did take notice of her. She could feel eyes on her every time someone passed.

She was, after all, the one who had brought this terror to light.

Charlotte gave up on the hallway and moved deeper into the castle, her left hand around the face of the Coleridge clock to keep it from view, feeling the etching dig into her palm as her knuckles paled with her grip. She ran the fingers of her right hand along the various ornate doorknobs she encountered. She kept finding herself hesitating to open them. She'd slow her pace when the hallway occupants thinned in spurts, tilting her head toward the door to see if she could hear anything. Most of the time she could hear voices. But she wasn't always certain that they were voices within the room or voices in the hallway.

She was wasting time.

Charlotte inhaled for a count of five, then exhaled for six. Then again. And again. It slowed her walking pace gradually as she continued her trek along the singular winding hallway. And at last, when her fingers moved from tracing the wall to resting on another doorknob, something made her pause. She felt that tightness in her chest dissipate completely, and her fingers slowly entwined to create a more secure grip on the handle. She tried to listen but couldn't really decipher if she heard anything from within or not.

She was getting a myriad of odd looks from the fae who passed her, and, longing for the inexplicable comfort this room's door seemed to promise, Charlotte smiled nervously before opening it just enough to slip within.

The room was empty: a large bedroom suite, lavish to be sure, but as it seemed in a similar theme to the rest of the castle, she didn't take much note of it.

Charlotte exhaled in relief, and her grip on the watch around her neck loosened enough to turn it in her palm and open it to look at the face. The golden hand beckoned her further inside.

The more she got a look at it, the only remarkable thing about the room was that it didn't seem very lived in. It had an almost abandoned sort of feeling, as if its owner hadn't taken a foot in it in some time. There was no dust—maids had clearly seen to that—but there was a sort of staleness to the air. Everything seemed uncomfortably in its place, like a catalogue photo.

Charlotte followed the little golden hand as it led her past the suite and into the bedroom to a large ornate golden-frame mirror. She swallowed and straightened her shoulders before turning the watch face in her hand, lining up the inside mirror with that of the one before her. The reflection pierced through the larger surface like a rock into a lake, and as the ripples moved outward, Charlotte watched the reflection of the room wane, and what looked to be a department store dressing room come into view.

Then the door of the room she was certain no one ever entered opened a crack.

Charlotte flinched and closed the watch in her hand, the portal closing simultaneously with it as she looked over her shoulder. She could hear voices, and so she crept a little closer.

One was Thorn. "And I'll be locked up until when?"

"I'm trying to protect you." That was Titania.

"With all due respect, mother, this family's idea of protection has made deeper cuts than most blades."

There was a pause and a long sigh. "If you wish to join the others when the time comes, you can. Just... Please. Indulge Oberon this once."

Another pause. The door opened fully and closed again.

Charlotte peeked into the front suite and saw Thorn standing by the door in frustration. They tried the door handle on a whim and confirming that it was locked, then turned to face the rest of the room.

"In my gilded cage again. Joy." And then they saw Charlotte. "Charlie?"

Charlotte cleared her throat and stepped out from the doorway. "Yes, um. Hello. How... Um... How are you?"

Thorn's eyes narrowed curiously. "Were you waiting for me here?"

Charlotte bit the inside of her cheek and met her companion's gaze, nodding. "Course. I wanted to see if you were okay."

Thorn chuffed. "Liar. You didn't even know this room was mine, did you?"

"So, they locked you in," Charlotte evaded. "Are you like… grounded or something?"

"Or something." Thorn walked toward her leisurely. "And you?"

Charlotte shrugged. "Robin is taking me back first thing in the morning…"

"And you thought you could hide from her?" Thorn mused. They leaned on the wall next to her, almost looming over her but not touching. "Quite a scandalous hiding place, princess, locked up with a bastard heir in a royal bedchamber…"

Charlotte's face flushed. "Well, I… um…"

Thorn's hand gently brushed from her cheek to rest on her shoulder, and Charlotte felt herself leaning her head toward it, savoring the touch for the brief time it lasted.

It left the girl feeling in a bit of a warm, comfortable haze.

"Robin doesn't know you have this, I take it."

Charlotte looked startled, and that haze cleared very quickly when her eyes opened and focused on Thorn now holding the watch face of the Coleridge Clock.

Thorn tilted their head slightly and gave Charlotte a look that indicated they'd been onto her from the very start, which made Charlotte feel a bit guilty about her thinly veiled lie. "So then, Treasure… where are we going?"

Charlotte's brow furrowed slightly. "Who says you're coming with me?"

Thorn grinned broadly. "The person who could help make sure you don't hop into the middle of the ocean again?"

Charlotte rolled her eyes and stepped away from the doorway, walking back to the mirror. "Nice try…"

"And the person who could break the mirror before you have a chance to go through it," Thorn offered in a sing-song voice as they followed.

Charlotte paused and looked back at them skeptically. "You wouldn't."

"There's still a lot you don't know about me," Thorn answered lowly, closing the distance between them once more.

"Is there?" Charlotte asked doubtfully in a flat tone.

"Will you really abandon me?" they asked dramatically, locking eyes once more. Their right hand tangling a little in Charlotte's hair, fingers playing with the golden griffin feather in her ear. "I'm literally a member of royalty locked away in a tower by an evil step-father. You wouldn't abandon a damsel in distress, would you?"

Charlotte watched them joke around, silent. They were breathtaking, there was no arguing that, but the gryphon feather let her see beyond that, to the underlying fear and concern wrestling beneath the thick layers of charm—fear of Charlotte leaving, and fear for either of them staying. "It's dangerous," she finally protested.

"So am I," Thorn purred.

"And stupid," Charlotte offered.

"So am—" Thorn stopped, glared, and huffed through their nostrils. "Nice try."

Charlotte took a step back and walked to stand in front of the mirror.

"I know the lay of the land better than you," Thorn argued.

"Learic…" Charlotte sighed.

"You'd miss me."

They were right, and so Charlotte didn't argue. "That seems irrelevant to the task at hand."

"I'd miss you," Thorn offered, stepping toward her again.

The gryphon feather didn't seem to protect as strongly against their allure this time, and for a moment, Charlotte wondered if they'd damaged it or if this feeling was not based around magic at all. "You'd be leaving your mother again."

"Someone needs me more right now, even if she can't see it."

Charlotte sighed in frustration, not sure what to do.

"Just tell me *where* you're going," Thorn asked gently.

Charlotte shrugged helplessly. "I don't know."

"Well, then you're sure to get there at least."

Charlotte ran her hands through her hair. "I'd thought I'd track down the vorpal blade, but…" She shook her head and dropped her hands to her sides. "Before I came here, I had this dream. This… huge library with trees for pillars, and a fretwork of branches covered with snow. It was… creepy. But there was this man—he's appeared in a lot of my dreams, all of which have had some kernel of truth up until now. He asked me to meet him there. I think it's important. I think it could help Mom... help the Dreamers. I'd nearly forgotten because when I met Smoke... I just assumed it was him—or that that library was here... but after all this... I don't know anymore."

Thorn thought for a moment. "I don't know about the snow... but it sounds like the Phrontistery."

"Alexandria's?"

Thorn nodded. "Huge place. Can't imagine it doesn't have at least *a* looking glass. She lived there even, so she'd need at least one to make sure her cravats were straight."

"*A* looking glass. One. We have to find *one* mirror among billions? Trillions?"

Thorn shook their head. "It's a better lead than nothing, Charlie." They paused and then added optimistically, "And we don't know that it's just one."

"Fine, at best, what, three?"

"Yes, but that doesn't mean there's only three on your side that lead there."

Charlotte frowned. "You said they were doors, not portals."

"I also said multiple doors can go to one room, didn't I?"

Charlotte blinked. "You did?" She tried to think back to their first conversation, and it did sound somewhat familiar. She shook her head. "Look, it's been a long couple of days. You can't honestly expect me to retain all of it."

"You're right," Thorn answered, stepping up beside her. "So, I should go with you."

Charlotte looked them over. "What about your wings? Those will cause a little bit of commotion, don't you think?"

"Haven't you ever heard of a fae glamour?" Thorn smiled.

"No one will see them?"

"I'll be as normal-looking as you."

"That's what I'm afraid of."

24

MIRROR SKIPPING

I t was for the briefest of seconds, passing through
the water-like surface of the mirror to the other side,
but Charlotte almost thought she heard... music?
But the notes were as quickly gone as they were heard.

On the other side of the looking glass, Charlotte and
Thorn found themselves standing in a lush dressing room.

It occurred to Charlotte that it wasn't clear if
they were in a men's or women's dressing room, or a
particular country, and knowing the answer to either
question could be "any," she grabbed Thorn's hand and
tugged them toward the exit, nearly bumping into a
tall elegantly dressed woman along the way.

"I'm so sorry," Charlotte apologized.

"*Stai più attento la prossima volta, questo non è un
parco giochi.*" The woman scolded, then warming up a
little. "*Ma i tuoi costumi sembrano grandi.*"

Thorn winked at her, and Charlotte watched the
woman's cheeks flush. "*Grazie, bella donna.*"

"So, you know French now?" Charlotte huffed
slightly and tugged the fae out into the racks of clothing.

"Well, yes, but *that* was Italian," Thorn answered impishly.

It would seem glamor or no, Thorn's charm was not one of the things that would be hidden from human eyes. She stopped, realizing Thorn looked no different from when they left Arden. "Could you try to draw less attention to yourself and lose the wings?" she demanded in a snap.

Thorn blinked at her, confused by the sudden shift in mood of their companion. "They are hidden, Treasure." Then, remembering. "Remove your earring."

Charlotte looked a little dumbstruck before she reached up to tentatively remove the griffin earring, setting it on the top of a clothing rack momentarily.

Before her eyes, the natural glow of her companion dulled and faded away, the iridescent wings vanished to nothing. Their clothing remained the same, and while different, it seemed somehow far less fantastical without being surrounded by their normal surroundings and natural aura.

Charlotte stubbornly put the gryphon feather back in its proper place, even more assured of its value. "Why didn't you change your clothes, too?"

Thorn shrugged and leaned toward her with a smile as the earring reverted her vision back to their true and breathtakingly beautiful form. "I didn't want you to feel alone."

Charlotte looked down at her own clothing and was reminded of the dress. "Right. This… will be frustrating to deal with."

"You look cute."

"I need to save the world, not look cute."

"I'm offended at the notion you can't do both," Thorn teased.

"Shut up," Charlotte grumbled, opening the Coleridge Clock. She took a deep breath and carefully moved the watch face in her palm. She was surprised to see that the little golden hand was not pointing directly behind them to the mirrors in the dressing room but urging them forward.

"You know," Thorn spoke lower. "If you're really uncomfortable... we are in a clothing store."

"I don't have any money," Charlotte dismissed, following the little golden hand while absently reaching for Thorn's behind her.

"I'm not entirely sure that matters once you hop through the next mirror."

Charlotte frowned. "Right... the five-finger discount perk of being forgettable."

"Charlie," Thorn's grip on her hand tightened, and she stopped to look back at them. "You're not forgettable. I'm sorry I suggested it."

"You didn't really suggest it, you just reminded me of a simple fact."

"Hey," Thorn pulled her closer and leaned their forehead against hers. "Stay with me. Think of why we're doing this."

Charlotte nodded. "You're right. I'm sorry." She looked back down at the watch face. "This way..."

It brought them down the escalator, and Charlotte caught sight of a name, La Rinascente.

"You know *I'll* never forget you, at least, don't you?" Thorn asked quietly.

"Yeah… the magic doesn't work on you the same," Charlotte answered distractedly, and they began to weave through expensive housewares.

"Right," Thorn conceded, hesitated, then spoke again. "But beyond that."

"Beyond that?" Charlotte stopped in front of a large, mirrored wall that reflected the countless crystal dishes and glasses, glittering under the lights and seeming to go on forever. "Ooh boy."

Thorn looked from Charlotte to the wall where the Coleridge Clock was pointing. "We can get around it."

"We're going to bump something."

"So, we bump something."

"It will knock over!" Charlotte whispered anxiously.

"And break into a thousand pieces, and no one will understand how because we'll be long gone," Thorn answered. They tilted their head to the side, studying the guilty expression on Charlotte's face. "What is that charming human expression? You can't make an omelet without breaking a few eggs?"

Charlotte looked dubiously at the display. "Those are some very expensive eggs."

Thorn shrugged a little and placed their hands on Charlotte's shoulders. "C'mon, Charlie. You can't save the world from an eternal deadly sleep without breaking a few Italian crystal dining sets."

Charlotte swallowed and carefully lined up the small mirror on the inside of the lid with the wall. It wavered, ripples in a pond stretching across the entire wall which caused the crystal pieces to lightly "tink" against each other as they moved ever so slightly. She looked around nervously, but none of the other shoppers seemed to notice. "How is no one seeing this?"

"You'd be surprised how little most humans actually see," Thorn answered, their eyes searching the forming image on the other side. "Looks like a ballroom of some sort. We might run into Nightmares on the other side, so you'll need to be ready to run, okay?"

"O-okay," Charlotte answered with uncertainty.

"Don't worry... I won't let anything happen to you. Now let's go!" Thorn pulled Charlotte forward, and Charlotte's grip on the Coleridge Clock tightened, making sure to keep it aimed at the mirror to keep the portal open.

Charlotte's eyes closed involuntarily a moment in fear but then—"Do you hear music?"

CRASH!

The sound of shattering crystal behind them was gone as quickly as it had been as the portal closed swiftly behind them once they were through.

Thorn released Charlotte's hand to draw their sword instinctively. "Stay behind me, just in case."

It was dark save for the dim sunlight pouring through dirty windows, empty, and cold— the once grand ballroom of some noble long gone. It had the eerie feeling of something beloved quickly abandoned in the face of danger.

Charlotte flexed her fingers and brought her hand up to breathe onto the glove to try to warm the fingers beneath. She looked back over her shoulder at their reflection as if she would be able to see the carnage that they'd left in their wake. She bit her lower lip.

"They'll be fine, Charlotte. Places like that have protections for accidents like this," Thorn assured, misinterpreting her look.

"No, I know…" Charlotte started.

"What's wrong?"

"I thought I heard…" Had there always been music? She would have thought she'd have remembered that from her first few jumps.

"Heard what?"

"Never mind." Charlotte shook her head and opened the Coleridge clock once more which had been gripped closed when she'd heard the impact behind them. The golden hand wavered slightly as if not knowing quite which way its "north" was before landing in a direction out one of the doors. "This way."

Charlotte stopped as they passed by a large golden ornate mirror behind a porcelain vase of wilted flowers. Her brow furrowed, looking from the mirror to the clock in her hand, which still pointed forward.

"What's wrong?"

"It's just… why not this one?"

Thorn shrugged. "Maybe that one isn't a door."

Charlotte was more bothered by this development. Weren't all mirrors doors that the clock could unlock? Or had she just been incredibly lucky before in her choosing?

The pair pressed onward, following the little golden hand. They wove down the halls, passing multiple mirrors before it took them to one in the basement of what must have been the servant's quarters. It was simple, but it would still do the trick with a simple beckoning from the Coleridge Clock.

On the other side was also dark, but an illuminated sculpture of a knight fighting a dragon that sat atop a dresser gave a soft glow that helped give way to details. There was a bunkbed, and while the top sleeper was not alight, the bottom bunk revealed the sprawled figure of a sleeping boy no more than seven.

Charlotte gripped Thorn's arm as they sheathed their sword. "There. Do you hear it? That music?"

It was faint, but the quiet tinkling of music, something out of a dream.

Thorn paused. "It's probably a lullaby the little guys listen to before bed," they hushed. They gently took Charlotte's hand and carefully stepped through the portal.

For a moment, the music was louder, vibrating in Charlotte's chest and mind. It sounded like a waltz of some kind. And then they were on the other side and the portal was closed, and the music gone.

Charlotte looked to Thorn expectantly but the fae hadn't seemed to notice the absence of what they'd attributed to the lullaby of children.

Instead, they walked over to the lit statue and chuffed amusedly through their nose before looking back at Charlotte. "I get it," they whispered, gesturing with their thumb. "It's a *knight* light."

Charlotte rolled her eyes and looked down at the Coleridge clock. It pointed out of the room, and so the pair carefully tiptoed their way from the small boys and around the corner to another door. Charlotte closed the door behind them. "Another unfamiliar bathroom," she whispered.

"You have to be joking," Thorn said, pointing to the mirror on the medicine cabinet above the sink. "How are we supposed to walk through that?"

Charlotte's lips quirked an amused smile. "You climb."

Thorn frowned. "What if there's a whole pack of toves on the other side?"

"Then you climb sword first?" Charlotte offered. She raised up the Coleridge Clock.

The reflection on the other side looked like a small cottage room full of sunlight. Warm colors, wood. A strange contrast from the dead of night on this side of the looking-glass.

"Look, no visible danger," Charlotte offered, then bowed slightly. "After you."

"Oh no," Thorn whispered back. "*I* insist, after you."

"If I go first, the portal closes behind me," Charlotte reminded smugly.

"You're enjoying this."

"I am."

Thorn glared before carefully stepping from the toilet to the sink. They adjusted their stance and paused. "Wait, Charlie, I hear that music again. Same tune."

"I know!" Charlotte said excitedly, then stopped, realizing she'd just exclaimed in an unknown house.

"You boys better not be out of bed!" A woman's voice called from downstairs.

Thorn cursed under their breath and fell through the mirror more than climbed.

Charlotte followed in their footsteps even less gracefully, trying to keep the Coleridge clock aimed properly. It didn't work, and so the portal closed. She had to open it again while standing in the sink.

"Who's in here?" The door began to open, and Charlotte dove through the mirror.

She landed on hardwood floor with an uncomfortable thump. "Ouch."

Thorn sympathetically leaned down to help her up. "I was worried you'd been caught for a moment there."

"I almost was," Charlotte admitted. "I need to work on my sneak."

"And your landing," Thorn teased.

"Your Majesty!" a voice exclaimed in shock, followed by a thwack and multiple thuds.

Charlotte and Thorn looked toward the doorway to be face to face with a simply dressed Seelie fae, a strongly woven reed basket on the floor at his feet and multiple escaping apples sprawled from it.

Thorn put a finger to their lips. "Not quite so loud, if you please…"

"I-I'm so sorry, I wasn't expecting royalty in my home—"

"And you shouldn't. In fact, we weren't here at all, yes?" Thorn asked.

"I…" The fae looked away, confused. "If you wish.

"Sorry about your apples." Thorn followed Charlotte out to the street. Then they cursed under their breath in a voice that only Charlotte could hear, and she was certain if she understood half of the words that came out of Thorn's mouth, she would have choked. "We're back in Arden."

Charlotte looked around at the street. It wasn't familiar in that she'd walked it, but the large trees and living buildings were rather unmistakable. "It's alright. We knew this was a risk. We'll be okay." She paused before reaching for the Coleridge Clock again to guide them. "Can you… grab one of the firefly lamps?"

Thorn gave her a strange look but flew up to carefully remove one of the orbs from the strings that laced around the trees. It was a few sizes larger than a softball, carrying two "fireflies" who were not currently illuminated, as they seemed to sleep during the day. "What's this for?"

"The knight light gave me an idea," Charlotte answered absently. "We'll need a few more... And maybe a bag to carry them."

"I'll see if our friendly apple picker has one to spare?"

Armed with a side satchel and five total "firefly" orbs, the two slunk through Arden once more, following the instruction of the Coleridge Clock.

"What do you think that music is?" Charlotte asked.

"I don't know. Certainly not in anything I ever read or heard about the Coleridge Clock," Thorn offered.

"Not something that was important to the original maker or...?" Charlotte prodded.

"Not that I'm aware of. Does it happen every time you open a door?"

"That's just it," Charlotte answered. "I don't think I've ever heard it until now. That can't be good, right?"

Thorn opened their mouth to make a smart reply but stopped themselves. "I honestly don't know. It seemed like a nice tune... but it could be related to the nightmares?"

"It could be something that could put people to sleep so they can feed off them," Charlotte offered.

"Then wouldn't we both be out cold by now?"

"Hmm. Good point." Charlotte stopped as the Coleridge Clock brought them to the front door of what looked like an enormous mushroom patch.

Thorn knocked on the door for them both. "And it doesn't make a terrible amount of sense for us to only be hearing it while going through the doors. That would only reach two of us, and I doubt The Nightmares even know what the Coleridge Clock even is."

The door swung ajar, and a voluptuous Unseelie fae blinked at Charlotte. Then her eyes widened as they rested on Thorn. "Learic?" She gasped.

"Kwenlas," Thorn purred her name. "What an unexpected and pleasant surprise… I don't suppose you would mind letting us discreetly use one of your mirrors, would you?"

The Unseelie blinked her thick dark lashes once more. "My mirrors?"

"I promise it will be quick," Thorn assured, "and for the good of Arden."

Bewildered, Kwenlas stepped aside to let them enter.

Charlotte entered first at Thorn's behest, stepping into a modestly sized but lavishly decorated foyer. Distracted momentarily from her mission, she let her eyes trace the walls, resting on a portrait of a handsome fae with sharp features and small horns at his temples. She took a few steps closer, peering at the piercing green eyes. He looked so familiar it actually bothered her. The plaque on the bottom of the frame confusingly read: *In begrudging memory of our beloved Jack. Knave & Martyr.*

Thorn cleared their throat. "Charlotte. Mirror."

Charlotte blinked and looked down at the clock once more. "Right, sorry." Following the Coleridge clock's directions, she walked down a hall toward a closed door. As her hand reached for the knob, Kwenlas stepped ahead of her and gave a strained smile.

"One moment, would you?" She gave a pained smile before turning around to the door and knocking a series of beats that didn't seem at all natural and then she paused, waiting.

It occurred to Charlotte this must have been some sort of code, but the door did not open for them. Instead Kwenlas seemed to count to herself before opening the door herself and motioning them to enter.

Inside was a room that seemed fit for no other word than "boudoir," but it did hold a three-way mirror. It reflected onto the bed, which was rumpled, suggesting its owner hadn't the mind to bother making it… or it had just been in use. Charlotte raised her eyebrows slightly. Just… exactly, where were they? She looked back toward the mirror and caught sight of Kwenlas draped against the wall with Thorn leaning over her to talk in hushed voices that she couldn't hear. She felt a sharp twinge in her chest and exhaled through her nostrils before consulting the Coleridge Clock.

It was pointing to the mirror on the right.

Charlotte positioned herself appropriately and cleared her throat loudly at her companion as the door opened.

The music greeted them again, louder this time, seeming to beckon them on the other side to a bathroom so large and luxurious it'd have to be a hotel. The large spa tub looked out to a snow-covered landscape.

"When this is over, we'll have to catch up." Thorn kissed Kwenlas' hand, lingering longer than what

Charlotte would imagine would be considered "proper" before they winked and sauntered through the door.

"If they live that long," Charlotte grumbled after.

"I think that music is getting louder," Thorn commented to Charlotte as she stepped up beside them.

"How do you know Kwenlas?" Charlotte asked, attempting to sound casual.

"Oh, I don't really *know* her."

"You knew her name."

Thorn grinned ever so slightly. "I know all of my subject's names."

"You didn't know the apple picker's."

"...So, I forgot *one* name. Where to next?" Thorn asked, looking pointedly at the Coleridge Clock.

"You didn't forget *one* name. I'm not an idiot. She called you by your given name in a very familiar context. You have a history with that woman. I want to know what."

"Aren't we being a little nosy?"

"No, we're being a LOT nosy."

"Excuse me, what are you doing in here?"

The two froze and looked toward an older blonde man with a mustache frowning at them. He looked rather intimidating, which was a feat considering he was wearing a white fluffy bathrobe and slippers.

"Um..." Thorn started, at a genuine loss for words. "We... aren't."

"We aren't doing anything in here," Charlotte clarified.

"Because we're illusions!" Thorn answered.

"What?" Charlotte snapped.

"Just go with it," Thorn whispered.

"I'm calling security," the man answered, moving toward his phone. "Don't move."

"Do move. Quickly," Thorn whispered, urging to the Coleridge Clock.

Charlotte looked down and took off at a run, following the clock out of the suite entirely into the hall.

"COME BACK HERE!"

"Doesn't want us in there, doesn't want us to leave," Thorn tsked. "That gent should really make up his mind."

"I really hope this is leading us to a public mirror," whispered Charlotte.

Instead, it led them to the stairwell.

"Shoot."

"It's just a few stairs."

"No, most hotel stairwells are locked, they're designed so you can escape in case of a fire but not go up unless you're staff."

Thorn shrugged and opened the door to the stairwell. "Risk we'll have to take."

"We're going to get stuck or thrown out in the snow."

"Maybe we'll get lucky," Thorn winked.

"You! Stop!"

Charlotte looked over her shoulder and saw two men in security uniforms coming toward them at a dead run. She squeaked and followed Thorn through the door, taking the steps upward two at a time. Her heart pounded as she scaled another flight, looking down at the clock to make sure they were still on the right track.

She could hear the door below them burst open and what sounded like a door above them.

"To hell with this," Thorn growled, and Charlotte felt their arms wrap around her the same way they had the day they pulled her from the sea, and suddenly her feet were no longer on the ground, and they flew up the gap between the winding flights of stairs.

She heard a collective and confused gasp as a blur of faces passed them on their ascent.

"I thought you got rid of your wings!"

"I hid them, I didn't cut them off!"

When they reached the top and could climb no more, the clock pointed through the doors.

Thorn gently set Charlotte down and moved toward the door, giving it a yank, but it did not budget.

"I knew it," Charlotte whispered, looking down the stairs where she could hear the rushing of the confused group coming after them.

"Have a little faith," Thorn answered. The fingertips of their right hand lovingly stroked the edge of the door jamb where it met the frame. Their left lightly traced the doorknob. "And remember I am very, *very* lucky…"

Charlotte wasn't sure if she imagined it or if she saw a little slip of glowing light between the lock and around the knob, but when Thorn tried the door knob a second time, it turned, and the door opened. Her brow furrowed. "How…?"

Thorn winked. "No time for secrets."

They entered what looked like the penthouse suite atop the hotel, overlooking the snowy expanse, with very few walls, only windows.

The brief serenity of the view was spoiled by a startled scream as a woman seated on the couch reading a book looked up and saw the two strangely dressed unfamiliar faces.

"Darling, what's—" A man entered from the bedroom, only a towel around his waist. He glared at them, but in comparison to the mustachioed bathrobe wearer from earlier, he seemed rather harmless.

"Wish we could stay," Charlotte apologized, following the golden hand past the man in the towel.

"I-I'm calling security!" The man threatened.

"Oh, they've been rung," Thorn assured, following Charlotte.

The Coleridge Clock opened a door through the mirrored wall opposite the windows in the bedroom.

The towel man followed them indignantly but stopped, blinking as he watched the mirror ripple into a picture of what appeared to be a darkened clothing shop, the same waltz pouring into the room like they'd opened a portal to a music box. "W-w-what is going on here?"

"It wouldn't matter if I told you," Charlotte sighed as Thorn stepped through.

They heard the stairwell door slam open as a crowd of clumsy urgent feet barreled into the main room, startling the same woman again and causing her to scream. And with that, Charlotte was through the door, as well.

In their wake they left two very valued guests irritated that security was interrupting their romantic getaway, three very confused security officers who couldn't remember *why* they had entered in the first place, and one who would never forget... He would rarely tell the story, but when he did, it was in the context of a ghost story.

When Charlotte and Thorn emerged on the other side, it was with a sigh of relief. It was a brief reprieve, as they quickly realized they were not alone.

There was a low guttural sort of growl, the kind of sound Charlotte had only heard in nightmares before.

Thorn straightened ever so slightly, drawing their blade and positioning Charlotte behind them. "Do you see it?" They whispered.

"I can't see anything..." Charlotte peered through the clothing racks, some toppled over, some still standing, massive amounts of fabric and not enough light to make out any shapes.

"Think of something happy..."

Charlotte reached into the sack and produced one of the orbs that held the "fireflies". She held it above her head and gently shook it.

The butterfly-like creatures stirred and ignited, casting warm light over the small room.

It danced across masses of fabric, stretching to fill what space it could, but in the far-left corner, the light seemed to die off before quite reaching it. The darkness did shrink back, and Charlotte could have sworn it hissed.

"Ah, good job," Thorn mused, rather impressed by this forethought.

The darkness squirmed uncomfortably and opened eyes so bloodshot they seemed to glow. It growled again and seemed to shimmy downward in a fashion that reminded Charlotte of a cat about to pounce.

"Learic," she whispered anxiously.

"I see it," the fae soothed, sword poised to defend or strike. "Where to next?"

Charlotte looked down at the hand that still held the Coleridge Clock. The arm that held the orb lowered to carefully wrap around Thorn's waist, both guiding them and pointing the light closer to the Nightmare. "This way…"

She led them out of the small shop to an abandoned market. Despite that she knew it had been a sunny day in Arden, here the sky was darkened by clouds. The hair on the back of her neck prickled, and her fingertips tingled. Was it harder to breathe?

"There's more out here," Thorn said through gritted teeth. "When I close this door, you take that light, and you make a run for it."

"What?"

"I'll be right behind you, but we have to move quickly."

"I can't—"

"We don't have time for a pep talk right now, Treasure. You'll go. And if you can't wait for me, you don't."

Charlotte felt cold, paralyzed. She looked shakily down to the clock, then up toward where it was directing her. It seemed to be to another small shop just down the way. Surely, it wasn't that far. Surely, they could both make it.

"Go," Thorn hissed, pulling their sword back out of the doorway and slamming it behind them. "Don't look back."

Charlotte released them and ran. She heard something scream unnaturally and thump against the door just behind them, glass shattering in its wake. Her heart hurt; her fingers gripped around the "firefly" orb so tightly they felt numb. The guttural scream from the temporarily trapped nightmare was answered by others from all directions.

She could hear Thorn behind her, but the sound of their exertion and whip of their blade was mostly drowned out by what she could only hope were the cries of pain from the nightmares.

She dared to look back and only caught a glimpse before the action caused her to lose her balance and trip, stumbling several ungraceful steps before she managed to return to her running stride. She'd seen four—maybe five—nightmares around them, but they were still standing—did they need help?

The clock took her up the stairs of a shop with a faded sign reading "Wool and Water." The door was thankfully unlocked, and she yanked it open and moved inside. It seemed a sort of kitschy shop, with knick-knacks, collectables, and fine wool hats and scarves. And standing in the back, she saw a full-length mirror.

The knick-knacks went flying as something burst through the shop window, a delicate porcelain sheep crashing against Charlotte's cheekbone, causing her to stumble back into a shelf of jeweled eggs, crashing more to the ground.

She felt both the Coleridge Clock and "firefly" orb fall from her hand, and then her face felt hot.

Shaking off her stun, Charlotte opened her eyes, seeing that the orb that had held the two "fireflies" had shattered. One had been crushed by the fallen objects, but not before starting a small fire right beside Charlotte's feet. The other was injured and flitted across the floor, leaving flames in its wake.

She took a step back, and now in the light could see that the creature that had burst through was none other than a tove, but it now shrunk away from the growing fire.

It waved its impossibly long tongue at her in irritation as if it could taste how close she was yet still out of reach. The tove stalked back and forth along the growing fire line between them before deciding she was not worth it and leaping back through the hole it had created upon its entrance.

469

Charlotte's cheek throbbed, and she waited a tense moment, expecting it to reappear at any moment. When it didn't, she blinked hard, regaining enough sense to remember she had dropped the Coleridge Clock. She looked down but could not see it—until she caught a glimpse of something brass in the fire. She looked around a moment before cautiously and quickly grabbing at it with her boot.

It seemed unharmed, miraculously, and the golden arrow was still pointing at the full-length mirror.

She reached down, cautiously patting it once, twice, before taking one of the scarfs to act as a barrier between her and the heat. She walked to the mirror, and with a ripple that reflected the growing fire behind her, it melted into what looked like an old shopping center, the music beckoning her through once more. It had become so oddly familiar now that it brought an involuntary smile to her lips. She paused and looked back over her shoulder to the door and broken window. "C'mon, Thorn…"

She waited. She waited far longer than she should have. She waited until the sound of the fire drowned out even the Tove cries, the smoke obscuring her vision, causing her to crouch to get under it.

Her eyes burned. She kept the clock pointed to the mirror. "Please…"

It was hard to breathe. She couldn't leave them. She wouldn't leave them.

Something rammed into her, wrapping around her as they both flew through the mirror, banging against the frame before emerging on the other side.

Charlotte coughed both from the smoke in her lungs and having the wind knocked out of her. Her ears ringing, she took a moment before she recognized the figure beside her, their arms and wings wrapped around her. "Thorn?"

"Fates' unholy predictions, girl, why didn't you go?" Thorn demanded angrily.

"And leave you there?"

"What if they'd killed me?" They sat up, gently bringing Charlotte up with them.

"I had faith?"

"You're lucky you don't have third-degree burns, you stupid…" They examined her face carefully, the anger melting away slowly. "Are you alright?" Their tone had softened.

Charlotte winced slightly as their hands cupped around her cheeks. "Yeah…"

"You're going to have a nasty bruise here by the looks of it."

As the ringing in her ears subsided, Charlotte realized something strange. She blinked and looked back toward the mirror they'd exited. The door was closed.

"Stay still, I'm trying to make sure you're in one piece."

"Thorn," Charlotte spoke quietly.

"You could have a concussion or worse, Charlotte, don't fight me on this," the fae insisted gruffly.

"No… It's just… do you still hear the music?"

25

FRANCIS

Soft, gentle, floating on the air as if beckoning listeners to wander until they found the source, was that same lullaby. That same music-box melody that Charlotte had become so accustomed to hearing as the portals opened. It accompanied the gentle dance of dust particles in and out of the golden rays of light that burst through broken windows.

Around them, strewn about the floor, were tipped over clothing racks, the walls themselves cracked, but still holding. What signs she could see were written in what might have been Chinese characters, worn by time and the elements.

They seemed trapped in a moment in time, just after the rush of danger had settled.

Charlotte looked back at the mirror once more. No cracks, a chip around the metal edges, but otherwise it seemed rather unaware of the chaos it existed in.

"Where is it coming from?" Thorn whispered.

Charlotte shakily pushed herself into a stand. "Somewhere outside, I think…" She turned to help Thorn to their feet, offering a hand, which they took.

"We should be careful."

"Of a song?" Charlotte laughed, carefully stepping around the fallen racks and shelves.

"You don't survive in the Fae Wylds without a healthy distrust of mysterious melodies, Treasure."

Charlotte delicately ran her fingertips over a deep crack in the wall, breaking past the paint to the cement beneath. "I'd be more concerned about what happened here."

"Structurally, perhaps," Thorn admitted. "But whatever happened here happened some time ago. See?" They pointed to a small bit of undergrowth reaching its way across one corner of the floor. "Nature has already started to claim what humans have abandoned."

Charlotte smiled softly, finding an odd peace in the evidence of life continuing even after tragedy. Serenely surreal. Like a dream. Her smile dropped. "Thorn."

The green-eyed fae looked back to her.

"If humanity has abandoned this place… then who is playing that music?"

Thorn's wings stretched out slightly reflexively, giving them a larger appearance briefly, like a bird attempting to intimidate a predator. "We should go. This could be a trap."

"A trap?"

"You've been hearing it every time we use your mother's clock. It might have been thought to lure her."

"You're being a little ridiculous," said Charlotte.

"You keep hearing this music, and low and behold, we find where it's been coming from. I think I'm being the more levelheaded of the two of us," Thorn insisted. "Give me the Coleridge Clock."

"You want to go back through? With the fire, and the nightmares?"

"What is that old Irish Proverb? Better the devil you know…"

"Fine, at least let me do it." Charlotte sighed and pulled out the Coleridge Clock. She frowned. It looked… dented. She opened the clock and the hinge fell off entirely, no longer connecting the mirrored inside to the clock face. And the clock face itself… the delicate hands had melted and bent, no longer able to turn. "Oh no."

"What happened?"

"It must have been damaged by the fire… it was too hot, when we fell on it, the metal must have been softer and…"

"It's broken."

"No." Charlotte held up just the mirror to the other mirror, lining them up the same way she always had.

The mirror rippled slightly, then solidified again.

"No." Charlotte adjusted her position in front of the mirror.

Nothing.

"No, you can't be broken. I've come so far!"

"Charlotte."

"It *can't* end like this. Not because of this. Not because of some stupid fuck up. I should have been more careful. I should have paid more attention."

Thorn took her gently by the shoulders. "Hey, it's okay."

"It's not."

"We can figure this out."

"Can you fix it?"

"No, but there are more ways into Terra Mirum than the mirrors. Your mother found her way into one of them."

"My mother wasn't in China!"

Thorn paused. "Yes, that will cause some potential hiccups." They smiled at Charlotte sympathetically. "But you're not alone. You have me. And while I may not be able to open doorways through mirrors, I am fae. That isn't nothing. It's going to be okay."

"How?"

Thorn gave her shoulders a comforting squeeze. "I don't know yet… but that's okay. Don't give up. We can do this." They looked around the abandoned shop, and their brow furrowed.

"You don't look so sure."

"It's not that… It's just… I'm realizing our best bet now probably *is* to go investigate that music. Who, or whatever, is playing it has to have some connection to the other side."

"Maybe they can help us."

"I wouldn't depend on them being helpful, Treasure. I'm still not convinced this isn't a trap."

The door proved somewhat difficult to open, but after delicate tugs, they stepped out into the evening sunlight. Or perhaps it was the morning. It was difficult to tell simply by the golden glow of the sun just above the horizon.

It was a small sort of little strip mall, each shop seemingly as ruined as the one they'd entered through. The music hauntingly filled the otherwise dead air of a city crumbling and overcome by greenery that had to have had years to grow and reclaim.

Deep ruptures in the parking lot caused asphalt and concrete to jut upward unnaturally like two wrong puzzle pieces shoved together.

"Earthquake," Charlotte said in a hushed voice more out of reverence than fear, "a big one by the looks of it. That would explain why they never came back to it. Too much damage." She pointed around Thorn to beyond the broken parking lot where the damage deepened, crumbled buildings, towers on their sides in pieces. "We're lucky the doorway was so intact."

"Mirrors are fragile, so if their environment crumbles, it's likely the doorway would be destroyed with it." Thorn held their hand up and tilted their head ever so slightly, listening. Then, wordlessly, walked down the walkway past a few shops, leading the way.

Charlotte followed, nervously considering the broken watch in her hands.

Thorn tilted their form slightly downward, creeping as they got closer to the sound, coming from what might have once been an antique shop. It was a bit more structurally-sound-looking than the others.

Thorn tried to peek in through the broken windows, but they had all been covered with cloth and even somewhat boarded up.

Whomever was inside had been for some time, or at least long enough to secure a residence.

Thorn rested a hand on their sword and nodded to Charlotte to take the door handle.

Charlotte put both pieces of the broken Coleridge Clock back in her pocket. She carefully ducked lower, wrapped her left hand around the doorknob, and pulled it open, allowing Thorn to duck inside first.

Charlotte, still crouched, carefully moved in behind them.

The antique shop was not clean by any sense of the word, but it had been organized. Someone had taken pieces and parts and sorted them into piles and boxes, and while it still felt cluttered and the building was far from repaired, it seemed somewhat separated from the untouched wreckage just outside its doors.

Clocks of all kinds were somehow working and had been re-hung on the walls, even if their outsides suggested they had taken a bit of a tumble and damage in the initial quake.

The glass display case had long shattered, but someone had swept up the glass and disposed of it, setting a board of broken wood atop the metal frame of the case to act as a new countertop. Settled on the makeshift counter was a music-box-like contraption, gently playing the lullaby they had been hearing. It was carefully wired to another contraption that looked like it might have been a radio, but it didn't quite look like any radio Charlotte had seen before.

There was a quick shuffle, and a woman in her early thirties stared back at them. Her dark brown hair seemed a bit shaggy and in need of a trim and cut asymmetrically. Her tall, lithe frame was adorned in dapper clothing that seemed out of time, topped with a bowler hat. Along her face there were two notable scars, one on her brow and forehead around her left eye, the other across her right cheek. Her left arm, however, drew the most attention, as it was fixed with a strange, geared contraption that, given the location of a linear actuator, seemed to assist with bending and extension.

Charlotte thought it looked as if someone had fashioned C-3P0's arm into a sling.

The woman's hopeful expression faded to disappointment. "Oh."

Thorn felt quickly self-conscious about their sword drawn and sheathed it sheepishly. "Forgive me—we weren't sure what to expect."

"Are you alright?" Charlotte asked the stranger.

"I thought you might be her," the woman confessed cryptically. Her voice was crisp, British, and deliberate in her choice of words.

"Her?" Thorn echoed in confusion.

The dapperly dressed dame dismissed her disappointment. "But you are you, and I will not fault you for that." She stepped forward and extended her left hand. "Hello! I am Francis Speke, daughter of the expired, world-renowned explorer Hanning Speke. Well, not this world, I suppose."

Thorn and Charlotte exchanged a confused glance.

"It is a pleasure to make your acquaintance," said Francis, her hand still extended.

"Um, likewise." Charlotte took the extended hand but found it difficult not to stare at the contraption on Francis' arm. It was unlike anything she'd seen in person. She almost expected it to be a costume piece, but as she retracted her arm, the cylindrical mechanism retracted with a quiet "whoosh" as it bent at the elbow.

Francis paused a moment, taking in her two unexpected visitors before gently urging, "I understand it is customary to provide your names, as well." She stopped, considered this, and corrected herself. "Or perhaps no. I have not been here long, and there have not been any signs of others in order to gather data on such things."

"Thorn," the fae offered.

"Charlie Carroll."

Francis paused at Charlotte's name as if she were remembering something. "Francis Speke, daughter of the expired world-renowned explorer Hanning Speke."

"You said," Thorn said dryly

"I did," Francis confirmed, her focus firmly on Charlotte. There was an awkward sort of pause. "Would either of you appreciate tea?"

"No th—" Thorn started.

"Greatly!" Charlotte chimed.

Francis nodded and walked toward the back, gently tapping her fingers on one of the built-into-the-wall shelves beside a pile of gears and springs. "Hanning Bird, we have guests."

The gears shifted, fluttered, and righted themselves, settling into a form of a mechanical clockwork raven. It took in its surroundings like a cat waking up from a nap, then seemed to sleepily ponder the two newcomers.

Thorn warily looked around almost as if to check if this was the sign of a bird army about to descend upon them. "Don't drink anything she gives you."

"Don't be rude," Charlotte hushed as she approached the clockwork raven curiously, admiring its construction and form.

"Then don't be stupid," Thorn countered petulantly.

"This is amazing," Charlotte called toward the back room where Francis had disappeared. "Did you make it?"

"Now who's being rude?" Hanning bird asked flatly.

Charlotte yelped and jumped back a foot. "Oh god, it talks."

The raven's metal feathers ruffled at that and he huffed loudly, a little steam rising from its nostrils.

"I don't think I've ever seen indignant clockwork before," Thorn commented.

"We call him Hanning Bird," Francis introduced, emerging from the back room. She held out her arm, and the raven flapped to her, resting on the forearm of her extended left arm. "And he has been my dear friend and traveling companion for quite some time now."

"We?" Thorn asked cautiously.

Francis simply nodded, but Hanning Bird lowered his head. "I do not always travel alone."

"But are you alone now?" Thorn pressed.

Francis looked at them blankly. "No. You are here."

Hanning Bird hopped up Francis' arm and settled down on her shoulder. There seemed to be a droop to his feathers.

"Did you mean my mother before?" Charlotte spoke up curiously.

Francis looked confused. "When?"

"When we first came in, you thought we were someone else… Did you mean my mother?"

"I do not believe I did," Francis answered. She thought for a moment. "I might have. Time is a series of variables, after all, but that would produce more questions than answers if I did in fact mean your mother."

Another glance of confusion between Thorn and Charlotte.

Thorn indicated to the radio contraption and music box. "We heard that melody when we were traveling through the mirrors."

"The *mirrors*," Francis repeated, seemingly genuinely surprised. "Fascinating; a variable I had not yet considered. Hanning Bird, we will need to recalibrate the frequency."

The raven flapped from Francis' shoulder to a pad of paper, where he clutched a pen in his beak and proceeded to jot down numbers to a formula.

Francis followed him and peered over the raven's shoulder thoughtfully.

Charlotte paused a moment and reached into her pocket, drawing out the Coleridge Clock as she approached the strange pair. "This used to be my mother's. Alys. Alys Carroll."

Both Hanning Bird and Francis seemed to freeze for the breath of a moment. When Francis turned to fully face Charlotte, the raven seemed to melt into the paper, as if he wanted to disappear but had no hiding place readily available in his current position.

"Alys is your mother," Francis stated. She looked Charlotte over. "I did not realize so much time had passed... or so little. How queer." She looked Charlotte in the eyes, almost searchingly. "What might have never been, had it all been undone."

"I'm sorry?" Charlotte asked, taking a slight step back.

"You broke the Coleridge Clock," said Francis.

Charlotte's cheeks flushed bright red. "Oh, I... well, no, I mean, maybe it's... I didn't mean to, but there were these nightmares and a fire..."

Francis patiently waited for Charlotte to trail off before asking, "Would you like it fixed?"

"You can do that?"

"I can," said Francis matter-of-factly.

Charlotte blinked and sheepishly held out the broken pocket watch. "Yes, please."

Francis gently set the Coleridge Clock on the surface of her makeshift counter and reached for a tool on her belt before carefully opening the watch face.

Thorn moved closer to suspiciously eye her movements, whereas Hanning Bird seemed too depressed to really show any interest at all in what was going on.

Charlotte watched in fascination, but other curiosities prodded her. "How did you know my mother?"

"I did not," said Francis, not looking up from her work.

The raven sighed deeply.

Charlotte looked at the distressed raven briefly before trying again, "You seemed to recognize her name. And this." She indicated to the watch.

"I knew of her for a time," Francis offered. "Passing acquaintances. We have a mutual…" She paused, trying to find her words and struggling for perhaps the first time, finally settling on "Echo."

"Echo?" Charlotte asked.

"There it is." Francis smiled and looked from her work to Charlotte. "That is a joke, you see. She would have laughed at that, I think."

"I'm afraid I'm not in on the joke. I don't know what a mutual echo is," Charlotte admitted.

"Not a what, a whom," Francis elaborated.

Hanning Bird chirped mournfully.

"Are you sure you know what you're doing?" Thorn accused Francis, now hovering over the counter from the other side.

"I am sure I will not break it further," Francis answered. "It is not my first encounter with a Coleridge Clock. And its make is not dissimilar to that of a common pocket watch."

"You've worked with a Coleridge Clock before?" Charlotte awed.

"Briefly," Francis admitted. "It only takes briefly. The construction is simple enough. It is the magic that is complicated, as I understand."

"Can you fix that too?" Thorn asked petulantly.

"Thorn!" Charlotte scolded.

"No," said Francis. "But the magic is not broken, it is the mechanism, and that in itself is rather simple." She reached over and gently stroked the raven's feathers. "Hanning Bird, could you find me one of those pocket watches we saw yesterday?"

Hanning Bird seemed to sink further into himself.

"I see we are determined to be of no use today," Francis tsked, then looked from Thorn to Charlotte. "Charlie, would you be able to search the boxes and find a pocket watch or two if you could? Or even a large wrist watch could be helpful for the inside. Nothing digital. Preferably gold gears, but they should be sturdy."

Charlotte nodded and began to hunt carefully through each pile.

"I do not understand what has got into you," Francis remarked to the sulking Raven, who seemed to glare in response.

Charlotte picked up a watch and began to sift through another pile. She found a small clock and decided to take that too. "Did you organize all of these?"

"The mess was distracting," said Francis.

"I don't understand. Are you hiding from something?" Thorn asked.

"No," Francis answered simply without further explanation.

Thorn's suspicion did not abate. "Then why are you here? In an abandoned city that could crumble down on you at any minute?"

"I did not wish to bother anyone," came the matter-of-fact answer.

Charlotte paused, confused by this. "Bother anyone? How would you be bothering someone?" She found an old pocket watch no longer ticking and walked back to the counter with her bounty.

Francis shrugged. "I manage." She gestured to the radio. "And the sound inevitably would cause some bother, and I would not want to interrupt the signal."

Charlotte looked to the radio and music box and her mind connected the details. "So, you *are* trying to broadcast that song."

Francis nodded.

"Why a song? Why not a distress call?" Thorn asked.

"I am not in distress," said Francis.

Hanning Bird huffed loudly, drawing everyone's attention for a long pause, as if they expected him to elaborate.

He did not.

"I am able to leave any time I wish," Francis continued. "The song is so when *she* hears it, she will know it's me—so she will know how to find me."

"Echo?" Charlotte asked.

Francis smiled and Hanning Bird whimpered.

Charlotte's brow furrowed, and she looked from Francis to the melancholy Hanning Bird. There seemed to be such a disconnect in their demeanors. Sympathetically, she reached out and gently stroked the top of the raven's head with the soft blade of her finger. "Is *she* lost?" she asked gently.

Francis did not answer. The silence that fell caused all three to look back at the tinkering woman, who had even paused in her work. Her eyes moved ever so slightly back and forth as if she was searching for an answer internally.

Thorn started, thinking Francis might not have heard. "She asked—"

"I do not know," said Francis. There was a slight break in her voice, and a look of what might have been confusion or even fear in her eyes, though whether it was for an unspoken reason or the mere discomfort of not knowing an answer, it wasn't clear.

"Why contact her from Earth?" Charlotte asked gently.

Francis, almost mechanically, seemed to snap back to her normal rhythm, back to questions she had answers for. Back to questions answers could be found for. "It was the most probable location."

"Is it?" Charlotte asked, her tone a little more disbelieving than she'd intended. "You don't really..."

"Belong here?" Francis almost smiled.

"I didn't mean it like that."

"It is quite alright, you are correct. I do not."

"You're from the other side then? Terra Mirum?" Thorn concluded.

"No," Francis shook her head, focusing on placing new gears. "Elsewhere."

"There are other elsewheres?" Charlotte awed.

"There are countless elsewheres," Francis smiled, "all held together by cosmic string, like drops of dew on a web."

"Is she, this person you're looking for, is she also from one of those Elsewheres?"

"Of sorts," Francis answered. "She's more from a nowhere."

"Is that like The Nothing?" Thorn asked warily.

Francis pondered this. "Very nearly, but not quite."

Thorn's eyes narrowed and reached for their sword once more. "It sounds like you're looking for a nightmare."

Francis's face fell. "Please don't call her that."

Charlotte's eyes widened slightly, and she took a step backward.

Hanning Bird jolted upright, feathers flustered, hopping slightly away from the hostile fae. "Put that thing away!"

"Who are you? Really?" Thorn growled.

"I am Francis Speke, daughter of the expired—"

"No, I mean what are you doing here? Are you with whatever caused the door to open?"

"I assure you; I have no basis of knowledge of what you are referring to," Francis continued, but she was hardly deterred from tinkering with the Coleridge Clock.

"Then why are you on Earth?"

"It was the last place we saw her!" Hanning Bird cried out desperately.

This startled all parties into an absolute stillness.

The raven looked from Charlotte, imploring, then to Thorn. "We just want to find her. We don't mean harm to anyone, and we certainly did not mean to lure anyone here."

There was another moment of stillness before Francis continued to work on the Coleridge Clock. "My initial calculations did not account for the frequency of the mirrors interfering."

Charlotte's brow furrowed in confusion. "Mirrors have a frequency?"

"Everything has a frequency, Charlie," said Francis, "even you."

Charlotte was struck by something in that moment, something she remembered her mother saying. "Some of us just vibrate a little differently."

Francis smiled encouragingly. "Correct."

"Please put the sword away," Hanning Bird pleaded with Thorn, who begrudgingly did so.

Charlotte soothingly pet Hanning Bird's feathers, as if she could smooth them down and soothe the agitated bird back into a resting position.

The fae took a deep breath and leaned against the wall, folding their arms almost petulantly. They watched Francis work a moment, and the delicate and precise movements of her hands, as well as the way the pressurized joint moved any time she bent or straightened her left arm even slightly. "What happened to your arm?"

"Thorn!" Charlotte scolded, not used to being the less mouthy of a pair.

"It's alright," Francis answered. "I fixed my arm."

"I meant before—"Thorn started but Charlotte cut them off.

"You made the sling? It's genius."

Francis shrugged slightly, closing the back of the Coleridge Clock. "It's what I do. I fix things. As a matter of fact..." She held the clock up to her ear, checked the ticking, then tested the hinge by opening it and held it out to Charlotte. "I fixed this."

Charlotte leaned forward in amazement to see the clock working as new... except— "Oh, no... I don't think... I don't want to be rude, but it's not supposed to spin like that."

Francis looked down at the watch in her palm, seeing the gold hand that acted as a compass to the nearest mirror endlessly spinning around and around. "No, it's fine. This can't be helped. What I'm looking for isn't in this world. There's no mirror it can take me through."

A beat.

"What do you mean by that?" Thorn asked.

Francis looked back at them. "*She's* off-world."

Thorn walked around to stand next to Charlotte. "No, I mean, what does that have to do with the clock? Mirrors are doors, not portals."

"True, but the Coleridge Clock is both a key and a compass," said Francis.

Charlotte nodded. "Right, it leads you to the closest door to the other side."

"No," Francis answered.

"No?" Thorn asked.

"That would be highly inefficient. What sort of compass doesn't tell you where you need to go?" Francis gently placed the clock in Charlotte's hand. "The only difference with this one, is north depends on what you're looking for."

Charlotte watched as the golden hand's spinning slowed to a stop, pointing in a deliberate direction. "So... this could take me to my mother?"

"If that's what you're focusing on. As this is new information for you, I can only surmise you heard the music while traveling and it pulled your focus, so the compass led you through a series of mirrors until you reached it. And consequently, me." Francis stood and proceeded to put her tools away. "It's fortunate you did, operating on incomplete data always has dangerous consequences. So many variables. So many things you cannot account for." Her expression faltered slightly. "I try not to do that anymore."

Charlotte's breath caught as she looked from Francis to the Coleridge Clock. "So, I just... need to focus on my mother."

"The library, Charlie," Thorn reminded gently. "Then we'll see about barreling into a world of nightmares."

"Right," Charlie sighed. "The library." She watched the golden hand shift directions ever so slightly and point in a new direction. To a new mirror. To a new path. No more random, desperate leaps of faith. She smiled slightly. It was a small victory, but it was a comfort. She looked to Francis, who was now gently petting Hanning Bird's chest with the back of her fingers. "I hope you find her. The one you're looking for."

Both automaton and engineer paused. Francis's smile didn't reach her eyes. There was a moment where she seemed to debate saying something, but instead she nodded. "I hope you do, as well."

26

GREY

They arrived at the Phrontistery with uncertainty, sword first, poking the thick white material that had hung over the mirror, pushing it away from the doorway. This seemed to work as they stepped through, but the fabric proved large enough that instead of slipping off the mirror before they'd fully passed through, they found themselves trapped beneath it like children whose blanket fort had just collapsed.

There was a moment of flailing before Thorn grabbed a swath above their head, pulled it taut against the pinned part of the fabric beneath their foot, and sliced it clean through, allowing it to fall on either side of the pair.

It was a storage room of some sort, or perhaps a bedroom that had gone neglected. It seemed covered in a thick blanket of fine dust.

As the falling fabric billowed and settled, it upset the coating of any surface it was near, and both party members coughed a minute, covering their mouths and noses with elbow crooks to try to shield themselves from breathing in more.

"How long has this been abandoned?" Charlotte choked.

Thorn shook their head, refusing to open their mouth, and very carefully stepped as to not shuffle their feet or disturb any more dust. Their sword arm reached out to carefully push down the handle of the door with their elbow, and they stepped out of the small, enclosed space.

Beyond the room, the air was sharp and chill. They could see their breath curl and twist in the air. Snow softly crunched beneath their feet as they stepped out into the great library of the Phrontistery.

Charlotte looked upward into the falling snow, the fretwork of branches that made the ceiling bare of leaves, which allowed great gaps in the roof and exposed a view to the milky grey sky. Her gaze followed the branches down to the trees along the perimeter of the room and scattered about like great natural pillars, as if this building had been grown rather than built. But the wood itself seemed grey, as well, gnarled and pet-rified. No sign of greenery or life. Just deathly stillness and cold. And Charlotte realized she knew this place from more than just her dream. "What... happened here? I can barely recognize it."

"You recognize it?"

"My mother has been here... It's... it's one of the paintings hanging in our home... but it... it didn't look anything like this. There were orchards of books and… what could do this?"

Thorn eyed their immediate surroundings with a great deal more suspicion than Charlotte, taking a few steps in either direction around her to peer down halls and around corners. "The Nightmares, I assume."

Charlotte reached into her pouch to produce one of the "firefly" orbs, both for warmth and visual aid. The warmth of the firelight somehow seemed to be eaten by their surroundings, as if the comforting hue could not survive the environment. "But… the villages and homes we saw were just abandoned. This place looks… almost like it's become a nightmare."

Thorn hesitantly sheathed their sword. "The Phrontistery is the home to every work ever written, as well as those that never will be. It thrives on the dreams of Dreamers. Since the Nightmares have been attacking Dreamers… perhaps the Phrontistery, too, has become infected as a result."

"An apt assessment," a refined British-sounding voice commented.

Charlotte had barely startled when Thorn swung her by the arm behind them, drawing their sword once more and brandishing it in the direction from which the voice had come, ready for any attack.

But no attack came.

Instead, a man in a grey bowler hat with an expertly tailored charcoal suit strolled out of the stacks with an umbrella he didn't bother using casually hooked over his right forearm. His hands were covered, but by the delicate stitching and craftsmanship of evening gloves, and while he wore a scarf draped about his neck, it was silk and for decorative purposes. He was utterly unperturbed by anything in his immediate surroundings, as if the cold, or more importantly the sword pointed toward his chest, were entirely inconsequential. "How can dreams survive if there are no Dreamers to dream them, no thinkers to think them…"

"You…" Charlotte's brow furrowed at the familiarity she found in looking upon this man.

The man in grey produced a silver pocket watch to note the time. "I've been waiting for you, Changeling."

Thorn's upper lip pulled back ever so slightly, and they took a few steps back, guiding Charlotte a few steps back and putting more distance between them and this newcomer. "How did you know she was coming?"

"I'd hoped." The watch snapped shut and was replaced in his pocket smoothly. "But hoping and knowing are much the same in desperate days."

The suit, the posture—she looked down to note his shoes, a stormy grey that faded to black at the toe-tip. She remembered falling to the stairs, she remembered that voice, and while she knew coming here might bring her face to face with him, she did not expect the anger that rose within her. "You're the one who's been sending me nightmares!"

Thorn's posture shifted, their back leg taking more of a fencer's stance to give them the leverage needed to launch forward.

"Visions," the man in grey corrected politely. "I'm the one who has been sending you *visions*."

"They were *horrifying*," Charlotte protested.

"Look around," the man said simply. He took the umbrella from his arm and used the rapier-like point to tap against the petrified bark of the tree nearest him. "The world isn't a very pleasant place to be right now."

Thorn and Charlotte exchanged a look before Thorn's stance relaxed slightly. "Who are you?"

"It changes by the hour," the man dismissed dreamily as he gazed up the length of the tree. He twirled the umbrella with his wrist, bringing it to rest on his shoulder as he turned to look at them. He clarified to Charlie specifically, "Your mother would have called me Grey."

"My mother knew you?" Charlotte blinked.

The man in grey paused, amused by a joke he had no intention of sharing. "No. I do not think she had wish to know me." Then he said to no one in particular, "Others call me a fool." Then, finally addressing Thorn: "My father called me Ikelos."

Thorn nearly choked on this. "Ikelos... as in the first prince to the White Throne?"

Ikelos shrugged and touched a grey glove to his chin delicately. "I bear occasional resemblance to him, I'm afraid."

Thorn struggled through their disbelief. "Your father was King Morpheus?"

"No, he fathered my twin brother, I was fathered by pure tenacity."

Thorn's sword arm dropped to their side. "That's not possible."

"That was sarcasm," Ikelos clarified dryly.

"No," Thorn insisted, raising their sword arm to point rather than threaten. "*You* are not possible."

"Yet here I stand. *Fascinating*, isn't it? What you don't know could fill a library. *This* library, in fact. Which does remind me…" Ikelos pivoted on his heels just enough to hone his attention tightly on Charlotte. "Aren't you looking for something in this library?"

"Looking…" Charlotte took a moment to collect her thoughts. It leapt first to the Bandersnatch, then the tunnel of brick, then to the library, and the shadows, and being bitten… her hand felt cold. "There was a book."

"Mm." Ikelos seemed to both agree and simultaneously judge this statement. "There are many books, but the one you need, you'll find over here." He turned and began to walk down the stairs to lead them.

Thorn and Charlotte looked at each other again before Charlotte gave a simple shrug.

For now, this Ikelos, or Grey, or fool, or whatever he was… would be trusted.

"I don't really know what I'm looking for," Charlotte called after Ikelos as she skipped a few steps to catch up.

"No, but the book will," Ikelos assured.

"The *book* knows what I'm looking for," Charlotte echoed doubtfully.

Ikelos chuffed a laugh through his nose. He brought them to an abandoned librarian desk, upon which a large snow-covered book sat.

Thorn looked from the book to Ikelos and jerked their head slightly to the side, to which the man shrugged and took several steps back to allow Charlotte a safe radius.

Reassured by the distance, Charlotte stepped behind the desk and reached to open the cover. She hesitated.

"What's wrong?" Thorn asked.

"In my ni... *vision*... the book bit me," Charlotte admitted.

"The *book* isn't what bit you," Ikelos commented. "And this won't either."

Charlotte glared at him before taking a deep breath, placing her hand on the book and opening to a random page.

Bandersnatch.

A cold shiver ran up her spine. The screeching cry from her nightmares echoed through her mind, and she nearly stumbled back a step as if the thing would pull itself up through the pages to attack her.

"It won't bite," Ikelos repeated, and Charlotte shot him a glare.

Thorn leaned over her shoulder to peer at the page. "Nightmares."

Charlotte looked above the Bandersnatch title to the small paragraph above it, which continued the text from the previous page.

The more information a Nightmare possess about a target, the more dangerous they become to their chosen victims. However, our own fears and insecurities pale in comparison to a Nightmare knowing and being able to speak your true name.

Charlotte's brow furrowed. "I thought you were being coy before." Her index finger gently tapped on a particular sentence. "This says certain Nightmares in possession of your name have the power to control you even to the fiber of your form and being." She looked to Ikelos. "Is that really true?"

"The book does not lie," came the simple answer.

Charlotte looked back at the book, feeling her heart palpitate. Should she have been going by a different name? Could she start going by one now? As soon as she thought of the idea, every name she'd ever known but her own seemed to fly from her recollection.

Her stomach rumbled.

Dinner. Dinah. Diana! She could go by Diana.

"Treasure," Thorn gently nudged her back to reading the book.

Charlotte's mind was swimming, and she attempted to keep reading, her eyes passing over the word 'bandersnatch' and then darting to the hand-drawn picture beside it. She could smell the musk of the tunnel. The cold air. The breath of the beast that stared down at her. Her heart wrenched.

Could that… happen to Thorn?

Charlotte swallowed and leaned forward slightly, reading sentences repeatedly before any information really sunk in. She was too anxious. Words were just meaningless marks. It took repetition and counting her breathing.

In for five. Out for six.

Repeat.

Fae. Both Seelie and Unseelie alike, capable of being driven mad by The Nothing.

Repeat. Breathe.

Murderous, cannibalistic, and motivated by an insatiable greed and hunger. These creatures are but hollow and savage incarnations of who they once were.

Breathe. Repeat.

Bandersnatches can smell fear. It was their keenest sense and how they tracked their prey.

In for five, out for six.

Laughter is the strongest weapon against fear. Its energy often covers the scent, making it difficult, if not impossible, for a Bandersnatch to smell you—however they then would likely be able to hear you.

She'd been holding her breath. She resumed. In for five, out for six. Repeat. Repeat.

Bandersnatches were hoarders, not of objects, but of the emotion attached to those objects. While it could include money and riches, it fed off the value the previous owner levied onto them rather than monetary worth. Loose in the waking world, Bandersnatch have been known to steal children, particularly those heavily doted on by parents. Myths around children being stolen by fae heavily stemmed from the horror of Bandersnatch.

The vorpal blade defeated The Nightmare Queen. It was once wielded by the only known Dreamer to enter Terra Mirum. Her mother. The Hero. The reverence around it alone must have made it irresistible to the Bandersnatch.

Charlotte's eyes moved up to the drawing, her fingers reaching out to lightly trace along the border and get a better look at the thing. Maybe if she could make herself used to the sight, it wouldn't unsettle her so much should she come face to face with one again.

It was a gaunt thing, to the point of emaciation.

Charlotte wondered how something known for its insatiable hunger, driven to feed, could be so emaciated. Skin and bones. Sharp. Haunted.

She felt Thorn straighten up to look back at Ikelos with a deep sigh.

"I don't like where this is going," they said, resting a protective hand on Charlotte's shoulder.

Charlotte attempted to keep reading, her gaze running over a strange word in a similar heading that Bandersnatch had been: Borogove. She frowned slightly.

Borogove: The horror grove. Born from the unex-
plainable shadows cast on children's walls and
the questionable bumps in the night. Like most
nightmares, Borogoves shy away from light, but
these particular horrors cannot stand any direct
illumination. Carry a torch and tread lightly…

Charlotte's mind trailed off, and instead of turning the page, she looked back to Ikelos, who met her gaze and did not break away from it. Still, she couldn't read him. He did not seem amused or conniving. He did not seem sinister or even concerned. He simply was. And that seemed even more unsettling. "Why did you bring me here?"

"Given your encounter with the one in your vision, you seemed rather at a loss for what to do when meeting a Bandersnatch. I thought it best to arm you with all possible available information," Ikelos answered.

Charlotte's stomach sunk. "So, I'm to fight a Bandersnatch."

"Absolutely not," Thorn growled, reaching for their sword once more. "Completely out of the question."

"I didn't ask one," Ikelos said levelly. Then, to Charlotte. "But I did provide you with the answer to yours."

Charlotte's brow furrowed. "What are—"

"If you want to defeat this, if you want to save the others, you needn't fight a Bandersnatch, but you do need to take back what it stole from Oberon. This is how."

Charlotte looked back to the book a moment before fully turning to face the man in grey. "Why me?" she asked simply. "I know my mother was a Hero for all of you... but I'm just me. I'm still a kid."

"You answered the call," said Ikelos.

"No," Charlotte grew bolder. "Why *call* me?"

"I called *many*, Changeling." Ikelos closed his umbrella and latched it closed so that it could once more be used as a cane. "Throughout time, I called them: humans, Dreamers—our pleas fell on deaf ears and were met with inaction or indifference." He leveled his gaze with Charlotte, being particularly deliberate in his words in that moment. "You were not chosen, Changeling; you were the only one who chose to act."

Charlotte felt her breath catch in her throat.

Ikelos continued, "Will you abandon that purpose now that you've come so far?"

Her mouth opened ever so slightly, trying to find the words to answer him, but instead they found another question. "How did you know my mother?"

"Very briefly in all but name, but with absolute entirety otherwise." Ikelos reached into his suit jacket pocket, and then, finding nothing, reached into the inside breast pocket. "We tried to warn her, my brother and I—well, *in our way*, we tried." His right hand then took the umbrella, and he reached into his left pant pocket. "I've found the more you directly hand some-one information, the more likely they are to reject it."

"And what information is that, exactly?" Thorn asked, suspicious.

Ikelos produced a dark orb from his pocket, and upon turning his palm so they could better see it, within, the darkness seemed to move, like a turbulent storm of night, ever shifting. "There is no such thing as black and white…"

"That's…" Thorn whispered.

"Part of it, anyway. Severed from the hilt some time ago. It's been in our family's possession ever since. I'm afraid the vorpal blade is rather ordinary without it."

Thorn glared. "So, fear had nothing to do with the theft?"

"Of course, it did," Ikelos answered incredulously. "This bauble vanquishes Nightmares; it cannot rewrite a soul."

A low growl echoed through the Phrontistery.

Charlotte swallowed. "Please tell me it also makes unnerving sounds…"

Ikelos looked around, not quite shaken, but clearly intrigued, as that was not something he had been expecting at all. "It's never done before…" He raised the stone up slightly and gave it a slight shake.

The growl shifted to what seemed almost a groan followed by an undeniable splintering of wood.

The group turned to the nearest pillar tree, which was in the process of wrenching itself free from the foundation, causing the building to rumble ever so slightly. The tree ripped its arms from the roof and fretwork. It was more gnarled than the rest, sharp and shattered, and as it shifted its weight, they gazed upon its face.

It was not a humanoid face but almost dragon-like. It consisted of overlapping sharp branches, staring at them with eyes that seemed merely like gaping holes into a nothing-like darkness. It opened its mouth, which was a battlefield of sharpened sticks; jagged spikes seemed to go on forever in a spiral down its throat.

"What the—" Thorn pulled Charlotte back a step.

"Borogove," Charlotte whispered.

More shattering as more trees twisted into the creature that towered over them some twenty feet away, and Charlotte began to understand the words "horror grove."

"They seem to be reacting to the hilt of the Vorpal blade," Ikelos awed.

"PUT IT AWAY!" Thorn yelled.

"We should run," Ikelos concurred, pocketing the orb once more.

Charlotte shrugged Thorn's hand off her arm, taking a few steps forward as she reached into the bag and her fingers clasped around a "firefly" orb once more. "They cannot stand direct illumination…" Gripping the lantern like a softball, she reeled her arm back and paused. "Don't mess this up, Carrol," she whispered to herself before chucking it toward them.

The glass orb flew towards the Borogove and broke at its feet.

"Damn it, I missed." Charlotte cursed before seeing flames catch to the stacks. "Oh, no…"

The Borogove screeched and stepped back before two flaming butterflies flew upward, twisting around the gnarled tree-like creature, flames dropping down from their wings, landing and catching quickly on the Nightmare.

"Oh," Charlotte realized.

"C'mon, Treasure." Thorn pulled Charlotte by the elbow, which was the only coaxing she needed to turn and run from the Phrontistery as it and its new terrifying inhabitants went up in terrifyingly fast flames.

27

AND GRAY

The Forest of Thought, as Charlotte had learned it to be named, was not a particularly friendly-looking forest these days, insomuch that she deduced if the trees were representative of any thoughts of the Forest, it might do well to talk to a therapist. She could feel eyes on them, like they should be moving quietly and without a word.

Ikelos had other plans. He was striding upright and proudly with his head back and high. He would occasionally raise his closed umbrella into the air to punctuate an encouraging, "Tut-tut!" that he would call back every time he felt Thorn and Charlotte were lagging. "Look lively now, look lively. Keep your eyes on the path. Don't let it wander away without you."

They walked in single file with Ikelos leading, Thorn behind him, and Charlotte bringing up the rear.

This forest seemed much like the Phrontistery, twisted, gnarled, haunted by the ghost of what it used to be. It reminded Charlotte of the sort of place princesses fled their wicked stepmothers before being found by kindly dwarves or elves or whatever else saved princesses in fairytales. But in the reality of staring scary faces and glowing eyes head on, she could only wonder if it might ever be the way it was before again… or if something like this could scar a place the way terrible things often scarred people. Would it heal and forget? Or would there always be an underlying sense of fear?

And if these nightmares could do this to the very landscape around them… what had they already done to her mother?

"Charlie?"

Charlotte stopped, her head swimming. She'd know that voice anywhere. Her heart in her throat, she turned slowly, and just beyond the closest tree off the path stood Alys. "Mom…" Charlotte breathed the word more than spoke it, tears welling in her eyes, but before she could take even a step toward her, a sharp tug pulled on her elbow, abruptly turning her back to face Ikelos and Thorn.

"What are you—"

"It isn't what it appears, Changeling," Ikelos answered calmly, unhooking the crook of his umbrella handle from Charlotte's arm. "Whatever this forest is showing you, it isn't the real thing."

Charlotte's brow furrowed, and she looked back to the tree where Alys still stood. Her eyes were sad, but she was dressed exactly as she had been before the slumber took her, slightly disheveled in her pajamas, a smudge of paint on her cheek. "No… she's… can't you see her?"

Thorn looked directly at Charlotte's mother, brow furrowing. They squinted and shook their head. "There's no one there, Treasure."

"What do you mean… It has to be. She's…" Charlotte paused, looking at the apparition in the shadow more closely. She could see the golden necklace hanging around Alys' neck, the necklace that she'd worn every day since before Charlotte was born, the necklace that Charlotte now wore around her own neck. "Exactly as I remember her…" She reached down to hold the pocket watch in her palm, to reassure herself that she did still have it, that if the figure before her was truly her mother… then she couldn't be wearing that necklace.

Ikelos' voice was kind. "This place often knows us better than we know ourselves. Deeply connected with memory and the subconscious…" He placed a hand on Charlotte's shoulder. "It knows what call you'll answer to." His back straightened, and he returned to his full height once more. "It called to your mother once in much the same way."

Charlotte's attention returned to Ikelos, and suddenly the path was clear once again. "What exactly is calling us?"

Ikelos resumed his walk, twirling the umbrella a moment before it again rested on his shoulder, but not before nearly hitting Thorn in the head, who ducked rather gracefully out of harm's way. "The Nothing. Those are the whispers you're hearing, that you've been hearing since the start."

Thorn paused. "I don't hear anything."

"Well, *you* wouldn't, would you?" Ikelos asked cheerfully. "You're not a Dreamer." He waved his fingers at Charlotte like she was a small kitten. "Watch her, would you?"

Thorn turned around to take Charlotte by the hand and give her a waltz turn and twirl to place her between them as they walked.

"*I'm* not a Dreamer," Charlotte protested.

"You're half," Thorn offered thoughtfully.

Charlotte couldn't argue with that, but something else occurred to her, and so she pressed Ikelos again. "Can *you* hear the voices?"

"Of course," said Ikelos.

"But *you're* not a Dreamer," Thorn said doubtfully, then, upon reflection, "are you?"

Ikelos smiled politely but cryptically over his shoulder. "I'm half."

Thorn's jaw dropped.

"You mean you're like me?" Charlotte asked almost excitedly.

"Very much like you," Ikelos answered, paused, pondered, and postulated, "and yet so vastly different, too."

"You're a Changeling?" Thorn asked in disbelief. "How can *you* be a Changeling?"

Ikelos looked back at Thorn with a somewhat dubious expression. "I certainly hope you're not asking me to explain copulation and genetics."

Thorn sputtered. "No! I just... There weren't supposed to be... How many of them are there?"

Ikelos looked back at his traveling companions and visibly pointed to himself and then Charlotte, mouthing numbers. "Plus my brother. That makes three."

"Our friend Smoke is, as well," Charlotte offered.

"Ah!" Ikelos nodded. "Four then. At least four."

"You don't know?" Thorn asked incredulously.

"I'm incredibly old, your highness, not omnipotent," Ikelos offered with a shrug. "A common misunderstanding, but I assure you they are very different and should never be confused."

"How old?" Charlotte asked curiously.

"Like the beginning of time old," Thorn answered.

"The beginning of Terra Mirum, perhaps. And even then, that was my father, not I." Ikelos waved a dismissive hand.

"Wait, your father," Thorn started. "If you're a Changeling... Was Morpheus... I mean, he couldn't have been, but was he..."

"Was the man who split the world in two, sealing Nightmares behind a door into their own realm, a Dreamer?" Ikelos asked dryly.

Thorn paused and shrugged, looking away and feeling almost petulant. "It seems a little obvious when you put it that way."

Ikelos smiled and tipped the brim of his bowler up ever so slightly with the point of his umbrella.

Charlotte shivered and changed the subject. "Thorn said you were the first prince of the... something."

"The White Throne?"

"Yeah, that."

"My father founded the line," Ikelos acknowledged, his pace increasing a little. "But I never really had any princely duties, if that's what you're asking."

"No," Charlotte answered. "It's just that I recently learned my father might be the current king of that... So... does that mean we're... related?"

Ikelos paused and looked back at Charlotte thoughtfully. "I suppose it does. My brother and I never sired children, but our mother remarried after my father quit the throne... and the line continued through her." He held up a gloved hand in concern. "But I will bore you with those details another time..." He removed his umbrella from where it hung and pointed it at a dark shadow perched atop a low branch. "If I'm not mistaken..."

"Jub-jub," Thorn acknowledged, placing a hand to the hilt of their sword.

Charlotte squinted up at the ominous and now familiar silhouette of the creature they'd seen far too many of when they'd first reached land. "Is he here because of what's happened?" Her eyes focused on the strangely familiar red brickwork just beyond the trees. "Or what's going to happen?"

"Thrilling possibilities, aren't they?" asked Ikelos.

"Not the word I'd use," Charlotte answered.

"If it makes you nervous, you could always move it," Ikelos offered casually.

"Like I'm getting ANYWHERE near that freaky thing," Charlotte answered.

Thorn stepped up beside Charlotte, scanning their immediate perimeter for any other Nightmares before letting their gaze land on the bird. "You know, you don't actually have to get near it if you use what Smoke was showing you."

Charlotte blinked and looked to Ikelos, whose mouth ever so slightly twitched at the hint of a smile before giving the faintest of nods. She looked back to the big ugly bird and remembered the feeling of the tove between her fingertips and shivered. "I'd rather not."

"Suit yourself," Ikelos said cheerfully before starting off down the embankment toward the brick structure in the near distance. He whistled a pleasant upbeat tune that seemed to ruffle the jub-jub bird's feathers and quite perturb it as he passed beneath unscathed and otherwise unnoted. "Might have been good practice for the Bandersnatch!" He called over his shoulder.

Charlotte gulped.

The jub-jub bird's focus shifted sharply, homing in on her. The strange sound from which it gleaned its name almost ribbiting up from its throat like a frog's croak: "Jub-jub."

"It can sense your nerves," Thorn said gently, reaching a hand up slowly to rest between Charlotte's shoulder blades. "Deep breaths. Show no fear."

"Show no fear," Charlotte whispered.

"Jub-jub," the nightmare bird rasped in response.

Charlotte closed one eye, and with her altered perception saw the large ungodly thing as something quite small as she brought her fingers up to her eyeline. Very small. Very light. Like a mosquito one could just flick away...

The bird let out a loud and unpleasant SQUAWK as it was knocked from the branch, catching itself in the air before it hit the ground and flapping off in a manner that could only be described as indignant.

"Nicely done," Thorn congratulated.

Charlotte exhaled slowly. "Now if I can just do that with the Bandersnatch..."

"The tunnel may not be the most structurally sound place to go knocking large creatures about," Ikelos pointed out, "but something like that should do."

Charlotte and Thorn took a few steps to catch up to him down the embankment into the clearing in the trees where the train tracks could be seen winding their way out of the brick structure and onward into the woods and disappearing.

"How do you even know the Bandersnatch is in there?" asked Charlotte.

"Once it took the vorpal blade, all we had to do was track it with this." Ikelos casually plucked the orb from his pocket and tossed it to Charlotte, who nearly fumbled it.

She starred into the pommel, and watching the shifting shades of darkness, something felt... off. Not good, nor evil, just... off, like the ground was no longer stable and she suddenly lost her balance. Charlotte tripped a few steps, her focus returning to the clearing around them and their approach to the brick structure, which was none other than the train tunnel, the very tunnel that had built around her in her dream as the horrific sound of the Bandersnatch chased her up the stairs. "What if it's not there anymore?"

"Well, that would make your task a great deal simpler, but I'm afraid we're absolutely certain it is still there," Ikelos answered.

"Why is that?" Thorn asked.

"Phantasos has made absolute certain of it," said Ikelos.

As they came around the mouth of the tunnel, they could see a man dressed in a slightly lighter shade of grey suit that was just as smartly tailored. His fedora was hanging from a brick that stuck out from the others just a little bit more than the rest. More remarkably, he was absolutely focused on a grey misty veil that blocked out the rest of the tunnel.

"Gray." Ikelos took a few steps toward the other man and tentatively rested a hand on his shoulder.

The man in gray turned his attention to Ikelos and smiled rather sleepily, the veil of mists dissipating as he turned from them. "You've returned. Am I happy or sad?" Unlike his brother, while it had a formal sort of clip, his accent was distinctly American.

"You are intrigued," Ikelos answered, then gently turned his brother with him to face Charlotte and Thorn. "Brother, may I introduce two illegitimate royal children, the daughter of the hero of Terra Mirum and the King of the White Throne—our very distant cousin, I imagine, and Titania's spite to Oberon." He beckoned the confused fae and Changeling to come a little closer. "Charlotte, Thorn, it is with absolute delight that I introduce my twin brother, Phantasos. Or Gray, as your mother would have called him."

"She would have called me a lot of things, given the chance, Mr. Grey," Phantasos mused.

"Undoubtably to us both, Mr. Gray," Ikelos answered cheekily.

Thorn extended their hand, and the man in gray shook it firmly. "It is a surreal honor."

"The feeling is entirely mutual," Phantasos answered. His attention shifted to Charlotte, and he extended his free hand to her. "You would be the one who chose to act."

Charlotte took his left land with her own. "Charlotte Carrol."

"We knew your mother," Phantasos answered.

"Probably better than she knew herself," Ikelos added.

"Oh, most assuredly," Phantasos concurred.

"She didn't mention…" Charlotte started.

"Oh, she wouldn't have," said Phantasos, now vigorously shaking Charlotte's hand with both of his own.

"She couldn't have," Ikelos pointed out.

"We gave her different names," agreed Phantasos.

"Wrong names," Ikelos corrected. "Wrong relations."

"It was meant to be a metaphor," said Phantasos.

"And a joke," said Ikelos.

"She didn't get it," said Phantasos

"She didn't get a lot of things," they said in unison.

"Maybe there were problems in the delivery," said Thorn through clenched teeth.

The man in grey and his brother in gray were still, and they looked back at Thorn as if both had completely forgotten they existed.

Charlotte cleared her throat. "Could… I have my hand back, please?"

Phantasos looked down at the gloved hand in his, and he frowned. "I'm afraid I'm not the one who took it."

Charlotte's brow furrowed as her eyes also settled on his hands clasped around her own.

Phantasos reached forward with his right hand, gripping Charlotte's bare forearm, his left sliding back to grip her glove at the fingertips, his own digging in slightly to take the fabric before giving a smooth pull to slip it from her.

Charlotte's breath caught. "What the…"

Her fingers were unrecognizable. The tips came to a claw-like point, pitch black as if they'd been charred, fading into the warm sepia of her skin just below her palm and knuckle. She moved them to prove to herself they were indeed attached to her. The fingertips felt cold, almost numb.

"Charlotte…" Thorn took a step closer to get a better look. "What happened?"

"She's been infected," Phantasos stated matter-of-factly.

"But the book didn't bite me!" Charlotte insisted.

"It never did," Ikelos reminded flatly, as if this was the time to get technical about the mechanics and meanings of visions and dreams.

"The tove," said Thorn quietly. "Back at Smoke's. It caught your hand, didn't it?"

"It was fine—you saw. Robin inspected it!" cried Charlotte.

"It may just take the poison longer to seep in," said Ikelos, "being only half dream."

"Poison?" Charlotte's eyes were wide.

"What's going to happen to her?" Thorn asked softly.

"Difficult to say," said Phantasos, raising Charlotte's elbow and consequently her hand so they could all get a better look. "Were she full dream, it would have fully corrupted her by now."

"But as a half-dreamer, she may be able to resist it entirely," suggested Ikelos.

"Or become a Horror the likes of which we've never seen as a nightmare with the power of a Dreamer," Phantasos offered.

"What?" Charlotte squeaked, pulling her hand back and recoiling from them, feeling her fingertips with her other hand. They almost felt tingly, like they'd fallen asleep.

"Could we not throw around unconfirmed possibilities?" Thorn asked calmly.

"Assessing all possible outcomes is how to best prepare for them," Phantasos answered.

"Or prevent them," Ikelos added.

"And terrifying her out of her wits?" Thorn asked.

"Some possibilities are terrifying," Phantasos shrugged.

"But it might not be the most constructive exploration right now given the circumstances," Thorn hissed.

"They do have a point, brother. She does still need to fetch the vorpal blade," said Ikelos.

"Uh, no, sorry, hang on. Charlotte is not going into that tunnel now."

"Why not?" Charlotte demanded.

"What do you mean, why not?" Thorn asked. "Look at your hand!"

"Nothing has changed! It was like this before; we just didn't know it was!" Charlotte argued.

"She does have a point," Phantasos agreed.

Thorn growled in frustration and turned to Charlotte. "Everything has changed, Charlotte. Now we know there's an added danger to you entering an already perilous situation. Robin is going to kill us when she finds out about this—assuming you haven't turned by then."

"Their Highness also makes a good point. Knowledge of the infection will breed fear and make her more susceptible to the Bandersnatch's senses," Ikelos also agreed.

Thorn whirled on the twin Changelings. "And you two, if this is the level of 'help' you provided to Alys, it's absolutely no wonder why she didn't understand you. You're absolutely infuriating!"

The brothers paused, and for a moment they looked offended.

Thorn sighed. "I'm taking Charlotte back to the capitol. It's too dangerous for her here."

"Ah, and what could be safer than surrounding her with untainted dreams?" Phantasos asked sarcastically.

"She should be with family," Thorn insisted.

"Her mother is family," said Ikelos.

"Her mother, for all we know, is trapped in the very heart of The Nothing!" Thorn countered. "If there's any hope for her now, it will be far away from ANY Nightmare!"

"Charlotte chose—" Ikelos started again.

"Charlotte doesn't understand what will happen to her if that infection takes her," Thorn growled angrily.

"Respectfully," Phantasos interjected, and Thorn shot him a glare that would freeze hell itself. The man in gray cleared his throat and pointed toward the train tunnel. "The one who chose to act appears to have chosen again."

Thorn turned to see that Charlotte had once again left in the throes of an argument about her but not involving her. They sighed and rubbed their face. "Of course… Dammit."

"She's marvelous initiative," Ikelos commented.

"It's going to get her killed," Thorn breathed, drawing their sword to start after her.

"If you value her life, you'd be better out here with us," Phantasos called after them.

"Your own concern for her welfare could trigger the Bandersnatch's senses and alert her to you both," Ikelos explained.

Thorn paused and sighed. "So, your suggestion is to what… just hope for the best and wait?"

"Or wildly speculate!" Phantasos offered.

Ikelos sighed, placing a hand gently on Phantasos' shoulder. "Brother, this appears to be not the time…"

"You're just saying that because she might die," Phantasos pouted.

"She *what*?" Thorn exclaimed.

"*Might*," Ikelos assured. "Might is a very mercurial word, your highness. She *might* also bring back the sword entirely unscathed."

"She might take control of the Bandersnatch and ride into the sunset," Phantasos added giddily.

"She might even heal her," Ikelos added with excitement.

"You can't heal a bander—"

Phantasos tsked with a raised finger. "Shades of gray."

"And grey. *Anything* can happen," Ikelos reminded.

Thorn looked from the brothers back to the tunnel opening helplessly. They sighed heavily and turned to sit on a rock and keep their eyes on the exit and any sign of Charlotte. It at least made them feel… somewhat useful. "Respectfully," they called over their shoulder. "I don't like either of you right now…"

28

BANDERSNATCHED

Charlotte gripped the cold orb of the pommel in her right, still gloved hand as she walked into the darkness. She could still make out the vague outline of the brick walls as she journeyed farther and farther from the light of the forest behind her. Her walking veered to the left, her hand finding the cool brick so she could use it to guide her as she lost the light.

She was fine. She would be fine. And even if she wasn't going to be fine, she was going to be fine enough to help her mother, and no one, not even Thorn and their concern for her wellbeing, was going to stop her from that goal. If they needed this stupid sword, then dammit, she was going to get it.

But the light never faded. She could see more than outlines, details, even though the tunnel's opening was too far to be still giving light. Her brow furrowed, wondering if this were some kind of passive changeling magic, but as she turned to face forward once more, the feathers of her earring brushed her neck.

Charlotte smiled despite herself. "Thank you again, Lark," she whispered.

This would be alright. She could do this. She could survive this. She'd already overcome several impossible obstacles. She could do anything. Even slay a Bandersnatch.

She swallowed hard.

Breathe in for five, out for six. Repeat. Repeat.

The clawed feet, the pale skin stretched over emaciated sinewy muscles, the hollow gaunt face, the eerily glowing eyes. In the dead of silence of the abandoned tunnel, all she could hear was the unholy screech of the Bandersnatch echoing through her memory. Her lips curled inward, pursing together.

The counts of five and six quickened, abbreviating her breath lengths. The oxygen was gone—she was sure of it. She was gulping for air and finding none.

No, not now. She told herself.

The world wavered as her vision faltered. Her head was too light; the oxygen must have been replaced with helium. She was going to float away. But no, her head was anchored to her body, which felt heavy and dragged her down to her knees. Everything was spinning. She needed to throw up.

It can smell fear.

Charlotte held her breath, hoping if she could interrupt the rapid rhythm, she could force it back to a slow and steady pace.

Her heart was too loud, surely the Bandersnatch could hear it. It was almost drowning out the sound of the memory of the screaming call of the demon she was trying to find.

Her hand dropped the pommel, reaching to her chest where a searing pain spread out from her heart, agonizing. She pressed her lips together roughly to keep herself from making any more noise. She was freezing and burning, and the world was deafeningly silent and garishly dark, it hurt to feel and see and hear and experience, and why couldn't she breathe?

Charlotte remembered to exhale. It was a gasp of the drowning as they finally broke their head above the surface, which caused her body to slump ever so slightly over itself in exhaustion. She focused on her breathing, ragged, her heart still pounding away but her breath too exhausted to keep pace.

In for five, out for six.

It could smell fear. She could not have a panic attack, no matter how devoid of medication she was. She must not fear.

Charlotte's lips twitched in a tired smile. "Fear is the mind killer," she whispered to herself, remembering being curled up in bed and reading *Dune* with her mother, one of many fantasy epics they'd devoured together. She tried to remember the rest. Something about... a little death bringing total obliteration.

Her nose exhaled the semblance of a quiet laugh. The French referred to the 'little death' as something quite different.

In for five, out for—giggle.

Laughter.

The book had said laughter was the strongest weapon against fear.

The noise of something being knocked over echoed from further down the tunnel, and Charlotte froze.

Slow, concentrated breathing. And then an inappropriate thought popped in her head.

Maybe the Bene Gesserit have a fear kink.

She closed her eyes and pursed her lips so tightly, her jaw hurt. Don't laugh. It could hear you laugh just as easily as it could smell your fear.

Because if it is, then really the little death could still mean the same thing after all.

Charlotte snorted quietly. She took another deep breath and for a moment had forgotten where she was. There was a lot of comfort, oddly, in her mental comparison between herself and the world of fiction to which she'd devoted so many late nights reading. After all, Frank Herbert's Bene Gesserit were about mastering themselves as humans. And what was the entire world of Terra Mirum to her, a changeling, but mind over matter?

If only her mind wasn't so often her own worst enemy.

Then maybe she wouldn't end up in detention quite so often. Or have a file that made *War and Peace* look like a brief description of events.

Charlotte smiled slightly, feeling just a little bit proud of that file folder. Then it dawned on her how absolutely confusing it would be to Mr. Blake to find that obscenely large file full of complaints for a student he would have absolutely no memory of.

Charlotte guffawed and clamped her hands over her mouth. Deep breaths.

She looked around for where the orb had rolled after she'd dropped it.

Mr. Blake would then be forced to inquire of Darrel Keats, the man whose litany of complaints would be the majority of the file's girth, and yet neither man would be able to recall just who the hell this Charlotte Carroll was and would likely conclude it was all part of some senior prank. But maybe, just maybe, when they were having trouble sleeping some nights, they'd think back to that file—they'd see their own handwriting and be haunted by a horrible and unanswerable "what if?"

Charlotte laughed again and dropped to a crouch to hold the pommel in her fingers. She could still feel the pulse, which now she realized was not her own, but the orb itself… and if it were used to track the vorpal blade, it was likely pulsing in reaction to her proximity to it.

Feeling far less lost, and far too amused, she pushed herself into a stand.

And that's when she heard the scrape of something sharp against the brick wall.

Charlotte's breath caught, and she looked up, seeing two bright green orbs floating in the distance.

Nothing was funny anymore.

Trying to move as slowly and little as possible, Charlotte slid her foot back in retreat and pocketed the orb in one fluid motion.

The Bandersnatch screeched and rushed forward, running on all fours along the wall, pushing itself off the brick to leap toward her.

Charlotte's now-free hand flew out in front of her to try to protect herself, not daring to take her eyes off the dreaded thing and wishing with all her might she could push the thing away.

As she'd lifted many objects, as she'd fought the tove and shooed the jub-jub, the forced perspective of her palm flying out was a giant force that caught the Bandersnatch and smashed it back into the tunnel where it had leapt, crushing the old brick around it and leaving a dent.

It was an action that stunned both parties.

The Bandersnatch fell to the ground, immobile.

Charlotte looked down at her palm and laughed. "That's right! I'm a changeling, bitch!" She crowed, her laughter triumphant albeit a tad hysterical. But as she looked at the crumpled heap before her, something wasn't right.

Her wings were ragged, and it was not out of order to describe the fae as even a little feral in appearance, but this was not the monster she'd stared down in her nightmare. Her features were unchanged. She was not some gnarled beastly thing; this was a person, a rather beautiful person.

"I don't understand…This isn't right," Charlotte observed to no one. "You're supposed to be…"

The orb glowed a little and continued to pulse in her pocket as a reminder there was no time to waste or guarantee for how long the Bandersnatch would be unconscious.

She pulled the pommel from her pocket once more and ran. She stumbled more than once but never fully lost her footing, though at one point she did jam her shoulder into the wall quite roughly while turning a corner.

She grimaced but pressed on, following the glowing orb until it no longer pulsed but merely glowed, humming in her hand consistently. She looked around, catching sight of piles of objects. Seemingly mundane things, objects of sentiment: photographs, paintings, teddy bears, books, clothing, strewn about in piles that seemed like something had been settled on top of them. Like a dragon of lore sleeping upon its bed of treasure.

Charlotte pocketed the orb once more so her hand could be free to sift through the piles, one after the other. She found love letters, necklaces, shoes, bassinets that thankfully held no babies… and a sword. She lifted it, triumphantly… but it still had its own pommel.

Wrong blade.

She moved farther in, feeling the vibration of the pommel in her pocket now. She glanced toward it, and the glow was permeating through the fabric. She dug, quickly at first, then more carefully, remembering she was looking for a very sharp object and it wouldn't do to come this far only to lose a finger by doing something stupid.

There was no question when she uncovered it. The blade was glowing as if it were made of moonlight, reflecting light even when there was seemingly none to be found.

Charlotte reached into the pouch, drawing the pommel out once more. She could feel a magnetic pull between them as she took up the vorpal blade in her left hand. Her fingers trembled, having trouble keeping hold of the pommel, and so she released it, watching it close the last foot of distance between itself and the hilt. There was a small flash of light between the orb and the metal, as if it were forging itself back together.

And then the hilt became unbearably hot.

Charlotte hissed and dropped it, shaking her hand to cool her fingers. "What the hell?" She raised her hand to blow on the skin… and came face to face once more with the unnatural claws her fingers had become. "Okay… so nightmare infection cannot touch reconstructed vorpal blade… got it." She looked around and reached for what looked like a baby's blanket, and using her unaltered hand, she wrapped it around the blade hilt, which seemed to protect her from being burned. "Works for vampires, works for me," she muttered. "Hey Charlotte, how did you save the world? Well, by watching too much *Buffy* with my mom, of course!"

She turned to go and saw the dimly lit, battered, and angry silhouette of the Bandersnatch blocking her path.

"…Why is it," she asked quietly, "you always seem to show up right when I start having fun?"

The Bandersnatch expanded her wings, filling nearly the entire tunnel height and width. The wings were battered—even ripped, but still translucent and beautiful. How could this be the horror she'd dreamed? That scared Oberon to his core?

Charlotte felt her chest tighten. "You… used to be one of Oberon's soldiers, right?"

The Bandersnatch let out a deafening scream.

Charlotte closed her eyes tightly a moment, her heartbeat increasing. Her ears rang long after the scream ended. *That* sound was as she remembered. She tried to control her breathing and slowly raise her hand to get the right perspective again. Maybe she couldn't squish her, but she could push her. Her hand trembled. This wasn't like the tove or the jub-jub. This wasn't just a creature from The Nothing, this had been a person. This *was* a person.

The Bandersnatch growled and shifted her weight.

Maybe she could make herself seem less appetizing. "Yeah, that guy seems like a nightmare to work with…" She swallowed. "Though I don't know if trading him in for a literal Nightmare for a boss is an improvement."

The green eyes blinked, almost as if confused, and she cocked her head slightly to the side.

Charlotte paused. Was she understanding her? "Do... you remember your name?"

Another blink. No response, but no further act of aggression.

Charlotte smiled weakly and brought her left hand to rest on her chest to indicate herself. "You can call me Charlie." She paused, remembering the multiple warnings Thorn had given her. "Though I'm pretty sure I was not supposed to tell you that."

The Bandersnatch said nothing.

"But I'm pretty sure you can't talk, so maybe that's okay?"

The great wings slightly lowered, not fully retracting, but almost as if she were uncertain if she was still attempting to frighten and intimidate this intruder.

"Maybe you don't remember your name right now, and that's okay," Charlotte kept talking, encouraged by the idea that she might be reaching this fae. "What if I call you something else in the meantime? Like... Fae... th. Faith!"

The Bandersnatch's lips pulled back and she growled.

"Ookay, not Faith," Charlotte answered quickly.

The Bandersnatch ducked her head ever so slightly, her wings following suit as she stalked toward Charlotte.

"Please don't," Charlotte asked quietly. "I don't want to hurt you."

But fear for someone else's welfare was still fear. And its call was too delectable for the Bandersnatch to ignore.

Charlotte's hand reached out, hurriedly trying to grip on to the Bandersnatch while there was still distance between them. She pinned the Bandersnatch's wings to her body for a few seconds, it writhed and wriggled against her before the strength of those wings not only pushed her hand away but did so with such a force that Charlotte stumbled back and fell into a pile of junk. Panic ran through her. She'd always felt a strange safety in this power, a false idea that she was untouchable, that if she could focus, nothing could stop her.

And then the Bandersnatch leapt.

The weight of the creature knocked what breath she'd managed to take out of her, sending her into a moment of shock which was overcome by cold and pain in her shoulders. Charlotte's heart raced. She could taste copper in her mouth, and her teeth began to ache. She flailed, clawing frantically at her attacker, managing to strike three scratches across the Bandersnatch's face.

Another horrifying shriek, and the Bandersnatch struck Charlotte in retaliation.

Cold fire stretched across Charlotte's face and neck. Something tugged at her ear followed by searing pain. Charlotte cried out and kicked her feet, trying to push the thing off her. Her nose burned. She could feel blood dripping down her neck. When she opened her eyes to try to find some way to deflect her attacker, she froze.

Without the gryphon feather, the woman she'd seen before was gone, and the nightmare creature that had haunted her memory now loomed over her; more gargoyle than girl, made of bone and teeth barely held together by flesh and sinew.

The Bandersnatch inhaled slowly through what remained of its nose, drinking in the cocktail of fear and pain exuding from the paralyzed teenager below her. And then she smelled something even more enticing: the importance of the golden watch necklace that hung around her neck. One claw released Charlotte's shoulder to grasp the Coleridge Clock.

Charlotte could make out every horrifying detail on the Bandersnatch's face, down to the strange, cracked texture of her skin and the glassy hollow glow of her eyes dimly reflecting the soft silver glow of the blade.

The blade.

Charlotte's hand tightened on the blanket-wrapped hilt of the vorpal blade and swung desperately at the creature above her, connecting awkwardly first with the wing, then the shoulder, and digging into the collarbone almost as if the creature was barely made of anything at all.

The Bandersnatch's skin sizzled and hissed, black goo seeping out of the surprisingly deep cut, the sword coming loose as if the oil-like substance repelled it. The Bandersnatch recoiled just enough for Charlotte to scramble backward.

The young girl found shaky footing. She gasped for air and gripped the blanket-wrapped hilt with both hands, stumbling forward to take another desperate slash.

It was more a batter's swing than any sort you'd take with a blade, but it hacked into the Bandersnatch's spine, knocking it from its crouch to crumple down to the ground. It let out a piercing howl as more black liquid spilled like a viscous ink.

Charlotte panted and stumbled back, looking at the wounded thing, hoping it would simply retreat.

Instead, the Bandersnatch looked at her, and those hollow green eyes seemed dimmer, but so much more terrifyingly human than even before. They were weeping. She pushed herself up slowly, just enough to let out a threatening scream, which passed through Charlotte like a great wind, blowing back her hair. Then her boney shoulders shuddered, and she collapsed again.

Charlotte's heart ached as she stared into those eyes. They seemed… pleading.

The Bandersnatch howled softly and swiped weakly in her direction with a clawed hand before letting it just rest on the ground.

Charlotte raised the sword again and hesitated. Everything up to this moment was out of defense, but this… what would this be? She tried to reason with herself that it would be putting the creature out of its misery. Out of *her* misery. "I'm sorry," she whispered, letting the sword fall to her side again. "I can't…" She looked down, feeling a deep shame as she took a few steps back. "I'm not my mother…" She moved toward the exit, keeping her eyes on the heavily breathing creature, making sure it wasn't going to attempt to follow before she turned to run down the tunnel back toward the exit once more.

"She's been gone quite some time," Phantasos remarked flippantly. "Do you think she's dead or having tea?"

"We'd know if she'd died," Ikelos answered, paused, then corrected. "I think. I am not entirely certain if that's true."

"How would you know?" Thorn growled angrily, long past their patience. They'd been pacing outside of the tunnel for quite some time now, feeling useless and without any distraction. "Am I supposed to believe that you can sense other Changelings? You didn't even know Smoke existed."

"Ah, that's right," Ikelos answered. "Never mind then."

"Are there four of us in Terra Mirum?" Phantasos asked.

"Apparently so!" Ikelos answered, throwing down a handful of cards. "Three aces."

"Would you two shut the—" Thorn turned on them, but they were focused on something coming out of the tunnel.

Charlotte was splattered in what looked like black oil and her own blood, the blade of the sword clanking against the train rails as it dragged beside her. Her limbs were heavy, and her cheeks tear stained. The earlobe that had once been adorned with gryphon feathers was bleeding but not completely cut through. She walked past Thorn to direct her glare at the brothers. She looked them up and down before with what remained of her energy and threw the blade at their feet.

"Now, you assholes are going to tell me exactly how we're going to use this thing to save my mother."

29

ALLIES AND ALL LIES

They'd argued about returning to Arden, Charlotte insisting they were wasting time by not directly going to The Nothing, Thorn being more pragmatic and reasoning they'd have better chances with an army at their back. Ikelos and Phantasos remained enigmatic and seemingly indifferent, and thus entirely unhelpful. One moment they'd seem to agree with Thorn, the next they'd agree with Charlotte, and at times they'd each stand with one foot on either side and argue with each other.

It was at the point when the twins seemed to be arguing with just each other that Thorn took Charlotte's hand in their own and led her behind a tree, just out of sight of the other two. "Please… I am begging you. Listen to me. You aren't thinking straight. How do you expect to charge in there like this?" Their voice was gentle but firm as they raised her left hand to bring her attention back to the nightmare infection.

"I defeated a Bandersnatch like this."

"You nearly lost an ear—or worse."

"But I didn't, and I'm fine. I will be fine. I was fine."

Thorn sighed, exasperated. "The Nothing is different, Treasure."

"Have you been?" Charlotte asked petulantly.

"No, and neither have you." Thorn's free hand gently ran a thumb over the nightmare-infected skin on her fingers. "You don't know what that kind of power could do to you—what it could do to this."

"Neither do you. It's possible The Nothing *could* do nothing to it. Or maybe it could give me an advantage. There's a lot it *could* do," Charlotte tried to reason. "You're just insisting on only looking at the negative outcomes."

"Fates," Thorn growled and released her to run their hands through their hair. "You're starting to sound like *them*."

Charlotte shrugged. "Well, they make a lot of sense."

"HOW?" Thorn didn't ask the word so much as expel it from their mouth with a force that made the forest almost seem quieter in comparison.

Another shrug as Charlotte's own frustration increased. "I don't know. They just do. Maybe it doesn't all make sense at once but there's something there that feels…" She gestured vaguely and shrugged.

"Feels *what*?"

"Like when you learn a word in the riddle you couldn't figure out has two meanings." Thorn's confused expression didn't clear, and so Charlotte attempted to elaborate. "And maybe you don't quite know the answer yet… but it's changed your perspective on what's being asked. And you realize you might have been looking at the question wrong this entire time."

Thorn paused and took a slow and even breath before speaking again. "Okay… what's the word in this case?"

Charlotte pursed her lips a moment. "…I don't know."

Thorn nodded slowly, maintaining patience. "Then what's the question?"

"I…" Charlotte fidgeted. "I don't quite know that either."

Thorn took a step back, blowing air through their lips.

"It's not a perfect metaphor," Charlotte defended. "It's just… It's how I feel, like my head has never been clearer."

"Well, you *sound* drunk," Thorn muttered.

"I don't *need* you to guide me, you know," Charlotte pointed out. "Ikelos and Phantasos must know the way to The Nothing."

"Now, there's sound judgement if I've ever heard it," came the sarcastic reply. "As if The Nothing wasn't dangerous enough, let's go by the guidance of two men who haven't been able to string a straightforward sentence together since you met them. Must be the blood loss talking."

"At least they're trying to help me."

"Is that what you think?" Thorn asked incredulously. "Charlotte, *I am* trying to help you!"

"Then why would we waste time going back to Arden?"

"Because we have no way of knowing what exactly we're up against, but I know we have a better chance with Oberon and Titania's forces than we do on our own!"

"Learic," Charlotte said softly. "Please... We've come this far, and we are running out of time. If I go back to Arden, Robin is going to send me back to my father to just wait this whole thing out."

The fae's brow furrowed, and their gaze turned skyward. The sun was on its descent. "I'm not going to change your mind, am I?"

"Stubborn as a mule is a Carroll Family trait, I'm afraid," Charlotte answered.

Thorn's lips pursed, and their gaze dropped to the forest floor. "Fine... *I* will take you to The Nothing... but you have to swear to me you will take every precaution possible."

"I swear," Charlotte breathed.

Thorn nodded. "I'll need the Coleridge Clock."

Charlotte's brow raised in surprise, and she looked down at the clock around her neck. "Why?"

"It's easy to get lost in the Tulgey Wood... but I know of a nearby mirror we can use as a lighthouse of sorts—should get us on the right track."

"Can't we just ask..." Charlotte turned back toward the clearing to where she expected to see the brothers still arguing, but instead, the vorpal blade, still mostly wrapped in cloth, lay on the grass unattended. "Wait, where did they go?"

Thorn followed her gaze, and the two exchanged looks before walking toward the blade once more. "Hello?"

"Ikelos?" Charlotte called. "Phantasos?"

Nothing.

"What the hell?" Charlotte muttered.

"Very helpful blokes," Thorn said dryly.

"Shut up," Charlotte answered. "They must be here..."

"Well, we can wait around looking for them," Thorn offered, "waste some more time..." They held out an expectant hand. "Or we can get going and try to reach the door before the sun sets."

Charlotte chewed her lower lip thoughtfully, looking from their perimeter to the sun's position, then finally down to the Coleridge Clock around her neck. Reluctantly, she lifted the chain over her head. She hesitated. "You're sure this will get us there?"

Thorn's jaw tightened. "You have my word."

The Coleridge Clock was placed gently in their palm.

"Thank you." Thorn wrapped the chain around their wrist a few times to secure it to them. They took a moment to focus before opening the watch to examine the golden hand that would point them toward their destination. They shifted their weight, changing direction as the hand moved until it settled. "This way," they said softly and began to walk. "Bring the blade."

Charlotte watched them start without her a moment, fumbling to replace a glove over her infected hand before she scooped up the vorpal blade. "Wait for me!"

It was a tense walk. They said very little to each other over the course of an hour or so, and Charlotte couldn't help but notice the way Thorn seemed to refuse to meet her eyes. When they'd first met, it might have made them seem mysterious, aloof… but now it just felt cold and distant.

They probably hate me.

Charlotte could feel the thought drop from her mind to the pit of her stomach.

I shouldn't have been so pushy. It was cruel to say they weren't trying to help; they've been trying to help from the start.

She swallowed.

They've been by my side since we've met, even when I tried to leave them behind. The twins didn't do that…

She chewed the inside of her cheek and focused on her breathing. She watched the way Thorn kept meticulously checking the compass and adjusting their path to ensure they were traveling as efficiently as possible and not going off course.

God I'm an asshole.

"I'm sorry."

Thorn looked a little startled, and for the first time, turned their head toward her. "What?"

"You have every right to be mad at me."

"What are you talking about?" Thorn asked incredulously.

"I had no right to doubt you—you've always been there for me."

Back to the clock with a dismissive shake of the head, eyes down and then forward, keeping an eye out for any approaching danger, then back again. "It's fine."

"It's not," Charlotte continued. "You had no reason to help me when you did... I probably would have died if it weren't for you. I'm so sorry."

"Oh, you do not even know the meaning of that word, little girl," Robin answered.

The two stopped dead in their tracks.

Thorn's fingers snapped the Coleridge Clock shut. "Robin."

The Unseelie dropped to the forest floor from her lookout perch in the tree above them. She was armored, and two curved short blades hung on each hip. "Where in the hell have you two been?"

"...East?" Charlotte guessed.

Robin pointed at her, anger seething. "I don't even have words for how stupid running off like that was."

Charlotte held up the Vorpal Blade. "How about 'thank you'?"

Robin's expression shifted ever so slightly to surprise. "You actually retrieved it."

"You're welcome," Charlotte said flatly.

"We didn't need this to win," said Robin.

"I hope Oberon is a lot happier to see this than you are," said Charlotte.

"You could have been killed," Robin scolded.

"I've been hearing that a lot lately," Charlotte answered. "Yet, here I am, still somehow breathing."

"Give me the damn sword," Robin growled angrily. She took the offered blade by the hilt, carefully unwrapping it from the dirty blanket. She paused, taking in the sight of it. She hadn't laid eyes upon the blade since Alys... She looked to Thorn. "And the Coleridge Clock."

Thorn looked down and reluctantly handed over the pocket watch, their hand snaking out of the chain loops with a few elegant movements of their wrist.

Robin shook her head at them disbelievingly before calling back up to the tree. "Hold the perimeter. I'll be back." Her upper lip curled slightly in disgust, and she turned on her heel to lead them through a glamor barrier, which, once breached, revealed an expansive camp, sleeping quarters in most trees and regular patrols. She barked at one of the passing units. "Find these two idiots a bed for the night. I'll deal with them in the morning."

The patrol merely saluted their understanding before moving to form around Charlotte and Thorn, guiding the two in a march in the opposite direction of Robin.

"You didn't say much back there," Charlotte said quietly.

"You seemed to be saying enough for both of us," Thorn answered.

"So, you *are* mad at me," Charlotte concluded.

"Fates, Charlotte…" Thorn muttered. "I just mean did you have to goad her? She wasn't angry enough already?"

"What difference does it make?" Charlotte shrugged. "She wasn't going to be happy no matter what we said."

"You can't expect people to treat you like an equal while you're acting like a petulant child."

Charlotte scoffed. "Like I haven't heard that damn piss-poor excuse for disrespect a million times."

"What are you talking about?"

"I'm talking about how people love to tell us to grow up and start acting like adults, but the moment we fucking do, they tell us we're children and we don't know anything." She shook her head. "Earth, Terra Mirum, Arden… Doesn't matter where I am, still sucks to be a teenager."

"You're tired."

"I'm pissed off," Charlotte snapped.

"I'm sorry." They meant it.

Charlotte sighed. "It's not your fault… Just rotten luck running into the army."

Thorn didn't say anything.

"Wait here," the unit leader instructed, placing them by one of the many trees within the Tulgey Wood camp.

The group then continued their patrol along the length of the camp.

Charlotte watched them go a moment before addressing her unusually quiet companion again. "Why are they camping now?"

"They have a better chance of victory if they mount the attack by morning light. Nightmares won't have as much strength outside of The Nothing during the day—will make the door easier to breach."

Charlotte nodded slowly. "And what are the chances we'll be able to join them in that attack?"

Thorn leaned against the tree. "Slim."

"Seems really dumb to give up soldiers who could be fighting just to escort us back to Arden," Charlotte criticized.

"They'll probably just keep us back with the healer's tents and mirror guard."

Charlotte blinked. "What?"

Thorn paused. "The Healer's Tent. It's where they tend to the wounded."

"No, I know what a fucking healer does, Thorn— what the hell is a mirror guard?" Charlotte demanded.

Thorn's jaw clenched, and they looked away and back again. "They carry doors into battle that link back to several varied evacuation points and medical facilities…"

Charlotte stared at them, unmoving. She remembered Thorn's rather extensive familiarity with the Coleridge clock… Mention of the symbol of the

Summer court... "That was the mirror you were using, wasn't it? You absolutely meant to bring us here."

Thorn didn't answer, didn't look at her.

Charlotte could feel her eyes burning, her hands balling into fists as her body trembled, though whether she was about to scream or cry she wasn't sure. Her throat felt tight. "You lied to me."

"I did what I had to," Thorn said quietly.

"To accomplish what?" Charlotte demanded.

"Save your mother."

"Like hell you did," Charlotte spat.

Thorn pushed off the tree to face Charlotte full on, meeting her eyes for the first time in what must have been hours. "You're not just a danger to yourself if you turn, you know that, don't you?" they asked. "The Bandersnatch was one thing, Treasure, but in there? Where those things *thrive*? You need to be fearless. And that, Charlotte Carroll, admirable as you are, is not you."

Charlotte scoffed. "So, you sabotaged me because you think I'll get scared at the last second?"

"No, I think they'll eat you alive," said Thorn gravely. "You've pushed through it every time, but you are riddled with anxiety. They feed on fear, Charlotte, and no amount of breath control is going to save you from that."

Charlotte's tears betrayed her resolve. "You don't know that. You had no right to make that choice for me."

"I do. You may be your mother's daughter, but you cannot be her savior. Not now, not like this."

Charlotte wiped at her eyes, feeling her throat tighten with a mix of anger and despair. "She's not going to remember me, Learic. Don't you get that? This was the last chance I had to do right by her, to fix all the stupid messes I've… It's my fault she's here!"

"I'm sorry."

Charlotte screamed in frustration, digging her fingers into her scalp. She was having trouble inhaling. "How could you do this?"

"Because, for possibly the first time in my life, I love someone more than I need them to love me," Thorn said quietly.

Charlotte couldn't speak at first, couldn't breathe. Struggling with hyperventilating, she managed a gasp for air, and with it she spat out, "I hate you!"

"I know," said Thorn. "And I know you'll never forgive me… But if it keeps you safe, that's an injury I can live with."

"Fu…" Charlotte wheezed. Her heart hurt, everything hurt. She couldn't breathe. She gasped and doubled over.

"Hey," Thorn said gently, reaching out to carefully grasp her arms. "Deep breaths. Slowly, slowly…"

Charlotte struggled against their embrace, gulping for air like she was drowning. She writhed, twisted around to fully face Thorn and slammed her fists down on their chest.

Thorn flinched upon the impact and felt a flurry of feathers and wind as the girl in their arms dissolved.

Their eyes snapped open in time to turn and see a murder of crows pass around them, flying frantically up into the sky, not quite in formation. "Charlie!"

The crows vanished from sight with a distant caw that echoed through the trees.

30

THE BREACH

Charlotte's understanding of what had happened was fractured at best. She'd felt the walls closing in on her, the world growing smaller. She was drowning, and the one person she'd been able to count on to pull her above the surface was seemingly holding her under the water. She'd flailed, choked, and just as she feared her lungs would give out...

The world shattered, or at least her vision of it. Giant cracks through her reality, as if she'd been staring at a reflection the entire time, breaking into dozens of pieces that all flew in different directions. Pieces of vision scattered about amid a void of darkness until her dizziness overcame her and the world went dark.

Her heart shivered, and she was overwhelmed by the sensation of falling, but unable to see in any direction, she wasn't sure if she actually was—or what she might be falling into. She felt a cold breeze sweep over her and with it an overwhelming sense of failure.

Why did you think you could do this?

Another chill and she found herself looking upward—or what she assumed was upward, feeling her hair whip around her face until that feeling, too, dissolved into the icy chill.

You're a fraud, Charlotte, and now everyone finally knows it.

She couldn't see her hands or legs, and when she tried to touch her own face, everything was so numb she wasn't sure if she was touching anything or had moved at all. Was she still even falling?

Maybe they always knew it. Maybe they were just too scared to tell you.

What was that sound? The wind?

What did you think was going to happen? That you'd barrel in and save the day? You? You're so much of a coward you ran away without even trying. It's pathetic. You're pathetic.

Not wind, *wings.* Flapping all around her.

They'd be better off if you'd never been born. Your mother would be safe. Happy.

Charlotte must have been getting some feeling back in her limbs because she could feel herself pulling against the cold, flailing in the air helplessly as the descent continued.

Thorn wouldn't have to babysit you. They'd be better equipped to deal with this if you'd never got in the way.

Her fists reached out to grab onto something, *anything*, and in doing so grasped what felt like a fist full of feathers. Charlotte's brow furrowed, and she tried to see what she had in her hand. But more feather-like objects blew past her, into her face and brushing against her skin in a flurry as warmth returned to her skin, letting her perceive even the faintest of touches.

You failed all of them.

Charlotte awoke with a jolt as if finally reaching the bottom of the endless pit she'd felt herself careening down just moments before. The world around her was bright, causing her to flinch and close her eyes as quickly as they had opened. She took a moment before shaking her head and opening them again, pushing herself up into a sitting position.

It was then that she noticed the circle of black feathers that surrounded her form, as if she'd spontaneously shed them herself. She blinked, once, twice, and took in the clearing in which she'd found herself.

It was unnervingly peaceful, sun dappling through the leaves from somewhere above. There was no sign of the Fae army, Thorn, or even a Nightmare. "What…"

"That really was a fantastic trick," Phantasos commented.

Charlotte looked behind her to see him leaning against a tree. "What trick?"

"Turning into crows to escape your situation," Ikelos explained. "Never seen anything quite like it. You must teach us how it is done."

Charlotte's brow furrowed, and she tried to piece together the fragments of what felt like a nightmare and everything prior… She reached down to pick up one of the black feathers curiously. "I... don't know how I did it."

"Truly?" Ikelos sounded genuinely surprised. "Pity. It seemed quite handy."

"And excruciating," Phantasos answered. "Splitting yourself into so many pieces, it must have been deliciously agonizing."

Charlotte brought a hand to her head, then to her heart, feeling the still racing beats beneath her chest. She took a moment to breathe. In for five, out for six. When her heart had slowed and she was confident she wasn't going to spiral once more, she turned her attention to the two men in suits. "Where the hell did you go?"

"Here," Ikelos gestured to their surroundings simply.

"It was more efficient to just meet you here," said Phantasos.

Charlotte blinked at this. "More efficient to meet... Did you *know* Thorn was going to take me to the camp?"

Ikelos waffled his hand back and forth at the word "know." "Given their affection for your safety, we saw it as a likely possibility."

"Why the hell didn't you try to stop them?" Charlotte demanded.

Phantasos shrugged. "Wasn't much of a point, really."

"In every scenario, you ended up here anyway," Ikelos elaborated.

Charlotte shook her head. "What?"

"The probability of you remaining in the camp was practically nil. Coming here first was hardly a gamble," Ikelos actually smiled.

Charlotte looked around, not seeing anything resembling the door or even a Nightmare. "Why here?"

Phantasos shrugged and adjusted his fedora. "You'll have to tell us."

"We only saw," Ikelos explained, "so, we came. Only you really know what's next."

Charlotte carefully pushed herself into a stand. "You saw. Do you literally mean you saw me coming here? Like a vision?"

Ikelos' mouth quirked in amusement. "Did you think we only gave visions?"

Charlotte didn't have any clever defense and found herself simply admitting, "…Yes."

"Bit narrow-minded," Phantasos muttered under his breath.

"Excuse me?" Charlotte glared toward him.

"Why here, Charlotte?" Ikelos prodded gently.

Charlotte looked to him, then to the forest around them. It looked like any other they'd traversed through, nondescript. "I don't know."

"You must," Phantasos insisted.

"I don't!" Charlotte snapped. "I've never been…" She stopped. Something *did* feel familiar. Vaguely. And the faint memory of her dream of her mother, wandering around with a frayed silver cord flowing behind her— just before she'd been snatched away. "I do recognize this place… sort of. This is where my mother was when I dreamed…" She looked to Ikelos. "It was part of your vision."

"Not entirely," Ikelos admitted. "My work was restricted to the Bandersnatch. I might have hijacked a vision you were already having by the sound of it."

Charlotte's brows raised, but she didn't quite know what to say. Was she also capable of visions on her own?

"You escaped from your perceived captors to retreat to the last place you saw your mother…" Phantasos said. "Did you think she'd actually be here? Or is this some sort of surrogate teddy bear?"

"What? No. I don't know. Shut up," Charlotte sputtered at him.

"Finding where your mother is would be a bit more productive than finding the last place she was, before she was taken," Ikelos offered.

Charlotte looked down at the scattered feathers around her. "I… don't think I can."

"Interesting choice," remarked Phantasos. "Come all this way, give up before the finish line."

"You didn't strike me as the sort to sit idly by while others fight the battle," Ikelos added gently.

"I just exploded into birds and blacked out because I couldn't deal with confronting a friend," Charlotte threw her hands up. "You really think I can handle The Nothing? Swarms of Nightmares? I want to help my mom, but Thorn was right. What choice do I really have here?"

"Infinite choices, really, most of which you haven't even thought of yet," Phantasos said flatly.

"I could *kill* them. All of them." She pulled her glove off her hand, and as she suspected, the infection had spread a little farther, now almost fully engulfing her palm. "Including my mother." Charlotte's shoulders slumped, and she stared down at her hands. "I really did fail them…"

The brothers exchanged looks, Phantasos nodding slightly to Ikelos, and Ikelos frowning in response. The man in grey took a slight side-step closer to Charlotte.

"'Could' is a *very* mercurial word, Charlie."

Charlotte's gaze raised from her hands to meet Ikelos'. "Meaning what?"

"Meaning there are many things that *could* happen," Ikelos answered levelly.

"Being responsible for your mother's demise is only one of them," Phantasos added almost a little too cheerfully, and Charlotte coughed in disgust. "There's several where others bring that about."

Charlotte's mouth could not find the words as she stared at the man in the fedora. Was this supposed to comfort her?

"There are also several 'coulds' where she doesn't die at all," Ikelos assured.

Charlotte exhaled in disbelief. "So… what? You're saying I should go?"

"We are suggesting," Ikelos began quietly. "That very often reality is what we make of it." He let his voice lower, settle into a register she had never heard from him before. "If you *know* where you are going, every road will get you there. Do you understand?"

Charlotte leaned back slightly in realization. The way they talked, never really settling on an absolute definite. "Like a self-fulfilling prophecy," she concluded.

Phantasos nodded ever so slightly, and the mirth in him seemed gone. "Now imagine what damage that kind of arrogant certainty could do in a place where an idea can quite literally shape the world around you."

Charlotte let this sink in, looking down at her hands again. If there was truth in this, then she absolutely had control over this infection. She could fight it. She wasn't defined by it. She nodded, taking a deep breath… Let's go."

The difference between the area directly around The Door and the rest of the Tulgey Wood had become like night and day. With every step closer, the sun's light became more distant, as if the air around was too thick to allow it through. It was the first thing Charlotte noticed.

Then the snow began to fall.

As if she was walking back into her dream, it floated down around them, eerily slow and inexplicably hot. Her brow furrowed as she looked up, taking in the sight of the charred trees all around them, embers pulsing beneath the blackened bark like a heartbeat. "It's… ash."

"They're always burning," Phantasos explained.

"Since the world was turning?" Charlotte asked facetiously.

"Since your mother went head-to-head with a Jabberwock," Ikelos answered sincerely, unaware of the joke.

"Epic, but not nearly as catchy," Charlotte commented before nearly tripping over a root. She looked back and saw a strange shape beneath the ash. She stopped and reached down towards the odd root, brushing off some of the ash. It was a hand. She recoiled quickly, taking a few rapid steps backward until her back smacked into a tree. "Shit, shit, shit... That's a body."

The two brothers looked down at the hand Charlotte had uncovered.

"Correction, that is a lot of bodies," Phantasos said gravely, pointing with his cane to the clearing ahead of them.

Soldiers lay crumpled across the forest floor, some cut and bleeding, others seeming drained of all life, skin and bones, as if they'd been dried out like flowers. There had to be at least three regiments worth of bodies. And just beyond them, Charlotte could see the crack in the sky that had haunted her since the start of all this. Her perspective changed. She could see it was not a crack at all but rather a tree, split and dead. She could hear the whispers calling to her as they had before. "Oh, god..."

Ikelos and Phantasos each drew a sword, one from the handle of an umbrella, the other a cane. They were thin, reminiscent of fencing weapons, but the blades themselves glittered and gleamed like moonlight.

"Vorpal blades?" Charlotte asked incredulously.

"You didn't think we were going to defend ourselves with wit alone, did you?" Phantasos teased.

"Rapier as they are, they don't always parry claws or steel very well," Ikelos commented.

"Why did I need to get my mother's if you both already had vorpal blades?" Charlotte demanded.

"Because there are *three* of us, Charlotte," Ikelos answered curtly. "Help us check the bodies. There may still be some living."

The three fanned out, careful not to step on any of the fallen.

Charlotte struggled to focus rather than follow the call of the whispers beckoning her to enter through the opening in the tree no longer obstructed by a door—it almost seemed as if it had been blown off. But amid the pleas of hushed voices, she heard crying. It took her a moment to realize it, too, wasn't a whisper on the wind. She looked around desperately, seeing a form trembling beneath the fallen leaves and ash. She dropped to her knees beside them. "Where are you hurt?"

The form moved to look toward Charlotte, and she found herself eye to eye with Queen Titania herself.

Charlotte's heart dropped into her stomach, and she looked down at the person cradled in her arms, terrified who she might see—but while it surprised her, she was almost relieved.

Oberon, the once great King of Shadows, ruler of the Unseelie, had fallen beside the men and women he swore to lead. It was surreal and uncomfortable gazing upon the man who, while not without fear, had seemed far too stubborn and arrogant to be capable of succumbing to any sort of mortal wound.

Charlotte looked from the body of the king to the queen who still clutched him to her. She had no words. She opened her mouth, searching for something to say to her, comfort her, perhaps reassure… but instead she found herself calling back to Ikelos and Phantasos. "Wounded!" The word croaked out of her, and Ikelos looked up from his search to move over to her to help.

Titania caught Charlotte around the forearm with a cold hand, gripping so tightly and desperately that her nails dug into the younger girl's skin. "Learic took the vorpal blade," she whispered, her eyes betraying the terror of what else she might lose that day.

Charlotte swallowed hard. She nodded slowly.

Ikelos knelt beside Charlotte, setting down his rapier on the ground to examine Titania's wounds.

Titania, however, never looked away from Charlotte, even then. "Find them," she whispered before finally releasing her arm. "Bring them back."

Charlotte looked to the ground and took up Ikelos' sword. "I'm sorry, I need—"

"Go," Ikelos said without looking at her. "We'll catch up."

She nodded shakily and turned to face the door. Her first step was unsteady, but no longer fighting its pull, she found walking directly toward The Nothing was far easier than she would have thought. She breathed slowly, feeling what felt like a wind wrapping around her back and pulling her in a cold embrace and into the void itself. The whispers grew louder and louder, a distant scream and cry interweaving between the discordant harmony until she crossed the threshold. It was so quiet; she could hear her own breath. A few dim lights—like fireflies—glowed not too far from her, but they were not enough to give any true illumination.

Her right hand tightened around the sword hilt. Without the earring she was blind by the sudden change in light. She closed her eyes and opened them. Still nothing.

She stumbled forward, blinking again against the darkness. he could dimly make out the shapes of five large wolf-like creatures. The firefly-like glow came from their bloodshot-looking eyes. Beasts of childhood nightmares, they bared razor-sharp teeth, and though her eyesight was still adjusting to taking them in, it was clear they needed no such assessment of her.

They fanned out on either side, intelligent enough to surround and attempt to corner her.

Charlotte's heart rate increased, but she remained focused on her breathing. If she believed she would fail, then she would. She had the power to fight this. She just needed to believe she did.

The creatures growled, but there was something in that noise that almost sounded human—even familiar. Her mother's voice? "You were right the first time," it was lower than her mother spoke, with more gravel and grit, and yet. "You aren't enough to win this."

"You can't use her against me," Charlotte warned.

"Afraid of everything, stupid, selfish little girl." Another guttural sound that carried the hint of Thorn's voice—but using words they'd never speak.

"I'm not afraid," Charlotte denied.

The pack surrounding her erupted into what sounded almost like hyena-laughter.

Charlotte gritted her teeth and lunged forward, drawing the rapier tip in an upward slash.

Immediately, one leapt from behind, knocking her hard to the ground. She could feel teeth sink into her wrist, biting down to either get her to release the sword or sever her hand.

Charlotte's heart was pounding. She could feel tears welling up in her eyes.

You've already lost. You've already failed them again.

No. She cried out and tried to push herself up. She couldn't give in to this. She had to fight it. She would not be weak. She would be fearless.

The pain rushed from her wrist and up her shoulder. She was bleeding, she could feel it. The pressure from the creatures on top of her, pushing her into the ground, restricted her breathing, and once more she found herself gasping for air.

She pushed against them with all her might, feeling as if her entire body was on fire until finally, she jolted upright, gasping for air as if she'd just broken the surface.

She looked around, seeing only darkness but feeling strangely safer. "Where did they go?"

"I thought they might be a bit distracting," said a friendly voice.

Standing just a few feet away was a boy not much older than Charlotte herself. He wasn't dressed at all like the citizens of Terra Mirum or Arden. No armor, no wings. Just a red hooded sweatshirt, jeans, and red converse. His smile was comforting, and while somewhat obstructed by blonde curls, his eyes were kind. "I was hoping we could talk."

31

THE OTHER CHARLIE

Charlotte stared, unmoving, eyes locked on the stranger before her. Her brow furrowed in confusion. He looked so familiar, but she couldn't quite place why. She'd seen him. She knew she'd seen him. A million times over, she had looked at that face, and yet...

Her brow relaxed in realization. "You're Charlie Lewis, aren't you?" She could barely speak above a whisper.

The boy smiled, and his chest puffed out a little proudly. "And you'd be my namesake, if I'm not mistaken."

Charlotte breathed a disbelieving laugh. "Yeah... I've... Mom talks really fondly of you..." She stopped. "Wait, aren't you dead? Oh, god, am *I* dead?"

The other Charlie laughed. "No. You are not dead."

"But you are?" Charlotte tried to make sense of the moment.

"By some definitions," Charlie conceded.

"Well, how would *you* define your current situation?"

"I'm…" Charlie mulled this question over a moment before grinning once more. He had rather perfect teeth and an impish energy that made Charlotte a little sad she'd never had a chance to meet him in life. "Redistributed."

"Redistributed?"

"Well, what are we really if not just energy buzzing about at various frequencies. And as I'm sure your science teacher has dutifully informed you, energy cannot be created or destroyed. So, we're… redistributed."

Charlotte looked around at the black nothing that surrounded them. "Redistributed to what, exactly?"

Charlie Lewis rocked back and forth on his heels to his toes. "I'm a fairy godmother of sorts."

"You're going to give me a makeover, a curfew, and tote me off to a ball to meet and eventually marry a man with a shoe fetish?"

Charlie snorted. "You've got your mother's smartass gene, I see…" He puffed out his cheeks in thought and attempted to elaborate on his role. "I'm an intercessor."

"For whom?" asked Charlotte.

"Truthfully? Alys." He paused and then gestured to Charlotte. "And you, by extension, of course." He shoved his hands in his sweatshirt pockets and began to walk around her, not circling like a vulture so much as just needing to move and not having a terribly varied place to go. "I wasn't happy with how I left things. So, I chose to stick around for a bit. Make sure she turned out okay. Right now? You're her best chance for that."

"Me? You're speaking to me from the beyond—can't you just wake her up?"

"Alas, no, I don't have that kind of power," Charlie shook his head. "I can't even reach out to her like this now."

"Why?"

"Because unlike the last time, she's not physically here. Just her consciousness is. Which means we can't exactly use it for a chat. When that consciousness is being held hostage? It's just... Well, it's still possible, but it's an utter clusterfuck, Charlotte. Pardon my language, but there's no real other words for it." He paused and amended this statement. "Well, there are, but they're hardly as satisfying to say."

Charlotte shrugged a little helplessly. "I don't understand."

"Where do you think we are right now?"

"The Nothing?"

"No," Charlie said gently. "That's where *you* are."

Charlotte's brow furrowed a moment before it dawned on her. "This... isn't real, is it?"

"It's really happening, but no, by your standards, this is not 'real.'"

"We're in my head?"

"Yes."

"I'm dreaming."

"In a manner of speaking."

"Am I just dreaming you?"

Charlie shook his head. "Let's say you're dreaming *to* me. That should help you separate the connection from the fabrication. Think of your mind as a physical location we could meet face to face. We're in your dream, but I am not a part of it. You could change the scenery, but you would not be able to change me."

Charlotte nodded, then stopped. "Does that mean my body is still being eaten alive by those… things?!"

"Momewraths, and I assure you, they're not really eating you, they're just… chewing, more or less."

"I'm being torn apart by literal Nightmares, Charles. I don't give a fuck about semantics," Charlotte spat, feeling her anxiety rising once more.

"Why not? Are you anti-semantic?" Charlie asked, then his eyes narrowed to a faux glare. "Nazi."

Charlotte was not amused.

Charlie exhaled sharply through his nose, greatly displeased. "…Oh, fuck you—that was hilarious."

"I'm dying!"

"Don't be dramatic," Charlie waved a dismissive hand.

"But you just said—"

"Let me tell you about Nightmares, Charlotte." Charlie's tone shifted, the playfulness gone. "The real danger? Are the lies they can tell you. The best lies. Lies that resonate in your bones. Because they're *your* lies. The ones we hear in our own voices. Our doubts, our insecurities." His mouth winced in a mirthless smile. "Repeating them back to you. That anxiety, that fear— they feed off it."

"Well then I'm screwed because most days I'm nothing BUT anxiety and fear. Anxiety, fear, thinly veiled sarcasm, and an unfortunate habit of laughing at my own jokes, none of which helps me here."

"Fear isn't inherently bad, Charlotte. In a healthy symbiotic relationship, we benefit from our fears as much as our Nightmares do. Fear can keep us safe in dangerous situations, act as a kind of alarm. Facing those fears isn't just courage—its what helps us grow. It even increases endorphins and serotonin—which incidentally helps your brain work more efficiently." He snapped his fingers, and the darkness faded into a muted sky, an uneven slope and even more lopsided concrete steps up to a dilapidated house. "Do you recognize it?"

Charlotte shook her head.

"This is where most of your mother's fears were born when she was your age." He sat down on one step with a crack down the center and invited her to sit next to him. "And this was our one safe space from them."

"…It's a concrete step."

"You don't need much to create one. Sometimes it's not even a place at all. Sometimes it's a person. Sometimes it's… just a thought. Even the smallest light can keep the nightmares at bay, if you believe in it enough. For us, it was the thought of leaving this behind."

An awkward beat.

"Not… how I did it," Charlie finally elaborated. "That was never the plan. That was me losing sight of…*everything.* Thinking it would never be enough to get away. That *I* would never be enough."

Charlotte nodded. "I know the feeling."

"That's one of those lies, Charlotte."

"Is it?"

Charlie smiled sympathetically, as if he saw some semblance of himself in that moment. He patted the stair next to him again, and this time she did sit down. "The most common, I would wager. We all hear it. Some days we even believe it."

Charlotte's nose scrunched in disbelief. "Mom doesn't. She's *fearless.*"

"I very much doubt that."

"Everyone says—"

"We have fears because things *matter* to us, Charlotte. You think nothing matters to your mom?" He almost sounded annoyed by the notion.

"That's not what I—"

"You don't think she was scared almost every day that she wasn't being a good enough mom to you? That somewhere deep down she wasn't terrified of becoming her own mother in some way?" Charlie shook his head. "You can't genuinely care about something and not be the least bit scared that you might lose it or mess it up."

Charlotte looked doubtful.

"Your mother is well-practiced in not letting fear stand in her way—and that *is* admirable, but that doesn't mean she's without. She's just honed that skill."

The idea that *bravery* was a skill struck her. She'd always assumed it a quality one was born with or not. There was comfort in the idea that not only could it possibly be learned—but that having her anxieties were a prerequisite to doing so.

"When we fail to practice that skill, we slip. And that's when those lies have a better chance of taking hold, and when Nightmares become dangerous."

Charlotte's brow furrowed. "What do you mean?"

"In normal circumstances, nightmares feed off our ordinary fears: running late, failing a test, saying the wrong thing in front of a crush. Sometimes they're more intense, depending on…" Charlie made a face and gestured to his own head. "What you're working with up there."

Charlotte hummed a laugh knowingly.

"The point is, they allow us to face our fears and dangers in a completely safe environment. It is, when maintained and healthy, a mutually beneficial relationship. They feed, we grow. The true terror of a *jabberwock*, is not *what* they are capable of, but *how*. They're forged by one life forcing itself on another with no regard for free will or thought. It's the product of ruthless pursuit for control and power. This is where an average nightmare and a jabberwock differ. There is no longer give and take. They stay with you long after you've awoken. Constantly lying to keep you on edge, never giving you a moment to question or even think about them. Intrusive lies—*violent* fabrications. All so they can feed more. And if you let them, if you shrink and back down, they will not hesitate. They will just take, and take, and take… until they swallow you whole."

"Is that what happened?" Charlotte didn't dare speak over a whisper. "Is that why you…?"

"No one forced me to do what I did, Charlotte. That was my decision." It was a firm admission of responsibility. One that did not leave room for misinterpretation. "But that *monster*? Did a fantastic job of convincing me it was my only option. That *everyone* would be better off if I was gone—that maybe they wouldn't immediately understand but eventually see it was all for the best." He sighed and shook his head. "It was a lie I'd told myself so many times, it was easy to believe when *he* started repeating it."

"The Jabberwock?"

"*My* Jabberwock," Charlie said. He paused, waffled with this statement, and corrected it, "Partly mine. My *nightmare*, anyway." He exhaled a laugh through his nose. "More than a decade later and your mom is still having to deal with my shit. Gods, I owe her such an apology. I was never particularly good at…facing it. Ever."

"You were a kid," Charlotte tried to comfort.

Charlie fixed the girl who would have been two years his junior were they contemporaries with a look.

"Not that you were any less valid," Charlotte elaborated quickly. "I just mean, you shouldn't have had to face that."

576

"There are a lot of things I never should have had to face. But if I'd *accepted* help... I probably could have." Charlie shrugged. "Then maybe my nightmare wouldn't have become a monster."

Charlotte scoffed and kicked a pebble down the steps. "You make it sound like it wasn't bad to begin with."

The boy waited, letting Charlotte's statement marinate in the silence.

Charlotte's back straightened slightly as a thought struck her. "They *aren't* bad... are they? At least not by nature?" She looked back to Charlie who just smiled encouragingly. Her mind raced, rejecting the thought as soon as she had had it. "But even when we're just kids, they make us scared of the smallest little things— stupid things—things that could *never* hurt us, *shadows* on the bedroom wall..." As her voice trailed off, she saw those moments with a different perspective. "So we can practice."

"You have to crawl before you walk. Climbing out of the comfort of your bed to turn on the light for a toddler is just as terrifying as standing up to a bully when you're older. Or interviewing for a job you want. Or moving to a new town when you don't have anything or know anyone. Nightmares give you a risk-free environment to practice being brave."

"Are you suggesting our nightmares are trying to help us?"

Charlie shrugged noncommittally. "I'm suggesting that perhaps nothing is so black and white as good and evil—that maybe we've been approaching our fear and nightmares with less understanding and compassion than we should."

Charlotte sat back, her breath caught in her throat. This was wrong. This was all wrong. "How do I fix this?"

"Take courage, Charlotte. Turn on the light."

Charlotte's eyes snapped open, and the pain returned to her arm. She clenched her left fist, curled inward, and then, with a snap, something felt like it expanded from her back, the force pushing the momewraths back several feet. She could hear crows cawing as they fled from her in all directions. She looked down—the darkness had spread up her entire arm to her shoulder. "This isn't real." She reached up with her uninfected hand and brushed her fingers down the length of her left arm, the skin changing back in her wake. "It's just another shadow on the wall." She flexed her hands, both now back to normal. She could feel the warmth in her fingers again.

The momewraths growled and pushed themselves up, moving forward toward their prey again.

"No," Charlotte commanded firmly, holding out her left hand.

The nightmares hesitated.

Her jaw clenched. "Sit."

They looked to each other, unsure. The smallest hesitated, then sat.

Charlotte looked toward it and almost smiled. "I was never infected because that part of me has always been there. I just didn't want to see it." She crouched slightly toward the smaller momewrath and held out her left hand as if offering food. "I study so much because I'm absolutely terrified I'll be called on in class, and won't know the answer."

The momewrath chomped down on air as if catching her words like a treat. It shimmied its shoulders, shaking its dark coat happily, and a sense of calm rushed through Charlotte.

The others of the pack immediately sat, looking expectant and wagging tails as if they were no more than a litter of puppies, impatient, but not wanting to do anything that would risk causing them to not be given a treat of their own.

"If I don't know the answer, my teacher will think I'm an idiot. And even though I dislike him, I care so much what he thinks about me. I'm afraid he'll think I'm an idiot."

They all chomped happily, as if being truly fed for the first time in days.

"Because deep down, I'm afraid I *am* an idiot."

The momewraths howled happily and moved to her, nuzzling their heads against her legs affectionately.

Charlotte chuffed in disbelief, a smile pulling at the corners of her lips. "Okay," she whispered, feeling her heartbeat slow and her anxiety dissipating. "Lead me to the Dreamers."

32

MIND AND MATTER

The darkness gave way to form and function around them. She looked down from her perch atop a momewrath, watching the void beneath their great paws give way into dark soil, indicative of volcanic ash. Though whether this terrain was forming as her mind made meaning of her surroundings or she could simply now see it she wasn't sure.

She gripped large tufts of hair and skin, holding on as they raced through the seemingly endless night and nothing. The terrain raced out from beneath them in all directions, creating roads and stones and an ominous skyline of jagged mountains and what Charlotte could only assume was some kind of fortress. As they got closer, she noticed an eerie similarity between the fortress and the grand palace of Elan Vital, almost as if she was looking at her father's castle through a warped piece of glass.

"So that's where he's keeping you…"

Subconsciously, Charlotte gently patted the mome-wrath's back to encourage it to move faster.

As they turned up an incline toward the fortress, gargoyle-like statues started to awaken and ready themselves as the pack approached.

Charlotte raised her hand, shakily adjusting her weight to make sure that releasing some of her grip on the animal beneath her wasn't going to result in being bucked to the ground. "I'm scared they'll never remember me again!"

The gargoyle-like creatures shifted back to relax in their perches, and with their calm, Charlotte felt her own strengthen.

Why had she never honestly voiced these before? It was such a relief, it was freeing, it—

The entire pack skidded to a stop as they entered the main hall, nearly colliding with a woman clad in black.

She was striking; militantly dressed, with features so sharp and precise they looked to be carved of marble. She stared at them with two black pools for eyes, hand upon her sword hilt.

Charlotte raised her hand soothingly. "I'm not here to hurt you…"

"*I think you are.*"

Charlotte stopped, confused. Was this a Nightmare? Or a Dream? "I'm here to save the Dreamers."

"*As I thought,*" came the cool reply. "*You seek to end our reign and dominance.*"

There was that question answered, yet it only sparked more. "Are *you* the Jabberwock?"

"*I'm a mirare.*" There was a strange cadence to her tone, a heartbeat like rhythm.

"Ah… You see, that answers nothing for me."

The mirare's lip curled in disgust. "*You thought us all just wild dogs to tame?*"

"No…" Borogoves, momewraths, jub-jub birds, toves—they were all animals—or at least animalistic. They didn't really speak, they acted on instinct—what did this new kind of Nightmare mean? Why hadn't she been warned? "Why kidnap the dreamers?"

"*Simple fool. For too long now have we been starved of air; condemned to grasp at scraps of fear and fright. While Dreams roam free, our lives cannot compare. The Jabberwock will grant us endless night.*"

Flawed as the plan was, she could understand the anger that fueled it. Nightmares had been sealed away since what seemed the beginning of time—and for why? A *Dreamer's* misunderstanding. "But what if it didn't have to be either way? What if we eliminated the door?"

The mirare sneered. She seemed frustrated, though whether it was by Charlotte's words or something else entirely, it was not clear. "*Fates, how your kind will lie so easily.*" She drew her sword.

"Please," Charlotte begged. "I don't want to fight you. I don't even really know how to fight using this thing, I just thought it would be stupid to not bring it."

The mirare hesitated. This was not a tactic she'd expected.

"I know what Morpheus did was wrong. I know we've *all* been wrong—we were just too scared to see it. But this isn't the way to fix things. We've upset the balance, yes, to put it lightly, but tipping the scales the other way will not solve what you think it will."

The mirare stepped back, taking a fencer's stance. Still, Charlotte could sense an uncertainty in her stance.

"I am so sorry about this…" Charlotte held out Ikelos' vorpal blade to the side as if she intended to charge the momewrath forward and strike down her determined opponent. Instead, with her left hand, she pressed forward as she had in the tunnel with the bandersnatch, as if her hand could just reach out and shove the mirare against the wall.

The nightmare screamed in surprise, the marble-skin knocking some pebbles from stonework upon impact before she crumbled to the ground. Prone, unconscious, but breathing.

"Oh thank god, I was really scared I was going to kill her," Charlotte breathed.

The momewraths barked a little before taking off at a run again up the stairs.

The momewraths barreled through a pair of double doors, which opened to a large chamber filled with trees—no, not trees, *borogoves*.

Their great limbs and branches stretched up to the ceiling into a network of what seemed like roots illuminated with a silver glow. The light pulsed, eerily moving outside of the room to continue the network out into the hall where, when Charlotte looked behind her, it continued out of sight, as if they were sending some sort of data or energy in that direction.

The source of the light became clear as Charlotte dismounted and carefully walked farther into the room. The women who had fallen ill, the sleepy sickness, dozens of them, at least, possibly more, were melded into the trunks of the borogoves, like haunting dryads, imprisoned in the bark. They all glowed ever so slightly, and that silver light traveled up the grains of the bark, up into the branches to the network of roots.

"Holy… shit…" Charlotte whispered.

The momewrath beside her whimpered.

That was when she saw the shadowed figure moving quietly to each of the women closest to the floor. Charlotte felt a spark of hope with the vague outline that seemed so familiar in that moment, but it wasn't until she heard a quietly hissed, "Wake up," from the figure that she was certain.

"Mom!" She took her cue from the other woman's volume, rasping a hushed yell as she tried to move quietly and quickly to her.

Alys turned her head, her face now illuminated by the dim silver light. She looked tired, but otherwise in good health. Her eyes widened only briefly before narrowing at her daughter. "Charlotte Aislynn Carroll," she scolded in a raspy whisper. "How the hell did you get here?"

Charlotte stopped a few feet short of her mother, unable to stop grinning. She knew who she was. She remembered, or at least she remembered her now—it was possible that would change once they moved to the other side, but in that moment, she couldn't be happier. "You know who I am."

"Of course, I know who my own daughter is. What in god's name are you doing here?" Alys demanded quietly.

With the most absolute sheepish of shrugs she said, "Saving you? Which... you seem to be doing surprisingly well on your own."

"Took me a while to wake up, but I... Is that a vorpal blade?" Alys asked, pointing to the sword in Charlotte's right hand.

"Yeah."

"Good, you can cut them free. I was trying to avoid disturbing these things by waking the others up one by one, but this will be much faster."

"Yeah..." said Charlotte reluctantly, looking from the vorpal blade to the borogoves. She thought on Charlie's message, Ikelos and Phantasos... and the mirare. "Or... I could... just ask." She dropped to her knees, placing her hand and closing her eyes.

"What are you—?"

"Shh..." Charlotte hushed, trying to focus. She thought of the shadows that frightened her as a child, of the strange things her mind would find to play tricks on her in the darkness, even now. She sent that energy across the floor to the roots of the borogoves. She took a slow and shaky breath, focusing on that uncertainty a barely lit space provided: the startled moment of a branch scratching against the window. She tried to remember mustering the courage to get out of bed, the inescapable curiosity that pushed her to slip from the protection of her covers to turn on the light switch.

The borogroves groaned slightly as if stirring from their own sort of sleep.

"Please let them go," Charlotte whispered. "I'll do everything I can to make this right."

One by one, the women fell away from the tree trunks, and as they did, they jolted awake. And as each gasped, waking from their own nightmares, they vanished from sight.

Charlotte's brow furrowed, and she looked to Alys, worried. "What's happening to them?"

"They're waking up," Alys answered reassuringly, "returning to the waking world."

Charlotte's brow furrowed. "Then why are you still here?"

Alys smiled softly at her daughter. "My situation is a little bit more complicated than theirs." She reached for Charlotte's hand, her brow furrowing. "What happened to your ear? Are you alright?"

Charlotte reached up absently to touch the dried blood on her neck and damaged earlobe, having completely forgotten the injury. She flinched a little as her fingertips touched the wound, but it was no longer bleeding. "Earring got ripped out. I know it doesn't look it… but I'm better than I have been in a very long time."

Alys was skeptical and gently rubbed her thumb over some of the dried blood on Charlotte's neck to confirm it wasn't hiding more wounds. Satisfied, she asked a more bewildering question. "How did you get them to let them go? Did you find a way to control them?"

Charlotte shook her head with a small smile. "The nightmare situation is just a little bit more complicated than we thought…"

Alys chuffed a laugh through her nose. "I can't believe you found me."

"We're not quite done yet," Charlotte answered, holding out the vorpal blade for her mother to take. "We have a jabberwock to stop."

"Jabberwock?" Alys took the blade by the umbrella-crook handle, her brow furrowing. "It couldn't be…"

Charlotte frowned slightly. "Charlie wanted to apologize."

Alys looked at Charlotte in confusion. "You spoke to…" She looked around the room, resting a hand to her heart. "They were all women. All Dreamers. From many times, but all increasingly like… me. It was after me." She cursed under her breath, taking a few steps back to pace in a small circle. "Of course. Of course, it would be that same son of a bitch… I should have ended it then."

"*You failed to strike, and he will take your life,*" rasped a voice from the door. The mirare from before seemed to have a crack in her cheek but had no other visible injuries. She was crumpled against the doorway like a bug that barely survived being squashed. Behind her stood more like her, some feminine, some not, some androgynous—a regiment of mirare standing behind their general.

"Ah, more familiar faces," Alys muttered, raising the vorpal blade.

"You know her, too?"

"I knew one like her." Alys' eyes narrowed. "She was his puppet, too."

The mirare glared and straightened herself as best she could. "*We chose to follow that which sets us free.*"

"Sets you free? Erebus doesn't give a rats ass about your freedom. Or your welfare." Alys used the vorpal blade to point to the now fading borogrove network. "Were you getting any of this? Was this being distributed to *anyone* but him? Did you even know this room existed?"

Charlotte looked from her mother to the mirare, who seemed to pause and take in the room around them for the first time.

"*The Jabberwock has come to set us free,*" the mirare repeated, but her rhythm trembled and faltered.

"*He'd have let you rot were it not for me,*" Alys countered.

The mirare balked, startled by a response spat back in her own magic.

"Erebus tried to control one of your kind in the name of his own arrogance and insecurity," Alys continued, "until it finally overtook him. And even as a Jabberwock, he tried to dominate Dreams for his own insatiable greed, *not* your liberation."

Charlotte extended her left hand. "If you can't take a Dreamer's word, take mine."

"Charlotte—"

"Mom, trust me," Charlotte asked softly, her eyes never leaving the mirare. "I think it's time we end this eons-old war, don't you? Started by an outsider who did not understand your world or even his own power—but sought to rule it all the same. I can't undo your pain, or what he did… But we can fix it. Together."

The Mirare looked suspiciously from Alys to Charlotte's hand, expecting to see a weapon or the same magic that had thrown her so far before. She finally spoke, but her cadence had changed once more, losing its rhythm. She spoke plainly. "Why should I believe you?"

"Because I am you," said Charlotte gently, looking from the general to those behind her. Her left hand shifted back to the same void-colored claw and then back again. "All of you. And I'm a little *them* too." Charlotte smiled slightly. "Two sides of the same coin, really, nightmares and dreams. Some real jerks on either side, but in general, people are people. Not wholly good or bad."

The mirare looked to the soldiers behind her, pondering this before asking another question. "What do you expect in return?"

"I only ask you to halt your assault on the Fae," Charlotte said. "Contain them if you must. You know The Nothing far better than any of them could. But please... let them *live*, and I will prove my word to you. I will petition The Dream King myself on your behalf. Morpheus was wrong. Doors were meant to open."

The mirare paused to mull this over. "Will you slay the Jabberwock?"

"Do I have any chance of convincing him for peace?" Charlotte asked.

The mirare nodded ever so slightly to herself, then turned to the others. "Alert the others. For now, we hold." She looked back to Charlotte. "I will go with you, and if you betray us... we *will* drain them all. Mark my words."

Alys blinked as she watched the other mirare walk away, in oddly perfect unison. Heels on a hard floor. Doom-tek. Doom-tek. Doom-tek. "What just happened?"

"You don't know a peace negotiation when you see one?" Charlotte asked with a small half-cocked smile.

"This way," the mirare general beckoned, leading them out of the room and down the hall. She pointed upward at the roots. "Follow these. They will take you to him."

"I thought you were coming—"

The mirare general cut Alys off. "Several steps behind. A jabberwock could end a thing like me without much trouble. But you… you I think he will not find so easy."

Alys nodded and led the charge down the hallway, Charlotte a few steps behind her. They followed the network of roots through a corridor, where they ran beyond two large double doors.

Alys looked to her daughter a moment, wondering if it was worth trying to convince her to stay behind. She could only imagine what she had gone through to get here, to be the person to apparently begin peace negotiations with nightmares and dreams, so instead she simply asked. "Are you ready?"

Charlotte took a deep breath and nodded, giving her a small but reassuring smile. "Let's save the world."

Alys turned the handles of both doors and shoved them open as hard as she could, creating a loud bang as they hit the walls they were hinged to. "Knock, knock, asshole!"

A man that Charlotte would have never described as "Jabberwock" sat upon a throne made from the roots that flowed down from the ceiling. A quite literal seat of power, it must have been where he'd been absorbing whatever it was the borogoves were draining from the Dreamers. He was by no means a pleasant-looking person, but Charlotte had imagined something more beast than man with such a title.

His features were sharp and unkind. As he opened his eyes, even from several feet away, Charlotte felt a

592

chill from them. "I suppose it was too much to hope you'd just died," he sighed, languidly drawing his attention to the two intruders.

"Sorry to disappoint you," Alys said in the least apologetic voice Charlotte had ever heard. "Afraid I had to cut your little soiree short."

The Jabberwock seemed unconcerned. "They'll be back."

"No," Alys tightened her grip on the hooked handle of the thin vorpal blade. "This time we end this, Erebus."

The Jabberwock smiled a wide grin with his uncomfortably white teeth. "Indeed, Dreamer. This time I devour you." He flicked his wrist, palm facing toward them, and with it the world around them shifted, the walls crumbling away, the ceiling crashing down in pieces that both Alys and Charlotte only narrowly avoided.

The sky above them flashed with lightning, rain pouring down from unseen clouds. With every flash of light, bodies littered the ground, impaled by weapons, drained of life. Among them Charlotte saw the body of Oberon she'd seen before, countless soldiers she'd seen in passing. At Charlotte's feet, she saw the body of her father, barely recognizable beneath the blood.

Alys looked down at the illusion of Oswin, and her nostrils flared ever so slightly. She glared around at the debris. "Come out and fight me, you spineless piece of shit. I'm not afraid of your party games!"

"But is your *daughter* so fearless, I wonder?" The Jabberwock's voice echoed with a laugh.

One of the gnarled bodies pushed itself up. Wings expanded, bat-like, flapped to bring the creature to its feet. The bandersnatch was undeniable in its features, though not quite as emaciated and unrecognizable as former fae as the one from the tunnel had been. It let out a horrifying screech, and Charlotte froze.

"Charlie!" Alys vaulted herself over the debris to try to reach her, but as she crested the peak of the crumbled wall, a great dragon-like creature slammed into her, grasping her with its taloned feet and carrying her up away from Charlotte. Alys flailed angrily, swiping her blade in an upward slash, the vorpal blade severing through the armored skin.

The Jabberwock let out a cry of pain and dropped Terra Mirum's Hero, where she landed on the peak of the fortress roof.

Charlotte jolted out of her paralysis the moment her mother was knocked out of her sight, and she looked from where she had disappeared back to the bandersnatch. "You're just an illusion," she whispered to herself as she took a few shaky steps back. "You're not real…" She raised her hands, trying to focus on clarity. "You're not real… *You* are just something I have to overcome." He'd used Nightmare magic to cloud her vision, all she had to do was turn on the light. A gust of wind expelled from her palm, blowing the bandersnatch backward a few steps, and with it, the bodies around them vanished in a curl of smoke.

But the bandersnatch remained.

Charlotte felt her breathing quicken. "Oh. Okay, you *are* real." She took a few steps back, taking in her surroundings. There were plenty of rocks to hide behind, but hiding only bought her time. But Charlie's words of wisdom, and the backward advice of Ikelos and Phantasos, did not help her here. There was advice for Nightmares… not a bandersnatch. Neither truly dream or nightmare, but a fae poisoned by the worst part of fear… It was a magic she couldn't reason with.

The bandersnatch screamed and leapt towards her, Charlotte narrowly evading by ducking around the stone debris that covered every inch of the former throne room, some chunks of wall as tall as a car.

"Think, Charlie, think…" There had to be another way. There had to be something beyond leaving that bandersnatch to die in that train tunnel. Something other than putting a fae out of its misery. Oberon had said there was no turning back, but Oberon wasn't right about everything. She crawled on her belly through the debris, hoping if she could hide, she could buy herself enough time to logic her way through this. She tried to quiet her breathing as she leaned against a large piece of rubble.

The bandersnatch in the tunnel… She *almost* understood her. Charlotte could feel that moment so keenly. And until it had been ripped from her, the earring had shown the fae's true form, which was no monster at all.

A clawed hand swiped down from on top of the rubble and Charlotte squeaked, narrowly avoiding the strike. She flailed, pushing herself up as the bandersnatch tilted its head unnervingly, skittering down the debris on all fours. It bared its fangs, which had not yet fully skewed in the mangled directions the one from the train tunnel had.

Charlotte scrambled backward like a crab until her back hit stone. She cursed and clumsily pushed herself to a stand but found herself sitting in the deep end of a wreckage-made crater. She'd be ripped apart. Or she would have to kill it. *Them.* Whoever they were, she would not let herself forget they had been—or even still might be—a person. She was out of time and had found no other options. She turned, shaking. She was not a killer. And this moment, if she survived it, she knew would haunt her until the end of her days. Her heart was pounding. Her breath short and shallow, unable to fully fill her lungs with air. Her eyes drew up the bandersnatch slowly stalking towards her, knowing it had her cornered and reveling in the fear it could smell from her.

Charlotte's breath caught. In her examination, she found herself halting at the creature's waist—the belt around it, and what was undeniably sheathed and hanging from it.

The vorpal blade.

Charlotte's eyes darted to the bandersnatch's face, and a new horror overtook her. Their cheeks were gaunt, but the bones still as strong as they'd ever been. Their lips hid fangs, but she knew the cupid's bow far too well from every time she'd found herself staring when they spoke. Their skin was paler, and they'd lost their indescribable natural glow... but Charlotte could not unsee the face she'd grown so used to having at her side. "Thorn?" she croaked.

The bandersnatch's head ducked down slightly as if they were considering how to devour their cornered prey.

"Please... *please* recognize me." Charlotte pressed herself against the stone, feeling behind her for anything she could use to try to put more distance between them without causing them any harm.

Undeterred, the bandersnatch hunkered down slightly, like a cat about to pounce.

Charlotte's breathing folded into hyperventilating. "Please, don't make me do this... I have to help my mother... Don't make me go through you." Tears streamed down her cheeks. "I don't know if I can..." She turned quickly and tried to climb up the tall broken stones but felt claws dig into her back and rip her back to the ground.

Charlotte screamed in pain as fire felt like it sunk into her wounds and through her bloodstream. The world spun, and she rolled onto her back in time to see the bandersnatch's claws dig into her shoulders, pinning her to the ground.

Kill them. Kill them before they kill you. You don't have a choice.

There were infinite choices, most of which she hadn't thought of yet.

Charlotte's hands reached for sword at their belt, tightening her grip around it, but before she could attempt to use it, the bandersnatch struck like a viper.

Fangs dug into her shoulder, drawing blood and shooting a pain so fierce through her she could no longer tell if she still held the blade. Everything felt sharp and buzzing.

Tears were streaming down her face as the bandersnatch pulled back up, blood dripping from their lips.

"I don't hate you," she rasped between gulps for air. "I didn't mean it. I was angry. It's no excuse... but I wanted to say I'm sorry, if I don't get another chance, even if you can't hear it. I wish it wasn't the last thing I said to you. I'm so sorry, Learic."

The bandersnatch froze.

This pause in its demeanor did not go unnoticed. Hope-fueled adrenaline and she reached up to grip their arms. "Did you understand that?"

They didn't move, they didn't respond.

Charlotte tried to push them off, but their strength was too much for her own. "Learic, please..." she panted. "Let me go..."

The bandersnatch retracted its claws, looking dumbfounded and confused as they sat back.

Charlotte's body shook with a sob of temporary relief, unable to piece together, between the poison of the bandersnatch and her own panic, why she'd managed to convince them to cease their attack. She pushed up onto her elbows. "Is this reaching you, or..." She pushed up onto her hands, staring at the unmoving nightmare-touched before her. "Are you just obeying..." She looked down at her hands, flexing her fingers in thought. "Nightmares and dreams, two sides of the same coin... Nightmares in possession of your true name have the power to control you even to the fiber of your form and being..."

She looked at the bandersnatch in a new light. "Fiber of your form and being..." She raised her hand out to them. "Does that mean... I can bring you back?"

Her fingers trembled, but the bandersnatch did not move, as if awaiting a new order.

"Learic..." she whispered, the word flowing more easily off her tongue now, like a song she'd always hummed to keep her anxiety away. She looked over their features, having caught herself studying them so often she could spot every alteration the nightmare's magic had contorted. "Give me your hand..."

The bandersnatch hesitated only a moment before reaching out a claw to rest it in Charlotte's.

Their hands were smooth, graceful but still strong, only calloused on the palms. When they flexed, she could see the tendons from their fingers to wrist. Their wrists... Dainty wasn't the right word—but they were somehow delicate. Their arms and shoulders… strong. So much stronger than they looked at first glance. She would never forget that first sensation of them lifting her out of the ocean the day they met.

She watched her memory rewrite their form before her, her hands almost tingling as she felt herself pulling out the nightmare magic strain by strain, like sucking poison from a wound.

Thorn's eyes were the last thing to change, shifting from the eerie, sickly green to the soft moss-like shade that encircled a ring of gold around the pupil. They blinked away the last hint of the bandersnatch that was before looking down at Charlotte. Their eyes widened, and they dropped to their knees. "Fates, Charlie, are you alright? Oh gods, what have I done?"

Charlotte choked on a laugh, or perhaps it was a sob. She was so relieved she wasn't sure what emotion managed to break through first. She used their hand as leverage to pull herself to them, wrapping her arms around their neck. "I didn't have to kill you."

Thorn paused and wrapped their arms around her slowly. "Um… thank you?"

"I don't hate you."

Thorn smiled slightly into her shoulder.

"I just wanted to save my mother."

"I know."

Charlotte pulled back abruptly. "My mother."

Thorn's brow furrowed. "I know, Charlie, that's what this whole thing has been about—"

"No," Charlotte insisted, trying to stand. "My *mother*. The Jabberwock has my mother."

Thorn stood immediately, helping Charlotte find her footing. "Where are they?"

"They vanished over the roof."

"Are you sure you're alright?"

"I can do this," Charlotte assured.

Without another word, Thorn wrapped their arms around Charlotte, their wings sending a gust of wind below them as they shot into the air, out of the debris and onto the roof.

Alys ducked out of harm's way of the green acidic flames that showered down from the Jabberwock's mouth. He was staying out of reach of the vorpal blade. And the surface Alys was standing on was about to give way.

Charlotte reached a hand out, even as she and Thorn were still in midair, and beneath them, like a great gust of wind, a sweep of smoke washed over the ground, forming into patches where the roof had burned through, trying to make it whole again.

Alys felt the gust beneath her and looked behind as if expecting to see another attacker, but it was just enough of a moment of distraction to allow the Jabberwock time to drop down on top of her, breaking through the roof just before it repaired itself beneath Alys. The repairs stopped short of the giant hole, a plume of dust exploding from below.

"MOM!" Charlotte screamed at the top of her lungs. Thorn set down on the roof, releasing Charlotte, who took off at a run toward the break in the roof. Great black feathered crow wings expanded from her back as she dove through the dust and debris to the bottom floor. She choked on the dust. "Mom!"

She heard the low guttural laugh of the Jabberwock before she saw him. What had first seemed like a dragon had evolved into what she could only describe as a near-skeletal hydra: multiple heads, each spiked with spines that reminded her of viper teeth, undoubtedly just as venomous. It smiled with what seemed to be five heads, flashing bright silver-like fangs. It spoke with a hiss, each head with its own voice yet almost in perfect unison. "Are you to fight me now, little girl? After the fearless have fallen? What hope could you have?"

Charlotte felt a white-hot anger rush through her. She didn't know where her mother was, and that fear alone sharpened her senses. "I don't need to be fearless to fight you," she answered.

"Isss that so?" the voices mused, quite pleased with themselves and finding no reason for concern in the small girl before them. "What nightmares might I pull from your brain?"

"Just simply not knowing what time it is gives me anxiety," Charlotte answered.

The Jabberwock hesitated, confused.

"I'm terrified everyone I've ever met who has shown me even a shred of kindness actually hates me but they're too polite to say it. I'm scared that my mother regrets having me. I have this recurring nightmare that I never amount to anything, that I just waste my life and am an absolute disappointment. I'm worried my father still won't want me now that he knows about me. I'm worried I won't recognize my own face, or that a natural disaster could wipe us out at any moment. I'm scared I'm not remotely smart, that I've just been parroting facts I've absorbed over the years because I'm terrified someone is going to find me out for the fraud I am. I try to pretend I don't care what I look like, but when gum was in my hair and I cut it, I absolutely freaked out. I was scared I'd be ugly—I am scared that I have always been ugly. I'm absolutely panicked about not liking or recognizing my own reflection to the point that I hate trying on new clothes. I'm scared about forgetting, about *being* forgotten. I'm scared of so many things I can't even name them all because I'm bound to forget a hundred or more."

The Jabberwock looked at her, amused, smiling.

"But even with all that, that should be paralyzing me... I still did everything I could to fight my way here." Charlotte's eyes narrowed. "And that's why you should be scared of *me*, Erebus."

The Jabberwock's heads all focused intently on Charlotte suddenly. "What?"

Her hand reached forward, and fingers clenched. She focused all her might on drawing out the nightmare, separating the dark from the light so she could evaluate to truly see what made this Jabberwock. Charlie had said what made a Jabberwock truly terrifying was one life forcing itself on another… but her mother had said Erebus had tried to control one of nightmares for his own gain. Which meant Erebus was *not* the Nightmare.

The Jabberwock screeched, flapping its wings to try to escape out the hole it had created as pieces of shadow pulled away from it.

"Stay, Erebus… If I must, I will be your judge, jury, and executioner!"

The Jabberwock screeched such an unholy sound and as it tried to fly upward, Charlotte found herself struggling to hold it. Her arms trembled.

A hand rested on Charlotte's shoulder, and then another.

Charlotte barely had to glance to see both Ikelos and Phantasos on either side of her. They each raised their own free hands toward the Jabberwock, adding their power to her own.

"Together, we form mind, body, spirit," said Phantasos.

"Together, the Oneiroi are complete once more," said Ikelos.

Charlotte grit her teeth as she felt a pulse of magic rush through her, her body trembling as a conduit for power she had never experienced before. "In the name of the court of Nightmares and Dreams, We try thee, Erebus, with the highest crime, a blatant disregard for the one thing we may truly claim in this world as our own: free will."

The Jabberwock flailed, wings flapping uselessly as one by one its heads shrunk back into its body, the body itself growing smaller and smaller, pieces dismantling and falling off into a dark smoke. The darkness twisted like smoke at the trio's feet, slowly forming into a shape of its own.

The growls and screeches of the Jabberwock faded into a man's screams, which, as he shrunk into his former state before them, devolved into sobs.

The once great King Erebus of Terra Mirum, now a shadow of whom he was, wept angrily on the floor, and a pile of stone that resembled a fallen statue lay beside Charlotte's feet.

She knelt down to look at it, her brow furrowing. "The remains of the mirare he devoured. Charlie's nightmare."

"Poor soul," Ikelos whispered.

"He is finally able to rest," said Phantasos.

Thorn dropped from the hole above, gliding at the last minute to land beside Charlotte, Ikelos, and Phantasos. "Charlotte," they pointed to the crumpled form of Alys beneath a small scrap of rubble.

"Mom!" Charlotte ran to kneel beside Alys. "Help me lift this…" Charlotte tried to push the debris off her mother with her hands.

Ikelos and Phantasos merely gestured, and the rocks lifted rather effortlessly off the fallen Dreamer.

"Mom?" Charlotte shook Alys.

Alys groaned.

"Oh, thank god," Charlotte could feel tears forming in her eyes. "How the hell are you alive? Are you okay? Can you get up?"

"The spirit is willing, but the body..." Alys trailed off with a strange little laugh. "The body isn't really here, so I guess it can stop complaining." She sat up with the help of Thorn and Charlotte, looking from the fallen Dream king shaking several feet away to the broken statue on the floor. "What happened?"

"Erebus imposed his will on a nightmare... I separated them, but unfortunately it looks like I was too late to save the mirare." Charlotte looked down at the broken pieces with compassion, then to Ikelos, Thorn, and Phantasos. "We should inform the others of what's happened."

"*No need. I've seen all that there was to see.*" The mirare general who had initially led them to the Jabberwock spoke from what barely passed for a doorway. She entered just enough to look at the broken pieces of her fallen comrade. "*He will be given proper burial.*" She looked to the trio of changelings before her, then the weeping dream, sniveling in his defeat. "*What will you do with he that took his life?*"

Charlotte looked to her companions as she helped her mother stand, an arm secured around her waist, while the other held Alys' arm around her shoulders. "I leave that to the judgement of you and yours."

Erebus looked up abruptly. "No. No, you can't leave me to these monsters! They're the ones who corrupted me! You have to believe me—I'm the victim!"

"How long until you needed to devour another nightmare?" Charlotte asked flatly. "Or was feeding off Dreamers enough to sustain that power?"

The King snarled. "You little bitch—"

"Will forget you the moment you are out of our sight." Charlotte looked from Erebus to Alys, and finally to the mirare general. "Have at. He's all yours." She nodded to Thorn, who took Alys' other side to support her. "Let's go home."

33

AND ALL SHALL BE WELL

The sun felt harsh to nightmare and fae alike as they helped each other through the doorway and into the Tulgey Wood. There was a strange uncertain calm that had nestled between the two armies, who regarded each other almost suspiciously, as if waiting for one to go back on their word.

But no one did.

Charlotte and Thorn carried Alys over the threshold, each squinting through the sun-dappled clearing. Behind them, Ikelos opened his umbrella, and both he and Phantasos huddled beneath it.

"Alys…" Smoke stepped out from the growing group of fae, momentarily leaving Titania's side to embrace an old friend. "Aren't you a sight for sore eyes?"

"Sore eyes, sore head, sore everything," Alys answered, untangling herself from her daughter and Thorn to take a shaky step forward into the tall man's arms.

Smoke cradled the woman's head to him with a hand. "I thought we agreed we were going to stop meeting during world-ending crises."

"Tell your world to stop having them," Alys huffed tiredly.

Smoke looked over Alys' head to Charlotte. "I definitely recall telling you that the world did not rest on your shoulders..."

Charlotte smiled tiredly and shrugged. "Like mother, like daughter."

"Is it really over then?" Smoke rasped in disbelief.

Charlotte shook her head. "Not quite. We've still got work to do. Both sides."

As the mirare gathered beneath the shade of the trees, they were joined by momewraths with lowered tails, padding over to them like puppies seeing their masters coming home.

The momewrath who had taken her all the way to the Dreamers scampered up to Charlotte and pressed his snout insistently into her hand, bopping it until it landed on its head so she could pet it.

"That's new," said Smoke, somewhat taken aback, and Alys released him to turn to look at her daughter and the canine nightmare that would have given the Hound of the Baskervilles a run for its money.

Charlotte smiled. "This little guy helped me get through my anxiety. Ate some of it right up."

The momewrath's tail thumped loudly on the forest floor.

"We are relieved someone finally understood," Ikelos chimed, bobbing over with his umbrella, his brother stumbling beside him to try to stay beneath the shade.

"It did take you far longer than we'd hoped," Phantasos added.

"You weren't exactly the most straightforward," Charlotte huffed. "It didn't really click until I spoke with Charlie."

"Ah, human to human," Phantasos said.

"We're part human," Ikelos defended.

"Yes, but it's been some time," reminded Phantasos.

"Oh, eternities. Truly. We will have to work on that, very rusty—"

"You two said something back there when you were helping me," Charlotte interrupted. "Mind, body, spirit?"

The twins smiled cryptically.

"Another time," said Ikelos.

"Another face," said Phantasos.

"Different duties, different space," the said in unison.

"I remember you two…" spoke Alys slowly, her eyes narrowing in recognition.

"My goodness, is *that* the time?" Phantasos asked, examining an imaginary pocket watch.

"Dear me, we'll be late for avoiding this uncomfortable conversation," Ikelos added, and the two walked at a fast but perfectly synchronized pace to disappear in the crowd.

"What happened to the Jabberwock? Slain for good?" Smoke asked.

"Dismantled in a way," Charlotte answered. "Stripped of his power and the nightmare he took control of. He won't be bothering us anymore."

Smoke looked at Charlotte in wonder. "If only we could strip the infection from the Dreams in the same way."

Charlotte's attention snapped out of its comfortable haze, and she turned abruptly toward the mirare, looking for the acting general she had spoken with before. She'd never gotten her name. "Um… whom would I speak to concerning further peace relations?"

A mirare slowly raised their hand, and Charlotte thought she recognized him as one who had initially stood behind the first when they confronted them in the horror grove of Dreamers. "I am Demetria's second."

"Ah," Charlotte took a moment to choose her words, careful to not offended. "Throughout the war, there have been Dreams who were… *altered* by Nightmare magic. Can these changes be revoked?"

"If handled by an experienced mage, any spell can be undone," the mirare answered simply.

"And would a tove's tongue… fall under that?"

The mirare took a moment before answering. "If they survived long enough to be transformed. A tove's poison is not deadly, but they themselves often can be."

Charlotte pressed. "And if they survived through the transformation? Would the toves still chase?"

"Fear is our bread, not our way, Changeling. A tove would have no sight for things that can no longer fear."

Smoke ensured Thorn could support Alys before he moved to join Charlotte. "Is there any way to find them if they did transform?"

The mirare blinked, not quite following this line of questions. "It would take some time, but it would be a very likely possibility."

Smoke bit the knuckles of a closed fist, and Charlotte rested a hand on his arm before continuing for him.

"My friend's wife and child went through a change after encounters with a horde of toves. We thought them entirely lost."

The mirare's face shifted slightly, but with such unreadable eyes it wasn't clear what he was trying to emote until he spoke. "I will gather the most talented of our people, and we shall find your altered Dreams and return them to their natural state." He looked to Charlotte and explained. "To be changed by such means is not to be Nightmare. A tove's poison is a sleepwalker's existence, driven by hunger as they are. They have their purpose, but all in all, they are unpleasant beasts, as I'm sure you have your own among the fae and Dream."

Smoke smiled despite himself. "Even some that wear faces not unlike our own."

"We will each tend to our wounded, and when Demetria is ready, we will escort you back to your castle."

"Where I will make a case to my father for a united future. Dream and Nightmare," said Charlotte.

It was Robin who made the initial negotiations, having to convince both her husband, Oswin, and the generals that it was safe to drop the shield around Elan Vital's castle—that though Nightmares stood at the gate, it was peacefully and hand in hand with Fae, Charlotte, and *Alys*.

They waited patiently, representatives of each faction: Titania and two of her own generals, as well as two of her late husband's, stood beside Thorn, Demetria, and two other mirare, not including the one who had taken it upon himself to help find and locate infected Dreams—Smoke had also gone along with him to help in any way he could. Alys and Charlotte stood off on their own as the misfits of the group, staring upward at the sky where Robin had vanished.

"So…" Alys started, eyeing her daughter almost drowsily. "Who is this Thorn person?"

"Mom," Charlotte grumbled.

"I don't have a right to inquire about my daughter's potential suitors?"

"Shouldn't you be more concerned with seeing my dad for the first time in sixteen years?" Charlotte deterred.

"Are we calling him 'Dad' now?" Alys avoided the question.

"I'm sorry, would it be less weird if I called him your lover?" asked Charlotte.

Alys's face skewed, and she looked forward. "No. No, I never want to hear that word out of your mouth ever again."

"That's what I thought."

Eventually, the shield faded away in a shimmer, as if it had only been a trick of the light glaring off a reflective surface, and as it vanished, the great palace doors slowly opened.

Robin was the first out, surprisingly energized for a woman who had just battled her way through hordes of Nightmares. Behind her, looking like a man who had long lost the concept of sleep was Basir, the polar opposite of his wife.

The strange party was greeted by Rhyme and Reason, one noticeably far more wary than the other but still managing a politeness that had been so bred into him it would likely have caused him physical pain to be any other way.

Introductions were made where needed before they were led inside, Alys and Charlotte heading up the rear.

There were hushed whispers from Dreams, watching from cracks in doorways, as the party entered the grand hallway where Oswin was waiting.

The King of Terra Mirum had fully intended on putting duty first. He knew through Robin how important reaching peaceful negotiations with the mirare would be, but as Charlotte and Alys entered into view, his world stopped.

Demetria and her fellows gave a strange flowing gesture of the hands with the slightest of bows of the head as a sign of respect. "Your Highness, I am Demetria of the Mirare. We have come to..." She trailed off, her eyes following his gaze. Her lips quirked in a knowing smile. "Perhaps my companions and I could be given a place to rest, and we may start negotiations after the sun sets. We do not often walk during such early hours, and I trust you will be better mentally equipped by then, yes?"

"What?" Oswin jolted slightly to bring his attention to the mirare who merely looked amused, like silently laughing statues. "I'm so sorry."

"Do not be," Demetria answered. "Mirare are without fear. Not passion."

"I...uh," Oswin flustered.

"Follow me," Robin interjected. "Your Majesties, if you would care to join us..." She gestured to Titania and Thorn. "We've all traveled so far; it would do our minds and hearts some good to rest before we take on another great endeavor." She looked pointedly at Basir. "Reason, if you would assist me?"

"If you cannot manage on your own, I should be drawing up documents to..." Basir took in his wife's expression, then glanced toward Oswin and Alys. "Ah. Yes. It would be my honor to help show our guests such hospitality."

The sound of steps vanished down the hallway, and Charlotte found herself awkwardly waiting beside her

mother in what felt like the strangest standoff she'd
ever witnessed.

"Oswin," Alys smiled timidly, and Charlotte could
almost see the nervous teenager she must have been
when the two had first met. "You look well."

"You're here," Oswin breathed.

"Well," Alys shrugged a little sheepishly. "Such
as I am."

"It's been..."

"Sixteen years."

"Eternities."

Alys bit her lower lip. "I'm sorry."

"Why didn't you tell me?" Oswin asked. "We could
have figured this out."

"Neither of us could have imagined an outcome like
this was possible..." Alys shook her head. "I couldn't
ask you to betray the trust of your people. And they
never would have supported a changeling heir, no
matter who her mother was."

"Should that changeling heir remove herself from
the room?" Charlotte asked, "or is this going to start
getting a lot less uncomfortable for me?"

They looked awkwardly at their child, suddenly
remembering her presence.

"Charlotte," Oswin began, "if I might have some
time alone... with your mother..."

"Wait, no," said Charlotte.

"No?" Oswin looked taken aback, genuinely not
expecting such an abrupt denial.

"No, I mean, later, but, Mom, we have to get you back to the hospital. We have to get you back in your body—I think it's shutting down, I overheard Diana talking to doctors before I left, and your vitals were dropping and—why are you looking at me like that?"

Alys' eyes were glossy, and she tried to force a smile, but it didn't reach past a faint upturn of her lips before it dropped completely. "Charlie…" She reached out her hands to take her daughter's. "I'm afraid I'm not going back."

Charlotte's brow furrowed in confusion, but she could feel that same pit in her stomach from when she first felt something was wrong in the house. "What do you mean?" She glanced towards Oswin. "Because of him? Mom, we can come back to visit, but we have a life there. We have a house."

"No, baby…" Alys said gently. "I don't think the bank is going to honor a mortgage with a ghost."

Charlotte blinked. Hard. "W-what?"

"I'm so sorry, sweetheart."

"I… I don't understand. You're not dead, you're here. I'm holding your hands. What do you mean a ghost?" Charlotte demanded.

Alys' grip on Charlotte's hands tightened, her voice remaining level and steady… but soft. "I was able to help the other dreamers because I woke before them. My connection to the other side had been cut completely, and so the Jabberwock had nothing left to drain… because I was no longer a Dreamer. Maybe it would be different if I'd never been severed previously... or maybe it would be worse. I might not be here at all."

Charlotte's throat felt tight as she tried to piece together what this meant. "No, no, you don't understand. You *have* to go back. Mom, you're the only one who knows who I am—everyone has forgotten. Kimiko, Diana—Diana doesn't know me. It's like I don't even exist!"

Alys released her daughter's hands to grip gently at her arms. "Hey," she bent her knees ever so slightly to be on the same eye level. "It's going to be okay; I promise."

"I can't do this without you. Please, I don't want to be alone."

"Oh, baby cake..." Alys breathed a sound somewhere between a laugh and sob. "You're not going to be alone. We'll always be together, you and me against the world, forever and a day."

"And I will need help with peace negotiations," Oswin chimed in hesitantly, "you being our resident expert on Nightmares."

Charlotte reached up a hand to wipe at her eyes. "Really?"

Both adults nodded.

"So... what, we'd just... live here? In a *castle*? Be *royalty*?"

"Or family?" offered Oswin uncertainly. "If... that's alright by you."

A strange sort of breath broke out of Charlotte and she covered her mouth with both her hands. She trembled. She looked from her mother to Oswin and her eyes welled with tears. hooked one arm around her mother, reaching the other out for Oswin, awkwardly pulling them both to her as she collapsed into sobs. It was an embrace of desperation, and an exhaustion brought on by an unending fear that life would never be the same.

And in truth, it wouldn't.

She wasn't sure if it meant better or worse, but for the first time, Charlotte found she wasn't paralyzed by the idea of change.

Alys kissed her daughter's tear-stained cheeks, hugging her tightly to her. "There is something you do need to go back for though," Alys said after some time. "Something I can't go with you to do, but it's important. It won't be easy… but I have every faith you can manage."

EPILOGUE

The door to the Carroll house opened, letting the sound of the rainfall fill the empty home. She stood just outside, staring into the dark unmoving, not daring to cross the threshold. She bit her lip and raised a hand to rest over her heart as if this would ease the deep ache. She focused on her breathing a moment before, with one large breath, as if she were diving beneath the waves, she stepped through the doorway.

Her hand reached out to the right for the light switch, and as she did, her hand caught under what felt like paper.

Diana looked toward the switch to see a Post-It note had been placed over half of it. She carefully took it from the wall.

> *It's going to be okay.*
> *(go to the TV room)*

It didn't look like Alys' handwriting, and her curiosity piqued. She walked into the den, flipping on that light, as well, where she found another Post-It note.

Have a seat on the couch.

Diana paused, pursed her lips, and looked around, wondering if someone had left these for Alys for some reason or if… It was too much to hope that these notes were for her. But there was something about following in the steps her friend might have taken for whatever reason—perhaps it was some kind of writing exercise—that made her feel like she might still be there.

On the couch, Diana found another Post-It note sitting on top of what looked like a photo album. She stopped, her hand over her mouth. She eased shakily down onto the couch, peering at the note.

Diana,
before you look at these photos, I need you to
watch the last video on your phone.

Her breath caught. No. This wasn't real. There was no possible way this could be real. She reached into the pocket of her crimson trench coat, finding her cellphone. Had one of the doctors somehow… or someone else?

The thumbnail made her pause. She could see herself, but she had no memory of recording it. Perhaps she'd accidentally turned the camera on while doing something else? She pressed play.

The Diana in the video tilted her head at
what must have been the recording phone. "Is

it recording?" she asked the person behind
the camera.

"Yes," a voice she didn't recognize answered.

"Okay..." The video image of Diana adjusted
her hair a little and ran her fingers beneath her
eyes to clear away any smudges. Her eyes looked
wet, but she was smiling. "Hi... this... Oh this
is strange... but I wanted to talk to you first, so
you'd know this wasn't some insane prank from
Benny to get your mind off things. She's going
to say a lot of things that sound crazy... but
you need to listen to her." She reached her hand
for the camera. "Okay, baby girl, your turn."

The camera was handed off, and for a moment
there was a flash of palms, and darkness, and
when it focused again, it was turned around
and focusing on a teenage girl. She was
dressed in a scarf-hemmed gauzy dress, the
light fabric contrasting against sepia colored
skin, and almost perfectly matching the wild
silvery-white locks asymmetrically cut around
a round face.

"Hi. My name is Charlie Carroll. You don't know
me... but you used to. You've known me longer
than I've known myself, since the day I was

*born. Alys was my mother. Is my mother. I'll try
to explain best I can, but suffice to say... While
she may be gone from your world, she still very
much exists in mine. She's okay. She's safe... And
I think, though she misses you very much... she
is happy."*

Diana gasped, unable to really process what she
was hearing—watching with her own eyes.

*"As you go through our old home, you're going
to find things that won't make sense, artifacts
from my life that you don't remember. You'll
even find photos of us together—as I'm sure
by now you've seen the ones at your own home.
Maybe you just dismissed them as photos with
a client."*

"Probably," Diana admitted behind the camera.

*"You did always make my hair fabulous,"
Charlotte looked beyond the camera lens and then
back again. "The photo album I've placed... or
I'm going to place, anyway, on the couch should
further provide any proof you might need, including baby pictures and some really weird ones of
mom pregnant... And at the back, I've done my
best, with your help, to write up what's happened
to us all."*

Diana looked at the album beside her, lifting the pages to see a yellow legal pad filled with the same unknown handwriting, and what even looked like some of her own.

> *"Mom says her executor will be calling you soon. She left everything to you and me. And... since no one will remember me... I wanted to prepare you for that moment of confusion. Just tell them the truth to the best of your ability. You can't remember the last time you saw me."* Charlotte cleared her throat. *"But more importantly, I'm telling you all of this, because you deserved to know what happened to us. And because even if your mind can't remember me, I will always remember you. This won't be the last time we talk like this. I imagine we'll have many videos like this one. So, you might want to save this somewhere, and maybe we can make it a tradition of watching them together. It's not going to be easy... but you're family. And I don't think there's a thing in the world I wouldn't do for family. I love you. I miss you. I will see you soon."*

As the video ended, a tear dropped onto her hand. She hadn't even realized she'd started crying. She reached for the book and moved it to her lap. As she pulled back the album cover, she was greeted by a self-portrait she'd taken with Alys. Diana was newly on hormones, and behind her Alys held a positive pregnancy test between her knuckles as if she were flipping off the camera. Beneath it, written in Diana's own hand—for a writer, Alys had no art for penmanship—were the words "And baby makes 3."

It was their first apartment together. She recognized the terrible '70s shag carpet that their landlord had insisted was 'newly installed' and they'd been too broke to argue too much about. And too young and dumb to care.

She turned the page and found shopping photos, making fun of strange onesies. How could she have forgotten all of this? How could her mind have forfeited these precious and ridiculous moments? They must have been so momentous in her life, and yet... it was like seeing them for the first time.

Page after page, there were new memories. Alys pregnant, her first book becoming a bestseller. Baby Charlie.

"I love you. I miss you. I will see you soon."

Diana rocked back and forth a moment, hugging the scrapbook of moments that had somehow been robbed from her to her chest.

She rewatched the video, letting it play in the background over and over again as she poured over each page. Eventually she picked it up and took it around the house, finding further evidence of this life.

Charlie's handprints in clay from kindergarten, framed photos, her room.

Alys' paintings were on the wall. There was a music box of a princess and knight from childhood days sitting atop a dresser littered with wrist cuffs, rings, jewelry, and a few odd cents as well as hair ties—some of which still had a small tangle of white hair in them. She lifted the top of the music box and the tinkling music began to play Stephen Foster's "Beautiful Dreamer."

Diana pulled the legal notepad from the back of the photo album. She flipped through the pages—at least ten explaining the "how" this had all come to be. She set it on Charlie's bed. She would read it... because ultimately, she did want to know why. And how. But right then, in the wake of Alys' death, she found herself also mourning the loss of a life she did not expect. Her own.

"I love you. I miss you. I will see you soon."

OTHER BOOKS FROM KIRI CALLAGHAN

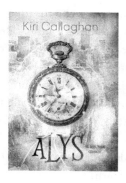

ALYS
The Terra Mirum Chronicles
By Kiri Callaghan

Following the death of her best friend, 18-year-old Alyson Carroll finds herself lost within the realm of Dreams and confronted with the challenge of facing her own fears or being trapped inside her own nightmares forever.

https://doceblantstore.com/collections/all/products/alys

CPSIA information can be obtained
at www.ICGtesting.com
Printed in the USA
BVHW041006100921
616443BV00028B/300